NATHANIAL

Nathanial: Western Promises Series, Book 3
ISBN-Paperback: 978-0-9991553-6-3
ISBN-Ebook: 978-0-9991553-7-0

 Published by:
Fig Publishing
www.jbrichard.com

© 2020 J.B. Richard .ALL RIGHTS RESERVED. With the exception of quotes used in reviews, no part of this book may be used or reproduced in any manner whatsoever without written permission from the author. This is a work of fiction. Names, characters, places, and incidents either are the product of the author's imagination or are used fictitiously. Any resemblance to actual persons, living or dead, events, or locales is entirely coincidental.

Editorial services by: Anne Victory, Editing and Gathering Leaves Editing

Cover and interior design by TLC Book Design, *TLCBookDesign.com*
Cover: Tamara Dever; Interior: Monica Thomas

Images © Depositphotos.com: cowboy & horse @ Bestgreenscreen, @ renatas76, mountain landscape @ broker; leather swirls @ Mario7. Cowboy walking forward ©iStockphoto.com/Kanyakits

Publisher's Cataloging-In-Publication Data
(Prepared by The Donohue Group, Inc.)
Names: Richard, J. B. (Julie Beth), author.
Title: Nathanial. [Part 1] / J.B. Richard.
Description: [Beaver Springs, Pennsylvania] : FIG Publishing, [2020] | Series: Western promises ; book 3
Identifiers: ISBN 9780999155363 (print) | ISBN 9780999155370 (ebook)
Subjects: LCSH: Adopted children—Family relationships—Fiction. | Runaway children—Wyomin—
    19th century—Fiction. | Custody of children—Wyoming—19th century—Fiction. | Human
    trafficking—Wyoming—19th century—Fiction. | LCGFT: Western fiction. | Historical fiction.
Classification: LCC PS3618.I343 N38 2020 (print) | LCC PS3618.I343 (ebook) | DDC 813/.6--dc23

Printed in the United States of America

WESTERN PROMISES
◦~BOOK 3~◦

NATHANIAL

J.B. RICHARD

FIG PUBLISHING

CHAPTER 1

NATE RAN A STEP BEHIND PHILLIP, racing along the boardwalk toward the Hendersons' general store. They were both hankering for a sweet, mouthwatering treat. And who better to ask than Phillip's pa, owner of the mercantile, for a piece of licorice? Sailing past the storefronts, Nate jumped quickly out of the way of smacking straight into Ned, the telegraph man, who was just stepping out the door of the wire/post office. His near brush sent Ned, wearing his silly blue visor, spinning a circle to catch himself from falling.

"Nathanial. Slow down, boy. Got somethin' for ya," Ned hollered, his words nipping at Nate's heels as he raced on. What good old Ned probably had for him was a big ear-chewing for pounding down the boardwalk, disturbing folks. That lecture he'd heard before.

"Got a letter," Ned called after him, waving an envelope.

Nate skidded to a halt while Phillip, who hadn't looked back once, kept running.

While Nate stood catching his breath, Ned hurried along at a healthy walk, shouting that he had gotten a letter from one Deputy Huckabee in Birch Creek, Nate's best friend. They hadn't seen hide nor hair of each other in months, probably four or five. He snatched the envelope from Ned's hand and quickly tore open the paper.

> *Howdy Nate,*
>
> *You're never gonna believe it. Birch Creek is having a big shindig. Rides, cotton candy, games—all of it in celebration of the Fourth of July. There's even gonna be fireworks. Ya just gotta come. Even if yer ma and pa say no, come anyway. I'll be watchin' fer ya.*
>
> *Your Buddy,*
Deputy

"Judging by your smile, I take it that's good news." Ned tipped his chin toward the letter in Nate's hands.

"Best news ever." He beamed. He had to ask Pa first, but he was going to Birch Creek.

Nate ran across the street, forgetting about Phillip and the licorice, and dodged a horse and buggy.

"Watch where the hell you's goin'!" The driver shook his fist.

Yeah, yeah, the old buzzard could go suck an egg. Nate had something important on his mind, and this matter needed tending to quickly. No time to spare. He had to have an answer this minute. He wanted to write Deputy back right away.

What a stupendous Fourth of July this was going to be. Birch Creek was twice the size of Gray Rock, lots more people, and he would get to spend time with his good pal. What could be better than that? His feet slapped the boardwalk in front of the jailhouse, still legging it at a furious pace. Through the door he burst, jumping up to sit on the corner of Pa's desk where he always sat when he came to the jailhouse.

"Can I go? Can I, can I, can I...please?" He waved the letter in Pa's face. Nate wasn't above begging.

"Nathanial, git that thing outta my face. You're makin' me cross-eyed." Pa pushed the letter away from the end of his nose.

NATHANIAL

Nate fanned air into Pa's face with it one more time. The invitation had to be addressed this instant.

"Boy, what is it?" Pa grabbed the paper and unfolded it, nodding several times while reading. So far, it seemed good, like maybe a yes. But then out of nowhere came a raised brow followed closely by a frown.

What didn't Pa understand? That would be a grand time. They couldn't possibly pass up such an opportunity. Good friends, lots of laughs. And Pa worked hard. He deserved a holiday. Maybe Nate needed to do some convincing.

He just could not hold in his excitement. As if he had no control over his mouth, at a hell-and-gone pace, the words rumbled out over his tongue, which wasn't keeping stride and spit his thoughts out all jumbled up. "Carousel, ice cream, popcorn." And the best, most ignitable word, "Fireworks," exploded off his tongue, reverberating off the four walls.

"Please." Nate bounced as he begged. Not that batting his long lashes over his baby blues ever worked on Pa, but it was worth a try. They just had to go. "Deputy really wants me to be there."

As a family, they hadn't visited with the Huckabees in what felt like forever. They could all go, even Jesse. Last time, he'd been away on official business.

"Ya know, Jesse ain't ever met Marshal Huckabee or Deputy Tate Horn." They were both better-than-good lawmen. Nate was sure the experience would be educational for Jesse, being that he was so green at his duties as deputy. It hadn't been quite a year since Pa pinned the star on him. "Jesse sure could learn a lot." Nate shook his head, giving the impression that if Pa said no, it would somehow be sorely detrimental to his deputy.

Pa leaned back in his chair, an amused grin spread across his face as he chuckled. Nate had a pretty good suspicion of what he was thinking: Nate was full of horse shit. Learning experience his ass. But Pa's face wasn't red, meaning he must not have been irritated, and Nate was determined.

This was no time to surrender. Pa hadn't said no, so he must've been rolling the idea around a little. Nate didn't know how else to sell it, so he kept running with what was best for Pa's deputy because it would benefit Pa. Nate smacked his palm on the desk like a preacher beating the pulpit with his Bible on Sunday morning, hellbent on saving Pa from making a mistake. This trip was necessary. Nate had to get him to see that.

"Come on. The marshal's your best friend."

After a minute or two of Nate's lips flapping nonstop, Pa raised a solemn hand. What if he did say no? He was probably recalling what happened at Council Bluffs the last time Nate and Deputy were together. That hadn't entirely been their fault. Deputy Tate was supposed to have been watching them. Instead, he'd had his eye on a pretty gal while Pa and Marshal Huckabee were busy testifying at the trial—lots of folks in town. What did any of them expect of two kids? Of course they had wanted to explore Council Bluffs on their own. It was more fun that way. An hour later, after the boys almost started a stampede of fifteen hundred head of cattle, Pa and the marshal had to do some mighty quick talking to keep that rancher from stringing up Nate and Deputy by their ears.

"Promise I won't raise any hell with Deputy." Nate put his right hand up.

Pa outright laughed. *"Come anyway, even if yer ma and pa say no,"* he read from Deputy's letter. "That sounds like a whole lot of *trouble* to me." He folded the letter, handing it back to Nate.

"Well…" Nate wanted to know if they could all go.

"I'll talk to your ma," Pa said with no hint of which way he might try to sway her.

Nate hopped off the desk. "Let's go." He was ready to ride home now.

Pa ruffled his hair. "Jesse and I have some business to attend to."

What Pa was really saying was he wouldn't be home for a while.

Nate slumped into a chair. Pa was always so darn busy with work. The town of Gray Rock had doubled in size since Nate had come to live there. But this was important too, at least to him. He couldn't fault his father. When it came to family and community, Pa never ceased protecting them or providing for his family, and nothing took precedence over the people he cared about. He somehow juggled it all. It wasn't fair for Nate to pout or hound him.

"Can I come with ya? I'm a better deputy than Jesse anyway." Nate flashed the star pinned on his shirt. He treasured his time with Pa, particularly when he got to be a deputy. There was no better lawman and no one he'd rather spend his days with, though Jesse was a close second. But he was more like a brother... annoying sometimes.

Pa chuckled. Before he could comment, in strolled Jesse, stopping to regard the door hanging wide open. In Nate's haste, he'd flung it but hadn't taken time to shut it properly. Jesse clapped it closed without a word of fuss.

"Where have you been?" Pa had been shuffling papers when Nate burst in. He must have been waiting on Jesse.

Jesse sheepishly grinned, and that's when Nate noticed the bright pinkness to his lips. "Kristy and her folks came into town, so of course I had to do right and talk a spell."

"I wouldn't call that talk. I saw ya kissin'." Pa pointed at Jesse. "That girl's respectable. Keep her that way."

A flush rose into his cheeks as he wiped a sleeve across his mouth as if that would remove the smooching he'd done.

"There's a new family. Moved into that ol' trapper's shack near Bear Meadow." Pa had a habit of introducing himself to those who rode into town, whether they planned on settling there or were just passing through. It was a nice way of saying he closely watched over Gray Rock and nonsense of the criminal type would not be tolerated. It kept the riffraff away.

"You think there's gonna be trouble?" Jesse worked too closely with Pa not to know what he was thinking most of the time.

"Mrs. Henderson." Pa sighed deeply. He had expressed on numerous occasions that he thought the wife of the store owner was a nosy, gossipy woman who ought to mind her own business. "Said some folks were in to buy supplies and had the look of trouble on them." Pa shrugged. "Won't hurt to ride out there."

Very true, Nate thought. What harm could come by saying howdy?

Jesse nodded in agreement.

As Pa rose from behind his desk, hitching his gun belt, Nate faced Jesse. "Guess what?"

"You got caught with lipstick on your face too." Jesse chuckled until Pa gave him a hard look. Apparently, he did not appreciate the wait.

Although Jesse was Pa's deputy, he was also like a son. That fact made it sort of rough on Jesse. Pa all around expected a lot from him, and like Nate, when Jesse stepped out of line, he got his ass chewed out for it. A plain deputy would only get a tongue-lashing if he did wrong at work. Lucky for Jesse, he was too old to get a whipping.

"Yuck!" Nate thought about what it would be like to press his lips against a girl's. He shook his head as if throwing off fleas. Why would he want to kiss a girl? Jesse had to be plumb loco. Yes, Kristy was pretty, but to smash his mouth, his face, to hers—how utterly disgusting. Nate shuddered. "No, silly."

"Let's go, you two." Pa headed for the door before Nate handed Jesse the letter. He took it as he grabbed Nate out of the chair, throwing him over his shoulder and carrying him out.

NATHANIAL

"You look thirsty." There was a boyish playfulness to Jesse's singsong tone. Teasing was one of his favorite pastimes. He enjoyed it thoroughly, and usually, it ended with the two of them wrestling, which was always a good time.

"Pa, help." Nate giggled without knowing what Jesse had up his sleeve. He wasn't worried. Sometimes Pa delighted in the hoopla. Then Nate became the monkey in the middle. Those were the best times. Nate loved his family.

Jesse flipped him over, and he was held dangling by his ankles just above the horse-slobbered water.

"You ready for a big drink." Jesse laughed as he dipped him enough that Nate's outstretched hands touched the water.

He let out with a tickled scream for mercy. Pa shut the jailhouse door with a smack, which Nate was sure was meant for the backs of their heads. He reckoned Pa was in a mood. He got that way sometimes when he desperately needed a break, always pushing himself too hard. A lot of responsibility came with his job, plus family duties, and Jesse acting like a big kid didn't seem to be helping.

"Put him down," Pa snipped.

In one swift twist, Jesse twirled Nate right side up and flopped him onto the back of the saddled mustang, Buck, Nate's other best friend.

At the hitch rail where the horses stood lazily, Jesse scanned then returned the letter. "Sounds like a fine ol' time to me...fireworks." He looked up at Pa, who was sitting on the bay, and judging by the veins throbbing in his neck, he was irritated that Jesse was moving at a pace that didn't fit his schedule. "Sheriff, you oughta go."

What? No. That wasn't how Nate imagined the trip. Jesse didn't seem to understand. He was supposed to go to Birch Creek too.

Nate huffed, crossing his arms tight. "You're part of the family. You gotta go with us." He looked between Jesse and

Pa for an answer, expecting to get his way, or maybe he'd have a fit.

Pa rubbed his temple. "Son, Gray Rock can't be without law for that long. One of us would have to stay. Who would keep the peace?" He was right, as always, and Nate thought a little more about it.

It'd take a week there, then back, plus whatever time they spent in town for the celebration. But it wouldn't seem right to leave Jesse. It would feel as though part of the family was missing. And it would be. He wanted Jesse to see the fireworks, and Nate had never witnessed the booming lights before.

"Pin a badge on Big John." Nate pushed with a feisty tone to get what he wanted. Johnny's Pa had helped his father out before. "Jesse just has to go." He wrinkled his nose up mean.

"If he goes, then I'll stay behind." Pa wasn't making him pick. Pa would make the choice and probably let Jesse go to Birch Creek. He did everything for them, even if it meant missing out himself. He was just like that. Nothing made him happier than making his family happy.

"You're forgettin' somethin'," Pa said. "Ma has a say in this."

Ma hadn't been feeling well as of late. She'd been gagging over a bucket three mornings this week and a few times after supper. Said the venison smelled funny and she couldn't possibly eat any. She had drunk mint tea to soothe her delicate stomach, then gone to bed early.

Jesse threw a leg over his saddle. "Kristy's ma and pa plan on havin' a big picnic on the fourth. Lots of folks from town are gonna be there. I'll be just fine spendin' the day eatin' her fried chicken and peach pie." He chuckled. "Havin' the house all to myself." He winked at Nate. "Two, three weeks without you jumpin' on the bed, wakin' me too early, might spoil me."

Nate rolled his eyes. Jesse never snapped at him for being underfoot, ever. To be honest, his partner doted on him. If Nate got his tail in trouble, Jesse always tried to bail him out. He never lied for him but would often expound on logical excuses until Pa was talked out of spanking Nate and he ended up with no more than a lecture and a wagging finger in his face.

"All right," Nate grumbled under his breath. Maybe Jesse would change his mind if he kept working on him. "Bet there'll be balloons and cakes and pies." He licked his lips as though tasting the yumminess.

"Bring me a red balloon, a big one." Jesse tweaked Nate's nose. "I am sorry I won't get to meet Marshal Huckabee or Deputy Horn." Both boys loved when Pa told them stories of the old days when he, the marshal, and Tate rode posse together. Jesse often said he looked forward to the day he'd finally get to meet them.

Pa shifted in the saddle, making it creak. "Ma still hasn't said yes. She's been feeling lousy lately. Might not suit travelin' that far." He lifted his hat, running his fingers through his dark hair. "A visit to Birch Creek does sound nice." He grinned warily. Dark circles rimmed his eyes, showing how doggone exhausted he was, but it seemed his mood was turning around. "Nathanial, you might have to work on your ma."

Nate knew exactly what Pa was talking about. He owned a sweet smile, long lashes, and big blues eyes, and he knew how to use them. They typically worked to get him what he wanted from Ma. They were going to Birch Creek. He'd bet the mustang on her saying yes.

"You go on home and do your chores. We'll see ya in a little while." Pa started to turn the bay, probably thinking that without Nate as a distraction, he could now get some work out of his deputy.

"But I wanna go," Nate blurted out, feeling gamy. He could do his stupid chores later.

Ma napped so much lately that she was probably asleep right now with Elizabeth, so he would be bored. Plus, he figured to ask her about Birch Creek when she was good and tired, at the end of the day when she was apt to say yes because she didn't want to be bothered with his pestering.

"Why not let him come? It's a homestead family...not exactly armed bank robbers." Jesse was figuring no harm would befall Nate. That slouched manner in the saddle definitely conveyed a no-worry attitude.

Pa gave him one of those hard looks, eyes narrowed, and Jesse straightened. "I don't need it explained to me." He was absolutely in a bad mood. It wasn't like him to just snap for no real reason.

Nate and Jesse exchanged that we-better-be-quiet look they gave one another when Pa was grouchy. He and Jesse had been working overtime lately. Word had come from a sheriff in another town that several young women in the area between had been stolen. That territory spread over four hundred miles across mountains, canyons, and grassy plateaus—too many hiding spots. Endless trails could be cut in any direction. Nate knew that from his days on the run with his father, who was in prison. No sign of those women, and Pa and Jesse had been looking from the time the sun came up until it fell asleep. Likely, that was another reason Pa wanted to check out these new folks—to warn them or see if they were involved.

Nate recalled those hellish days before he had become Nathanial Crosson, when he'd followed after Deegan Jones, a smuggler who had specialized in stealing woman. The man had killed Jenny, the sweet girl who had taken care of Nate long before Pa and Ma adopted him. Then Pa caught that bastard Jones. Still, none of those bad memories kept Nate from wanting to go.

His baby blues pleaded with Jesse to keep angling for him.

"I didn't mean insult. Just be nice to hear my partner's chatter." What Jesse was saying in a nice way was that Pa indeed was a man of few words. It was a fairly long ride into the mountains until they would reach Bear Meadow. "My ears sure do git lonely." He sadly shook his head.

Nate joined in with a desperate pout, a plea to escape the misery of chores.

"You boys are shysters. That act might work on Ma." Pa let out a defeated sigh. Had they broken through? Was he going to bend this one time? "If I let him, could we git goin' on our way?"

Nate answered by wasting no time turning Buck and falling into pace between Jesse and Pa. Jesse winked. They both knew they had gotten very lucky. Pa wasn't one to give in.

"Race ya!" Jesse wildly spurred the gray he was riding.

"That's not fair!" Nate hollered while madly kicking his mustang.

CHAPTER 2

NECK AND NECK, they rode up through the hills, the horses stretching their legs, running as though their tails were afire. Nate was holding on tight, his fists wrapped in the reins. The gray was snorting, falling back half a stride while giving chase as Jesse's shirttail flapped in the wind. Pa wasn't far behind, handling his rushing horse, having a little fun himself. Buck leaped a downed limb and kept flying. Were his hooves even touching the ground? They were splitting the air. Nate was positive Buck had never run faster. He threw a glance over his shoulder. The gray was fading. Jesse tugged on the reins, slowing the horse until it fell in next to the bay.

"Buck's gotta be the fastest horse in the territory," Jesse said to Pa. Dapple, an appaloosa Jesse had owned, had been a fast horse. Then it was killed. Now he was stuck with the old gray. It didn't have near the same stamina as the mustang.

Pa nodded. "I know ya miss Dapple."

Nate wheeled Buck, pulling up on the reins. "I won." He threw down his bragging rights with a fat, satisfied smirk on his face, pumping his arms above his head. Nate congratulated Buck on a job well done with a hearty pat on his neck.

A quarter-mile later, they stopped at a stream and let the horses drink, then walked their mounts in a line along a path that was barely wide enough for a wagon. There were tracks from the wheels, and the tall grass was pushed over from the wagon bed rubbing against it. Nothing else could have done that. Nate was good—actually great—at reading sign. Pa had taught him everything. Too much, Pa had said at times when Nate got in the way while trying to help.

They were almost there when Pa looked over at Nate and Jesse. His face was without expression. Were they in trouble for something? Nate waited to hear it, his gut coiling.

"Why would anyone want to claim that old trapper shack as their home? If you recall, the place is mighty rundown." Pa was silent then but still holding his gaze, waiting for one of them to answer.

Jesse snickered. "They're idiots. Got no sense."

Nate chuckled.

Pa's face pinched tight, his lips pressed in a thin line. Nate slipped a boot out of the stirrup closest to Jesse and gave him a nudge. A hissing noise escaped between Pa's gritted teeth. Jesse seemed to have taken notice, clearing this throat.

"Sorry, sir." He held eye contact with Pa. "Does seem odd, unless you're a trapper, but that don't appear to be the case. Most trappers don't have families. Typically, they're loaners, but not all. Maybe a squaw."

Pa nodded, his face relaxing. This was the logical thinking he wanted to produce in them, forever teaching what he knew, getting them to figure it out rather than just giving away the answer without any work. Nate liked learning, but sometimes he liked being silly with Jesse more.

This wasn't the time to play around. Pa might not let him come along again.

"Doubt they're sodbusters," Nate said. "Mountain soil ain't good for plantin', and besides Bear Meadow, there's no field to raise stock."

"Very good." Pa grinned. "What kind of people hide themselves far away?"

There was only one type Nate could think of—outlaws. He'd done that too many times with his old pa to forget.

Jesse must have had the same revelation. "But Mrs. Henderson said it was a man, woman, and thought she'd counted five youngsters, a baby for sure. Maybe they're plannin' on fixin' the place up, openin' a trade post or something similar."

"Could be." Pa agreed. "Don't rule out the possibility of criminal activity just because a man totes a woman and kids. Do I have to remind ya of Nathanial's early upbringing? What looks normal, peaceable, can be a great cover."

Nate didn't need any reminding. His old pa had used his innocence to cheat folks more times than he could count.

"Reckon you're right," Jesse said. He no longer slouched, his demeanor replicating Pa's serious side.

The dank shack appeared through the thick, leaf-covered trees. It was aged black with rot, and moss freckled the exterior walls and a large portion of the saggy roof where bundles of thatch weren't missing. Gaps in the side planks let more than just light spill inside. The place probably rattled every time the wind kicked up. What about coons and opossums and such? No doubt lots of critters had to be shaken out of that drafty dump before it was livable.

"Mrs. Henderson must have heard wrong." Nate glanced at Pa.

No way was there a family living in that heap. Plus, the one room hardly looked big enough for two grown-ups, let alone a passel of kids. Ma had muttered on occasion, usually on a rainy day when they were all trapped inside, that it felt as if

NATHANIAL

their house shrank, and it was only him and Elizabeth to get underfoot.

"Hush." Pa pressed a finger against his lips.

"I was wrong. They are trappers," Jesse said in a whisper. There were animal skins everywhere, staked and stretched out on the ground, other furs tacked to a small shed.

Nate wrinkled his nose. "Phew-wee, that stinks." He fanned the air in front of his nose.

Near the shed, a wagon stood ready for its next job. Two mules were picketed not far away. Someone dwelled there. By all accounts, it looked like a trapper had made a home, not some family.

A baby cried from inside. Nate's eyes widened as he looked over at Pa and Jesse, who both seemed just as shocked. After initially seeing the condition of the place, none of them had expected to actually find a brood.

"Hello to the house," Pa called.

There were some shuffling noises inside, along with murmured voices. Then the lopsided door whipped open with a screech from a rusty hinge. A thin, pale-faced woman with brown hair and dark eyes and a squawking baby on her hip stood squarely in front of them as if she owned that mountain and no one was about to run her off, not that it was what Pa aimed to do.

She glared at the men. "What?" she barked.

Around her bony hips was a holstered pistol hanging opposite the baby. Nate had never seen the like and sensed all-fire quick that she rightly knew how to use that gun. This was no homestead family. Plenty of folks had settled around Gray Rock. Never once had Nate met a clan like this one. He would have remembered because he was a little bit scared of getting shot.

For being a wee thing, she was a fierce-looking woman. Not much weight or height to her, but she threw a shadow that had both Pa and Jesse sitting strangely quiet. No one seemed to know what to think of her. A staggered line of four dirty-faced kids peeked around their mama's skirt and stared wide-eyed at him, Jesse, and Pa. Their big eyes fastened on the badges.

Pa tipped his hat. "Howdy, ma'am. I'm Sheriff Crosson." He nodded toward Jesse. "That thar's my deputy, Jesse Adams."

Before he could introduce Nate, the woman clutched her chest, nearly dropping the baby. She stared at Nate with an air of disbelief.

"Nathanial." She spoke as if confirming to herself that she was honestly seeing him. Her voice suddenly choked up, eyes welling with tears. "You gotta be Lucinda's boy." She blinked rapidly. He reckoned she was clearing her vision to make sure she wasn't hallucinating. "Come here, child." The sharp tongue she had chopped at Pa with was gone, and her soft coax was luring.

Who was this lady? How did she know Nate's birth mother? He slid out of the saddle.

"Nathanial, git back on your horse." Pa sounded none too happy. It was the same tone always used as Nate's last warning before he got a licking. Those uncomfortable memories seemed far away, and she and that warm smile were right in front of him.

Nate wasn't one to warm up to strangers, but this lady seemed to know him. People who showed up out of his past usually brought trouble. She didn't exactly look innocent or even kindhearted. There was a raw edge to her the same as the mean men Nate's old pa, Jim Younger, had ridden with. She was a woman, though. What trouble could she bring to him? For pity's sake, she had kids of her own, so he didn't feel threatened.

Pa's warning from two minutes ago was shoved to the back of his mind. The bony lady didn't look at Pa or Jesse, but smiled warmly at Nate.

NATHANIAL

"Boy, if you don't git on your horse, I'm gonna open them ears by tannin' your ass." Pa was steaming, heard in his barking tone, but Nate didn't even look back.

Not that he was ignoring him, but he couldn't help himself, completely intrigued. He didn't know much of anything about his birth mother, just that she had been a whore. She'd died when he was so young. He barely remembered her. Sometimes he did wonder. That was his secret. He would never want to hurt the mother and father he had now by asking questions. What if they thought he wasn't grateful for what they had done for him? He loved them more than anything and too often wished he'd been born of their seed like Elizabeth. But that didn't sway his curiosity.

Nate stopped a step in front of the raggedy woman, her hair unkempt, her clothing wrinkled and soiled, not unlike his own, except hers were homespun, every stitch. There were smears of dirt from her day's work on her face that matched those on her children's thin cheeks. The oldest kid, a boy, was probably Nate's age. They smiled at each other.

"Holy shit." She chuckled and fingered his snowy hair while wearing a shitty smirk. "Your mama had those same white strands. Hated them. Always wanted dark hair."

Nate hadn't known that and kind of liked learning a little something about the woman who brought him into this world.

A strong hand clamped his shoulder and turned him.

"Excuse us, ma'am." Pa's nostrils flared as he silently scolded Nate with a hard stare. He didn't tolerate disrespect, and not listening when Nate had been told to get back on his horse was grounds for a tongue-lashing, if not an ass smack. Pa marched him toward Buck.

"Your man home?" Jesse asked, breaking the tension.

The woman seemed as displeased about Pa interrupting her storytelling as Nate was, or at least she was hatefully glaring.

"He's off trappin', or so he said. I never really know what he's into." Her temper flared. Gone was her soft voice.

"You expectin' him to return anytime soon?" Jesse had taken over while Pa flopped Nate on Buck, then swung a leg over his bay.

Pa turned his attention back to the thin woman.

"I don't know when that dog'll come 'round. Likely when he gits the itch to make another brat." She snubbed her nose with her fist. "If you's worried about us botherin' any of those so-called good folks in that thar town, don't be. We ain't much on being neighborly. Stick to ourselves."

The way she had spit out the words "that town" had Nate believing she silently just slapped Jesse and his badge right in the face. And if she got the chance to actually hit him, she likely would. Pa, too, for that matter. The lines on her face were hard as she eyeballed the two like she had an old score to settle. Maybe she just hated lawmen. Seemed that way.

"I ain't keen on self-proclaimed righteous folks tellin' others how to live. That store owner's a bossy bitch."

Nate slapped a hand over his mouth, holding back his chuckles. He'd overhead Pa relaying those exact words about Mrs. Henderson to Ma a few times.

"Well, that explains it," Jesse whispered over Nate's head. "Somewhere along the line, someone did something and left a mean mark on her, or she wouldn't be so mad."

She huffed at the whispering as though she were about to put her head down and charge.

"Could be she's referring to us comin' to talk to her man, wantin' to know his business, judgin' her husband in a way." Pa's voice was no louder than Jesse's had been. "But one busybody doesn't mean everyone in town is like that."

Pa was right. She was jumping to conclusions, being judgmental herself. Nate pondered if her man was a good one, trustworthy, honest. He knew half a dozen in Gray Rock that straddled that fence daily.

The mountain woman breathed in snorts. Reckon she figured it wasn't up to them to judge, that they had no business being there, and she was tired of looking at them.

Pa and Jesse were still leaned together. "Just because a fella's mean and miserable don't make him a criminal. All the pelts are evidence enough that he's a trapper, or at least some of the time he is. Don't forget she said she's not always sure what he's up to. We need to keep an eye on them."

Nate was soaking it all in. The woman had called her man a dog.

"It ain't polite to whisper. Say it to my face, or shut the hell up." She smacked a hand against the door to grab their attention as though what she'd just said wasn't enough.

Pa and Jesse glanced at one another as if neither was sure what to make of that gun-toting spitfire of a woman.

"If there ain't nothin' else, I got cookin' to do." She tapped a foot impatiently for a few seconds. "Oh, one other thing. You might like to know that my boy"—she jerked her head at the kid about Nate's age—"was out huntin' and spotted a war party. Said they were carryin' scalps. I certainly wouldn't want any of those unwelcoming pricks in that town of yours to get their hair lifted. That'd be a damn shame." Then she spun on her heel, and the door slammed.

They all just stared at the empty doorway. Pa scratched his head. He hadn't even found out her name or that of her man. Jesse looked just as taken aback by her brassy manners. Hands down, that woman had balls, big ones. Nate chuckled. He wasn't so sure that she was even the same species as Ma.

Ma would have strung up any of them, including Pa, had they slammed a door in someone's face. She was all heart. Everyone around Gray Rock knew it. She'd do anything within her means to help a friend or neighbor. There were no hard edges on her. Rarely did she even raise her voice. This woman, on the other hand, was all bite, teeth, and claws to her very core.

"Reckon that hellcat's done talkin'." Jesse snorted out a chuckle.

Pa let go of a deep sigh as if he had just slipped a tangle with a grizzly. They turned their horses.

"As soon as we rode in, there's one thing I observed right away," Pa said. "Do either of ya know?"

"Yeah, the place is far too small to cage stolen women."

What Jesse said led Nate to look around a mite closer. The outbuilding with furs tacked on it was also too tiny to hide much of anything. But that didn't mean those folks weren't involved. The woman sounded as if her man might be up to something other than trapping, and Pa had reinforced that to Jesse. Nate knew firsthand how kids could be used as a decoy. His old pa had forced him lots of times, practically his whole life, to smile sweetly and bat his lashes, pulling the wool over the eyes of his prey. It made Nate wonder what kind of man would leave his woman and children alone in a rat trap, not even fit for animals, way out in the mountains without much to keep them well. Pa would never.

There was no guesswork. Nate knew the answer. The man was no good, just like Nate's old pa. He hoped she wasn't a criminal. He wanted to talk to her more and learn what she knew about his ma.

CHAPTER 3

A FEW LENGTHS BEHIND THE BOYS, Nolan rode into the ranch yard just before dark. Nate and Jesse prattled over one another, planning a fishing trip. Jesse promised to take the boy to the Platte River near Fort Laramie.

"The huntin's good there too," Jesse said. "Maybe we'll kill us a bison. We can pack the meat, or most of it, and skin the hide and make ya a big blanket like the Injuns keep warm with."

At that, Nolan's little boy was all smiles.

Nolan's mood was not so good as those two, irked with himself for riding the whole way to Bear Meadow and coming out with no information. Where had that woman's man gone and so soon after getting supplies in town? Had he been out checking traps? Why not take the boy that was around Nate's age and teach him? The woman would have given a better excuse, other than not knowing, had her man's work been the day-to-day sort. Then again, she'd been so defensive she might say anything to protect him. It certainly made Nolan think those two were involved in breaking the law, possibly those abductions.

"Pa, you should come campin' with me and Jesse when we go."

"Nathanial, not now." Nolan needed quiet. His mind was rolling with too many questions, too many possibilities where that couple was concerned.

"You're a grump," Nate fired back.

Nolan twisted in the saddle, giving his son a hard look.

Jesse angled his mare, slipping between them, pushing Buck and Nate out of Nolan's reach. Not that he was going to take hold of the child. However, he would not tolerate disrespect.

"Don't speak to your father that way." Jesse scolded the boy.

It was a clear sign that Nolan needed rest, not just a good night's sleep. He was in desperate need of letting go of work for a while. Not long. A few days would do to step away from his sheriff's duties and breathe in some fresh air. But he couldn't, not now, especially with him thinking that couple was involved in something illegal. Birch Creek would be just the ticket, except the trip would take more than a few days. He couldn't spare that. Perhaps another time. Nate would be disappointed, but he could take off a few hours and they could go fishing.

Kate stepped out of the house, giving a holler from the porch. "Supper's about ready. Come wash up."

A good hot meal might put his mood to rights.

"Pa, can I jump the fence?" The boy was prancing Buck, ready for the word go, and he would be off. He'd been told no countless times before this. That son of his would push and push if he thought he could get away with something. And in this case, he could end up breaking his darn fool little neck if the mustang didn't make the jump. How many times did Nathanial need to be told?

"Hell no." Nolan could feel the heat in his cheeks, and he was near ready to grab hold and shake the brassiness right out of the boy.

Jesse snickered.

NATHANIAL

Nolan shot him a hard glare. Laughter would only serve to encourage Nathanial. At the moment, he didn't want to deal with either knucklehead. A soak in a steamy tub and a shot of whiskey was what he wished for.

Nathanial snorted, but the boy did pull up reins at the corral fence instead of doing as he pleased, which sometimes his orneriness led him to do. At those times, Nolan was forced to take a hand to the child.

"We'll jump the fence the next time Pa ain't lookin'." The disobedient cuss hadn't whispered softly enough into Buck's ear.

"I oughta spank ya for even thinkin' about jumpin' the fence." Nolan shook his head.

Nathanial quickly looked at Jesse. They were partners, and the boy wanted out of trouble.

Jesse put his hands up. No help there. "Sorry, little partner. I don't wanna see ya break your head. I can't believe ya asked in the first place."

With a long pout on his face, Nate slid out of the saddle and led the mustang into the corral. Nolan carried Nate's saddle, plus his own, into the barn, the child on his heels. While he stored the tack and then the entire walk to the house, Nathanial pestered about going to Birch Creek.

"When ya gonna ask Ma?" He anxiously bounced up the porch steps next to Nolan. They stepped inside behind Jesse.

"Suppose after supper." Nolan hung his hat on a peg just inside the door. He wouldn't be able to go with this new development, but Jesse might take the family. Though, he was looking forward to the Shorts' picnic with Kristy, so it wasn't a guarantee.

The child's impatience turned from bouncing into something vastly different. He stiffened and stomped his feet.

"Why can't you ask before we eat?" Nate's voice was pure whine, which he knew did nothing but annoy his father.

Nolan was one breath away from unbuckling his belt. If he got one more boo-hoo about anything, that would be it. Nate was awful close to having his behind warmed.

"No." The word cracked off his tongue like a whip.

Jesse pushed his little partner toward the table. Nathanial threw himself into his chair.

"Go wash your hands," Nolan barked. He wanted to talk to Kate privately about going to Birch Creek. It had sounded like fun and would get her out of the house, be a break for her. He figured he'd at least mention it, but he wouldn't allow her to travel alone. So unless Jesse agreed to go, no one would.

Kate had him worried. At this very moment, she was green around the gills. That seemed to be happening more often, though she didn't appear distressed about it at all. There was one other time he could recall she'd had the same symptoms. Surely, if it was that, she would have told him. They hadn't had much couple time lately, barely a few words. He'd fall into bed at night, exhausted, and if she wasn't already asleep, she was tending to one of the kids. They needed to talk, and not just about a getaway trip.

Kate had just sat down at the table with her plate of barely anything when Nate loudly cleared his throat.

"Pa has somethin' important to ask ya." Their rotten brat was batting his eyes at his mama. "You look real pretty, Ma." He smiled oh so sweetly.

Nolan was none too happy. And if he wasn't so blasted tired, he would have dragged Nate away from the table and blistered his hide. Instead, he just gave him a hard glare that the boy ignored by not looking his way, his long lashes still fluttering at his ma.

"I was gonna pick ya some wildflowers, but I got busy with my deputy duties." Nathanial shook his head as if sorely disappointed in himself. "To make up for that, Jesse'll do the dishes tonight while you relax or knit or whatever you choose to do." He offered Jesse up as a slave for the evening. The boy had laid it on a mite thick, irritating Nolan further.

Kate outright laughed. "What do you want, Nathanial?"

Before he could recover from the shock of being called out, Jesse came awake and looked up from his plate with his mouth stuffed full of stew, his cheeks like a chipmunk's.

"What?" Jesse protested. Food particles sprayed over his lips and across the table. "Partner, if you wanna go to Birch Creek, then you do the dishes." Jesse gulped down the glob, maybe unchewed.

"Birch Creek!" Kate was flabbergasted and stared past the boys at Nolan.

At no time had Birch Creek ever been a spur-of-the-moment trip for them. It took planning. They had a ranch and stock that required daily tending. It was a long journey, one that required a fair amount of supplies when traveling with a family. Though, Nolan would be at home this time and could take care of things around the house and in town. The rest of them could manage to go last minute if she had a mind to.

"Give your ma the letter from Deputy," Nolan said.

The boy pulled it quickly out from under his shirt and excitedly handed it over.

"Deputy Huckabee. I might have known." Kate's eyes traveled over the script as she read. *"Come anyway, even if yer ma and pa say no."* Her lips thinned severely, and Nathanial slid down in his chair.

Nolan reckoned no would be the answer. Those two yahoos were too often trouble when they got together, added to the poor way she'd been feeling lately. Although, her long silence after folding the paper and handing it back to their son was a good sign that she was seriously considering it. Every second of that time, Nate kept begging with his big blue eyes. Kate and Constance, Marshal Huckabee's wife, exchanged letters several times a month. Women liked the company of other women, liked to talk of lady things, kids, recipes, and dress patterns and such. It'd be nice for them to have these conversations face to face for once instead of waiting a week or two for correspondence.

A growing excitement made Nathanial's little face glow as he waited for Ma to say the word. His fingers crossed on both hands, and no one at the table could mistake his giddiness for anything but joy at the thought of seeing his good friend. Even Jesse, who had volunteered to stay behind but would be going if Nolan could convince him, had stopped making a hog of himself and was on the edge of his chair. Nolan found that he, too, was holding his breath.

She gently placed her hand over his. Was he about to hear a list of reasons why she didn't want to go? Was she sicker than she was letting on? If that were true, then right away tomorrow morning, he would take her to see Doc Martin. Nolan would then at least find out if she was expecting. Maybe it was too early for her to be sure, but Doc... Well, he'd delivered lots of babies. He would be able to diagnose her symptoms. And Nolan wasn't about to ask in front of Nathanial, who had acted out in the past when jealous.

"We should go." She flashed a stunningly beautiful smile. Nolan would never tire of it. He was just sorry he couldn't go. Time alone with her and the kids sounded wonderful.

"There's one thing." Nolan didn't know how to say it. His wife would want him at her side, especially since she wasn't feeling well. "I have to stay here."

Nathanial jumped up, nearly knocking his chair over backward. "Thought you said... Now you're not going either?" He smacked a hand on the table.

"Nolan, why bring it up if you can't go with us?" Kate's eyes glistened. "Then we won't go."

"What?" Nathanial shoved his plate away. "Jesse can be sheriff. He knows how. You taught him."

NATHANIAL

"Nathanial, settle down," Kate snapped.

"I was hopin' Jesse would change his mind and take my place." Nolan glanced at his older son.

Jesse shook his head. "I'm sorry. I got somethin' special planned on the fourth. Been meanin' to talk to ya about it. Just haven't had the chance."

Nathanial turned and ran out of the house. "I'm going," he hollered over his shoulder. Then the door slammed behind him.

Jesse stood. "I'll get him." He turned back after a few steps. "I can handle things here. I understand that watchin' over the town is a huge responsibility. I won't let ya down." He stared straight into Nolan's eyes, his gaze never wavering. "If you're worried about that couple, I'll keep my eyes on them. Planned on tryin' to trail him tomorrow."

"Son, it's not that I don't trust you. I do. I'm just worried there's more goin' on than we initially thought. That couple's trouble. If anything should happen to you and I ain't here, I'd never forgive myself."

"Yes, sir... But might I remind you that I am your deputy? Let me do this. You go with Kate and the kids. If I run into any problem too big, I'll have Ned send a wire. And Big John is always willin' to help at the jailhouse. If I would need more assistance than that, Shorty and some of his men can help. You know they would."

Jesse was a bright young man, a fast learner, strong as an ox, and had enough nerve for three men. No one could forget that boy's skill with his Winchester. At almost nineteen, he was practically a legend. Nolan had sent him alone on assignments, but never out from under wing for more than a week. It was just scary since Jesse was like a son, but he was right. He was capable of handling things there. They hadn't actually found any sign of that couple being involved in the stealing of women. What he was feeling was a strong hunch, believing they were guilty of something.

"I'll help you track him tomorrow. Depending on what we find, maybe I'll take the family to Birch Creek."

Jesse grinned.

Kate reached over and squeezed Nolan's hand. By the smile on her face, he could see she was pleased. As much as he would hate to make that shine fade, if he wasn't certain there was no threat to the citizens of Gray Rock, including Jesse, they wouldn't go anywhere until this matter was settled. And Nathanial would have to understand that.

"Partner will be happy to hear it." Jesse rushed out the door.

CHAPTER 4

AFTER BREAKFAST, Nolan and Jesse hit the trails, steering their mounts toward Bear Meadow while Kate and the children headed into town. Flour, coffee, and a few other items were on her list of supplies for traveling—if Nolan's work didn't keep them at home. That morning before the rooster crowed, Nate had landed in bed with them, bouncing as he pestered, going on about packing, adding a few pleases and batting those long lashes. Plain and simple, that boy was a pain in the ass sometimes. But Kate had a good point. All the necessities, common goods, could be packed in their pantry.

Nolan wasn't sure what they might find today, and he'd given no hint of going to Birch Creek, not wishing to overexcite Nathanial. He had okayed Kate buying the supplies, and she seemed nearly as excited as their son.

Jesse pulled up reins a hundred yards from the shack, his eyes studying the ground. "Single rider." With a finger, he pointed, drawing a line in the air to the south.

Indian country. According to the mountain woman, the Cheyenne were on the prowl. Not a good time to be riding that way. A desperate or wanted man might, though. Nolan didn't know that the fella they were hunting was either. That sassy woman could have warned her man, and he probably figured they'd be back. Was this sign of him hightailing it out of there, slipping away from jail time or a noose?

"Bet our man's gone. These hoofprints are right in line with that shack." Jesse nudged his mare toward the little house. Smoke puffed out of the chimney and over the treetops. "I say we talk to her first, then trail him." Jesse nodded, agreeing with himself.

Nolan touched spurs to the bay. That was exactly his thinking.

No kids were running around. The wagon that had been there during their last visit was missing. The dozen or so pelts that had been lying around were all gone. The house was too quiet, not a single noise coming from inside. Odd, given that five children resided there.

Nolan tossed his reins to Jesse. He stepped up to the door and pounded two, three times. A bird called from a branch somewhere behind the shack. Where had she gone? No one that he knew of in town dealt in furs. He jiggled the knob, opening the door.

The room was clean, spotless. Quite a surprise, given that the brood he had seen wore strong evidence of outside chores. Wood crackled in the fireplace. That fire would have been outed had everyone left. Someone had it jumping. Strange since it was the end of June and hot as hell. Sweat trickled down his back.

Four chairs without occupants sat on each side of a small table, center room, but tin plates had been laid out. A pallet of three or four patchwork haps was stacked all messy in a corner. He pushed the door farther without stepping inside, that sense of being watched making him breathe rapidly.

Without warning, a boy—the one about Nate's age—swinging a sizeable chunk of kindling leaped from behind the door, aiming at Nolan's belt buckle.

He sprang back, hands flying up as the kid missed and whacked against the doorframe, sending a shudder through him and causing him to drop the slab. Nolan, accustomed to reacting quickly, grabbed the little bugger, who let out hollering as though he were being whipped. He had not recovered swiftly enough to run and hide, which scared kids would do. Poor boy. His eyes were stretched grotesquely wide, and Nolan swore he could hear the child's heart pounding even over his shrieks. God only knew what he'd been told about lawmen. The wetness in his round eyes indicated a fear of staring helplessly at his demise, which was the furthest thing from the truth.

"I ain't gonna hurt ya, son." Nolan slowly released his grip on the boy's shoulders.

The child stood stiff as a board, not even blinking. He was obviously alone, or he wouldn't have been so frightened.

"Where's your ma and pa?" Nolan had no intention of petrifying the kid more by hounding him with questions he probably didn't know the answers to anyway.

The boy wiped at his eyes while glancing between Nolan and Jesse, who was off his horse and stood nearby. Given a chance, that kid still might run. He seemed to be considering it.

"I ain't supposed to talk to you, either of ya." His little voice was so soft Nolan barely made out the words.

Nolan hunkered in front of the kid, who stared at the ground as though he could dig a hole with his mind and disappear, shifting from one foot to the other repeatedly.

"Son, look at me."

The kid hesitantly raised his head, even slower to make eye contact.

"Do you know when your ma and pa will be back?"

The little fella shook his head. Nolan glanced over his shoulder at the wagon tracks that rutted the yard. The boy's mother would return. It wasn't likely that she just up and ran, leaving him behind. What kind of woman would do that? Besides that, why have five if you didn't like kids?

"Ah-choo, ah-choo, ah-choo…" Three sneezes in a row, then a blow horned from inside.

Nolan's head spun on his shoulders. He stood, staring into the blackened room. Sunlight overhead made it appear as a cavern would. He could see no farther than a foot inside. Eyes narrowed, he searched every dark inch. He had started backward at the kid's earlier swing, which put him three or four feet from the open doorway.

Jesse had drawn his pistol, and Nolan's right hand, of its own will, came to rest on the butt of his revolver.

The kid suddenly bounded forward with one great leap, tearing Nolan's hand away from his holster. "She's sick. Don't hurt her." Tears cascaded down his face.

"Willie," a frail, quivery voice called.

"Settle down." Nolan pulled the youngster off him. "I ain't gonna hurt anyone."

Nolan entered, the kid on his heels, and Jesse followed close. At first glance, Nolan hadn't noticed, but wrapped in the stack of patchwork quilts lay a small girl. Six years old maybe. The blankets covered her little body so well he'd thought her to be a wrinkle. Sweat glistened across her brow and beaded her lips.

"Fetch some water."

The boy rushed out.

Jesse shoved his pistol into its holster. "The woman probably went after Doc."

"Reckon so." Nolan squatted, picking up the rag the boy must have been using to sponge his sister's head. He pressed the damp cloth against her cheeks. Damn, she was hot.

NATHANIAL

The kid returned with a bucket, sloshing water as he hurried and plunked it next to Nolan. Nolan dipped the cloth, then placed it on the girl's forehead.

"I'll wait and see to her until their ma and hopefully Doc gets here. You go on and follow that single rider. If you don't catch up to him before he gets too far into Indian country, you pull back. Understand?"

"Yes, sir." Jesse ran through the door. A few seconds later, his horse's hooves pounded the ground at a run.

No longer shying away, the kid stood next to Nolan, but his eyes were on his little sister, listlessly moaning, her head turning side to side, eyes closed.

"She'll be okay, won't she?" He looked up at Nolan.

That was for Doc to say after he examined her, whenever that would be. Hopefully soon. Nolan had helped nurse his kids through sickness, but he didn't have a clue what was going on with this pale, hacking child.

"How long has she been like this?" None of the kids had presented as ill the other day when he'd seen them. Of course, they hadn't been there long, and he'd only glanced at the children while trying to do his job, sidetracked by Nate and his uncanny fascination with the kids' mother.

"Woke in the middle of the night fussin' and bawlin'. Been like that since." The kid flopped down next to his sister. "Pa should've stayed and helped us. He couldn't take the cryin' and left like he always does. It ain't right, but Ma don't say anything." He smacked the wall with a fist.

Nolan felt bad for the boy. From hearing stories of Nathanial's past, he understood all too well what this kid was going through. No child should ever feel unwanted. It alarmed him that the boy's mother had been part of those early years that Nate hated to talk about. She had recognized him at a glance. That for damn sure didn't sit well with Nolan. She'd just left him with a bad feeling. But at the moment, his main concern was these kids.

"I'll split some wood to keep the fire going. You keep sponging her head." Nolan straightened. There was an ax sticking in a log in a pile at the side of the house. He wrenched it free, then gave her a wide swing over his shoulder, striking the wood. Splinters flew.

If the boy's pa had left in the middle of the night, there wasn't much chance of Jesse catching up. The best Nolan could hope for now was to get some answers from the woman when she returned.

When he finished, he sank the ax. Sweat soaked his shirt. There on the ground behind the log pile was an indent, a partial impression of a horseshoe. It wasn't the same as the one Jesse had spotted while riding there. Nolan was positive about that.

He squatted, touching the edge. A nail was working its way out, making a slight peculiar mark, but his keen eyes caught it. If not soon fixed, the horse would no doubt lose a shoe, slowing the animal's pace. That would help if Nolan had to traipse God knew where after the rider. There was no place around for miles to get a shoe mended.

Hopefully, he could learn what he wanted to know from the woman.

Nolan walked toward the well. A bucket hung on a string, a ladle tucked inside. Drips of sweat stung his eyes. Anything wet would bring relief to his parched throat.

Down the lane, approaching at a trot, a wagon rattled. There was the woman at the reins. Two little ones sat next to her, one of them clutching the baby, all of them bumping up and down. Doc was in his black buggy behind her, both carriages swaying over the rocks and ruts.

She jerked up on the reins in front of the house. Her mean glare and stiff neck were enough to tell Nolan that her disposition toward lawmen hadn't changed overnight, not that he'd expected it to.

"What the hell do ya want? I told ya before my man ain't here. And I don't want bothered with your bullshit right now." She hopped down, then turned, being handed the baby by a little boy who proceeded to jump down, followed by another small boy.

The pistol was on her hip, but the leather thong remained over the hammer spur. Her words had sounded threatening, edgy, ready to snap. Nursing an ill child could wear on a person. Nolan experienced that himself, and he only took over when Kate needed a rest from caretaking. This woman was on her own. And now she'd had plenty of time to slip that leather strap off had she meant any real threat.

Doc, carrying his black bag, his brow curiously wrinkled, walked up. "Hello, Sheriff. I didn't expect to see you here."

"This ain't the time for chitchat. Git on your horse and git out." She pointedly stared at Nolan. To Doc, she said, "Penny's in the house." She jerked her head in that direction but continued to hold her hateful gaze on Nolan.

Doc hustled, disappearing inside. That mouthy rip turned to follow, the baby in her arms. The other two had gone inside before Doc.

"Wait a minute." He knew she was worried about her daughter. He'd be acting no different had it been one of his kids, but he needed answers. Some things needed explaining.

At the door, she spun on her heel. Her lips pursed, ready to give him another earful. He put up his hands. Causing her more of a headache at a time like this wasn't his intention, but that didn't negate the nagging feeling pecking at him. If she and her man were involved in something illegal, he would stop them. Arresting her meant those kids would be without a mother—and, it seemed, a father—but he would do it. Had to. Laws applied to everyone, not just those without children.

Perhaps it wouldn't come to that. For the little ones' sake, he hoped not.

He was there to gather information, not take her to jail. "I'll wait out here. Do what ya need to inside, but I won't leave until we talk."

The door slammed.

A few minutes later, out ran three boys. Nolan swallowed another ladle of water, then sat in the shade. The rowdy youngsters tussled in the yard, squealing and carrying on. It made him wish even more that he could go to Birch Creek and have time alone with his family.

He also wondered how Jesse was making out. Had he caught up with the single rider, maybe this woman's husband? But he could have been the other rider. Why had two different men been there, or were they working together but had split for some reason? Could be they were still allies but had needed to separate for a purpose Nolan could not guess.

The door flew open. "Willie, take your bothers. Catch us some fish for supper."

All three boys sprinted toward the shed. Within a few seconds, the older two each had a rod, and then they tore off in the direction of the creek.

The woman stepped outside, closing the door behind her.

"What do you wanna know?" Her hands were squarely on her hips, expressing her annoyance that Nolan was still there.

He stood, brushing the dirt off his pants, then joined her at the house. She wasn't wearing the pistol, but there was nothing soft about her stance, as if ready for a brawl. He wasn't one to beat around the bush, blunt at times, and she seemed to want to get this questioning over with.

"Two men rode out from here." Nolan pointed south, then east. "Who are they? Why were they here?"

"My visitors ain't any of your damn business. I don't have to tell ya nothin'."

NATHANIAL

A proper mother wouldn't want to leave her sick child or any of her children. Nolan hoped his bluff would work. He grabbed one of her wrists, and with his other hand, he pulled a pair of shackles out of his pocket and slapped them on her before she realized what he'd done. One hard jerk and she stumbled beside him as he dragged her toward the bay.

"You son of a bitch. You can't lock me up. What about my kids?" She twisted in his grasp. He squeezed harder.

This was exactly the response he'd wished to provoke.

"For the time it takes for you to open up, I think they'll be fine all alone here in the mountain. Does your oldest know how to shoot in case those Cheyenne you seen come snoopin' 'round?" He grinned, knowing he'd have Jesse guard the place all night if need be, and Doc could stay with the sick girl.

Her eyes twinkled with a fiery hate. She spit at his face, but he ducked.

"Now, now, that might cost ya a whole extra day in jail. Let's be civil."

She wrenched to escape, but he was far too strong for her, keeping her at arm's length.

"Names?" He waited.

"I don't know. Honest. I burn a red candle in the window. I can always use the extra money." She took a deep breath, sticking out her chest, bellying up to Nolan, and keeping those pert breasts right under his eyes. "One was a trapper, the other a fella just passin' through. I don't ask names." She pressed against him. "I seen that wife of yours in town. Looks like a prude. I bet I can pleasure you in ways she's never dreamed of."

Nolan laughed, shoving her away. She stumbled backward, tripped when she stepped on the hem of her skirt, and fell on her ass. Apparently, she'd used her looks to get out of trouble before and had no shame in doing it again.

He stepped in front of her and leaned down into her face. "I know you're lyin'."

He wouldn't tell on the boy. The kid wasn't supposed to talk to Nolan, and he didn't want him getting into any trouble for innocently stating his concern about his father leaving. The rest of what she'd said, he chose to ignore. The ring on his finger symbolized love. Part of that was trust and loyalty, and he had no interest in breaking that commitment with this whore or anyone else.

"It's true," she screamed at him.

He yanked her to her feet. His patience was wearing thin, and the fact that it was hot and he was tired wasn't helping.

"I ain't ever hit a woman, but you're pushin' me damn close to it." Nolan's jaw clenched. "Your husband, what's his name?"

"John Smith." She spit it out awful quick, too fast, as if rehearsed.

John Smith was a bland, run-of-the-mill name, and it was probably a lie. An honest man didn't have to hide who he was or have his woman do it for him. It was obvious the skank wasn't going to give him any good information.

"There was a second man. His name, what is it?"

She glanced around at the shack, the rickety buckboard, the poor conditions in which she and her children survived. "Just some ugly trapper who wanted to grunt over a woman for once instead of using his hand." She lifted an elbow toward the woodpile where he had found the second horse print. "My kids need warmer clothes before winter."

It was possible for her to do some whoring in the bed of the wagon or the shed. The house was but one small room, and her children would have been in there. Her face was without expression, and Nolan was leaning toward believing her. But it was hard, given that she'd boldly lied to him once already. Maybe she'd just switched her tactic. Her voice had been softer, more ladylike, which might have been a trick to get him to feel bad for her.

He didn't feel any pity for her, but he did remove the cuffs.

"Ma!" Willie came running out from among the trees. Held high in one hand was at least a dozen trout. "Fish were really bitin' today."

The other two caught up, huffing and puffing.

She smiled. "Go on and clean 'em. We'll have us a fine supper."

The boy hastily handed his rod to one of the others, then spun, about to take off running.

"Willie." Nolan called him back, and the boy halted. "Your ma was just tellin' me about your pa." Nolan snapped his finger several times. "What's his name?" He rubbed his head as though he couldn't recall.

"Walter," the boy said.

Nolan wished he had mentioned a last name too, but one honest word was a start. "Does he like to take ya fishin'? He teach ya how?" he asked before the boy's mother, whose face was bright red, could say anything.

Nolan wanted to get a sense of how often Walter came around. Earlier, the boy had mentioned his pa leaving when things were tough, and it seemed that was more often than not. If Walter was an outlaw, the woman knew it, or she would not have lied. But that didn't mean she was directly involved. She definitely had her hands full there.

"No. Ma taught me. Pa's away more than he comes 'round."

She waved the boy to go, and he did, his little brothers on his heels.

She turned on Nolan. "You sneaky bastard. Stay away from my kids. Don't involve them."

"Involve them in what?" He picked up the reins of his horse.

"Whatever you're dreamin' up that my man, John Smith..." She drew out the name. "Is supposedly involved in." For the second time, the door slammed.

Nolan stepped into the saddle, his horse already walking as he steered the gelding toward town. He would search every wanted poster for anyone named Walter.

CHAPTER 5

IT WAS AFTER DARK by the time Nolan got home. He'd found no papers on anyone with the first name Walter. At the barn, he dismounted. The door of the house behind him opened with a squeak. He glanced over his shoulder. Kate stood in the doorway, looking breathtaking as always.

Nate pushed past her, running out.

"Pa!" The boy hightailed it across the yard, then skidded to a halt at Nolan's feet. "Can we go to Birch Creek? I helped Ma fold blankets, put them in the wagon, and packed my clothes."

Nolan grinned, ruffling his son's hair. "I need to talk with Jesse first. But when I do decide, you'll be the first to know. I promise."

"Jesse ain't here. He ain't come home yet." Nate took the reins of the bay and led the horse into the barn where Nolan helped him strip the heavy tack and store it properly.

All the while, he pondered where Jesse was. He should have been home by now. Honestly, Nolan had expected him to show up at the jailhouse. When he didn't, he had assumed he'd come there instead.

The likeliness that he'd had trouble with Walter was

NATHANIAL

slim. Too many hours between when that man had left his family and when Jesse had started after him. It was more presumable that he had a run-in with the Cheyenne.

Nolan was just about to grab his saddle and throw it on the bay when the sound of a horse trotting into the yard carried inside. He hustled toward the door, Nate right behind him.

"Jesse!" Nate bounded off.

Jesse reached down and scooped Nathanial up, plopping the boy in the saddle in front of him.

Both boys were smiling, but Nolan took a closer look. Jesse's shirt was bloodstained on his left shoulder. "What happened?"

"Damn scalp hunters. Almost had me." Jesse stepped down.

Nate stayed sitting on the mare.

"Nathanial, take Jesse's horse inside, brush her down, and give her hay."

"Yes, sir." The boy and horse disappeared into the barn.

"Go on and let Ma patch ya up," Nolan said. He would help Nate.

"I'm all right. It ain't that bad. Just a mean slice." Jesse rolled his shoulder.

"You see anything of our man?" Nolan didn't expect he had but wanted to know for certain.

"His tracks go straight south. He's running. I trailed him the whole way to Black Mesa before I turned around. He didn't show any signs of stopping."

Black Mesa was a place where, when the light was just so, the rocks took on a deep purple, almost black color. It was miles farther than Jesse was supposed to have gone.

Nolan grabbed his hat and smacked his leg with it. "I told you to pull back. Not to go that far into Indian country. You're damn lucky to have gotten out of there."

"Yes, sir. But I wanted to be sure of where that fella was headed."

"Well, we ain't gonna follow him. Not now while the Indians are on the fight." Nolan shoved his hat on.

"That ain't what I was thinkin'." Jesse smirked.

"Are you gonna tell me or make me guess?" Nolan lifted the saddle off Jesse's mare. Nate had the pitchfork, throwing hay into the stall the mare would soon occupy.

"Now that we know he's gone, you can take the family to Birch Creek without worry."

Nolan chuckled.

"Please, Pa." Nate had finished his chore. The fork stood against the wall. The boy's hands were tightly clasped in a praying position, fingers intertwined, showing hopefulness.

It did seem things had worked in their favor. Based on what both the mountain woman and her son had said, Walter's routine was absence rather than homecoming. Black Mesa was quite a distance, and he was still running south. The next town was Buttonwood. Sheriff Berk was a hard man, a good, honest lawman. He didn't tolerate much trouble in his town, so if Walter was headed there and was involved in anything criminal Berk would figure it out. Plus, he had two smart deputies. Nolan had nothing on the mountain couple, no evidence of wrongdoing, though he still believed the man was guilty of something and she was willingly going along with it.

As far as Gray Rock, Jesse had been right. He was quite capable of handling things and could easily round up help or a posse if need be.

Nolan smiled. "Let's go tell your ma we're going to Birch Creek."

The boy cheered, jumping up and down. Jesse gave a whoop and clapped Nolan on the shoulder.

After a later supper of warmed-up stew and after Nate was tucked in bed and Jesse got a few stitches, Nolan finally had a minute alone with Kate. He slipped into bed next to her. Her head rested on a pillow, her red hair spread everywhere,

NATHANIAL

eyes closed, and blankets up over her shoulders. He scooted over until he was pressed against her and gently placed an arm around her. She was thinner, except for the roundness of her belly. Her eyes fluttered open. They smiled at one another, then kissed.

"Why haven't ya told me about the baby?"

She pushed up onto her elbows, looking him in the face. Her pale-blue eyes glistened. "I've wanted to. Lots of times" She touched his face. "There always seems to be an interruption. Elizabeth is cutting teeth, and now that she's toddling, I hardly get a moment's peace. And Nathanial's been such a handful lately. He acts up every time you and Jesse have to work extra hours. He misses that time with you and doesn't seem to know how to explain it, so instead, he turns into a brat, pushing my buttons every chance he gets. I had to give him a licking the other day. I forgot to tell you."

"I'm sorry, Kate." He would give their son a good talking to.

She kissed him. "You're the sheriff. It's your job...and Jesse's. Nathanial's old enough to understand that."

Nolan lay back on his pillow, still focused on Kate. She was quiet for a minute, then slipped her arms around him.

"I'm glad we're going to Birch Creek. All that time together, perhaps Nathanial will settle down. And I know you're busy, but I miss spending time with you too." Kate had never been a clingy woman. She had a good mind of her own, had organized a ladies' auxiliary, filled in as teacher once or twice, and when Mrs. Henry, wife of the hotel owner, took sick, Kate had stepped in as cook for a week. At the end of the day, though, they had always come together as a couple and discussed the day, even if they had spent time with one another. The past two weeks hadn't been that way, and he was sorry he failed her.

When Nolan woke, it was to the sound of a little someone's feet pounding up the stairs. Sunlight streamed in the windows. He rolled over, and down the hall chugged Nathanial at full steam. With a fat smile on his impish face, he sprang onto the bed right on top of his father's guts. Nolan instantly curled, rolling Nate off, which led to a tussling match while the breathless child was trying to spit something out.

"Pa, I can't wait no more. Let's pack the wagon." Nate wiggled to free himself from Nolan's arm lock around his waist. His son grabbed a pillow, playfully whacking him with it.

"I surrender," Nolan said, letting go of his son. "I need coffee before we do anything."

Nathanial leaped off the bed. "I'll get it." And just that fast, he hopped onto the banister and swiftly rode the rail downstairs.

Nolan barely had his breakfast eaten before Nate collected everyone's plates, then helped his ma scrape them clean, which he never volunteered to do. That child hated doing dishes maybe more than getting a whipping. His cheeks were rosy, as was Kate's face, giving off a happy glow.

CHAPTER 6

WITH JESSE ON ONE SIDE and Nolan on the other, they pulled the canvas cover over the wagon. Nate had his little hands in there helping. Everyone was wound up with excitement, chattering about what needed packed, what last-minute supplies they would have to stop in town and get. The sky was sunny, so making miles before dark shouldn't be hard.

Nolan had wanted to put off traveling for another day. Kate had hugged a bucket twice that morning, so he'd thought she would want to rest and feel better before being bounced around inside a wagon. But she insisted they leave today, saying the fresh air would do her good.

They came and went from the house and loaded everything they needed. It was more than Nolan would have packed, but

he wasn't about to argue with Kate about anything. It was true that lately, they hadn't had much time for talking. With all of life's distractions, they just weren't doing a good enough job of finding time for each other. Elizabeth, now that she'd found her feet, was getting into everything she shouldn't, pulling stuff out of cupboards, making messes everywhere.

Nate...Well, he was ornery day or night, Monday through Sunday. And Jesse still needed guidance while learning the job of deputy and taking on more responsibility at the jailhouse.

That was not the kind of marriage Nolan wanted, and he knew for certain that Kate would agree. This trip could help change that. He was devoted to family, but at times, duties outside the home pulled him away. He was guilty of not taking time for only Kate. She needed him too, as much as he needed her. They were a couple, after all, not just two separate people raising kids together. While traveling, there would be less to separate them from one another. He, too, was looking forward to this and had no complaints about leaving earlier than expected.

Finally, everything was in the wagon, including Kate and Elizabeth. Nate rode in front of Jesse, who trotted his horse alongside as Nolan drove the team out of the yard and turned onto the coach road toward Gray Rock. There was no reason to list Jesse's responsibilities while Nolan was away. As deputy, he knew what was expected.

They bought their few extra supplies, got them packed in, and Kate and the kids tearfully hugged and kissed Jesse goodbye at least a goldarn dozen times. It wasn't as though they would never see him again. Kate's emotions had been hitting peaks and valleys the last few weeks, anger to sadness in the blink of an eye, and so far today, it seemed worse because their oldest son was staying behind by choice, old enough to make his own decisions. But Nolan wasn't about to rush Kate. This trip, he hoped, would start and end well. She doted on their kids, nurturing them a little too much. Doing so while she was sickly always seemed to make her feel better, brightened her face. Though, presently, she was sobbing about who would cook for Jesse and so on and such. She couldn't bear the thought of him going hungry.

"Kate." Nolan called her attention. "Jesse's a grown man. If he starves, then it's his own stupid fault."

Her mother bear claws showed as she smacked one fist to a hip while holding Elizabeth perched on the other. Her lips pursed and Nolan expected to hear it, but Jesse intervened.

"Now, Ma. The sheriff's right. I ain't no boy." His charming grin was contagious, and Kate smiled. Jesse took her hand. "Let me help ya into the wagon." He gave her and Elizabeth a lift up. Then he peeled Nate off his back and handed him over. "Good-bye, sir. Safe travels." They firmly shook hands.

Nolan slapped leather to the team, the wagon jerked forward into a steady roll, and Nate waved out the back flap until Jesse was no longer in sight. Mile after mile, the wagon creaked along, making good time. The road wasn't rutty from rain because there'd been none lately. The horses kicked up a little dust, but nothing choking. It didn't even reach into the air as far as their noses. Nate was reading aloud from a dime novel Jesse had ordered for him. Kate had her arm around the boy's shoulders, and their daughter was on her lap. This was exactly what Nolan needed. Time like this was worth more than gold, but every other thought reverted to that mountain couple.

It was possible for the man, Walter, to return instead of going on to Buttonwood. Jesse had a good head on his shoulders and by nature, like Nolan, was a cautious man. He'd be leery of any stranger. So far, no women in close proximity to Gray Rock had been snatched, and they wanted to keep it that way. Other than folks passing through town on the stage, that couple was the only new people to plant themselves in Gray Rock. Why set up a home if they planned on stealing women?

"Nolan, stop. I'm gonna be—" Kate leaned over the side, retching.

With a mighty yank, he halted the team. Nate and Elizabeth nearly went flying off the seat. He threw out an arm, stopping them from falling.

How much longer could this sickness go on? He should have gone with his first instinct and stayed home today and traveled tomorrow. He'd even thought about taking her to see Doc. Why had he let her talk him out of resting for a day before a week of riding in a jarring wagon? Sometimes he was a darn fool when it came to that woman.

Nolan jumped down and hustled around to the other side. She was climbing down, and he gave a hand. Sweat beaded her head, and he couldn't recall her ever being so pale, not even when she was carrying Elizabeth. Now that Kate was steady on her feet. He took Elizabeth from Nathanial.

"Nate, get me a blanket," Nolan said.

The boy hopped over the seat into the bed and tossed Nolan a groundsheet in a matter of a few seconds. It seemed their son was also worried about his mama. Nolan spread the piece of patchwork on the ground under the shade of a tall block of trees. Kate immediately lay down, closing her eyes. For a first, he noticed how ill-fitting her clothing hung on her, or maybe it was just that dress. Either way, she had lost more weight than he'd realized, and she wasn't a big person to begin with. That worried him.

A shallow creek snaked through the meadow where ash and maples were rooted, and long branches overhead supplied the needed canopy of shade. Near the water, the air was slightly cooler. It might be good for Kate. A body could breathe easier when the air wasn't sticky, and the day was warm.

"Kate, we're turning around. I'm taking ya to see Doc. Birch Creek is a far trip. It might be too much for ya." He gently dabbed at her head with a handkerchief.

Nate came over with a canteen, thrusting it toward his ma, who had opened her eyes and sat up. "Maybe this'll help." Then he turned on his pa. "Pa, I wanna go to Birch Creek." He stomped his feet. "What about Deputy?"

NATHANIAL

Nolan understood that Nathanial wanted to play with his best buddy, but he would not risk Kate's health or that of the baby. It twisted him up inside seeing her so sick. There would be other opportunities to visit the Huckabees. Yes, the holiday celebration would be lots of fun for everyone, but it wasn't worth risking Kate possibly getting sicker along the way and no doctor being close. What if this illness turned out to be a complication with the pregnancy and not just morning sickness?

"We're not going home, sweetheart," Kate interjected, reaching for Nate's wrist, pulling him down next to her and patting his leg. She coddled their kids too damn much at times. It wasn't a sin to take care of herself, especially when she was obviously ill.

"The hell we ain't." Nolan was firm.

Elizabeth began to fuss, reaching for her mother. Maybe she'd felt his muscles tense or sensed the shift in mood. Kate reached up and took the baby.

Nate jumped to his feet, kicking at the dirt. Of course their son didn't want to go home, and Nolan was in no mood to put up with a fit.

"I'll walk if I have to." The boy smarted off.

"There will be none of that," Kate said as though she were really saying they were going on. Since when had she become the head of this family? Mostly, they talked things out together, not usually in front of the kids, for good reason. "Kate we're turning back. Nathanial, water the team. Then get in the wagon."

"No." The boy stood his ground next to his ma.

Nolan grabbed their son's arm, twisting him around, and with the flat of his hand, he smacked Nate's ass three hard swats. Tears streaked down the boy's face. His bawling made Elizabeth cry, and she had her little face tucked into their mama's bosom. Kate hugged all over their daughter and gave him the evil eye.

He ignored that for the moment and looked hard at the boy. "You don't talk to me that way. Now I told you to go water the horses."

Nathanial shot off in the direction of the team while wiping at his eyes.

"There's no reason to go home." Kate pertly sat up straighter as if he didn't have reason to be concerned. "I'll be fine."

"Ya don't have me convinced. This is every day. And it seems to have gotten worse since we left." He jerked his head toward the mess of puke on the ground near the wagon.

"There's nothing Doc can do for my condition. We both know that. Not until the end anyway. Now let's drop it." Her lips had smartly thinned into a straight line of annoyance.

Drop it! How could he? She and the kids were everything to him. He couldn't believe her nonchalant attitude. What the devil had gotten into her? "What if this is more than just the typical sickness that goes with pregnancy?" he said with profound irritation.

"This ain't the time, husband." She glanced over at Nathanial, who had the team unhitched, leading them toward the stream well within earshot. Her eyes welled. There was fear in them. "I don't want him running off again like he did when I was carrying Elizabeth." Kate squeezed their daughter tighter.

"I don't think he will. He's got a helluva jealous streak, but things are different now. Our family is more settled, and he knows his place." Nolan had confidence.

Nathanial was a Crosson through and through. The boy rarely brought up his old life and those who'd been part of it. All he ever talked about was following in Nolan's footsteps and becoming sheriff. In part, that might have been so he could boss Jesse. Though, Nate couldn't have been any more of a shadow had he actually grown from Nolan's seed.

NATHANIAL

"Later, husband. Please. Let me rest." Her voice softened. She began to lay her head down, red strands of hair falling out of the loose bun on top, Elizabeth still drawn in her arms. Their daughter had stopped crying and was now half asleep.

"We need to talk about this now. I'm scared we might lose the baby," he blurted out. A proud father he was, and they both wanted more children.

Kate snapped into a sitting position, her gaze on Nathanial, whose head reared up from where he was squatted picketing the team on a thick patch of grass. His eyes widened, a fresh shimmer of insecurity showing. How could Nolan have been so clumsy with his words? It wasn't often, but their son did need reminding from time to time of how their feelings for him were no different just because he was adopted and Elizabeth wasn't. He'd been raised without care until they had filed the legal papers and claimed him. Before then, he'd never known a gentle touch or kind word. Beaten on, neglected—those were the harsh affections his outlaw father and others had shown the boy.

When Kate was carrying Elizabeth, Nate had gotten so scared that they wouldn't want him, would give up loving him, he had run off three hundred miles to Buttonwood and gotten himself in some serious trouble. Their love for him didn't need reinforcing as often as when Nathanial had first come to live with them. Things had gotten much better, but that frailness was still an issue now and then. Lots of time had passed since then, and Nate had the reassurance of experience. Nothing had changed after Elizabeth had come.

From what Nolan could see, Nate was in shock, slowly, stiffly standing, but Nolan still didn't believe he'd run away. He'd maybe be upset for a short spell.

Nate began to step away from Nolan and Kate. It was clear by his panicked expression that he didn't want to hear that he was getting a little brother or sister. In particular, a brother.

Nate wasn't good at sharing his time with his father, not that Nolan didn't spend time with Elizabeth. However, his time with her and Nate was spent differently. Nate was often called "Little Nolan" by lots of folks in Gray Rock, and he made no qualms about telling anyone and everyone just that, how much he wanted to be like his father.

"Sweetheart…" Kate's voice was soft and filled with concern.

Nate scooted farther away, two or three more feet, separating himself from them.

Those bastards—the men who had long ago been part of Nate's life, the scumbags that hit him, treating him worse than a dog—infuriated Nolan anytime the ugliness of Nate's insecurities reared up. Kate looked heartbroken as her little boy scurried backward another foot or two. It was a remnant of the mess caused by those men. The couple was used to dealing with it, accepted it was an outcome of Nate's past, but neither of them liked it. They loved their son enough not to let anger about the boy's past show on their faces.

Nolan took a step toward his son. It was all it took. Nathanial spun on his heel, except Nolan was faster and caught hold of his arm, not letting the pup squirm away.

"Nathanial, settle yourself." It was said firmly, but not an uncaring warning.

The child held still, his head down, staring at the ground around his feet. Nolan lifted his chin. Nate's little face wrinkled up mean as though the news of the baby was meant to upset him.

"Just 'cause your mama's gonna have a baby doesn't change anything." Nolan pulled him in close, hands on Nate's shoulders so they were face to face. "You should be happy. If it's a boy, you can teach him to ride a horse as good as you." It was a fact that Nolan was proud of. Nathanial could ride a horse as good, maybe better than most men. Though, he liked to jump the corral fence on the mustang, which did nothing but irk

NATHANIAL

Nolan. He didn't want to see him get hurt and whipped him more often than not for doing that.

Nate's muscles relaxed a mite under Nolan's grasp. "You sure?" What the boy was really asking was would they give up being his pa and ma because he hadn't been born to them.

Nolan saw Nate as his blood, always had since the day Nate had taken the Crosson name—actually before. Nothing would ever change that.

"You're my son. I'd never give ya up, ever, not to anyone." Nolan winked. "I think ya already know that."

Nathanial nodded, grinning from ear to ear, then looked at his ma for the same reassurance. What they saw was a big, loving smile, teary eyes, and arms stretched wide. Nate threw himself into her embrace, and they held one another.

Nolan made lunch while Nate played with Elizabeth at the creek and Kate rested. Her nausea had passed, but she complained of being so tired. With their stomachs full, except Kate's, Nolan loaded everyone into the wagon.

"Pa?" Nate sweetly turned his face up, batting his long lashes.

"Don't say a word about goin' to Birch Creek." Nolan warned.

The boy threw himself back on the seat.

Kate reached around him and touched Nolan's arm. "Husband, why don't we go? I'm feeling much better. I shouldn't have eaten those eggs at breakfast. Cooking them, just the smell alone, turned my stomach." She grinned. "There's a doctor in Birch Creek. I'll go see him as soon as we arrive." Kate was as bad as Nathanial, both of them giving him sad eyes. She didn't usually resort to such immature tactics, so she must not have thought she could appeal to his senses any other way, really wanting to go herself.

Good Lord, he was a weak-spirited man at times. Only when it came to his family. It made him wonder about Jesse, and he hoped that mountain woman stayed out of town and didn't cause his deputy any trouble. Jesse, no doubt, was out on the trails, hunting for some sign of whoever was abducting women, and that was enough weight to carry.

Nolan slapped leather to the team, and they were off. Kate and Nathanial cheerily began to sing, "She'll Be Coming 'Round the Mountain," but switched out the word she'll with we'll. Elizabeth squealed, Kate, hand over hand, clapping to the tune with their daughter.

Nolan kept a close eye on Nathanial during the following days. The boy was a little quieter than normal and stuck close to his ma as though it were the last minutes he would spend with her. Apparently, he was apprehensive, more so than Nolan had first believed him to be. There might be a half-cocked idea brewing in that little head about running off. Birch Creek was a big town, almost a city compared to Gray Rock, and with lots of folks in town for the celebration, it would be easy for the pup to slip away. Maybe being reunited with his pal would keep him grounded; although, Deputy had run off to Buttonwood with Nate. Those two together were something else. Knuckleheads. Nolan would just have to be overly watchful.

CHAPTER 7

NOLAN STEERED the team into Birch Creek around midmorning. Nate stood on the seat between him and Kate and shaded his eyes, searching for Deputy. Deputy hopped off a bench in front of the jailhouse. His face lit up with a big, fat smile, and he waved with wild exuberance.

"Pa, they're here!" Huckabee's son hollered over his shoulder.

Nolan pulled up on the reins, then locked the wheel chock in place. The jailhouse door swung open. Marshal Huckabee strolled out, extending a hand, and they shook firmly. It was good to see each other.

Nathanial bounded off the seat feet first past Nolan, getting a push. The boys happily eyed one another for half a second, then shot off pounding down the boardwalk toward the Huckabee home. Probably, they were headed for the pond behind the house. It was a favorite spot—mud, frogs, and occasionally a harmless water snake. What else could two little hoodlums long for?

"Nolan, Kate, glad y'all could join us. The missus is looking forward to having ya." The marshal looked closer, studying Kate.

She wasn't standing too tall—not that she was tall, the average height for a woman. But today, with her gills green, she stood hunched over and weary-looking, feeble, as though she'd pulled the wagon from Gray Rock to Birch Creek.

"Ma'am, no offense, but it appears the long travel has not agreed with you. Constance has your rooms ready if you'd like to go to the house and rest a spell."

Kate weakly nodded.

"Where's your doctor?" Nolan slipped his arm around Kate, holding her steady.

Huckabee pointed down the street. "I hope it's nothing serious. Is there anything I can do?"

Nolan was about to burst, anxious to share the glorious news. He smiled at his friend. "Kate's with child."

He received a hearty spank on the shoulder.

"Congratulations. That is fine news." Huckabee picked up the reins of the team. "I'll take your wagon to the house and tell Constance. We'll wait for ya there." He clucked at the horses, and the wagon lunged forward.

A half hour later, Nolan and Kate were given the news they'd both been waiting to hear. She was fine, the baby healthy, and sooner or later, the sickness would pass. Kate just needed to take it easy and rest whenever she could. Doctor's orders—and Nolan would remind her.

After Nolan and Huckabee had the wagon tucked inside the barn and Kate, along with their loaded trunks, squared away at the house with the marshal's wife, Nolan and Marshal Huckabee headed for the jailhouse. Joseph had to keep his eyes on the town. With so many folks coming in, crowding the streets, hotels, and boarding houses, it could mean trouble. Even bigger trouble could be a jammed-full saloon. There were even people camped out in wagons along the outskirts. Nolan would guess forty or fifty Conestogas. It looked like an entire other town. As lawmen, both men were comfortable in a room with cells and could use that time to catch up.

Nigh to the town square where the jailhouse sat, Nolan happened to glance across the street. Buckboards holding families rolled by, along with single riders, all of which kicked up dust. On the other side stood the Songbird Saloon, a yellow-painted building named after an actress who had stayed after the show she'd been involved with moved on to the next dusty cow town. She claimed to have fallen in love with the owner, Sam, a right smart fella whom Nolan had spoken to numerous times when visiting the Huckabees. The actress's given name was Lola, and Nolan had been fortunate to have heard her sing and hoped maybe he would get another chance during this stay in Birch Creek.

A prim-looking couple stood at the swinging doors of the saloon, the woman trimmed in lace. She was wearing pearls the size of pennies and carried a folded parasol. Fancy. On tiptoes, they both poked their heads over the threshold and peered inside. The man's tailored, pinstriped gray suit fit to perfection. Glinting in the sun were his diamond cufflinks. Dandified. They seemed hesitant to step inside but were intently watching something or someone, the lady's fingers curled over the door. Was the songbird singing?

Lola drew quite a crowd. Even the respectable would gather in the den of gambling, whores, and whiskey to have their ears caressed by that lovely soprano, which usually carried into the street. Though, nothing but the creak of wheels, the swish of horses flicking away flies, and the hum of lots of people filled the air.

There was something else about those two that caught Nolan's attention, more than the fancy duds. They seemed far out of place. Easterners he would bet. The other folks around him were all of the western variety. The men, even if dressed in broadcloth suits, wore guns. The ladies were mostly sensible in attire, unlike that woman who, even in her impractical high heels, was short. The couple appeared polished in a way that folks who lived west of the Mississippi were not, even the wealthy ones. Hereabouts, it was mostly cattlemen who held big money, rough men who handled cowboys, broncs, cattle, and sometimes rustlers. Their wives might have enjoyed big houses with bought furniture and none of them probably wore homespun clothes, but they cooked, cleaned, raised kids, stood by their menfolk, and fought next to them if need be. That's how it had been when the area was thick with Indians. Sometimes a woman had to be as tough as her man was.

This lady was tiny, almost doll-like, with porcelain skin. Probably, she never got out in the sun, the fresh air. Certainly, she'd never fought off anything more than the heat, and even that was questionable. They were big city folks, not that Birch Creek wasn't large. It was by all accounts when compared to all the little one-horse towns all over the Wyoming territory. It was bigger than Gray Rock but smaller than Laramie or Cheyenne. It seemed silly, those two being there. What could Birch Creek offer that a big city fandango wouldn't have ten times over? Why did he even care? Oddly, it was the lady's fair hair that drew his eye. Not as white as Nathanial's, but unusually light for anyone over the age of five.

Nolan owned a canniness for sizing up folks, and those two were too sterling for this place. Not that they weren't welcome. Everyone was. Birch Creek was a friendly town, but an agenda had probably brought them there, business maybe, traveling through on their way to San Francisco or some important port along the coast. Nolan wasn't here in any official capacity. This was time to get away from his job. But he couldn't get away from his instincts, and there was just something about them that bothered him.

About then, the doors flung wide, smacking the couple, which caused them to stumble back, flailing while trying to

NATHANIAL

keep from falling in the dirt. Nathanial and Deputy, snickering like all get-out, plowed straight through without much notice of the couple brushing themselves clean. The man's face instantly lit up red, his brow furrowed, and he glared at the mischievous boys. Deputy was juggling a big old bumpy bullfrog. The critter was croaking and bucking, doing its best to get free. Those little troublemakers must have been teasing Tate. Nolan chuckled.

Tate Horn was a tall, lean man, faster than most with a pistol, who liked to drink and flirt with women, and no matter what, there was always an easygoing way about him that matched his happy-go-lucky grin. No mistake, though, Tate was a hell of a tough man, one to have beside you in a fight, a loyal friend. One thing was strange about him—his almighty fear of frogs, big ones. He hated them. Wouldn't go near them, not even those served up in a frying pan.

Nolan reckoned that Deputy had played that prank on Tate before, and now he'd gotten Nathanial in on the picking. Kids would be kids. Nolan stepped off the boardwalk toward the saloon, the marshal at his side, and he, too, was shaking his head. Not in town an hour and the boys had already stirred up trouble. They were streaking away and quickly disappeared into an alleyway, likely returning to the pond.

The highfaluting woman ogled after them. Her eyes stretched wide and stuck on the spot where the boys had ducked between the two buildings, her mouth slightly hanging open, showing she was baffled, maybe angry. Perhaps she wanted to give them an earful.

Nolan smirked and pushed through the swinging doors. There was always a good time to be had with Tate.

CHAPTER 8

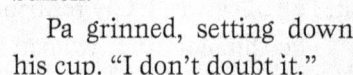

THAT HAD TO BE THE BIGGEST, ugliest bullfrog Nate had ever laid eyes on. Slimiest too. Neither he nor Deputy could stop giggling. What a joke, flopping that fat sucker on the table right smack dab in front of Tate, almost on his lap. He was up out of that chair like a honeybee had stung his behind. Boy oh boy, had he cursed until they grabbed that frog and ran out. Everyone in the Songbird got a kick out of it.

That night at supper, both families were seated at length on each side of the Huckabees' table. Tate was like a brother to Marshal Huckabee, the same as Jesse was a son to Pa. It was great, them all together, and Nate and Deputy sat near Tate, ribbing him hard about the frog. It made him miss Jesse.

He looked over at his father. "I bet Jesse misses me a whole bunch."

Pa grinned, setting down his cup. "I don't doubt it."

The next day, Pa and Tate took them fishing while the marshal kept an eye on things in town. The carnival people were supposed to be coming in soon, and Nate wouldn't forget the red balloon he promised to get Jesse. After lunch, their fathers took

them hunting for a few hours, and they came back with a mess of rabbits, which was a fine supper. Tate was a little sore that he hadn't gotten to go since nothing broke out in town. The worst that had happened was some drunk stumbled out of the Songbird and passed out in the street.

Two more days passed with a sunny sky and fluffy white clouds overhead. It was great entertainment, watching the carousel being built. A boxing ring and dunk tank were set up. There was an area roped off for a sporting show claiming the shooter could cut the end of a cigar held in the mouth of a beautiful young woman. Along with that, there would be trick riding. Food stands were taking shape, and a man was walking around on stilts. It was all so exciting. Nate could just pop out of his skin with anticipation.

Earlier that evening, Nate and the rest of the kids were stripped down and made to bathe. Since he and Deputy were the oldest, they got the fresh water. Then in went Miles, Deputy's little brother, then Ada, his baby sister, and—Ma always said, "Don't throw the baby out with the bathwater!"—Elizabeth was last. It had been decided that both families would take supper at the Royal, a restaurant too elegant for Nate's liking, but he wouldn't complain. Maybe he and Deputy could slip out early and go sneak a peek into the cage that supposedly held a goat with not two, but three horns growing out of its head.

Pa held the door at the Royal as their party filed into the dining room.

Ma pulled aside Nate. "You and Deputy better behave, or I'll have your pa take a hand to ya." There was no joke in her tone. During the last visit, there had been an episode when they got to wrestling in their seats, bumped a waiter, and a serving platter filled with loaded plates was spilled and crashed all over the floor. Hell of a mess. Ma hadn't forgotten that.

"Yes, ma'am." He raised his right hand. All he could do was his best, and he glanced at Pa, who patted his shoulder as though saying all would be fine.

They were seated in the middle of a noisy room. Waitresses buzzed past with water pitchers, pots of coffee, and plates of steamy food. Utensils clinked in all corners, and a mushed-together hum of voices almost strangled out the clank of pans coming from the kitchen. The place was packed. Nate reckoned they were lucky there was no wait. His belly growled.

Of course he and Deputy sat together, and they had sneakily chosen chairs to space themselves from their mothers, which wasn't hard since Ma would need to feed Elizabeth and Mrs. Huckabee had to tend to her two younger children. Pa and the marshal where next in the line of seats, sitting across from one another. Then Nate and his best pal sat on the end.

The food was ordered, and while they waited, they conversed the same as everyone else in the dining room. Nate took a good look around and recognized the man who'd been on stilts. Then he noticed some woman at a table between them. She was openly staring at him. How rude.

He nudged Deputy under the table. "Ain't that the same lady from outside the saloon? The one we almost ran over."

His best friend nodded.

Nate once again looked over. His gaze met hers. She lifted her chin a mite, and there was a snooty air about her. Nate didn't like the smell of first class. Anyone who thought they were better than everyone else could kiss his big toe. Besides, her gawking was irritating. She needed to knock it off. A grown-up should know better. He'd show her. He stuck out his tongue, which earned a tap on the head from Pa.

"Ignore her," Pa said, but then he did the exact opposite. His dark-blue eyes were fastened on the uppity-looking couple, and the hard look he gave was none too friendly.

NATHANIAL

Pa was protective, but Nate sensed it wasn't only that. Who were those people? He hadn't seen Pa or even the marshal talk to either one, but now that he was thinking about it, he'd seen them both around and always a little too close. But there were lots of folks in town, and he had crossed paths with hundreds of them over the past few days. Everyone seemed to buzz all around, watching the happenings before the big shindig. It was probably just a coincidence.

Nate ate his plate clean, his gut about to burst. Ma would chew him out if he unbuttoned his pants there, but then again, he'd be able to breathe easier. When the waitress asked if anyone would like dessert, Nate vigorously shook his head. Maybe if he walked around, got some fresh air, he'd feel better. Under the table, he tapped Deputy's shin. When he put down his glass of milk and looked across the table, Nate subtly pointed with his chin at the door. Deputy winked.

It was doubtful they would be set loose at that hour, even if they promised to stay on the bench just outside. But that's not what either of them had in mind. To two boys of their age, the forbidden nightlife that went on around them while they were stuck in bed seemed far more exciting than everything they saw during the day. Tonight, the songbird was to perform, and there'd been talk of a dance outside town where all the wagons were parked, where those folks who had come too late to get a room at the hotel or boarding house were camped.

"Pa," Deputy said. The marshal looked over while chewing on a hunk of steak. "I gotta use the outhouse." He squirmed in his seat just enough to hint that it was an emergency.

"Go on."

"Nate should go with me."

Before Deputy could give a reason, the marshal's brow shot up. It was a definite sign of suspicion. Deputy better come up with something good or they'd be stuck there through dessert, and none of the adults seemed to be in a hurry. Nate's pa wasn't even done with his meal yet.

"Why? Does he suddenly have to relieve himself too?" the marshal asked dryly, a knowing look on his face.

With a lawman for a father, it was hard to get away with anything. That didn't mean Nate wouldn't try.

"Well, sir." He cleared his throat. "When a book ain't available,"—meaning Deputy would not be using the outhouse at his home where reading material was at hand—"some company outside the door might do instead."

He had another thought that quite possibly might be more convincing, because the marshal's brow was still arched as if he didn't believe a single word Nate was shoveling.

"Plus, the sun's going down. Kinda scary sittin' in thar when it's dark." He shivered for added believability. They were just children, knee-high to a grasshopper, and what he'd said was a little bit true. He'd pestered Jesse on more than one moonless night to guard the outside while he did his business.

They turned on their best pouts, pleading with cute faces for permission. This usually never worked on Nate's pa. Maybe the marshal would fall for it, but he laughed and glanced at Pa, who put an arm around Nate's shoulders and gave a small squeeze.

"What are you boys up to?" Pa wasn't going to let them leave the table without knowing the truth. It was time to fess up, as if Pa hadn't already guessed.

"We just wanna go look around…by ourselves," he added in a soft tone.

Pa did something strange then. He looked across the room at the snooty couple, the one that had been staring at Nate earlier. They were watching him again, then glanced away as soon as they realized their odd behavior was noticed.

NATHANIAL

"Stay where I can see ya." Behind their party was a window. If Pa angled his chair just a mite, he could see nearly the whole length of the street.

They quickly promised, then swiftly zigzagged between tables and glided out the door. Nate glanced then waved at Pa watching them, coffee raised to his lips.

From among the campers, a fiddler made music that flowed into the street, creating a sense of peace as the orange hue of the sleepy sun hugged the skyline. Someone tooted on a jug. Shadows blanketed the ground in places, and soon, the land would be covered in black. Lights were being lit along the street, and one by one, lanterns came on inside the dwellings that stood among the businesses.

In the square stood a tree with a crooked spine, long, twisted branches reaching out over the street. There was a well pump near there, a short bench, and some other kids horsing around. Hoots and hollers flew every which way, making the fun sound good. He and Deputy skipped along, following after the giggles.

"Bet ya can't climb to the top." Deputy dared him.

"Got a nickel says I can." Nate pulled the coin out of his pocket.

"Fine, I'll take your money." Deputy smirked, too sure that Nate wouldn't make it up there. The tree did look flimsy near the top. The branches were thinned out, not so many, and definitely not as thick around. But he was a featherweight for his age.

He hopped up on the bench, then grabbed the lowest branch and, with a grunt, swung his legs up. A minute later and almost halfway, he was feeling confident. After all, he was the best tree climber at recess back in Gray Rock. Deputy didn't know that, and Nate would soon be five cents richer. Though, he'd probably just buy them both gumdrops.

"I insist you come down from there this instant!" Below, the voice was one he didn't recognize, and Nate glanced down. His foot slipped and his hands caught on the branch above.

It was the prissy lady. The other kids had scattered, perhaps afraid of getting in trouble for something. The pert way she dressed made her look like a bitch.

Deputy stood at the base of the trunk, looking up, although he, too, had moved out of arm's reach of the lady.

"If you come down, I win." Deputy boasted.

Nate was no quitter.

"Ya ain't my ma. I don't have to listen to you." Nate turned his back on the woman, thinking of winning, and headed for the top. With his next step and closer to the finish line, a skinny branch groaned under his weight. The cockeyed tree seemed to lean even more. Oh lordy, he hoped he didn't fall. His hands were sweaty.

"Boy, git your hide back on the ground." That warning came from Pa, and he sounded mad.

Nate's gaze turned downward. The lady was gone, and there in her place stood Pa, his neck red right up to his ears. Nate hustled to get out of the tree, though he made sure he had a good grip so he didn't fall and break his head wide open. His heart was pounding. Getting his ass smacked in the middle of the street, the center of town, with so many people around wasn't something he wanted to happen.

"Over there on the bench." Pa pointed as Nate's feet touched the dirt. He and Deputy were marched near to the front door of the restaurant. "Don't move." Pa wagged a finger at the two of them before returning inside.

"Whew." Nate wiped his sweaty brow. "Thought I was gonna git it."

"So did I." Deputy held out his hand. "Pay up."

There was no use complaining. A bet was a bet, even if Pa had stopped him from collecting on what could have been a win. Nate dropped his money into Deputy's greedy fingers, who then triumphantly grinned and shoved his winnings into his pocket.

"I'm glad to see you made it down safely." The woman had reappeared.

Where she had come from, Nate wasn't sure. He hadn't heard the restaurant door open or close, not since Pa had gone inside. This woman had made herself scarce when his father had come to talk to him, and now that he wasn't right handy in sight, she showed herself once again. Nate popped up closer to Deputy, who was standing next to him alongside the bench. When would Pa look out that window and notice her? Nate didn't like being alone with her, a stranger, and Deputy didn't count because he wasn't any bigger than Nate. But they both could holler real loud if Nate couldn't scare her off.

"Git away from me, or I'll spit on ya." He hocked up a big, juicy glob, rolling the snot on his tongue.

"What's your name?" Her voice was silken, a devious caress to get what she wanted. She'd even batted her lashes, lashes as long as his. He knew a dupe when he saw one. He'd been taught those types of ploys. She had ignored his warning, and that pissed him off. The last thing he would tell her was his name. Wasn't any of her business. Though, he might just tell her to go live with the devil.

Pa would blister Nate's hide if he saw what Nate was about to do. God willing, he'd never find out. Nate arched his neck and spit. The woman belched a quick scream. Her hand, the one holding a beaded clutch, flew up, stopping the green wad from splattering her frilly blouse. She waved her little bag violently until the slime fell off into a dollop at her feet on the boardwalk. Nate and Deputy giggled.

She didn't need to know Nate's name, and she hadn't asked for Deputy's. Who they were wasn't important unless she planned to tell their folks, but why wait so long if she had a mind to yell at them for nearly knocking over her and her man a few days ago outside the saloon? It had been an accident. No harm done.

Strangely, she didn't seem to even notice Deputy. Her big blue eyes were all on Nate. His heart began to pound.

"Lady," he said with some serious huff, "I'm a deputy. So is he." Nate puffed out his chest, showing his spit-shined badge. "If you don't leave us alone, we'll lock your ass in a cell."

Her mouth fell open. "What kind of language is that for a child to be using?" She crossed her arms. "I'm not going to hurt you." A ripple of amused laughter shook her shoulders a wee bit. "You remind me of someone, someone that was lost to me. I'm trying to find him." Her face lost any glee, and there was a cold, hard look about her. Her stance had become rigid, the picture of a stuffed shirt. Likely, she was used to getting what she wanted, judging by the giant-size brooch pinned to her bodice. Whoever she was hunting, it was obvious she wouldn't give up.

She leaned down, looking him in the face. Her smile was soft, but Nate didn't trust it. A wolf in sheep's clothing was what she was. He had a sixth sense for those things. It was his outlaw upbringing, before becoming a Crosson, that made him leery of most strangers. And more times than not, he was right to trust his gut instinct. This woman made him fidgety. He didn't like her. He pushed her hand away from touching his hair as she stared. His strands were the same color as hers, nothing special, certainly nothing to be so fascinated with. Deputy was a towhead, and she wasn't trying to touch him.

"It won't hurt to tell me your name." She reached again, this time to touch his arm, and he sprang away, knocking into Deputy. Both of them hit the boardwalk one on top of the other, and both stared at this stranger who was now bending, offering a hand.

Where was Pa? Nate was just about to scream.

"Excuse me, ma'am. Is there a problem?" Pa hauled Nate up by an arm and lifted Deputy with his other hand, pushing them behind him. They peeked around his hips. He was firmly planted between them and the woman. Thank goodness for that.

Would she have tried to snatch him, maybe kidnapped him? There'd been some of that going on back in Gray Rock—not kids, but grown women. Criminals sometimes did the unexpected. She didn't fit the image of the average outlaw, but who knew? Maybe she was a kid snatcher. Asking his name and telling him that story might have just been a way to get him to feel bad for her, to trust her, a conniving way to get her hands on him. But why? He was probably just letting his imagination run away with him after hearing all that talk about abductions for weeks. Likely, she was just one of many odd idiots in this world.

Her pale eyes were wide. Pa had come out without notice, an expert at walking softly. It was part of being a good lawman. He could sneak up on an outlaw nice and quiet so as not to get shot.

The woman breathed heavily and fanned herself with her dainty little handbag. Her face was crimson. Talking to Nate was obviously meant to be a secret or at least meant to go unnoticed. Getting caught hadn't been part of her plan, if she'd had a plan at all. Maybe she was just a well-dressed loon.

"No. Everything is fine," she said hurriedly while stepping past Pa toward the door. "Excuse me." The words were thrown at them over her shoulder as she was halfway inside. Glancing back, her gaze met Nate's.

"Pa, who was that?" Nate tugged on his father's sleeve.

Pa was still watching after the woman. He shook his head. "Just stay away from her."

Nate wouldn't have to be told twice. He had no intention of going anywhere near her. It was just creepy, her staring at him through supper and even days before that and then wanting to know his name. Why would she think he was that lost someone? He wasn't lost. He didn't know her, had never met her before, and he hoped to hell he never laid eyes on her again.

"Pa, can Deputy and me go to the house?" Nate felt safe to leave Pa's side to do that.

The strange couple was inside the restaurant. Pa would soon be in there, and without a doubt, he would keep a close eye on them. Nate and Deputy could be at the Huckabee home in three minutes, long before those city folks came out looking again.

That lady had been shaking when she flew inside. Nate felt a little quivery himself.

Pa ruffled his hair. "I'll walk you boys home." Before they turned to run off along the boardwalk in front of him, Pa put a hand on Nate's shoulder. "What did she say to you?"

"She asked for my name. I didn't tell her." He figured he'd done right, given she was a stranger and all.

Pa nodded thoughtfully, then waved them off as Ma and the rest of their party filed out the door.

Nate couldn't get the question out of his head. Who did that prissy lady think he was?

CHAPTER 9

NATE WON THE RACE TO THE HOUSE. He and Deputy were both puffing when they got there. Pa and everyone else weren't too far behind. The evening was cool. The outside air felt good.

Nate and Deputy were playing jacks on the porch when Tate joined in the lounging, taking a seat on the swing next to Pa and the marshal. Nate overhead Pa quietly talking about that couple and how the lady had followed him outside. Maybe he didn't want Ma to overhear and get worried, but she'd probably seen all the commotion out the window at the restaurant and that's why everyone came home. She and Pa didn't keep secrets. Pa had explained that and some other things about marriage to Jesse while Nate had been playing in the barn and listening. So he'd probably tell her at some point.

Ma was in a delicate condition, or so Pa had said. That meant Nate had to try real hard not to upset her. Hopefully, that couple didn't cause them any more trouble and possibly upset Ma. She wasn't one to get angry too easily, but she might get mad at Nate since he was the source of their curiosity. What if Ma didn't want bothered with all that, bothered with him? What if the new baby took his place? What if she didn't want him anymore?

No, he couldn't let himself think like that. Everything had been okay after Elizabeth was born. Nothing had changed between Nate and his mother and father. Besides, he always had Jesse. Unless Jesse started to like the baby better. Nate hoped it wasn't a boy.

"I won." Deputy swiped up the last jack.

Nate's mind hadn't been on the game. He needed to forget those people and enjoy the time with his family and friends. Too soon, Pa would be back at work.

Tate retrieved a guitar from inside the house, then took a seat on the stoop and strummed. Everyone sang, and before they knew it, there were millions of stars twinkling in the sky.

Ma yawned. "Nathanial, it's time for bed." Elizabeth was asleep on her lap. They sat next to Pa on the swing, his arm around Ma's shoulders.

Nate didn't want to go to sleep, but he wasn't about to argue. The last time he bickered, Pa had swatted him before Nate realized he was even thinking about giving him a licking. Instead, Nate crossed his arms sharply in silent protest. Deputy huffed loudly because his ma had followed suit and was shooing her children off to bed.

They stomped up the stairs side by side, giving each other that look of knowing better. It was easy to read the other's mind when they thought so much alike. There was fun to be had outside those walls, and they would find it.

As soon as Ma kissed Nate's head and the door clicked shut behind her, he threw off the blankets and tore off his nightshirt. In all of two seconds, he had his clothes back on, as did Deputy. Quietly, they heaved the window open. It couldn't have worked out any better. The back porch roof ran the length of the house just under Deputy's window. When they had been forced inside, Pa and the marshal were still sitting on the front porch, sipping sweet tea. It was a specialty of Mrs. Huckabee's, and it was good.

Nate was the first to the edge, curling his fingers around and swinging down toward the post. He caught it and slid down, touching his feet quietly to the ground. Deputy followed a few seconds behind. They skirted the pond where tall grass swayed in the breeze, and flowering bushes and a tree here or there kept them well hidden while making their way to a night of forbidden fun.

They kept to the alleyways and behind the buildings so as not to be spotted if Tate was making rounds. Voices poured out of the saloon, laughter boomed, and the cigar smoke was so thick it blurred their view through the window. How many bodies could be shoved in one room?

"Lola hasn't started yet. Let's go find a spot." Deputy tugged on Nate's sleeve. They turned toward the door. In the meantime, the keys of a piano were tinkering. It was music, not truly pleasing to the ear, but Nate hadn't ever been out this late, so all was good.

They slipped in under the doors without making them swing. No one, not a soul, looked their direction. In a room so crowded, they just sort of blended into all the noise and moving about that was going on. Nate smiled and nudged Deputy, who was also wearing a fat grin. Cards were being tossed, bets made, money lost and won. Fancy painted ladies danced around and slung drinks. The bartender, Sam, was pulling tabs and filling mugs as quick as he could. Men lined the bar. Every table seat was filled. Others stood around jawing or watching the gambling.

A cowboy gave a hoot and swung around a lady in a ruffled skirt, then kissed her. Nate and Deputy giggled. That was gross. They bellied up to the bar, sort of. Shorter than the top, they stood on the toe bar and still had be on tiptoes to look over. There wasn't much room, so they were squeezed tight together on the very end.

Sam slid a foaming beer mug down the bar, then turned, his eyes fixed on them. "Deputy, git the hell outta here. Your pa's gonna skin ya." He shook a straight finger. "And ya brought a friend." Sam pulled a rag covered with smears from his waistband and wiped the bar top where whiskey had sloshed. Deputy ignored Sam as if it were just friendly advice he'd given them and not a warning and slapped his nickel and the nickel he'd won from Nate on the bar.

"Two drinks." Deputy winked at Nate as though to say, *Don't worry.*

Sam pulled a dark bottle out from under the bar. The parchment on it was red, the letters too small for Nate to read without holding it himself, which wasn't going to happen. Sam didn't look happy, so Nate wasn't about to open his mouth and ask. Deputy was smiling. Sam dropped two glasses, one in front of each of them, then poured a shot of syrupy-looking liquid into them.

Nate picked up his, taking a whiff. He grinned, then toasted. "To a night of fun."

They clanked their glasses, then tossed back their shots of sarsaparilla.

"Now leave." Sam picked up the ten cents and left them. Apparently, Deputy was a frequent customer, whether his ma and pa knew it or not. Sam obviously kept sarsaparilla stocked.

Nate followed Deputy over to the piano, where he sat down, stretched his fingers, and began to play right along with the sharp-jawed man sitting there, fingers dancing across the keys while belting out "Oh Where, Oh Where Has My Little Dog Gone?" followed by "Oh My Darling Clementine." Nate had forgotten that Mrs. Huckabee was a fine piano player and had taught her son. He banged the ivories, and the entire place was roaring out "When Johnny Comes Marching Home Again."

NATHANIAL

Nate grabbed the hand of a passing dove. He bowed. "Would ya do me the honor of this dance?"

She lit up with giggles, set down the empty platter that had been carrying whiskey and beer, and took his hands in hers. They two-stepped, whirling around the room.

Men were clapping as the songs played on. A holler rose, then died off. Someone was having a good time. It seemed everyone was.

Nate was breathless. Deputy must have thought he was having too much fun, so he hopped off the piano stool, grabbed a dove for himself, and spun past Nate and his gal. So far, it was quite a night. Ma was all wrong about these kinds of places. Some of the men were stumbling around, drunk on their toes, but it wasn't a sin to sing off-key or even the wrong words.

"Ya mind if I cut in?"

Nate instantly recognized that deep voice, and the dance abruptly halted. Nate swallowed hard. He didn't say a word, balling up inwardly.

The whore smiled at Tate. "Hi, sugar."

Tate ignored her and grabbed Nate by the arm. In three huffing strides, he had a tight grip on Deputy and was dragging them out the door just as Pa and the marshal walked in. A look of utter confusion passed between the two fathers. In no time, Nate and Deputy were marched across the street and into the jailhouse, and Tate actually locked them behind bars.

Tate was stretched back in a chair behind the desk, his feet propped up, when Pa and Marshal Huckabee stormed in. It must've taken a minute for the shock to wear off, and now here they were, looking none too pleased, nostrils flared and faces red.

At that moment, Nate was kind of glad there were iron bars between him and Pa. His ass was feeling the sting of the belt already.

Tate grinned as their fathers eyed them. "We're good here. Everything's under control. Why don't you two go on over and listen to Lola? Her show should start soon. You can pick up these little scoundrels afterward."

"I didn't even know they left the house." The marshal picked up the keys off the desk. Deputy whimpered. He knew what was coming. It was the same thing Nate would get—an ass tanning neither would ever forget.

"Sam sent someone over. Said the boys here were dancing with the girls so they couldn't make him money, if ya know what I mean." Tate smiled at the marshal and Pa, who both grinned. "From what I was told, they did a little singin' and dancin', harmless really." Tate shrugged it off, although he'd been mad just a few minutes ago when he'd dragged them out. With his easygoing manners in charge, the mounting tension as the marshal and Pa decided the severity of the punishment dissipated quickly.

Pa pulled a chair next to the bars, giving them a little bit of a shake. "Don't tell your ma about this, any of it. She'll skin us both."

"No, sir. I won't." Inwardly, Nate was celebrating. He wasn't going to get his ass smacked.

Tate was too much like Jesse. He'd been plenty mad, but he didn't want to see either boy in trouble. They would probably get an ear chewing once their fathers left. If that was all they got, Nate would thank his lucky stars.

"If there's a next time, I'll bare your ass and give ya a whuppin'." Pa had never done that, never even threatened it. It was a bold indication of how serious he was.

"Don't ya worry, Nolan. I'll give 'em both a good talkin' to," Tate added.

Pa and the marshal left, the door banging behind them. Being stuck in a cell for a few hours wasn't the worst punishment they could have gotten.

NATHANIAL

"Tate." Deputy squeezed the bars, his face pressed tight between two. "Why don't ya let us out? You can lock us up before they git back."

Tate laughed. "Boy, that is the one place I know I won't lose track of either of ya. You're stayin' put." He pulled open a desk drawer, then tossed a deck of cards still in the pack to Deputy. "Entertain yourself with that. And no poker. Play Old Maid or Snap."

Nate sat back on the cot. Like Jesse and even Pa, Tate was trying to keep them seeing themselves as kids. It wasn't normal for every child to be around criminals, cages, and Nate looked through the wanted posters daily. He was going to be Pa's deputy someday, just like Jesse. Deputy also had a star pinned on his shirt. But Nate reckoned going into that saloon, they had crossed a line. They were just kids, and that was a place for men.

"Sorry, Tate." Nate meant it. He hadn't thought beforehand about the worry they might cause. He'd only seen the fun in it and was sure Deputy had taken the same view.

Tate nodded. "All right, I won't lecture ya since ya seem to have learned your lesson." He dropped his hat on the desk and eased his arms behind his head. "How 'bout you, Joseph Huckabee the second? Have you learned your lesson?"

"Yes, sir." Deputy stopped counting out the cards for a breath or two until Tate agreeably nodded.

When the door opened a minute later, it wasn't who any of them expected, least of all Nate. He didn't know who he thought it would be. Maybe somehow Ma had found out they had sneaked out. Or it could have been Pa, leaving the show early. Instead, it was that stately city dude. His black hair was combed perfectly and parted on the right. He had a longhorn mustache that curled just a mite on the ends. What did he want?

Nate instinctively pushed back, distancing himself.

The man's eyes narrowed as he stared into the cell holding the two boys. Then he turned his ugly scowl on Tate. "You have children locked in a cell," he said as if Tate didn't know, as if they had just appeared there out of thin air.

"No shit. I'm the one who put 'em there." Tate chuckled as though this man were a fool.

He wasn't. Nate could tell that. This man was a thinker, probably a university-educated man. He reminded Nate of Judge Prescott, who was here in town. He had signed the paperwork for Nate's adoption.

This man silently, shrewdly eyed Tate, who didn't seem to care. His face hadn't changed to show signs of worry or anything else. Tate was Tate, and that easygoing way did make Nate feel a little less scared.

"Where are their guardians?" the fella demanded, shaking the walls. Why was he so mad? They weren't his concern. Besides, they were just fine. Nate and his friends sometimes played in the cells at home.

The chair under Tate squeaked as he shifted his weight while keeping his feet propped on the desk. His hands glided down from behind his head, and he hooked his thumbs inside his waistband. "If you mean their fathers, well…" Tate pointed out the window. "They'd be in the saloon, listening to Lola. I'd like to be there myself." He grinned, but some sense told Nate it wasn't friendly.

"Let them out." Whoever he was, he wasn't asking.

Nate supposed he was used to getting his way, being rich. Judging by his glossy shoes without a speck of dust, he must've been a king. People probably fell all over themselves to please him. Maybe he even had servants. Nate had heard tell of rich folk having butlers and maids to wait on them.

When Tate didn't move, the man's fists balled at his sides, his face reddening. "I'll have your badge for this," he snarled, baring straight white teeth.

NATHANIAL

"And just what would you do with it?" Tate ran his fingers through his hair without concern. "You gonna protect this town and its people?" He grinned, knowing by the looks of that man's smooth hands, he had probably never held a gun or been in a knuckle-busting fight. "I'm gonna give ya a bit of advice, mister, and I'll even give ya a few seconds to take me up on it. If'n ya don't,"—Tate looked about at the dusty floor—"I'll mop this place with your hide. I'd surely hate to dirty that clean, starched coat, but then again, it'd do to get all the crust off the floor. Bet I could make her shine."

The man spun on his heel. The door slammed behind him. Tate stood, went to the window, and watched him go.

"Do ya know him?" Nate didn't believe the couple was local. He'd never seen them during any of their visits, but he thought he'd ask just the same.

Tate shook his head, keeping his gaze out the window. Pa had talked about the man, so Tate knew something was up or the feller wouldn't have come to the jailhouse. How did he even know where they were? Nate thought real hard. The Songbird. It'd been so jampacked that he must have been in there and seen them, maybe watching Nate the whole time, maybe close enough to reach out and grab him. That gave him the shivers.

An hour later, Pa and the marshal burst through the door with an arm around the other's shoulder, singing the last stanza of "Beautiful Dreamer." The marshal had a cigar stub held between his lips, and there was the flush that came with drinking too much whiskey on their cheeks. They bumped into the desk, knocking over a stack of papers.

"Ya missed a heck of a show." Pa snatched the key ring off the desk, twirling it around his finger.

"Sober up," Tate snapped. That wasn't like him. Nate couldn't recall a time when Tate was overly serious.

"Don't be sore. We could've just smacked their asses, sent them home. Then you could've come with us. Lockin' them up was your idea." Pa gave Tate a friendly elbow to the ribs.

"That man you were telling Joseph and me about was here tonight."

Pa sobered in one breath. The crimson from the whiskey drained from his face as he and the marshal separated from their good-humored hold on one another. They both stood straight as a board. These were men who could smell trouble before it got too close. All three of them sensed something, and that made Nate bite his nails. He didn't understand the interest in him.

"What did he want?" Pa plunked down on the corner of the desk, and there was no masking the raw irritation in his voice.

"He told me to release the boys."

"That all he said?" Pa's brow rose.

"Purdy much." Tate nodded.

"Pa." Nate pressed his face between the bars next to Deputy, who was also gripping the rods tight. "The lady said she was lookin' for someone. Said I reminded her of him. She didn't say who."

Pa unlocked the cell. A strange look passed between Huckabee, Tate, and him. Nate threw open the barred door and stood close to his father. He didn't want to look like a baby in front of everyone. He respected these men more than any others, besides Jesse. But he couldn't help it. Inside, he was shaking. This was the second time those people had interfered in his life.

"Can't you make 'em go away?" His voice quivered.

"They haven't broken any laws, so all we can do is keep an eye on them," Pa said.

"I'll check the register at the hotel. They certainly aren't camping in a wagon. I'll have a name by morning." Tate opened the door. "See ya at breakfast."

NATHANIAL

"Nolan, if ya don't mind takin' Deputy along to the house with Nate, I'll stay here while Tate is out lookin' around. I might do some diggin' of my own." The marshal scooped the fallen papers off the floor.

"I should stay too," Pa said. He wasn't one to let others do all the work, especially when it was his so-called fight.

Huckabee shook his head. "You've had a lot to drink, and I don't want your temper gettin' in the way." He stacked the papers neatly. "We don't know who these people are or what exactly they want. We only know that it seems to have something to do with Nathanial. As the boy's father, I think it's best you stay out of it for now. Tate and I will find some answers. We need to know more."

Every word the marshal said was true. Besides, Nate wanted Pa to stay close. The Huckabees had a big house, and he didn't want to be all alone with just Ma and the other kids. What if that man snuck in and tried to take him? He kept hold of Pa's sleeve until they got in the house and he and Deputy were tucked deep under a quilt. Though, he doubted he'd sleep.

Each time he woke, he thought about crawling into bed with his folks. The strange couple must have thought he knew something about that missing person. Why else would they keep tabs on him?

Pa and Jesse would follow any lead when they didn't have a good solid one to solve a case. Maybe those people were doing likewise. Only, they were being weird about it. Just because he looked similar to the person they were hunting...

He nearly choked on the air as his mind led him to another thought. Did they believe he was who they were searching for? That couldn't be. Why? Lots of people had lookalikes. He rolled over, tucking the blankets tight around him.

CHAPTER 10

THE GREASY SMELL OF BACON put a smile on Nate's face as he and deputy thumped down the stairs, tussling into the dining room. Nate yawned. He was tired from not sleeping well. They plopped into seats while pushing at each other. Ma was serving the other kids, and Mrs. Huckabee strolled in with a platter of meat.

"Where's Pa?" Nate looked into the other room.

Deputy's father wasn't there either, nor Tate. That fancy couple sprang front and center into Nate's mind. He didn't want to focus on them or how scared he'd been last night, but they were hanging in his brain. He wasn't going to let the thought of them ruin his good time. That was easier done when Pa was near to protect him. The sooner this mess got straightened out, the better. It just felt like a heavy cloud was hanging over him.

The front door opened, and in came the three absent men.

"Where were ya?" Nate fired off at Pa. His face wrinkled up, irritated that Pa had gone away without him, especially with that couple around.

NATHANIAL

He ruffled Nate's hair as he sat next to him. "I got some good news."

Nate couldn't wait to hear that the couple had packed up and left town. Pa had probably come to the same conclusion Nate had and explained everything about the adoption, and Huckabee and Tate were witnesses to officially confirm Pa's story. So it looked like he wasn't who they were searching for.

He smiled. "So they're gone?"

Pa cocked his head, seriously studying Nate. "No. But I got a name, and we'll keep looking into this. We can talk about it later. Let's not start the day on the wrong foot. I know you're worried, but your Ma and I, the marshal, and Tate have all discussed it, and you must stay in sight of one us at all times. Understand?"

"Yes, sir."

"I don't think they mean you any harm. They've only tried to talk to you, but we're not going to take any risks. If you happen to see them, run to one of us."

"So what's the good news?" Nate needed to hear something cheery.

"I met a man who has an appaloosa for sale. Thought we could go have a look-see. Wouldn't Jesse be surprised?"

Nate jumped out of his seat. This wasn't just good news. This was great news, the absolute best. Jesse missed Dapple so much. He compared any horse he rode to that appaloosa of his that had been killed. Nate could clearly imagine the surprise on Jesse's face if they came home with a good, solid horse for him, especially if it happened to be spotted like Dapple.

"Let's go." Nate was ready, first grabbing a few pieces of bacon off his plate.

"Keep your britches on. Eat. Then we'll go." Pa picked up his fork. Ma had just piled lots of eggs, a slice of bread, and meat on his plate.

The marshal and Tate were digging in too. At the moment, Pa didn't seem a bit flustered about that couple who'd been watching Nate. If he wasn't nervous, Nate wouldn't be either. Pa could handle anything, always had.

Nate sat in the saddle behind Deputy as his horse moved at a spanking trot. Pa was on one side of them, the marshal on the other.

They rode about five miles from town, turning east at a dusty split in the road. A few rippling hills of grass waved as they passed by. Then a ranch nestled down in a little valley came into view. Pretty spot. Leaves and trees of varying shades of bright green, flowers abundant throughout the yard—all of it reminding Nate of home. Although, this place didn't have a picket fence. The house sat under the shade of some almighty tall maple trees. The well-stacked stone foundation of a bank barn showed on three sides, the fourth set hidden into the side of a hill, hence the name. A large oval corral connected to the front of the barn where four horses huddled, swatting flies with their tails. It seemed to be a lazy day for them.

A man came out of the house, giving a friendly wave. In town, Pa had agreed on a time to meet. It only took the fella a few minutes to gather a lead rope from inside the barn, catch up to the horse they came to look over, and guide the animal out of the corral. Pa rubbed his hand along the appaloosa's neck, then over its back, then inspected each leg. He opened the animal's mouth, checking its teeth, and agreed with the age of five.

Mr. Tyson hadn't raised the colt from a foal. He'd taken the appaloosa and the other three as payment due to him instead of demanding cash. Nate wasn't surprised. Mr. Tyson had a kind face. Though, he walked like a man who took business in hand, and the .44 on his hip was a guarantee he would not be taken advantage of. That wasn't the case here. The marshal and Mr. Tyson were friends, so he had introduced him to Pa.

NATHANIAL

Pa threw his saddle on the spotted gelding and tried him out. He looked like a smooth mover, and his hair shimmered in the sunshine. Jesse would likely fall in love as soon as he laid eyes on the animal.

Pa pulled up on the reins right in front of them. "How much?" He looked over at Tyson.

The man rubbed his chin all thoughtful like. "Hundred dollars."

Pa huffed. "Indeed, this is a fine animal, but that's a lot of money. How about seventy-five?"

They went back and forth for a few minutes until finally settling on eighty-five dollars. Pa probably would have paid more than a hundred, knowing how happy the appaloosa would make Jesse. He had a good poker face, so the gent probably didn't realize he'd held all the cards. The horse was definitely worth more than what Pa had to pay.

"Can I ride him back to town?" Nate bounced excitedly on a fence rail as Pa and Mr. Tyson shook hands.

"We can race." Deputy nudged Nate. That sounded like good fun.

Pa's eyes narrowed. "Yes, you can ride him." He then wagged a finger. "No runnin' him."

A horse was like any other creature. It needed to get to know ya before it showed trust. The appaloosa was young, broke to saddle, but not used to Nate's riding. It might act up. Though, if Pa thought the horse was too green, Nate wouldn't have been allowed to ride him at all. He should probably take it easy until it got adjusted.

In no time, they rode into Birch Creek. The marshal pulled up in front of the jailhouse.

Tate was leaning lazily against the porch post. "That's a fine-lookin' hoss." He stepped into the street, and Nate halted. The appaloosa hadn't acted up once on the return ride. Tate patted the animal's neck.

"Tate, why don't ya take a break? I'll take over for a while." Marshal Huckabee stepped down out of the saddle, then tossed his reins over the hitch rail. Pa hopped down too and tied his horse.

Tate nodded. "See you boys at supper." He winked toward Nate and Deputy, then was off, halfway across the street, heading for the saloon.

"Nathanial, I'm gonna stay and help the marshal keep an eye on things. Put Jesse's horse in the corral."

Nate knew Pa wasn't talking about the livery. He meant at the marshal's place on the far edge of town. "Yes, sir." He turned the appaloosa, and Deputy's horse fell into pace.

It was the day before the big Fourth of July shindig, and even more folks appeared to have somehow crammed into town. There was a harmonious buzz along the street. Everywhere, people were smiling, greeting one another, and the consensus was excitement for tomorrow's events. Nothing this grand had ever come so close, certainly not right among them. It might be the one and only time, so no one was apt to forget it. The street was overloaded with fancy black carriages and plain or simple-painted wagons. Dust hung in the air. There was hardly room along the hitch rail. And foot traffic along the boardwalk was heavy.

It was a shame Jesse couldn't be there with them.

"Follow me." Deputy turned his paint pony into an alleyway. They came out behind the row of buildings. The path before them was wide open.

Nate felt like he could breathe again.

"Nobody's watching." Deputy grinned. There was a glint of ornery in his eyes.

They were about to get into trouble for something, because Nate couldn't say no to his best friend. Whatever it was, he was all in. Then he recalled Pa's threat of taking down his pants and slapping his bare ass.

It was too late. Deputy kicked his pony. No time for Nate to change his mind. Deputy's horse leaped forward into a run.

"Race ya home." The dare flew over Deputy's shoulder and into Nate's ears.

No way would Nate lose a horse race. He was too good of a rider to get bested. He sank his boot heels into the appaloosa's sides and madly kicked. The gelding stretched his legs, neck thrusting forward, ears pinned back, and caught that paint in no time. Neck and neck, they tore along the wood line, tails flapping in the wind. Nate squeezed the reins and shrank tighter, shoulders hunched, skimming the air, maybe going a mite faster. They were almost to the house.

Deputy wasn't letting up, so Nate kept kicking. The horses ran faster. Into the yard they flew, heading toward the barn. Thirty yards and closing in quick on the corral fence. Nate wasn't afraid. How many times had he made a jump just like this one?

Deputy skidded his horse to a halt. Nate was going to win with a celebratory liftoff and really show his bud. All of a sudden, the appaloosa threw its head down, forelegs out straight, plowing the dirt in an effort to stop. They hit the fence. Nate went airborne, high over the top rail, doing flips. Sky then ground, sky then ground. Then he smacked the dirt with a god-awful thud, his face leading the way as his elbows and knees shredded across the rugged ground, tearing his clothing.

When he stopped rolling, Nate couldn't move a muscle. He could cry, and he did at the top of his lungs. His skin where he'd dragged across the lumpy dirt burned like hell. His face was bleeding, as were his arms and legs. His one arm wouldn't lift. It just hung there, and his hip had a big, bad heartbeat pounding inside it.

"Ma!" Deputy hollered. He hunkered beside Nate. There were tears in his friend's eyes.

Not only was Nate hurt badly, but they were going to be in all kinds of trouble. They'd been warned about how to treat that horse, all horses really. Pa was serious when it came to taking care of his bay and Nate's mustang. Nate liked to jump fences, but he knew better. Likely, Pa would tear the rest of his hide off. Deputy was probably afraid the same would happen to him.

Ma ran out of the house on the heels of Mrs. Huckabee. Both women gasped. Nate lay bleeding and crying in the middle of the corral. The trail through the dirt and the horse standing freely on the opposite side of the fence told a gruesome story.

When Ma bent over him, her eyes were flooded with tears. Tears and a spark of anger that reddened her face, almost matching her hair. "Deputy, go get Nolan and the doctor."

"Yes, ma'am." He shot off.

A few minutes later, Pa arrived, followed closely by the marshal, and Nate was still lying in the dirt, crying. Pa's face was pruned as hard as bark, his neck veins pulsing. He scooped Nate off the ground, carrying him into the house with the other adults bunched around in case Pa needed assistance of any kind. Nate expected to hear it. Instead, he got silence. Pa must have been seething, boiling under the surface where it wasn't so noticeable.

"I'm sorry." Nate wiped at his eyes as Pa sat him on the table and began stripping off his shirt. Pain tore through his weak arm as Pa lifted that sleeve, and Nate let out with a high-pitched yelp. Fresh tears sprang from his eyes, blurring his vision.

The door opened, and in ran Deputy, Tate a hustling step behind. Following those two was a man carrying a little black bag. The doctor looked over Nate's cuts and bruises as Ma and Mrs. Huckabee fetched hot water and towels to wipe off the blood and dirt.

"You'll need stitches, and that arm is very badly bruised. You're lucky it's not broken." The doctor had a sour look on his face. He appeared to be just as unhappy as everyone else in the room. Perhaps he was too familiar with Deputy's shenanigans.

Nate had followed along. Racing had sounded like a good idea until now.

He wailed the entire time the doc sewed. Pa and the marshal held Nate down, one over his shoulders, the other holding tight to his feet. Ma and Mrs. Huckabee fashioned a sling, per doctor's instructions. Nate was bandaged up but still hurting something awful when Pa carried him up to bed. It wasn't even lunchtime yet, but he could barely keep his eyes open.

Pa pulled back the quilt, then gently laid him between the sheets. "Why'd ya do it?" His voice wasn't hard like when he was mad. Disappointment was what Nate heard.

Nate shrugged the arm that wasn't throbbing. He liked to go fast on his horse and thought he'd try out Jesse's new steed against what Nate knew about his mustang. It had been meant for fun. No one was supposed to get hurt.

"Son, if anything happened to you..." Pa wearily shook his head. "You had me scared. Pissed off and scared."

"Don't worry, Pa. I inherited that tough Crosson hide."

Pa grinned. "Suppose ya have."

Nate closed his eyes and it was strange, but his getting a new baby sister or brother popped into his head. Maybe he wouldn't be Pa's favorite anymore, and that would hurt, but he was Nolan Crosson's son. Nothing could change that.

"Nathanial."

Nate opened his lids.

Pa was holding the door half open. "You'll have extra chores to do at home." The door clicked shut behind him.

When Nate woke, voices drifted in the window from the porch below. Squeals and giggles made him lift his head off the soft pillow. He cringed with the least little movement, nearly in tears before his feet touched the floor, but he wanted to join the fun. Missing out wasn't something he intended to do, even if it killed him. And the way his arm was screaming with pain, it just might. It took him awhile on his gimpy leg and he stopped to take a few deep breaths, but he did make it downstairs.

That's where he was when Ma walked inside, a pitcher of tea in her hands. She smiled sadly when she saw him. It was a look of pure, sweet pity. She kissed his head. "Nolan." She called Pa.

Pa carried Nate out and sat him on the steps where Deputy sat churning ice cream.

"We're gonna catch lightnin' bugs later." That was Deputy's way of asking if Nate thought he would be able to help.

Nate wasn't so sure. He'd try. He hadn't been taught to be a quitter.

"Nathanial, why don't you read something for us? Your ma's been bragging about how good you are. I wish Deputy liked to read." Constance Huckabee disappeared into the house and returned a few minutes later, carrying several books.

Nate was happy to oblige. He loved to read. He opened the pages of *Through the Looking-Glass*. Tate joined them, and everyone sat quietly as Nate turned page after page. He was on the fourth chapter when Deputy announced their treat was ready. Nate laid aside the book. They all ate ice cream and talked. Then, at Deputy's urging, Nate pushed up and gimped behind the other little ones, all trying to snatch a firefly out of the evening air. He was too slow to catch even the low-flying ones, but it was fun anyway.

"Nate," Ma called. She had a plate in her hands. He had missed supper but wasn't really that hungry. He hadn't even eaten all his ice cream. But to make Ma happy, he sat on the porch and picked at the food until she was satisfied.

"How's your arm feelin'?" Pa sat next to him.

NATHANIAL

Nate didn't want his folks to take him home early, and they would if they didn't believe him well enough for all the activity happening tomorrow.

"Hurts a little." It actually hurt like the devil, but he wasn't about to complain. He didn't mention his hip either.

"What about your leg?" Pa eyed the bloodstains on the knees of Nate's pants.

He should have known that Pa wouldn't forget a thing like that. He didn't miss anything.

"It's okay." And the truth was it didn't ache near as bad as his arm, so he hardly noticed it until he took a step.

No more was said, and Nate leaned back against a porch post, resting his head. The kids were running all over the yard and putting their catches into a glass jar Deputy's ma had given them. Nate yawned. He had slept most of the day away, and still, he was doggone tired.

Stars began to come awake in the darkening sky. The moon was full, and everything around Nate seemed peaceful. He was glad he hadn't seen hide nor hair of that nosy couple today.

CHAPTER 11

NATE WOKE IN BED. Pa must have carried him inside last night. Deputy was sprawled out next to him, soundly sleeping, his mouth hanging wide. Drool had formed a puddle on his pillow. Nate thought for a second about rubbing Deputy's face in the spit.

The door swung open, and Tate strolled in with a big, cheery grin on his face. "Time to git up, lazybones. You boys are gonna miss the horse race." He roused Deputy by rubbing his head into the wet pillow. Exactly what Nate had been thinking about doing. He grinned.

Deputy groaned and, with one hand, weakly pushed at Tate to leave him.

The horse race was the first event. The start of the whole shebang.

Nate pushed back the quilt. No way did he want to miss Tate's race. He rode an all-red horse that had long legs and ran like the wind. Nate eased himself to the edge of the bed with a few stifled moans. His leg was awful stiff, and the bruise had turned a darker shade of purple. His arm wasn't thumping yet, but the day was young.

Deputy sat up all sleepy-eyed, his hair mussed in every direction, and he wiped the spit off his cheek.

Tate chuckled. "Yous two git dressed and git breakfast. I'll be waitin' at the startin' line. Don't be late." He was gone as quick as he'd come in.

Deputy was no good at helping Nate get his shirt on. He kept bumping Nate's arm, making him ouch.

"Ma!" Nate called.

It only took her a few minutes, and he was dressed. Everyone was at the table when they took their seats. Breakfast was served and cleaned up in no time. Nate didn't fuss about how much Ma had put on his plate. He knew her ways. He had to eat good food, a full meal, or she wouldn't let him have sweets at the celebration. And he lived to satisfy his sweet tooth.

They left the house as a group. There was a cheeriness to everyone's voice. Everybody was smiling. Deputy was skipping along in front, his little brother a few steps behind, doing the same. Pa was carrying Elizabeth, and Ma had her arm strung around Pa's. Her health had been much improved since they had settled in at the Huckabees'.

Mrs. Huckabee held Ada on her hip while Pa and the marshal took bets on the race. Mr. Tyson had entered one of his horses, a black filly said to be thoroughbred.

Nate hobbled at a fast pace, trying to keep up with Deputy. His sore leg wasn't cooperating, and he stumbled off the edge of the boardwalk into the street, one arm swinging to keep him from hitting the dirt. Smacking himself up again wouldn't help any of his aches. A hand slapped against his back, stopping him from falling. Nate looked up, expecting Pa to be there. Instead, it was the city lady. Nate took a quick glance around. The prim dude wasn't with her.

Nate jerked away, sending a jab of pain through his stove-up arm. He stumbled forward, bumping into Pa.

"Ma'am, I'm gonna ask ya to leave my family alone." There was irritation in Pa's tone. This was to be a day without worry or headache or bother. A holiday that, as a family, they could just enjoy being together.

"Hello." She didn't extend a hand. "I'm Deloris Fletcher," she said as though the name should mean something to them.

Nate wasn't familiar with anyone with that name.

Pa tipped his hat. "Is there something I can do for ya?"

Ma and the Huckabees were all bunched around, waiting, listening.

"I believe there is. My husband and I have traveled west, searching for our nephew. We've been through every dusty little town between here and Missouri. The only reason we've stayed here so long is that I think he is my sister's child." She pointedly looked at Nate.

Ma gasped. Mrs. Huckabee grabbed her arm, steadying her. Nate clung to Pa's sleeve.

"Don't approach my son again." Pa turned, nudging Nate along.

"I'm not sure he is your son. From what I've been told, he was adopted." Her nose was in the air. "I've already asked to see the paperwork."

Pa abruptly halted. The marshal was quick to his side.

"Let it drop, Nolan." Huckabee gave Pa a push, and they all moved off down the street toward the starting line.

Nate glanced over his shoulder. She was still intently watching him as if he were the prize in some strange game. It scared him. He kept a tight hold on Pa's arm. Pa must have sensed the spine-tingling prickles running through him. He handed Elizabeth to Ma, then scooped Nate up and sat him on his shoulders.

"You got the best seat in the house." Pa patted Nate's knee. "You let me worry about her."

NATHANIAL

"I don't know her or her husband," Nate stated, trying to hide the shake in his voice.

He knew Tate and the marshal had done some investigating. But then he had hurt himself, and he and Pa never got to talk over the details. Could he really be that woman's nephew? And what exactly did that mean? They'd been searching, and people only looked for things they wanted, valued. But how could that be? They didn't know him. He'd never once been around them.

"Her husband's name is Lem. Do you recall ever hearing either name?"

Nate's past was filled with lots of bad people. Most of them, he'd rather forget. He would have remembered those two. They were too wealthy for the likes of men Nate used to ride with when he was with his old pa. The Fletchers were the kind of folks that Jim Younger and his gang would have robbed, not hobnobbed with.

"No, sir. I ain't ever met them before."

"Forget it," Pa said. "We're gonna have a jim-dandy of a day, and nothing's gonna ruin it."

Pa was right, of course. Why let circumstances or other people tramp down your mood? There was always a way out, a way up. No reason to sulk or stew on it. They would go on about their day and just forget those rotten Fletchers.

So what? She'd read over his adoption papers. She'd also learn he was born to an outlaw, a notorious one, and, like many others who had found out, she would probably never look his way again. He wasn't high society. This had to be a case of mistaken identity. Tomorrow, they'd head home, and he would never think about the Fletchers again.

"What would you like to do after Tate's race?" Pa patted Nate's leg.

"Ride the carousel." Nate was quick to speak up.

"All right, then."

They found an open spot along the crowded boardwalk near the starting ribbon. They all bunched in. A red ribbon was stretched tight across the width of the street, marking where the horses should line up. Deputy was already cheering on Tate. All the horses pranced nervously.

Nate was thankful Pa had put him up on his shoulders. Perhaps his leg wouldn't get bumped. There were people everywhere, shoulder to shoulder. They must be five deep along the whole length of the street. Lots of people passed by, trying to find a hole that would allow them a good view of the race. Ma stood close to Pa and held Elizabeth on her hip. The marshal and his wife were standing on the other side of her. They all watched as the riders jerked the reins, lining up their horses.

Nate cupped a hand around his mouth. "Go git 'em, Tate."

Tate gave them all a confident wave.

The starting pistol fired. The line of horses sprang forward, taking off at a run, breaking through the red ribbon. Shouts and cheers rose from the onlookers. The street roared with voices, everyone elevating the name of their chosen rider. They all clapped loudly for Tate, except Nate, whose right arm was still in its sling. Tate's horse pulled a length ahead of the others, dust flying off the heels of the horses. Down the street they flew, almost to the finish.

Nate felt Pa jerk under him. The sudden tug twisted Nate, and he squirmed so he could stay facing the race. Nate brushed off the distraction of the moving crowd, figuring someone had bumped Pa.

Tyson's horse had gained on Tate. It was gonna be close.

"Tate won!" Nate threw his one arm up.

Deputy was bouncing. Everyone cheered. Some clapped or shook hands. A few exchanged dollar bills. The marshal gave a sharp whistle.

Pa was quiet. Nate looked down. Pa was eye to eye with Lem Fletcher, and he had a mean grip on Pa's arm.

NATHANIAL

"How did he get hurt?" Fletcher demanded as though Nate's welfare were his personal business.

No one in their right mind laid a hand on Pa. He wasn't one to be pushed, nor was he tolerant of being questioned about his own affairs.

"Git your hands off me." There was a definite edge in Pa's tone, a stern, icy warning, his stature stiff, and there wasn't a friendly line on his face.

The marshal stepped between them, shoving Fletcher off.

Pa lifted Nate over his head, setting his feet on the planks. "Kate, you and Constance take the children. I'll be along in a few minutes."

Nate wanted to go congratulate Tate, but he didn't feel okay to leave Pa's side. Not that Pa needed his help. Quite the opposite. Nate felt safest with Pa.

Fletcher was in Pa's face, not as tall, not by six inches, but he held himself in an austere manner that made one believe he was a big man in a different world, wherever he'd come from. "I understand my wife spoke to you earlier and explained why we're here." He thrust a tintype toward Pa. "The woman on the right, do you know her?"

Pa pushed the picture back at Fletcher. "Can't say that I do."

"Well, let me enlighten you. Her name is Lucinda."

Nate stiffened. His grip on Ma tightened. This couldn't be. That name he knew. So did Ma, and she began to pull him away from there.

"The other woman is my wife. That photograph was taken before Lucinda came west, where she fell in love with a killer, a man by the name of James Hardin Younger. I have letters to prove what I'm telling you. As I'm sure you know, they had a child, a son."

Nate twisted and tugged against Ma's grip. Pa and Fletcher were having words, lots of them, angry and loud. And Nate wasn't so sure Pa was winning that battle. That frightened him.

People were starting to watch, stopping and listening. Tears flooded Nate's eyes. What if they got into a fight? He didn't want to see Pa get punched, though he could probably pound that slick fella into mincemeat.

"Were you drunk like the other night in the saloon? Were you even watching him or anywhere nearby when that happened?" Fletcher pointed a straight finger at Nate's bandaged arm.

"I don't see how any of that's your concern. He is my son." Pa's fists balled at his sides.

"You're very wrong. I know for certain that is Nathanial Younger. The boy we are looking for," Fletcher snapped with an air of indignance as if Pa had no right to know, had no right to Nate, as if he were doing Pa a favor by telling him.

"Pa." Nate didn't like that pressed suit knowing his name. Fletcher's sharp bow tie was perfectly squared, and his short-brimmed hat was without a speck of dust.

Mrs. Fletcher, who had slipped through the crowd, stood back a foot or two and was gowned in lace, holding her parasol overhead.

"Kate, git the children outta here." Pa kept his eyes on Fletcher.

Ma looked stunned at all the commotion and was surely stunned by what they'd just heard. Besides his uncles—and he didn't count Jim Younger's brothers—Nate and his folks believed he had no other relatives.

Ma snapped to and turned Nate. He struggled against her tug, standing his ground. Maybe he could get rid of these people. He wasn't supposed to lie, but he had no choice. He wanted these people to leave him alone.

"My name's not Nathanial. It's Matthew," he screamed.

No one moved or maybe even breathed. Ma and Pa and the Huckabees were all aware of who Matthew was, Pa's first son who had been killed during a stagecoach robbery led by Jim Younger.

The Fletchers' faces hardened. Nate was shaking, so maybe they saw through his fib. Maybe if they had been looking into who he was, then they knew the story about Matthew.

Ma scooped Nate up. Mrs. Huckabee had Elizabeth on one hip and Ada on the other, the boys hanging on her skirt. They hustled them away down the boardwalk.

Nate sobbed into Ma's shoulder. He wanted Pa.

CHAPTER 12

"I SEE YOU'VE TAUGHT him how to lie," the Fletcher man snipped like an uppity bitch.

Nolan had his fill of this arsehole, drawing back to throw a punch. Knocking the man's teeth down his damn throat might turn his day around.

Nolan's arm got caught by the strong arm of another. He and the marshal struggled against each other's strength, evenly matched until they both pushed off, breathing heavy.

"How barbaric," Fletcher spat. "You're practically a savage, resorting to fisticuffs. You should know that Nathanial's story is still talked about—a lawman adopting the son of a murderer. How else do you think we pieced our way out here? A snippet of information here and a fact there. We learned a lot about the boy's life along the way. Those clues led us this far. And I know that Nathanial's father killed your son, Matthew. No doubt, your behavior here will certainly help our case."

"What the hell does that mean?" Nolan lunged.

The marshal was quick to throw himself between the men. Lucky for Fletcher, because round two would have been very short-lived.

Nolan had a mean notion to knock that smug son of a bitch on his ass.

"Nolan, this ain't the time. Our families are waitin' for us. Let's go." Joseph gave him a hard nudge. His friend turned and eyeballed the Fletchers. "I'll throw ya both in jail for the day if I see either of ya near this man or his family."

Fletcher made a hacking noise in his throat. It sounded like a retort to Nolan. "On what charges?" Fletcher chuckled in the marshal's face. This man didn't know too much about western law.

Yes, there were sanctions and rules to be followed, jurisdictions, and steps to be taken in certain procedures, but mostly, the men who wore badges got their positions because of their bravery, being good with a gun. Most times, they had sound judgment when it came to right and wrong. They very clearly saw the line between the two. That didn't mean they weren't a rough lot. Most were and could handle themselves with fists, guns, or otherwise. Nolan was no exception, nor the marshal. In this case, he could enforce his rule, and not a damn thing could be done about it. He could toss those two in the pokey for a few hours, and exactly jack shit would be done about it.

Judge Prescott was in town, but until the Fletchers contacted one of the two lawyers who worked at the courthouse to have them released, the day would be gone. Besides, every business in town was shut down for the celebration. The Fletchers had best step lightly because the marshal was a man of his word.

When Nolan and Joseph got to the finish line, Tate had a blue ribbon pinned on his vest. The boys were ogling over it. As soon as Nate noticed his pa, the boy practically crawled into Nolan's pocket.

He gave Tate a hearty clap on the shoulder. They talked easily for a few minutes, then took the kids, as promised, to the carousel. The painted horses spun in a circle. Was there anything better than the laughter of children?

It was irksome that Nolan's mind wasn't where it should be. Did the Fletchers have a case that would stand up in a court of law? It was how men like Fletcher fought. What did those letters Fletcher claimed to have say?

Nolan watched his son, all smiles. He and Deputy were yapping excitedly over one another as the ride twirled. They waved at each pass. Nolan didn't want to think about good-bye.

The Fletchers had recognized Nate right off, so they must have possessed enough evidence in those letters that they were able to correctly identify him from that damn tintype. But why now after so long a time? Nate's mother had died when he was but three, leaving him in the hands of Jim Younger for a few years, then Mr. Harper before Nolan adopted him. The boy had been kicked around so often. Why would anyone even entertain the idea of uprooting him from a stable home? And it seemed that was what the Fletchers were thinking. That Nate was somehow theirs.

Nolan needed to get it out of his head and make the most of today with his family.

They all had a try at the dunk tank next. It was pitiful, but Nate did his best with his left arm, missing the target by at least three feet. Nolan missed by an inch, and the marshal sank the clown. Cheers erupted from all the kids.

"Constance and I are going to watch the judging of the baking contest. She used my cherry pie recipe." Kate kissed his face. Then she and Elizabeth turned and walked off with Constance and baby Ada.

Nolan and the marshal had the three boys. They went to the arena to watch the trick riding and, after that, the bronc busting in which Tate was entered. Nolan sat Nathanial on the fence post next to Deputy, Miles, and the marshal, then leaned heavily on the top rail, watching as the first bronc was let loose. Five seconds and the cowboy hit the dirt. The next man held tight for a few seconds longer, then was tossed into the air, falling flat on his back. The boys cheered each rider. Nolan whistled as Tate climbed onto the back of a big snorting, pawing black stallion. That beast looked downright evil.

"I wasn't aware that your deputy had so many talents." Nolan ribbed the marshal.

"I told the fool I was in no hurry to find a new deputy. Likely, he'll bust his noggin open." The marshal shook his head. "He's got his sights on a pretty filly by the name of Betty Sue. I tried to tell him that gettin' hisself kilt wasn't gonna impress her."

Nolan laughed, thinking of Jesse and Kristy Short. In the past, the Shorts had hosted some good times. Their parties were always full of food, drink, and laughs. Jesse was probably having the time of his life.

CHAPTER 13

Jesse turned the mare into the yard of the Short ranch, both sides of the lane lined with buckboards. In all his born days, he hadn't seen so many people. Little heathens, all Nate's friends, were running amuck everywhere. Squeals and giggles floated in the air. The whole town must have turned out for the Fourth of July picnic.

Near the barn sat a wagon with three keg barrels on the bed and a line of men waiting. Around the food tables, women were busy placing platters filled with every garden vegetable in season and frosted cakes and apple pies. A pig roasted on a spit.

It all smelled wonderful, making his mouth water. He hadn't eaten a decent meal since the Crossons had left for Birch Creek. With the sheriff gone, Jesse's duties as a lawman had doubled, keeping him busy nearly every minute of the day. He and Kristy hadn't spent much time together lately, but he aimed to change that. Soon, if she gave the answer he expected her to, they'd be making a lifetime of memories.

Among the lively music, boisterous conversations, laughter, and kids yelling as

they chased one another between the mingling groups of men and women, Kristy appeared at the side of the house, between the trellised rose bushes. In each hand, she carried a pitcher of lemonade. The breeze lifted her hair off her shoulders, exposing the graceful curve of her neck. Jesse was a lucky man.

He raised a hand, giving her a wave. What a smile she had, beautiful, simply lovely. Her eyes twinkled. He tied his horse, then headed straight for her, a definite giddy-up in his step. The dress she wore was a peach color, tight at the waist, and lace trimmed the bodice. The brooch he'd bought her last Christmas was pinned there. Honestly, she could have been wearing a burlap sack and he wouldn't have cared.

Kristy hurriedly plunked the pitchers down, probably slopping some of the liquid over the lip. On her heel, she spun to face him, reaching out. He swept her into a close embrace and planted a big one on her. She giggled. They kissed again.

Mrs. Short loudly cleared her throat. Jesse was familiar with the sound, so there was no mistaking who was interrupting.

With a broad smile, he turned, facing his soon-to-be mother-in-law. "Good day, ma'am. Exceptional weather we're having... Fine day for a picnic," he offered in a genial tone.

At best, Kristy's ma tolerated Jesse, not exactly disliking him, but she'd made it clear a few times that his job as deputy put her daughter at risk for becoming a widow too young. He should instead go back to being a cattleman. Quit being a deputy before contemplating marriage. Hell would freeze over first.

Mrs. Short, remaining silent, glanced up at the wide blue yonder. Fluffy white clouds floated overhead, and the sun was not too hot for July.

Jesse's star wasn't just a tin fixture pinned on his shirt. It symbolized a truth, a core belief that he had adopted and internalized while working every day with Sheriff Crosson. Even before that, when he was just a boy, a sense of justice had been born in him. He reckoned that was why he had never fallen into his pa's thieving ways and had left home at fourteen. Too bad Mrs. Short couldn't understand that. It didn't bother Kristy that he was a lawman, and he was glad of it. Or if she did share her ma's attitude, she'd never said anything.

Mrs. Short's gaze fell away from the bright welkin and fixed on Jesse. Her grin was not so welcoming. "Let's not spoil the day by having us a shotgun weddin'. You two …" She pointed a finger at Jesse, then turned on Kristy. "You're not married yet, not even engaged. Conduct yourselfs properly."

Perhaps holding Kristy in his arms in a public setting the way he'd done had been a touch fresh. "Sorry, ma'am."

"Shorty's over there." The cattleman's wife nodded. "Why don't you go say hello? I need to speak to my daughter." There was a hint of something, annoyance perhaps, in her tone, which led him to believe the conversation about to take place would not be a pleasant one.

Jesse's gut tightened for Kristy's sake, but what could he do? Kristy might not marry him without her ma's blessing. Her pa already referred to him as son, so there were no worries there. Jesse hated to leave her, knowing she'd heard the lecture before. It was a sore spot between them.

Kristy loved him, and her intention throughout their courtship was never to upset her ma. Jesse did what he could to get along with the woman, but damn, if she didn't make it difficult. Anytime she could, she'd point out how dangerous his job was. One time, he had his fill of her big mouth and countered that stampedes, rustlers, and lightning could get a cattleman killed just the same. They'd bickered until Kristy ran from the room in tears. He didn't want that to happen again, ever.

He gave her hand a little squeeze before he turned to go. Suddenly, the ring in his vest pocket felt like a lead weight holding him in place. There was something he could do for

NATHANIAL

Kristy and himself. Once they were married, he'd have the say, not Mrs. Short. Kristy would be his wife. Mrs. Adams. He grinned and spun on his heel to drop on one knee directly before the woman he'd been in love with since the first moment he'd set eyes on her.

Mrs. Short gasped. Others around them all held still, all eyes on them. The buzz of conversations halted. Jesse didn't care who saw him profess his love. This was a proud moment. He only wished the Crossons were there.

He gently took Kristy's hands in his. She seemed to be holding her breath. A smile spread across her face, and she squeezed his hands.

"I love you, Kristy Short. Will ya marry me?"

Kristy screamed, "Yes!" about ten times. She threw her arms around his neck just as he began to stand. He swung her around a few times. Cheers rose around them. The band struck up a lively tune, and the hum of people talking was louder than before. This was indeed a celebration.

Jesse pulled Kristy back, then reached into his vest pocket, producing a gold ring. On it was mounted her birthstone, opal. He slipped it onto her finger. Then at least a dozen men, if not more, came forward, giving Jesse's shoulder a pat and congratulating them both. Kristy beamed and kept glancing at the sparkling stone on her hand. Jesse believed he stood taller than his normal height of six two.

Shorty pushed through the crowd. Standing in front of them, he lifted his beer. "To my daughter and her future husband. I couldn't ask for a finer son-in-law. I'll be proud to call you family." Shorty clapped the top of Jesse's shoulder. "Here, here!"

All their friends and neighbors repeated the toast, raising their cups. Mrs. Short wiped at her eyes, but she drank ceremoniously. Folks began congratulating Mr. and Mrs. Short as well. Her smile seemed forced, but it was hard to tell. What mother wouldn't be excited over the happiness of a beloved child? It made him think of his family, the Crossons.

Mrs. Crosson, Ma, would have been crying her eyes out, happy of course. And she'd probably do just that as soon as he relayed the good news. No doubt, the sheriff would offer lots of fatherly wisdom—he always did—and Jesse would accept all of it. Partner…Jesse wasn't so sure how the boy would react. They'd grown close, tighter than most brothers. The kid might cry a fit at the realization that Jesse would be leaving home to start his own family. Not that he and Kristy would be going far. Neither had a longing to leave Gray Rock, but Jesse and his little partner would no more be living under the same roof. He expected the kid to be upset, but maybe with the promise of him having his own room at Jesse's place, he'd be okay.

As the enthusiasm lessened, Jesse faced Kristy's ma. Kristy was next to him, but her back was turned and she was showing off her ring to the huddle of girlfriends surrounding her, all chattering at one time, going on about how beautiful the stone was and how Kristy was glowing. Shorty was nearby, pouring brandy into small glasses for a group of men. Another toast, Jesse supposed. Everyone appeared elated but one.

"I reckon I should have asked permission before proposing to your daughter." No one ever accused him of being refined, though he always did the best he could. That didn't seem to be enough for Kristy's ma.

She didn't blink, just stared a hole through him. He shifted uncomfortably.

"You know very well my husband would have given his blessing." She glanced at Shorty, who was boasting loudly about the coming nuptials and what a shindig they'd have there on the ranch. The whole town would be invited.

More drinks were poured.

"It's your blessing I'd like to have," he said sincerely.

"If I were you, I wouldn't hold my breath. If I can talk my daughter out of this marriage, I will."

The blow of those words hit Jesse hard right above the belt, knocking the wind out of him.

Without thought, he took a staggering step back, putting space between them. "I don't understand. Kristy and me have been courtin' nigh to a year. Where'd you think that was leadin'?"

Jesse knew for sure that Shorty had been aware of his intentions. A man didn't keep coming around for no reason. He ate supper with them twice a week. How could a future wedding not have crossed that woman's mind?

"I hoped it would fizzle out on its own. When it didn't, Shorty forbade me to intervene. I wanted to talk to you privately. You're a decent young man, and I believe you will take care of my daughter. But you hunt criminals for a living, men who'd rather put a bullet in ya, kill ya rather than go to jail or hang. That gun on your hip scares me." She dabbed a napkin to the corner of her eyes. "On top of that, there's your reputation for being a rifleman. No one better. Every person in this territory and beyond has heard stories of you and that Winchester. So tell me. What outlaw wouldn't want to brag about cutting down the best?" Her eyes were reddening as more tears welled up.

A man could die performing in any occupation. Plus, accidents happened. In his mind, he called her irrational, but he'd never say it aloud. She was truly upset, and he didn't want to start a real argument. It was a fact that he did interact far more frequently with outlaws than a man not wearing a badge. He had learned well from Sheriff Crosson, who was one of the best. Jesse was still learning, but he wasn't as green as he had been when he was brought there to the Short ranch some time back, full of bullet holes after chasing a killer. Mrs. Short and

Kristy had patched him up. Apparently, that awful memory had never left her mind.

"Jesse, let's go dance." Kristy had her arm looped around his and swished her skirt, showing her eagerness. Her happiness had obviously blinded her to her ma's stern face, and he suspected he appeared just as sober, but not to the beaming bride-to-be.

He kissed her cheek. "Give me a minute with your ma. You go on. I'll be right there."

She fluttered off, and folks congratulated her a second time as she breezed past on her way to the music. He couldn't imagine having anyone else at his side or seeing her married to another man. The very thought of it stirred jealous anger in him. He'd marry her without Mrs. Short's consent if he had to, but that wasn't what he hoped for.

"I'd hate to see anything ruin Kristy's good mood. How much of this have you told her?" He was aware of some belittling of his job because Kristy had poured out her heart to him. She didn't want to see him get hurt or worse, which was natural due to the love they felt for one another, but she'd said yes. So him being a lawman wasn't enough of a practical worry for her to end their courtship.

"I never told her I was against marriage." She glanced around. Folks everywhere were enjoying themselves, drinking, eating, and dancing. Kids playing tag. "Shorty will give ya your pa's ranch. You and Kristy could live there, work cattle, combine with this spread, and raise your children. Think of your future family. This is the largest cattle spread in the territory or any of the surrounding areas. There's a lot of responsibility in running it. My husband is capable, but I'm sure he would enjoy giving some of those duties to you. And being a boss here would be a lot less dangerous than hunting killers." Her face tightened, lips thin. "It's your choice. One is a little more selfish, but either way, your family will always be provided for if something should happen to you."

Jesse had his fill of her trying to talk him out of being a lawman, a job he was good at and enjoyed. And what made her think he'd ever give up working side by side with the man he admired greatly? There was no choice. Kristy accepted who Jesse was. Her ma would have to learn to do the same.

No one planned on dying in the line of duty, but it did happen. God forbid he left behind Kristy and a passel of little ones to grieve. Jesse wasn't haphazard about catching outlaws, modeling the ways of Sheriff Crosson. He would have thought that would give Mrs. Short some relief. Instead, there was tension between him and her that always seemed to be present to different degrees. Shorty and the rest of the family somehow were able to overlook it. Kristy felt it sometimes. He knew because that's when she had complained. For Kristy, he was willing to do what was necessary and, within reason, to keep the peace, but he was done being pushed about dropping his badge.

"I'm a lawman. That's all there is to it. You'd best get that straight in your mind, or you'll end up hurting your daughter." He tipped his hat, then headed toward where Kristy was waiting.

They danced a few songs. When they rested, others who had not congratulated them earlier did so. Jesse's stomach rumbled, reminding him that he hadn't eaten. He and Kristy each filled a plate. On the porch, seated together on the swing, they ate and made plans for their future. Kristy wanted a late-spring wedding when the blossoms were in full bloom and it wasn't yet too hot. He didn't care what time of year they exchanged vows as long as she became his wife.

He was thinking about filling his plate a second time while Kristy talked between bites about having a lace train that would hang to the hem of her wedding dress. He glanced over the porch railing at the food tables. What the hell was she doing here? Who were the two men with her? Probably one was the man he'd trailed to Black Mesa.

"Jesse, are you listening to me?" Kristy turned his chin.

Heat rose in his cheeks. "Sorry." He grinned.

She shook her head. However, she did return his grin, so he knew he was forgiven.

He glanced again toward the food tables. "You know those three?"

Both men wore their pistols tied down. They weren't cleaned up, dusted in trail dirt, unlike the folks at the picnic, including Shorty's ranch hands. Even the tough men who worked for the cattleman had slicked their hair and were wearing their spare shirts, which Jesse knew from being a cowboy himself were saved for special occasions. The woman hadn't even tided up her hair. They weren't there to celebrate, so why come?

Shorty had posted a notice that everyone in town was invited. Perhaps it was the free food and drink that brought them. Or being new in town, they wanted to meet folks, get to know them, but that hadn't been the impression that spitfire of a woman had given when Jesse and Sheriff Crosson had paid a visit. Where were all her kids? Surely, she hadn't left them alone at the cabin.

"No. I don't recall ever seeing them. They weren't here earlier. I'm sure of it. Pa's good about making introductions."

Jesse stood. He'd bet one of those two men was that woman's husband. He and the sheriff had failed once to get a name and, the second time, had come home with only a first name. Walter. Jesse would introduce himself and find out who they were. There was probably a wanted poster back at the office with one or the other's face on it. It wouldn't surprise him to learn that both men wore a bounty, though the sheriff had found nothing by checking just the name.

NATHANIAL

Jesse's gut had tightened at the sight of them. The sheriff had taught him to follow that instinct. These two were trouble. The woman too. Her relaxed manner while standing between those shaggy-looking men led Jesse to believe she was right at home. The whole group, their nonchalant air, seemed queer since they were strangers there. They'd just moved into the area a couple weeks ago. Being around new people in perhaps an unfamiliar situation usually made one feel nervous. That wasn't what he was seeing.

"Stay here." He strolled down the stairs, leaving Kristy to finish her potatoes.

Shorty had come over and was shaking the hand of one of the two men. The woman was eyeballing the other ladies. She was dressed in nothing fancy or even what he'd refer to as nice. Even girls such as Kristy's sister, Hattie, were all dressed in their Sunday best. It could be that the many styles caught the woman's attention. Women fancied having new clothing. Such a simple thing made them shine.

"How are you folks?" Shorty shook hands with the other fella, whose eyes weren't focused on Shorty. The man stared past him.

Jesse glanced over his shoulder. Kristy was standing near the gate in the yard, talking with several of her friends and their beaus.

"We're just fine," the first man said.

Jesse plunked his empty plate on the table. The group of outsiders and Shorty looked over at the sudden interruption. "I see that dog you mentioned showed up. Which one is he?" Jesse's gaze shifted off the woman to flick between the two men. Both had stiffened. Neither had a hand near his pistol, yet their eyes narrowed on him, and he got the distinct impression they would enjoy nailing his hide to a tree, especially the tall, lean one. His jaw twitched, and his hands balled at his sides.

Shorty choked on his drink. His eyes widened. "Boy, what's gotten into you? These are our guests." The burly cattleman turned, facing what Jesse perceived as trouble. "Excuse my soon-to-be son-in-law. We've all been drinking. Reckon he forgot his manners." Irritation deepened his voice.

Jesse hadn't forgotten anything, nor had he touched any booze. The hardest thing he had to drink was Kristy's sugary lemonade, which left him a touch jittery. He'd be damned if he'd give an apology. The group was silent. An explanation later likely would settle any misunderstanding as far as Shorty was concerned.

The taller one glared down his nose at the mountain woman. So he was the dog and must have been the ringleader, used to giving orders. He didn't cotton to Jesse's blunt words being shoved in his face. Bosses didn't typically put up with that. The other one's neck veins were throbbing, his skin reddening. That one glanced sideways at his tall partner, silently questioning, *What now?*

"I told ya the sheriff and his deputy came callin'. Maybe you should try listenin'." The wench was frank with her man.

The tall fella shifted his gray eyes onto Jesse. There was a glint of raw hate. It could have been the badge he disliked or the fact that Jesse had prodded at him. Whatever the reason, they were both edgy.

"Why don't we all have a drink?" Shorty's words were slightly slurred, and he made a misstep as he fetched the tray of bourbon, nearly spilling it across the table.

Since day one under the tutelage of Sheriff Crosson, Jesse had begun to develop a keen sense of whether a man was on the up-and-up. This fella, the tall one before him, was posed to pounce at any minute. Honesty probably wasn't in his vocabulary. Those three had to be scheming something, but what? No reports of any more stolen women had crossed the sheriff's desk, and Jesse had been riding to the outskirt ranches, checking in, seeing if folks noticed anything suspicious or had any kind of trouble. He had also ridden to the shack where the mountain woman was squatting. No one had been home then or the two days following. He hadn't seen hide nor hair of her until today.

Jesse didn't offer a friendly hand toward any of the three. "What are your names?"

Shorty was a very wealthy man. Maybe they were sizing up the place. A robbery now, or anytime really, would be risky. At all hours, cowhands could be found all over the ranch.

"I don't like you," the tall one said through gritted teeth.

Jesse grinned. "The feelin' is mutual."

Suddenly, Kristy was at his side, slipping her arm around his. "Missy and Patrick would like us to go for a buggy ride with them on Sunday. Sounds like fun." Her smile faded as she looked at all the unhappy faces.

Her pa pushed off the table he'd been leaning against, keeping himself from falling. He wavered as he stood there. The missus was shaking a finger at him, right in his face. Some cowhands nearby snickered. Other folks politely ignored the couple by turning away.

"I've seen enough. Let's go." The tall fella turned, and the two with him followed.

Jesse grabbed his arm, spinning him. Kristy immediately backed off. The other two twisted around.

"I asked you a question."

"Boy, git your hands off me." He jerked his shoulder.

"There'll be no fightin'." Mrs. Short, all of five feet of her and round as barrel, shoved between them, giving Jesse a mean look.

"Ma'am, we'll be ridin' now." The tall fella tipped his hat, then smirked at Jesse. "By the way, the name is adiós." The son of a bitch chuckled.

At the corral, the threesome mounted.

Seen enough. What had that meant?

"Jesse." Kristy's soft voice called his attention away from where those three were headed. "I have met that woman before in town, at the Hendersons' store. Hattie and I were doing some shopping, then met Ma and Pa for lunch at Henry's hotel. Remember, we ran into you afterward."

Jesse nodded. That was the day Sheriff Crosson had given him guff about kissing Kristy when he should have been at work. "Did she say anything to ya?"

"No…" Kristy thought a minute. "But every time I looked up from the catalog, she was staring at Hattie and me."

"You didn't think that was odd?"

Kristy shrugged. "We were wearing new dresses. The latest style. Beautiful satin material. Shipped all the way from New York. Mrs. Henderson raved the minute we walked in."

Kristy wasn't the bragging type. She had a comfortable life. Even so, she was modest, recognizing that not everyone could afford the same luxuries her pa was able to provide for her and her siblings. That pampered upbringing did make her naive at times. Normally, that didn't irritate Jesse.

Not even her pa had perceived danger, welcoming those three right into the party. Shorty was half drunk, though.

"Let's get some cake. Too bad Nate's not here. I made chocolate." Kristy seemed to have already forgotten about the thin woman and her two rough-looking companions. Nothing was going to spoil her day.

Jesse picked up a plate, though his mind wasn't on dessert. His instinct was to trail those three. But he'd just gotten engaged, and Kristy's face was still lit up brighter than the sunshine overhead. She put a wedge of cake on his plate, then handed him a fork.

They joined another young couple, sitting on a blanket near the music, watching men spin their ladies. Jesse picked at his food. Kristy and Missy jabbered about wedding plans. Nearby, some fellas tossed horseshoes. The clang of the iron smacking the metal stake was giving him a headache. Yet his mind was clear about one thing. To protect Kristy and these other ladies, he needed to know for sure that those men weren't part of that ring trafficking women.

"I'll be back." He stood.

Kristy looked up from where she sat. "You're not leaving, are ya?"

He nodded.

She gathered her hem, then followed him to his horse. "You're going after them, aren't you?"

Maybe she wasn't as naive as he'd thought. "Yup." He swung into the saddle.

"I suppose I'd better get used to this." She grinned. "Be careful."

Jesse leaned down and kissed her. "I don't know how long I'll be." He turned his horse.

Hopefully, Kristy didn't mention to her ma where he'd gone. Those three somewhere in front of him were smart enough to know he would track them. An ambush might be waiting.

CHAPTER 14

JESSE PICKED UP THE TRAIL of the thin woman and the two men without difficulty. They stayed on the road into town. He crossed over the bridge into Gray Rock. The place looked deserted. Everyone was at Shorty's ranch, whooping it up. Exactly where he should have been, celebrating the holiday with a beer in his hand and now and then kissing his bride-to-be. But it was his responsibility to watch over the town and the folks who lived there, especially with the sheriff in Birch Creek.

Sheriff Crosson probably had thought about what was going on back home at least a hundred times. Jesse knew that man too well, and they'd been investigating these disappearances, trying to find a pattern or some clue that would aid in catching the men who were stealing women right out of their homes. Sometimes in broad daylight when least expected. Nightfall would give better cover, but the outlaws committing those crimes seemed to hit randomly.

Their tracks halted in front of Pete's saloon. On the door, a paper was tacked. *At picnic. Open tomorrow.* Around the side of the building, their trail led him to where the back

NATHANIAL

door was kicked in, hanging wide open. Pete wasn't careless. He'd never leave the place unlocked.

Inside, the register drawer hung open. Not something Pete would have overlooked. Plus, it was empty. The saloon keeper did quite a business. There wasn't another bar around for miles and miles.

Under the counter, the shotgun Pete kept was gone. He wouldn't have toted his weapon to a neighborly gathering. Jesse would bet some bottles of whiskey were missing too, but he had no way of telling without having Pete check the inventory. He wouldn't pull the man away from the celebration. The barkeep was the surly type, not one to mess with. He'd be fit to be tied the minute he realized he'd been robbed. Keeping Pete from taking the law into his own hands would be a headache Jesse didn't want to deal with. He suspected that the men who did this crime were involved in much worse transgressions, so he wanted nothing getting in his way of nailing them for the bigger offense.

He closed the rear door behind him. From there, the robbers' trail skirted the tree line. Then they had ducked into the trees at the far end of town. That's where the hoofprints stopped being so easy to follow. They'd gone into the creek, leaving no horseshoe marks to track. He suspected they would eventually end up at the shack. But he would trail what sign he could find in case they moved camp.

Along the ridge side, he rode. Two, three miles later, weaving among the juniper, he topped the summit. The mare was holding up fine, just a little winded. He let her breathe a few minutes. Sun glinted off the rocks that formed the skyline of Jumping Fish Canyon across the valley six or so miles farther ahead. Down off the ridge, he steered his horse. The brush was thick there, and he slowed his pace to a walk so as not to make noise. The thought of an ambush hadn't left his mind. Likely, they were watching their backtrail, or at least they were taking time to sweep away their tracks with a branch. He'd found such markings twice.

Jesse veered around Jumping Fish Canyon. The trail into that gorge was a harsh one, unforgiving to any horse that didn't have sound feet, and a perfect spot to snare a man. If he made it inside without getting shot, the trail out was too steep for the mare to climb. She wasn't as sturdy as his last horse that had gotten gored by one bitch of a cow.

Twenty minutes later, on the other side of the canyon, he pulled up reins. There in the dirt was a hoofprint. They'd missed erasing that one. Soon, he would be at the shack. This was the long way around, but that trio had obviously taken precautions.

The shack was empty. No woman, no kids. Nothing but a few fur pelts stretched out and drying in the heat. Jesse mopped his brow. The wagon was gone, and the tracks of the rickety thing were hours old. How could that be? She'd been at the picnic. Not enough time had passed. Which meant someone else had been there with the kids. Another man probably. How many were in this lot?

Jesse searched the ground. Boot tracks had stamped the dirt, men coming and going out of the shack. If he counted right, there were four. The prints were all too big to even consider that a second female was involved. The wagon tracks should be easy enough to follow, but now there were kids in the middle. Extra precautions would have to be taken. He thought of his little partner likely having lots of fun in Birch Creek, eating too much sugar and getting himself into trouble. Jesse didn't want any shooting around the young ones.

The sun had moved farther to the west. Blue Sky Lake wasn't far off, and the wagon tracks were headed in that direction. Only, there were no other hoofprints in the dirt other than the team horses in line with the trail of the wheels. Somewhere, Jesse had missed where the tall man and the men he rode with turned away from the wagon. He'd covered a lot of territory. Too much to go hunting for a needle in a haystack. Tracking was the one skill he wasn't altogether good at, but usually, the sheriff was with him and that man was a hound dog. So Jesse's ability wasn't often solely relied upon.

Voices, squeaky ones, carried on the breeze. Hoots and splashing drew his attention to the water's edge. The thin woman sat on the bank, her skirt hiked above her knees and her feet soaking in the cool wetness. It was hard not to notice that the buttons in the center of her low-hanging neckline were unfastened, exposing the sweaty flesh underneath. He swallowed hard. For a little-bitty woman, good God, she was blessed in that area. Quite a distraction, one he'd bet she knew how to use to her advantage, which could get him killed. Jesse glanced elsewhere.

The wagon was tucked under the shade of some mighty tall trees. The two team animals grazed on a patch of grass where they were tethered to a limb. No other horses. Not a surprise since he'd lost their trail, but that didn't mean they had left her. They could return.

He pulled up reins. "Where are your friends?"

The thin woman twisted around, her eyes narrowed. "I knowed we'd be seein' ya. All you lawmen are the same. Don't know when to quit." The corners of her mouth curled into a wicked grin.

This woman was evil, but Jesse had seen her be kind to Nate and she appeared to treat her kids well. What a contradiction. One person one minute, and the next, she was a heartless bitch. It could be she was just out of her damn head, plumb crazy, having moments of sanity.

"You pissed him off, my man. The next time he sees you, you'll get a bullet in the face." Her gun belt lay on a flat rock within reach of her right hand. At the moment, her hands were sifting through her hair, rearrange the loose bun on top of her head. "Can't say I'd cry." She pressed in a pin, then a second one to hold all the brown strands up.

If she didn't want to tell Jesse where the others were, then he'd bait them. "Get up. You're under arrest for the robbery of the Blue Star Saloon."

Mad cackling burst out of her. She didn't move from where her ass was planted in the dirt. "Kids, the deputy's gonna take us to town, feed us a free meal, and y'all will get to sleep on a soft bunk tonight." She pointed toward the baby splashing in a shallow pool. "He's still on the tit, so don't get any ideas 'bout placin' him in a home unless someone's willin' to wet nurse. As for the other four, they're all skittish around folks, so have fun findin' anyone to watch them."

The kids had all come running. Dripping from head to heels, they all huddled around their mother, but their innocent doe eyes were on him. Nathanial had lived a similar life to these kids, and Jesse felt bad for them. Nate had lots of scars that were connected to bad memories. Jesse wouldn't lock the mother of these kids up in front of them, and worse, that bitch knew it.

"Tell that dog of yours that I'm lookin' for him."

"Tell 'im your damn self."

Before Jesse could argue, the thin woman drew the baby into her arms, and he went to nursing.

"Go play." She shooed the other kids.

Jesse wheeled his horse. If she had expected him to follow, then the men she'd been with probably wouldn't show themselves, not today anyway. Especially since so many at the picnic had seen their little altercation. They'd be the first suspects if Jesse were killed. That'd be a hanging offense.

Did Jesse want to waste what time was left in the day hunting men who, as far as he knew, had stolen a gun and what probably amounted to petty cash? Pete housed a safe in his room, or so Jesse had heard tell. Hopefully, he'd stashed away any bills.

Jesse didn't know that those fellas had anything to do with stealing women. Until he had more proof, or at least a name, to check if any of them had a record, he was at a standstill. Although, he would keep hunting them on the charge of robbery.

Jesse touched spurs to the mare. The rest of the evening belonged to his beautiful bride-to-be.

CHAPTER 15

AFTER THREE KICKS, a hop, and a snort, the animal's neck was arched to buck again. Tate came flying out of the saddle, hit the ground, and got up, limping toward them. When the event was done, they met up with Kate and Constance. The kids wanted to ride the carousel again, which turned into four more times. Then they drifted through the stands and got a late lunch.

They laid out a picnic blanket in the grass near the edge of town where lots of others were doing the same. Corn on the cob, pulled pork, fish, chicken halves, cake, and slices of watermelon were being served. There was a man making popcorn and a woman selling squares of fudge and pieces of pie. Nolan had caught sight of the Fletchers a few times, but they had kept their distance. He didn't want any more trouble with them, especially in front of Nathanial. The boy was having a good time, and Nolan didn't want anything to ruin it.

"Pa. May I get another piece of watermelon?" Red juice dripped off Nathanial's chin. His face was nearly buried in the rind, hands covered in the sticky liquid. He had eaten everything else on his plate.

NATHANIAL

Nolan tossed him two bits. The booth selling the slices was not far, thirty, forty feet away at most. Nolan could see the line clearly, maybe five, six people, and the Fletchers weren't there or at least not in sight.

"Why don't you go with him?" Kate squeezed Nolan's hand.

"The Fletchers haven't bothered us since the marshal warned them. I don't want Nate thinkin' those folks got us so scared that we can't relax at all, or he'll just be anxious. We're all here to enjoy ourselves." Nolan was worried. Fletcher had mentioned a "case." That could only refer to one thing. Court. Was it possible they had pinpointed the wrong kid?

A whore, an outlaw, the offspring of the two... Nate's story probably wasn't all that uncommon. However, the fact that a notorious killer, one of the infamous Younger brothers, had fathered the boy did make him unique. That was one reason his son's past was talked about, so well known.

"I need to tell you something." Kate set aside her plate. "Right before the pie judging, Constance sent a wire to some of her business associates back east. She got a reply. I wasn't sure I should say anything in front of Nathanial." She glanced at their son standing in line, licking his lips.

"They're from New York City, but they own an oil field down Texas way. Three of them to be exact. Lem Fletcher inherited them, old money. He also owns stock in the UP and a few other very profitable ventures. They have more money than we could ever imagine."

What Kate was saying was that the Fletchers had immeasurable resources if this feud went on, and it likely would. They had traveled out west from a far city to find their nephew. No one endured that many miles for weeks on end to engage in a day visit.

There was no reason to doubt the information. Before becoming Constance Huckabee, the marshal's wife was married to a man named Pierce. He'd been a very successful businessman before he died.

"Do you think they want to take Nathanial away?" Kate wrung her hands.

Nolan doubted she was really asking. It was the only logical explanation. Why else would they be following him? More so, Kate was looking to have her fear, their fear, confirmed. She glanced over her shoulder toward their son.

"Nolan!" Kate nearly screamed.

Nolan jumped to his feet. Fletcher was shoving something at the boy, and he dropped the watermelon in his hands.

Nolan ran.

"You ass!" Nate lit up with a blue streak of curses, kicking away the dirty piece of food on the ground, firing splatters at Lem Fletcher, his trouser legs catching the brunt of it.

Deloris Fletcher threw down a coin, quickly producing another piece. She held it out with both hands toward Nathanial, appeasing the fiery tongue.

Nate hesitantly took the food from her.

Nolan's boots pounded the dirt. Fletcher looked up. Their eyes clashed. One man against another. Only, their terms of engagement were very different. Nolan was charging. If he got his hands on that son of a bitch... But Fletcher snatched his wife's arm, whirled her in the opposite direction, and quick as a blink, they disappeared into the crowd. More people had flooded the area to satisfy their hunger, inadvertently forming a hedge.

Nolan hunkered in front of Nate. "You okay?"

The child nodded, then spit a seed. He didn't seem shaken, just concerned about eating dessert. After Nolan and Mr. Fletcher's earlier altercation, the boy had been clingy. Not this time. Maybe because there'd been no shoving or loud words. Nolan took an easy breath.

NATHANIAL

"What did Fletcher give you?" From the picnic spot, Nolan hadn't been able to make out exactly what the man had pushed on Nathanial.

Nate handed him the tintype that Nolan had seen earlier and a sealed letter. Nolan wasted no time tearing open the envelope. As he silently read, his blood began to boil. He was right. There would be a court hearing, a custody battle. He needed to discuss this with Kate immediately.

"What's it say?" Nate cocked his head, staring at Nolan. "I ain't ever seen that vein in your neck thump like that."

"Son, this is serious." Nolan wagged the letter. "We need to go back to the house with your ma and talk about it."

Nathanial threw down the rind. "I don't wanna. I didn't get Jesse his balloon, and me and Deputy wanna ride the carousel again."

It was hard to be upset with him when his little cheeks and all around his mouth were painted with pink juice, resembling a clown. And he had a right to be a kid. This sudden intrusion in their lives was something none of them foresaw. They'd come there to share in good times. He didn't fault the boy for feeling slighted.

Kate appeared next to Nolan. "What did they want this time?" She pulled Nathanial into her skirt, holding him close.

The boy peeled away and looked up at his mother. "Can we stay? I don't wanna leave the celebration."

"Nathanial." Nolan scowled.

His son knew better than to play his mother and father against one another. If one of them said no, then the answer was just that. He wasn't to go to the other and try to get away with something. Nolan had already told the child they needed to take time out and discuss this new development.

"What?" Kate's gaze flicked between them, looking lost.

Nolan handed her the letter and picture. As she scanned each line, he watched the color drain from her face.

"Do you think they can prove that?" She replaced the letter into the envelope, then stared at the photograph.

"Prove what?" Nate jetted onto his tiptoes, leaning in, staring at the picture the same as Kate.

Nolan recalled Fletcher mentioning correspondence between his wife and her late sister. Perhaps one of those letters contained Lucinda's last will and testament. Would an old letter stand up in court when, by all accounts, it could be disputed as a false document? According to the paper he'd just read, the Fletchers were claiming she'd granted them guardianship.

"Honestly, I don't know."

"I do look like her." Nathanial touched the image of who they believed to be his birth mother. "But I don't really remember her. Just that we lived above a saloon and it was always noisy." Nate was quiet for a long minute. His gaze seemed faraway, not in the present.

"Sometimes, I would have to wait in the hallway all by myself while Lucinda entertained a customer in our room. Strange men was always kissin' her, touching her, or tryin' to. I remember weird sounds. There was another woman. I can't recall what she looked like, but if she saw me millin' there in the hall, she'd take me in her room and give me a book full of sketches to look at."

Nolan touched his son's shoulder, wishing he could collect every bad memory and throw them so far away that Nathanial would never be troubled again. The boy stared up at being pressed. His eyes were glassy. None of them could be positive that wasn't Nate's birth mother. None of them had ever seen her, and Nate had only a vague inclination of her, never recalling the woman's face to them.

"Why'd they have to find me?" He wiped a sleeve across his face.

NATHANIAL

Nolan squatted. "All that photograph proves is that this Lucinda and Deloris Fletcher were sisters... that you may have an aunt." He hated to say it. "I want to talk to Judge Prescott. I can't fathom that an adoption ruling could be reversed on the grounds of what some obscure relative who shows up unexpectedly after almost nine years has to say. And that is if she is actually kin. We don't know that."

"I hope you're right," Kate added.

Nathanial grinned at the two of them.

"I saw Judge Prescott with his wife earlier at the baking contest. Maybe he's still around." Kate's head twisted in every direction.

"So can we stay?" Nate's grin grew into a hopeful smile.

Nolan couldn't help chuckling. He nodded. For now, Nate had enough details. The last thing Nolan wanted was the child getting stuck in those memories that caused him to shrink up inside himself, and as the boy's father, he could hardly take the tears. The more Lucinda's name was brought up, the more his son might mentally drift off to those awful times.

They returned to the picnic. Only, Nolan had lost any urge to eat.

After studying the photograph, there was no uncertainty. The Lucinda in that picture was Nathanial's birth mother. The facial and size similarities were stunning, but a picture taken years ago... Was it enough evidence to take Nate from his folks? Nolan wished he could read the other letters, the ones supposedly from Lucinda to Deloris. He didn't question that sisters would write one another. It was the content in those lines that had him skeptical.

After everyone ate their fill, they got balloons for the kids. Nate insisted on a red one for Jesse. Nolan couldn't get him to understand that Jesse had been funning him about the balloon. He was too old for such things.

The afternoon passed without any more tricks from the Fletchers. The way they had gone right for Nate the moment he wasn't close to Nolan and Kate had his senses attentive. Of course, Nolan wasn't letting the boy wander more than a foot from his side, and both he and Kate were keeping an eye out for Judge Prescott.

The kids played a ring toss game. Then they all watched an archery event.

Evening was coming on when Nolan spotted a familiar face among the throng.

"Nolan, how are you?" Judge Prescott extended a hand. "Kate." He greeted her with a polite nod.

The Huckabees were turned and talking with another couple. Between them, Nate, Deputy, and little Miles sat on their knees in the dirt, drawing pictures in the dust with their fingers.

"I swear, in all my born days, I ain't seen so many people...Two in particular have caught my attention." Nolan pulled the tintype and letter from his pocket.

Thomas J. Prescott was a hanging judge. The law was the law, and he made no exception. He was a fair man, couldn't be bought, and freed the innocent. He'd been a high-powered attorney in Chicago. Then a close friend had been murdered while buying cattle during a trip west. It was the reason Judge Prescott landed in Birch Creek. He quickly acclimated to the climate, the breed of men around him, and took it upon himself to stay and see that enforcement of laws was brought into the territory. Few towns had a sheriff, let alone a judge. Birch Creek was lucky enough to have both, and good ones at that.

"I wouldn't worry. Nathanial doesn't remember his birth mother, and one photo and a few letters don't seem like much of a case. If the letters are that old, are they legible? It could be that Mrs. Fletcher is reading into them, missing her sister more as the years pass instead of healing, wanting to hold on to a little piece of what she lost." Thomas patted Nolan's shoulder. "She was a whore. I can't imagine anything she had written about was all that pertinent. Most women in that profession, if you will, don't want a child." Prescott whispered over the kids' heads. "They have their ways of taking care of such situations, but I understand she was deeply in love with Jim Younger."

Kate, standing tight to his side, squeezed Nolan's arm. He knew what she was thinking, and it was a mistake. Not all women were like her and loved their kids. They might have loved the men who fathered the child, deceiving themselves into believing that a baby would force his love, bring them closer. That was rarely the case, or so he'd encountered a few times. Then she'd take her hate out on that child. Kate needed to remember what Nate had said earlier. That he'd been left on his own in a dirty saloon while his so-called mother screwed men within earshot. Nolan wouldn't call that caring. So the chances of her leaving behind a single word specifically announcing what should be done with Nathanial in the case of her death were slim to none.

Thomas Prescott looked at Kate, who kept glancing down at Nate with tears in her eyes. "Even if, say, this Lucinda did write something down about Nathanial, without a reliable witness to connect all the parts, it would really just be Mrs. Fletcher's word. Anything of sustenance in letter form could be disputed as a forgery. For heaven's sake, it's been how long? Almost nine years? As a judge, I would certainly be questioning the lag of time between events. And Mrs. Fletcher would have to provide more proof than a picture as to her blood relationship with the late Lucinda in question. How do we know this is even her? Yes, she does resemble Nathanial, but all Mrs. Fletcher has that I can see is an outdated tintype and a story."

Nolan nodded, and Kate eased up on her neck-breaking grip. Nathanial was giggling, as was Deputy. They had written

Tate loves frogs in the dirt. He was glad to see his son was not allowing a few sour minutes to spoil his day.

"Thanks. I needed to hear it rationalized."

As a lawman, Nolan was levelheaded. As a father, he could be excitable at times. Not often, but this was a direct threat against his family. And before talking to Prescott, he felt all twisted up inside. He was now breathing easier. The judge would be the one to know if the Fletchers had a genuine case.

"Not a problem." Prescott touched the brim of his hat. "Enjoy the rest of your day." He began to turn, looped an arm with his wife's, then stopped. "If the Fletchers come before me and present their evidence—and it sounds like they will—I don't want to mislead you. An investigation is not entirely out of question, but from what you've told me, I don't foresee a trial unless they have proof that hasn't been unveiled."

Nolan had thought hard about that too. He bid the judge good day.

As the sun began to fade, they bought the kids popcorn, and as a friendly group, including Tate, they headed for the pond behind the Huckabee home. It would be the perfect spot to watch the fireworks.

Kate laid out a blanket, as did the Huckabees. Tate being there reminded Nolan that one member of his family was missing. Jesse was probably still at the Shorts', eating his fill, maybe drinking too much, and probably staring into Kristy's eyes all moonstruck. She was just as hopelessly in love.

Nolan suspected that the special thing Jesse had to do today was pop the big question. The young couple had been courting seriously for a spell, too long in Nolan's mind. What was the boy waiting for? Something had to have him stalled. It wasn't cold feet, because his mouth flapped like a duck's ass when it came to that girl of his. Sometimes Nolan got sick of hearing it.

If he had to guess, the trouble was Mrs. Short. She'd never taken to Jesse, and frankly, it pissed Nolan off. His son was a fine man. Shorty could see that. And the rest of the family liked Jesse. That woman was just trying to hold on to her daughter. Grown children were meant to be set free, to make their own choices, to cut out a life of their own. Forcing her ideals on her daughter wasn't right, and from what Jesse had told him, that was exactly what Mrs. Short was doing.

Hopefully, she wouldn't spoil any part of Jesse and Kristy's day, even if they didn't get engaged. Nolan just hoped Jesse was using that brain of his while at Shorty's place. An engagement or even spending an entire day together—picnicking, socializing, having laughs—would be reason to celebrate, and he didn't want them to commemorate in the way that a young couple might. He had caught the two getting frisky in the barn loft just a week before this trip. Kristy had gone home in tears, probably figuring he planned to tell her folks, which he had no intention of doing. Kristy and Jesse were old enough to be married and coupling came with the territory, yet they weren't officially engaged. So Nolan had given Jesse some stern fatherly advice. Shotgun weddings were not a good thing. He was to get a ring on that girl's finger.

Nolan wanted it to be a surprise, a wedding gift. He and Kate planned on giving the young couple a plot of land on the ranch to build a home.

"Pa, when will the fireworks start?" Nate scanned the blackening sky.

"Reckon after dark."

A few minutes later, the boy asked again, then again, and kept pestering, and for the hundredth time in twenty minutes, Nolan said he didn't know.

"Keep watching the sky." Nolan ruffled the boy's hair.

Nate squeezed his tiny bottom between Nolan and Kate. Elizabeth was asleep on her mother's lap. Nolan slipped an arm around her shoulders. He was a happy man.

His little boy jumped near out of his skin at the first boom lighting up the dark sky with red, blue, and yellow sparkles. Nathanial pressed against Nolan's side. Maybe he was a little afraid. His eyes were wide and stuck on the bright, colorful lights making their magic sprinkles, illuminating the black. More booms filled their ears. The display of fireworks was like nothing Nolan had ever seen, and the children were all in awe. To his surprise, Elizabeth slept as lights flashed and the thunder shook the air. An entire field filled with people sitting on their blankets stared into the sky. Then after the grand finale, applause, hoots, and whistles rose off the ground from every direction.

Kate with Elizabeth and Nolan carrying Nate, they collected the blanket and followed behind the Huckabees toward the house.

After tucking the kids into their rooms, Kate changed into her night clothing. "Nate was asleep before his head touched the pillow. Do you believe Elizabeth slept through all that noise?" She slipped into bed, wrapping her arms around Nolan. "I'm pretty tired myself." She kissed his face, then looked at the paper in his hands. "Why don't you throw that thing away? I don't need any reminders."

Nolan rolled to sit up at the edge of the bed, crumpling the letter in his hand. Then he pulled on his pants and boots.

"Do you think they'll follow us home since they have been keeping a close eye on our son? If they see us leave, they won't want to lose sight of him." Kate nearly choked on the words. This wasn't an easy thing to think about. Gray Rock was their hometown, and Nate should feel safe there, be able to play with his friends and run around without worry of being harassed.

Nolan stiffly shrugged. Who knew what that couple would do? He hadn't expected any of what they'd done so far, but if it was a court battle they wanted, there wasn't a judge in Gray Rock.

NATHANIAL

"I think they'd have to stay in Birch Creek long enough to file paperwork with Judge Prescott. Unless they've already hired a lawyer."

"I don't understand. Why now, after years, would they come trying to find him, especially if they had gotten a letter almost a decade ago? When he was a baby and needed someone, no kin had come forward to claim him, to take him in, to protect and care for him. I can't believe Deloris didn't know what kind of a woman her sister was. Did she think that was the best environment for him? No one in their right mind would think that a child living in a bar with a whore was okay. It makes me not believe them." It didn't need to be said. Kate was a mother bear. They wouldn't give up their son without a helluva fight if it came to that.

Nolan hoped it wouldn't. Just handing Nate over would never be an option in either of their minds.

"I'm glad Nathanial doesn't seem worried," she said.

"Yes, but our son knows how to hide his feelings. Don't forget he's been taught how by Younger."

Nolan removed the photograph from his vest pocket. He stood, walking toward the door. "I'll be back in a few minutes."

In short time, Nolan walked into the hotel. "What room are the Fletchers in?"

The clerk looked at the badge on his shirt. "Eight."

Nolan tipped his hat, then walked up the stairs, stopping to stand squarely in front of the door centered with the brass number eight. His fist pounded the wood. Anyone inside was sure to be woken.

The door opened.

Nolan didn't say a word. He hadn't come to talk. He threw a quick, hard punch, hitting Lem Fletcher square in the nose, knocking him to the floor.

The woman screamed. She quickly knelt beside her husband, fussing over his bleeding nose.

J.B. RICHARD

Nolan tossed the wrinkled-up letter and tintype at the two of them. "Stay the hell away from my son." Then he turned, walking down the stairs and out of the hotel.

CHAPTER 16

NATE HATED TO SAY GOOD-BYE. It felt as if they'd just gotten there, and now it was time to go home. He missed Deputy already, and Nate wasn't even in the wagon yet. He was sure Pa might have to put an arm between Ma and Mrs. Huckabee, hugging and crying all over one another, and pull them apart. Nate understood, though. There was just something sad about packing up and leaving those you cared about. Instead, he thought of Jesse and giving him his new horse and balloon.

Pa and the marshal shook hands. Then Tate did the same. It took a few minutes, but Pa finally got the women to separate, and Ma was helped up onto the wagon seat. Nate crawled up and plopped down in the middle. Then Pa stepped up and took the reins. They all gave one more wave. Pa slapped leather to the team.

Deputy ran beside the wagon until they reached the far edge of town. Nate turned forward once his friend was out of sight.

He looked up at his father. "Pa, when's the marshal gonna bring Deputy to our house to go huntin'?" Nate had heard their fathers discussing it.

"Maybe in a few weeks." Pa grinned.

Nate supposed that would satisfy him. At least it wouldn't be months until he saw his best friend again.

The weather was perfect as the days passed and they drew closer to home. Ma hadn't gotten sick once while bouncing along in the wagon over the rutted roads. Nate's leg wasn't stiff anymore, but his arm still ached if he tried to move it too much. He would remove the sling and slowly stretch out the stiffness every now and then.

At night, Nate and Elizabeth slept under the canvas while Ma and Pa got to view the stars from their bedsheet on the ground. Tomorrow, they would be in Gray Rock, and that meant seeing Jesse. Nate had missed him a lot and wasn't sure he would sleep a wink.

The sun was overhead when Pa steered the wagon into Gray Rock. Nate took a deep breath of mountain breeze. Home was the best place ever.

Where was Jesse? And as if he'd heard the wagon coming amid the others on the street, Jesse stepped out of the jailhouse, and he looked as tall and strong as when Nate had left. Nate jumped in front of Ma, got a toe up on the wagon lip, and before Pa could catch him, he took a flying leap into Jesse's arms. Nate wasn't wearing his sling and forgot about his sore arm until Jesse caught him and spun him around. He yelped, but at the same time, he was happy.

Jesse lowered Nate to stand on the boardwalk. "What in tarnation?" He eyed the sling Ma thrust toward them.

"It's nothing." Nate wanted to shrug it off but knew he'd get in trouble for that, so he snagged it but ignored the stern look to put it on. He didn't care about his arm and wanted more than anything to give Jesse the appaloosa so he wouldn't say he fell off that horse and give away the surprise too soon.

"It don't look like nothin'." Jesse turned then as Pa had stepped down, came around the wagon, and patted Jesse's shoulder. They were pleased to see one another. "Hello, sir.

It's good to have ya home, all of ya." Jesse looked up at Ma who had stayed planted on the wagon seat with Elizabeth squirming to get down. "Ma, I've missed ya." Some time ago, Jesse had taken to calling her ma. Her bright smile showed that she loved it.

"We got a surprise for ya." Nate grinned sheepishly.

"My balloon." Jesse winked.

"It's better than that. Now close your eyes." Nate could hardly keep from bouncing. He was going to burst if he had to wait another minute to give Jesse his new horse.

"Jesse's a mite old for that. He doesn't have to close his eyes. He ain't a kid." Pa rolled his eyes and headed toward the back of the wagon where the horse was tied.

Nate put up both hands, keeping Jesse held back.

"It's not as fun if ya don't close your eyes." He begged a little.

Jesse grinned, then gave in and closed his eyes. "Don't ya run me into anything or I'll box your ears." He blindly held his hand out for Nate to lead him. Nate was careful and watched Jesse's every step. Good thing they didn't have to go far. This was taking too much time, and he didn't want Jesse to peek and ruin it.

Nate stopped within a short reach of the horse. "Surprise!"

Jesse opened his eyes. Nate would have sworn that someone had punched the wind out of Jesse's gut. His eyes widened, and his mouth fell open. Then hesitantly, as if the horse wasn't real, he reached out and rubbed the appaloosa's neck.

"Are ya gonna cry?" Nate chuckled as he socked Jesse in the arm.

"Got dirt in my eyes." Jesse rapidly blinked.

"Sure ya do, crybaby." Nate looked over at Pa, who wore a broad grin.

Jesse gave Nate a bump with his hip. It was one of the ways they spoke. That bump meant shut up, and Nate socking

Jesse was him calling Jesse a girl. On the outside, Jesse was a tough man, hard as nails, but at times, he could be a big softy. Of course Nate enjoyed teasing him about that tender side. Brothers picked on one another, harmless, and Pa seemed to get a kick out of it.

Jesse wiped his eyes. "I gotta surprise for y'all." He cleared his throat, stood a little taller, and let out a deep breath. "I asked Kristy to marry me, and she said yes. We're gonna have us a weddin' come spring."

That big news brought Ma right down off the seat, hugging and kissing all over Jesse. She was a proud woman. Nate, though, was a little bit sad. He didn't want Jesse to move out of the house. Jesse's room was where Nate ended up if he had a bad dream. They had lots of good times together and Nate would miss that, but he put on a smile 'cause Jesse was so happy. So were Ma and Pa. Pa was now shaking Jesse's hand as though he were trying to rip it off.

When all the excitement subsided, everyone but Jesse got into the wagon, and they headed home. Nate hung out the back flap. Ma and Pa couldn't see him from the front. The closure was drawn shut. On the street, Jesse was changing his saddle over to the appaloosa and would soon be following. Nate was tired of riding in the cranky wagon and wanted to spend time with Jesse now that they were home, even if it was only two miles to the ranch. He would rather ride with Jesse on his new horse.

Nate slipped out the flap, dropped to the dirt on his feet, and shot off toward Jesse. For sure, he'd catch hell later. When Nate skidded to a stop, huffing and puffing, next to Jesse, Jesse turned his gaze on the wagon as it rattled over the wooden bridge on its way out of town.

He grinned, shook his head, and ruffled Nate's hair. "Partner, I missed ya too, ya little rascal."

NATHANIAL

Jesse stepped up into the saddle, then gave Nate a hand, swinging him up behind. Jesse nudged the horse, and it took to his leading. They began to trot. A few minutes later, before even reaching the wooden bridge, he sank spurs, and the gelding cantered as smoothly as sipping buttermilk. Out ahead, the wagon was rolling at a dull pace.

"Hold on," Jesse said over his shoulder.

Nate tightened his grip the best he could with one strong arm as Jesse kicked. The appaloosa took off a'hellin'. The rush of air almost tore off Jesse's hat. He pushed it down, and Nate pressed into his back, keeping a tight hold around his waist. The fast horse thundered past the wagon. Nate didn't dare to glance back. He'd probably hear it from Ma about how he could have gotten hurt and for sneaking out of the wagon. If Pa said anything, it would be what Ma wanted him to say, or if she was really mad, she'd make Pa give him a spanking. Pa knew how good of a rider Nate was, even if Jesse was at the reins, and he was an outstanding rider too. They went riding together nearly every day.

Ma must have been glad just to be home, because Nate didn't get a tongue-lashing when she got down off the wagon. Without being asked, he helped her carry stuff to the house while Pa and Jesse unhitched the team and stored the canvas. It was nigh to suppertime. With Ma in the kitchen, starting the meal, Nate went back out to see if he could help Pa and Jesse get the wagon and such put away.

When he stepped inside the barn, Jesse had a pitchfork raised and was mid toss. Hay spilled into the stall where Pa's bay stood lazily.

"Shorty left on a cattle drive a few days after the picnic. I gave him my word that I'd look in on his family while he's gone. I should be back by supper."

Pa nodded, although Nate could see the disappointment on his long face. They had just gotten home, excited to see Jesse and spend time with him, and he had to go. Although, Nate had heard Pa say many times how proud he was that Jesse took his duties seriously. He was a man of his word.

"Can I go?" Nate pleaded with his blue eyes.

It felt like such a long time since he'd seen his friends, Lenny and Norman Short. He was sure they would want to hear all about Birch Creek. Plus, Nate couldn't wait to throw a leg over Buck and go for a ride in the mountain air.

"We could take the path past Blue Sky Lake and see how good your new horse is on the trails." Waving a good run of the animals under Jesse's nose as bait might just hook him into taking Nate. But he knew that probably wasn't necessary. They were partners, and Jesse hardly ever said no to him.

"Heck yeah, you can go. Sounds like fun." Jesse ruffled Nate's hair.

"I'll see you boys when ya get back." Pa left the barn, heading for the house.

A few minutes later, the horses were saddled, and soon after, Nate and Jesse were on their mounts, running up across the ridge side toward Blue Sky Lake. Near the top, they slowed their heavy-breathing animals, and Nate explained his accident. Shaking his head in displeasure, Jesse told Nate he would have tanned his hide had he been there. The rest of their ride toward the lake was filled with bits and pieces of their time spent in Birch Creek, and Jesse ate it all up.

"So those city people, the man and the woman, the Fletchers...They just kept bothering ya?" By the stiff way Jesse was now sitting in the saddle, Nate could tell he didn't like the sound of that, not in the least. He, like Pa, could sense trouble a mile away, but Nate figured he didn't have anything to worry about anymore. The Fletchers were in Birch Creek or had returned to the city, wherever they lived, and Nate was safe at home in Gray Rock.

"Yeah, they did. I thought Pa was gonna throttle 'em a few times." Nate chuckled.

Jesse snickered too. "I'm surprised he didn't. When it comes to family, it don't pay to rile your pa."

Out ahead, the sound of water being splashed and voices carried on the cool mountain breeze. "Maybe some of my friends are at the lake." Nate wanted to say hi. He nudged Buck and trotted ahead of Jesse's appaloosa.

At the water's edge, Nate pulled up on the reins. There, ankle deep in the water and bent over a washboard with a full basket of linens waiting onshore, the thin woman from the old trapper shack was scrubbing away at a dirty shirt. Her kids, all five, were playing in the water, including the baby, which was being held by a young girl who was soaking the infant's feet for a touch of coolness.

The thin woman looked up from her work. The sharpness in her eyes left as soon as her gaze met his, and she grinned.

"Hi," Nate said.

She lifted her chin to greet him. The kids all kept playing, paying him no mind.

"We just got back from Birch Creek." Nate beamed.

Then he recalled how this woman had said she knew his birth mother and thought of how strange it was that within a matter of a few weeks, he had come across three people who said they knew Lucinda. He'd gone years without ever hearing her name. Now, suddenly, people associated with his past were popping up everywhere.

"Ya ever been to the city?" Nate was doubtful that this dirty-faced mountain woman knew the Fletchers, but he wouldn't have guessed her to know his birth mother either.

He should just forget about the Fletchers. They were out of his life now, but they'd known his name and pieces of his past and believed they had known his mother. He wasn't so convinced. Why would a rich lady come west and become a whore, giving up a pampered life to live in a gutter, to smell stale cigars and cigarette smoke day and night, to reek of cheap whiskey and the cologne of different men? It was strange the details that would just come forward in his brain, but never Lucinda's face.

This woman, her brash attitude, was familiar with what he was able to conjure of those days living in that hole of a saloon. She was the type of woman he pictured his birth mother to be, so he didn't doubt her friendship with Lucinda.

If Mrs. Fletcher really was the sister of Nate's late mother, then wouldn't this lady know about her? Maybe by some chance, she had met the Fletchers and would know something about them, other than they were rich and didn't live west of the Mississippi. Anything that might help prove he was not their nephew. Only to himself did he admit being curious about his birth mother's life before she fell in love with an outlaw.

"Do I look like a city dweller?" She smacked her hands to her hips as if to say he'd just asked the stupidest question she'd ever heard.

"Partner, let's go." Jesse was waiting on the trail and gave a sharp wave.

Nate ignored him and would probably hear it later.

An interest prodded him to know the truth, not that he planned to do anything with it once he knew. His inquisitive nature was getting the best of him. Maybe this woman could clear up at least one question for him. "Do you happen to know a Deloris Fletcher?"

The thin woman straightened, eyes narrowed. "I don't know her personally, but I sure as hell know who she is. You stay away from that bitch. Your mother cut ties with her, never really liked her."

"Why?" Nate swallowed hard, hoping she had the answer.

"Just because two people are kin don't mean they're gonna see eye to eye. Deloris and Lucinda were very different people."

NATHANIAL

She sighed deeply as if recalling something unpleasant. "They used to write. Too often, one of 'em would get mad and stop writin' for a while. It was like a catfight on paper."

"So they were kin." He wasn't really asking.

Nate's heart sank. Even after Pa had said it might be true, Nate hammered in his mind that it wasn't so. He didn't want to have any ties to those people. The thought of it worried him. His old pa, Jim Younger, who was in prison, had to sign over custody for Nate to be adopted. Being blood relation, would the Fletchers have any right to him? Nate felt suddenly weak and sweaty.

The thin woman cackled. "They was sisters. Deloris Fletcher's your aunt."

Out of nowhere, the reins were jerked out of Nate's hands. Jesse's face steamed red. "Excuse us, ma'am. We gotta be on our way." Jesse kept ahold of Buck's reins and turned both horses toward the trail leading to the Short ranch.

Nate wiped at his eyes. How could those city folks be his aunt and uncle? It just didn't seem possible. He looked over at Jesse, who was still red around the ears.

"Jesse, did you hear what she said?" Nate wanted to know what he thought. If the Fletchers had been looking for him as they said they had been, then it only made sense that they might pursue him to Gray Rock. And if they found him again, then what would happen?

Jesse stiffly nodded. "I think we need to tell your pa about this." What he was saying was that Nate wouldn't get to spend much time playing with Lenny and Norman.

Jesse's demeanor had become all business. He sat straight in the saddle, and his gaze was forward. Nate could tell he was thinking over all that information, and judging by his wrinkled brow, he didn't like the framework that was building toward conclusion.

He tossed Nate's reins back, then spurred the appaloosa. They ran the horses along the trail toward Shorty's until they crested the hill behind the ranch house.

All was good, and they left for home within a half hour. Nate had promised his friends he'd return tomorrow. For nearly a week and about the same time each day, after he was done with his extra chores, which included soaping saddles and cleaning tack, Nate and Jesse would run their horses along the trail near Blue Sky Lake to the Short ranch.

Nate had gotten a lecture that first night after Jesse told Pa about the meeting with the thin woman. He had been made to promise not to speak to her, or he wouldn't be allowed to go to the Shorts' with Jesse and Pa would find more extra chores for him.

They topped the hill behind Lenny and Norman's house, slowing their mounts. In a patch of trees off to their left stood five saddled horses tethered to a low-hanging branch. Why wouldn't Shorty's ranch hands take their mounts to the corral? Nate looked harder. Those horses weren't wearing Shorty's brand.

"Dammit." Jesse cursed under his breath, and Nate knew why.

There was but one reason for men to hide their horses. They didn't want to be seen, to be caught. Nate had ridden with his old pa too long not to recognize it. And he and Jesse were in a bad spot. They were slowly walking their horses down the hill toward the house. The closest cover was fifty feet away. That was a lot of space to be dodging bullets. Likely, there was a lookout who had already spotted them and was watching, waiting to see what they would do, and Nate wasn't sure himself.

"I bet they've come for the women." Jesse's words were a serious warning to Nate. He had better do exactly as he was told when he was told, or one or both of them might die.

NATHANIAL

"What are we gonna do?" he whispered without moving his lips. Fifty yards and they'd be in the ranch yard. They couldn't up and run without getting shot at. What other option was there?

"When we get closer to the barn, you take the horses and go hide yourself somewhere inside." Jesse was pure calm on the outside, and for good reason. They couldn't let on that they suspected trouble, or whoever those five horses belonged to might rush them or shoot them. But Nate figured Jesse's heart was banging with the same ferocity as his.

"Then what are you gonna do? If you pull either of your weapons, rifle or pistol, they'll likely shoot ya down." Nate had to push aside his fear and focus on whatever he could do to help. He didn't want to see Jesse get hurt or killed. Whoever was hiding there, if it was criminals—and he and Jesse weren't sure yet—they might kill Jesse anyway. The sun was shining, and the glare of both Jesse's and Nate's badges couldn't be mistaken for anything but a lawman's star.

"I gotta get into the house. Kristy and her little brothers and sister are probably in there. And Mrs. Short." Under the brim of his hat, Jesse's eyes were searching all over the yard for just the right path to keep him from getting killed.

The barnyard was too quiet. Usually, ranch hands were working about somewhere. Were they all on the cattle drive with Shorty? Or maybe the ranch hands that stayed behind were in the fields, watching cattle. It looked like Jesse was alone against five, or at least there had been five horses tied yonder in the trees.

Nate had an idea, and as he hopped up feet flat on the seat of his saddle and stood straight up, dropping the reins and spreading his arms out like wings, he hoped to hell this worked.

"Look at me. I can fly." He forced a wide smile and subtly winked at Jesse.

Jesse needed some kind of distraction to get them out of the open and help him sneak closer to the house without much notice. If anyone was watching—and Nate was sure someone was on lookout—he would do his best to keep their eyes on him.

Jesse returned the wink, then turned in the saddle while yanking up on the reins. The horses halted at the bottom of the hill. From here, they were twenty feet from the larger of the two barns. A corral jetted out from there to within five feet of them. It was some cover, and the barn was not unreachable. Thirty feet to the other side of them was the house. They had approached from the rear of the homestead, and it was likely that only one man was positioned to watch this direction. But they didn't know where he was, so they couldn't take any chances. Maybe in an upstairs window of the house, or he could have an eye on them from inside the barn, perhaps the loft. That way, he could probably watch the horses. Most folks that might stop by for a visit would come up the lane from the coach road and ride up to the front of the house. That's where the heaviest amount of lookout would concentrate. So it was possible for Jesse to maybe slip into the house somewhere on the rear side.

A breeze kicked up, and Nate spied an open window at the back of the house. The white curtain was flapping out over the windowsill. Hopefully, Jesse had seen it too.

"Ahh!" Nate faked losing his balance in the wind, his good arm failing. He'd pulled the hurt one in tight, protecting it as he pitched himself toward Jesse's horse, grabbing at Jesse's rifle in its boot, knocking it to the ground. Nate hit the dirt beside it. Pain really did shoot through his bad arm, and he let out crying. But his plan had worked.

Jesse was off his horse and picked up the Winchester as if retrieving it without a purpose. Now his gun was in hand, and Jesse was a true rifleman. There wasn't a better shot.

He owned lots of skill with that rifle, and suddenly, the odds seemed more in Jesse's favor. Hopefully, whoever was watching wasn't suspicious that he was now ready for them.

"Boy, I've told you before not to fool around on your horse." It was a fake scolding, but no one else would know it.

Nate pushed up off the ground, and just like that, Jesse gave him a swat on the bottom, then flopped him on the mustang. None of it really hurt, but it looked convincing.

"You get on home. I'll deal with you later."

Nate knew from his days of riding with his old pa that criminals usually picked towns where they wouldn't be recognized. That also meant whoever was lurking here wouldn't know that Nate and Jesse were not father and son unless they were up close and realized how young Jesse really was. He was as tall as Pa and just as broad-shouldered. There were lots of dark whiskers on his chin, but Jesse was only eighteen.

Nate turned Buck away from the house and ranch yard, knowing the plan was for him to run and get Pa as fast as he could. A hundred yards behind, the boom of a rifle shook the air. As Nate raced away, the Winchester retorted with a mean bark.

CHAPTER 17

BUCK THUNDERED into the yard with Nate hanging on tight and hollering his lungs out for his father. "Pa!" Pa had just stepped out of the outhouse and turned toward Nate's cry. On the porch swing sat Ma, and a man was sitting in one of the chairs near her. The porch roof cast shadows on their faces, so Nate didn't recognize the man at first. But he had captured their attention, and the man stood. Nate caught a glimpse of the star on the man's shirt. It was Marshal Huckabee. Nate didn't have time to think about him being there, not so soon after them leaving Birch Creek, and he didn't see Deputy.

"Nathanial, what's wrong?" Pa hustled toward him.

"It's Jesse. There's some men at the Short house. He thinks they're the ones stealin' women." Nate was breathless after spitting it out so quickly.

Pa was hightailing it toward the corral where his bay was standing. The marshal was off the porch, hurdling the gate, and in no time at all, he was swinging a leg over his horse. Ma, with tears in her eyes, was on her feet, gripping the porch post and watching the flurry going on in the yard.

NATHANIAL

Pa threw his saddle on the bay. "Nathanial, get my rifle."

Nate jumped off Buck and sprinted up the porch steps. Before he got to the door, which was open, Ma was running out with the rifle. She quickly handed it to Nate. When he turned, Pa was waiting atop his horse just outside the gate. Nate hurried and lifted the rifle to him.

"You stay here with your ma." Pa jerked the reins, turning his horse, and the marshal fell into pace as they ran their horses toward Shorty's place.

Nate watched until they were out of sight.

Elizabeth suddenly burst out crying from inside the house. Ma, who was standing on the porch and watching as Nate had been doing, wiped at her eyes, then hurried inside. Nate lumbered up the stairs, touching the badge on his chest, wishing he was old enough to ride with Pa and the marshal. He had helped in a small way by fetching Pa.

Nate flopped into the chair that the marshal had been sitting in. There was a thick stack of papers on the small table Ma had there to hold drinks when they took in the cool evening air. Nate took a peek. Why was his name on those papers? He picked them up and smoothed them out so he could actually read them. It was a summons to appear in court. Nate read fast, scanning over the first three in the stack. He didn't understand all the legal terms. Some of the words were really big. But he understood the gist of it. The Fletchers wanted custody of him. He had overheard Judge Prescott in Birch Creek telling Pa not to worry. It would take an eyewitness to link Nate with the Lucinda in that picture, and there had been uncertainty about those letters.

The thin woman popped into Nate's head. She knew Nate's mother and could surely identify her from a picture. What if the Fletchers somehow found out about her? If they had tracked him down from where they lived in some state back east, then they might find her. Her word might be enough to get Nate unadopted and sent away with his aunt and uncle. There was only one thing he could do. Run away. He'd come back after the Fletchers forgot about him. He could take Jesse with him. He wouldn't say no to this.

Nate dropped the papers, and the breeze scattered them across the porch floor. He ran toward Buck, feeling mean inside, wiping at the hot tears in his eyes. He couldn't say good-bye to Ma or Elizabeth. Ma would never let him go. She would make him stay and give him a talking-to about them being a family and fighting to keep Nate. He couldn't do it. That summons had him too spooked. And a court proceeding might be too much stress on Ma in her delicate condition. Then that would worry Pa to a frazzle. Nate didn't want to leave his family, but he would be with Jesse, so Ma and Pa wouldn't fret that much. Someday, he and Jesse could come home, when the Fletchers gave up and went away. Hopefully, that wouldn't take too long.

Nate kicked Buck into a run and took the mountain trail the same as he had earlier. But this time, he was in a rush to get to Shorty's place. He needed to find Jesse in one piece. Then they needed to skedaddle out of the territory. If he had to be ripped from Ma and Pa, then Nate would do it on his own terms.

As he trotted Buck past Blue Sky Lake, he thought briefly about turning around. Maybe he could somehow get the thin woman to promise not to tell about who he was. But he'd already made the mistake of telling her the Fletchers were following him, and a trial like this would bring folks down out of the hills. This would be big entertainment for some. She knew the connection between his birth mother and Deloris, and she was aware of how wealthy the Fletchers were. She and her kids were very poor. What if she used what she knew as a bargaining chip to gain something more than an old rundown shack for her and her five children? It didn't seem he had any other option than running away.

Nate steered Buck through the trees where the five horses had been tied earlier. There he left Buck, then slipped silently down the hill on foot and right up to the side of the house. He peeked around front. Where were Pa and the marshal? Their horses weren't there and neither was Jesse's appaloosa. Nothing was moving in the yard. All was quiet, including the house. No sound carried out through the open window on the sidewall. Nate slipped over the sill and into what was Shorty's office. He didn't know who or if anyone was there. But he'd been taught from day one to be cautious and had been a mite scared to knock at the front door.

Sniffles floated in the air from one of the other rooms. Nate stood stock still and listened.

"Hurry it up, boys. The sheriff told us to get to town. We'll stay at the hotel 'til your pa returns." Mrs. Short's voice was quivery, and there was an air of urgency in her tone.

Nate recognized Norman's cry. He'd heard it lots of times. Out of the bunch of his friends, poor Norman was the crybaby, but this time he had real reason. Outlaws had broken into their home. Nate hoped none of the Short family had been hurt.

"Ma, I don't feel right leavin' without the girls. Do you think Jesse and the sheriff and Marshal Huckabee will find them?" Lenny choked up while the words were still coming out.

So Jesse had been right. Those five horses that they'd seen earlier, hidden among the trees out back, belonged to the men who were stealing women. And it sounded like Jesse, Pa, and the marshal were all on the trail after the bad guys.

Nate slipped back out the window and hurried toward the buckskin. No way would Mrs. Short let him run after Jesse, Pa, and the outlaws. Had he shown his face, she would've dragged him to town, then sent him home. And he wanted more than anything to run home, throw his arms around Ma's waist, and give her a big, loving hug. He missed her something awful already, but he couldn't go back. The Fletchers would get him, and he wasn't moving east to a city.

Nate waited a few minutes until Mrs. Short had her sons packed in the wagon, along with several carpetbags and some blankets. She slapped leather to the team and rolled quickly out of the yard. Nate trotted Buck up to the front of the house, searching the dirt for the track that Pa's horse made. He wasn't yet familiar with the print of Jesse's new mount. Although, he thought he'd found that one too and studied it.

The sun was low in the sky when he left the Short ranch and headed south, following the bay's print. Buck was a sure-footed, fast horse with lots of wind. Nate was a featherweight, so the mustang didn't have to rest as often as Pa's bay or the marshal's horse. Jesse, too, would have to give his steed a breather now and then, and Nate hoped to use that to his advantage.

Pa, no doubt, would skin Nate if he caught him following, but that wasn't why Nate didn't want to catch him or the marshal. Pa had taught him to face his trouble, but this time, he just couldn't. The trouble with the Fletchers was too big. Maybe Pa couldn't even handle it. Jesse was a different story. Pa had taught him to face his problems head on too, and that was exactly what he did when the state of affairs pertained to him. This situation with the Fletchers was Nate's worry. But knowing Jesse the way he did, he would probably come up with some plan for them to get away together. Or at least that's what he was counting on. He tried not to think about how sad his folks would be without the two of them. He made a silent promise to come back home as soon as possible.

The moon was bright and lit the trail fairly well. There were dozens of stars twinkling overhead. Good thing it was a warm night because Nate didn't have his coat. It made him sad for the things he'd left behind at his house.

NATHANIAL

A flicker of light out ahead of him, not far in the distance, caught his eye. It was back among the trees just off the trail. Was it Jesse, Pa, and the marshal? It could just be some men traveling through the territory, or it could be Shorty and his men on their way home from the cattle drive. Nate turned the mustang off the trail. The ground was darker there under the trees, too many shadows, and he wouldn't risk breaking one of Buck's legs. He slid out of the saddle with his reins in hand. Every step was taken with care to miss any rock or holes that might trip his horse as he wound his way closer to the camp. He didn't want Buck to whinny if he smelled another horse, so he picketed him behind an evergreen, then went forward on foot.

Just outside the firelight and hunkered down among a thatch of tall grass and milkweed, Nate listened as Pa and the marshal talked. Jesse wasn't with them, so he must have taken after the outlaws and been on their trail before Pa and the marshal got to Shorty's ranch. It was the only reason that made sense. He could get to Jesse first and explain everything about the Fletchers. Then once Jesse saved Kristy and Hattie, he and Jesse could light out on their own. Hopefully, in that time, Pa didn't catch up. Then Nate would have to return and be part of a legal trial, a terrifying thought.

Nate turned to go back to Buck when the name Fletcher caught in his ears and stopped him dead in his tracks.

"I'm sorry to mention the Fletchers, but we need to talk," Huckabee said.

"Honestly, Joseph, I can't think about that right now. Judging by the tracks we've been following, my deputy ain't too far behind those five armed criminals. Let's get the girls back. Then we discuss that other matter. I just hope Nate doesn't see those papers." Pa sounded worried, his voice cracking.

"Nolan, this is urgent. Prescott told me to advise ya to get a good lawyer, and if there isn't one in Gray Rock, then he'll give ya the names of a few that he considers top of the line."

"Dammit. I mean it, Joseph. Let it lie."

Nate had never heard Pa snap at his best friend. The marshal was quiet then, and like Pa, he stared with a sad, glazed-over look into the flickering flames.

Nate walked a mile or so, leading Buck by the reins, skirting around Pa's camp. He'd be damned if the Fletchers would snatch him. They probably wouldn't even let him keep Buck. Mr. Fletcher, when Nate had seen him in Birch Creek, looked real smart, like a bookworm. He might make Nate study twenty-three hours of the day, and if he failed to get straight A's and mind his P's and Q's in every situation, the Fletchers might lock him in his room or whatever uppity people did to punish their kids.

He needed not to think about it anymore. He looked down at the badge on his shirt and thought of how upset Mrs. Short and his pals had been. He needed to focus on helping find Kristy and Hattie. It was what a deputy should do, and it would make him feel better.

CHAPTER 18

NATE WAS IN THE SADDLE at sunup, and the mustang seemed to be holding up just fine. They'd stopped a couple times to drink and rest a few minutes. Pa and the marshal would be on the move again since there was a little light in the sky, so Nate needed to keep trailing Jesse. If Nate calculated right, he was ahead of them by five, six hours if they hadn't started out before daybreak. Nate pulled up reins on a little butte. There were a lot of miles stretched out before him, and every inch of it seemed lonely. It made him think about how frightened Kristy and Hattie had to be. And they weren't the only ones. Ma, most likely, was worried sick since he hadn't come home last night, nor Pa or Jesse.

Nate searched the ground, and after a half mile or so, he spotted a hoofprint belonging to Jesse's appaloosa. At noon, he happened to sight a berry bush. He let Buck eat grass while he ate raspberries as quick as he could pick them. When he crawled into the saddle, his fingers were stained purple. He wiped them down the front of his shirt and on his pants, but that didn't help take the color off his hands, so he got down

and tried wiping them on the grass, finding a fresher print from Jesse's horse.

A few hours later, Nate pulled up next to a trickling spring.

In the dirt at Buck's feet was a clear shoe mark of the appaloosa, and it was fresh, minutes old. Nate slid out of the saddle, looked around, then bent down, cupped water with his hand, and drank. He let Buck drink too. Then Nate took a few steps, following the appaloosa's prints. The trail went into the tree line, which appeared to lead up and over a ridge side. The ground there was rockier, and that would make it harder to track Jesse, though not impossible. Nate got on his horse and started up through the trees.

When he got to the top, out of ahead of him and down in the green valley below, a single line of gray seeped up from someone's camp or cabin. Nate nudged the mustang. He figured that was where Jesse would head. It certainly drew the eyes and made one want to turn that way as though following a beacon.

He'd gone no more than two hundred yards. Tucked under some flowering trees was a tiny cabin. There was nothing polished about it. One window, one door, and four ugly wooden walls, aged gray from withstanding the change of seasons year after year. Yet it was a good place for anyone on the run or just traveling through to rest. Nate sat his horse inside the tree line and watched the cabin for any sign of life.

The door swung open. A scruffy, unshaven man in a red shirt stepped into the doorway. "Flynn, what's taking ya so long? Hurry up with that horseshoe. Walt ain't gonna like waitin' fer us."

Nate couldn't see the fella called Flynn because of the heavy tree cover that hemmed the rear of the cabin, but out of nowhere, the bang of a hammer rang out. A few minutes later, a tall, lean fella walked out from the tree line back there where the horses must have been hidden, and he and the man in the red shirt had words. They both stomped inside, and then the cabin door slammed shut.

Nate didn't have to wait long before the door peeled open again. This time, Kristy was marched out, Flynn holding tight to her arm. She was wiping at her eyes with her other hand. Nate's breath caught, and he froze. If he had caught up with these men, that meant Jesse had to be around somewhere. Jesse's fresh tracks, the ones Nate had found not twenty minutes ago, were not far from this place.

The man in the red shirt dragged Hattie by an arm toward where Nate suspected the horses were hidden. A third man, a big, blubbery-looking brute of a fella, wobbled from the house. His stern face told of having a surly disposition. There had been two more men at Shorty's ranch, or at least there had been five horses. Maybe two of the horses had been there so no one rode double, which would tire a horse out quick. That way there was one for Kristy and the other for Hattie.

A shot rang out from across the stretch of grass that separated the cabin and the next set of tree-covered hills. It had to be Jesse. He'd put himself in the outlaws' path. If he turned them back, they would run right into Pa and the marshal, but Jesse didn't know that. He only knew he was stopping them from going forward with his woman and her little sister.

The man holding Hattie pitched forward and hit the ground with a hole in his chest. He didn't move. Jesse must have killed him with one shot. Hattie was screaming as if someone were shooting at her, and it might have seemed that way. She took off running away from the fat one, who was definitely too round to be fast enough to catch her on foot.

"Run, Hattie!" Kristy screamed while struggling under Flynn's restraint as she tried to get free.

Flynn threw Kristy on his horse, then swung a leg over the saddle and spurred his mount, disappearing quickly among the trees. He obviously wasn't so stupid that he'd try escaping across open ground where Jesse's Winchester might send him to the devil's doorstep.

Another rifle blasted from the other side of that small valley. Jesse's Winchester boomed. A ricochet of gunfire rocked the trees and everything else nestled between those ridges. That made four men: one dead, Flynn, the fat one now on his horse and disappearing into the trees, and the fourth engaged in the rifle battle with Jesse. So where was guy number five? Nate hoped Jesse had eyes in the back of his head. This one might be keeping him busy while the fifth fella snuck up on him.

There was one thing Nate could do to help. It would be one less worry for Jesse.

"Hattie! Over here!" Nate kicked Buck. The sudden thump against the buckskin's sides made him leap forward at a run. Nate ran his horse out into the open area and straight toward Hattie. She was running headlong for him. Her eyes were red, and tears streaked her face.

Gunfire blasted overhead. Nate kept his head down and his shoulders curled, not wanting to get shot. He slowed Buck just enough to pull Hattie with a great grunt, helping her into the saddle behind him. Then he gave a hard cluck, and Buck took off flying into the tree line where they would be covered by all the branches and hopefully wouldn't get captured or killed.

Nate didn't bother to look for Jesse. That might have been the smart thing to do, but the Winchester was still battling the other rifle and Nate didn't want him or Hattie caught in the crossfire. Plus, with Jesse tied up in a fight, those other men were getting away with Kristy.

Nate made a snap decision to follow. He'd do his best to keep Hattie safe. How he'd do that, he wasn't sure, but his thought was to leave a clear trail for Jesse to follow. That way he could catch up quick. As long as he didn't lose that fight he was in. Jesse was a master with the Winchester, but if it was two against one and that fifth fella was back there somewhere,

NATHANIAL

then Jesse did have his work cut out for him. Maybe soon, Pa and the marshal would catch up. That would be a big help to Jesse. Then he could catch up to the men who still had Kristy.

"Where are you going?" Hattie screeched in a quivering voice. She held tight around Nate's waist as Buck hustled along the path. The poor girl was shaking all over. He didn't want to scare her more than she already was, but he wouldn't lie to her.

"We're going after your sister." Nate was blunt but honest.

A funny squeak slipped out between Hattie's lips, and her eyes swelled with more tears. She shook her head. "Let's go back to Jesse."

Nate kept Buck moving forward. "Listen to me, Hattie. I know how these outlaws work."

Everyone in Gray Rock knew the name of Nate's birth father, and the entire country knew details of Jim Younger's crimes. Hattie might not know that once upon a time, Nate had helped rob banks, but she was aware that he had been raised for a time by an outlaw.

"The one back there fightin' Jesse means to kill him, and while they're battlin', it gives these two time to get away with your sister. If I can help it, I ain't gonna let that happen."

"What if they catch us?" A flood of tears streaked her face, and the boom of Jesse's Winchester could still be heard.

Nate grinned confidently. "They won't. Buck's too fast, and I promise I'll not get that close. We'll follow at a distance. I'm good at reading sign, so if they turn direction or try to trick us somehow, I'll spot it."

The men ahead of them did switch directions about ten darn times. And each time, Nate got off Buck and scratched an arrow in the dirt for Jesse to easily follow.

Nightfall was coming on when the tinkering of ivories danced on the wind and into their ears. Out of nowhere, two buildings, a small barn, and a corral appeared. If this was a town, it wasn't much of one. There were several horses in the corral, and an empty wagon sat under the eaves of the barn. One light then another came on inside the place pitching out the gay melody. Several saddled horses stood tied just outside the swinging doors. In the ever-fading light of dusk, Nate couldn't tell if those horses were lathered from running. He could only tell that they were darkish in color. The windows of the other building were black, which made it seem spooky. No lights shone out from inside the barn either.

"I don't think we should go in there." Hattie's gaze was fixed on the lively joint that Nate assumed was some sort of saloon. She squeezed him harder around the middle, nearly cutting his breath off, and in a way, she was letting him know just how frightened she was.

"Those horses might belong to the men that have your sister. Maybe they have her locked up in one of the buildings or even maybe the barn." Nate's thoughts were such that they should do what the two of them could to locate Kristy. It was worth a look.

"We should wait for Jesse." Hattie's voice quivered.

Nate didn't want to say it and put the fear of God into her, but Jesse should have caught up by now. He had all too clearly marked the trail for him to follow, so he shouldn't have had to waste time hunting sign to track them. Jesse might be in a bad way, injured during that gun battle. As good as he was with his rifle, he, like any man, could catch lead.

Nate put his hand over the badge on his chest. Every deputy repeated an oath before pinning on that symbol of justice. Pa had never sworn Nate in because he was too young, but Nate had the words memorized and had repeated them to himself a hundred times or more.

His heart was pounding. "I'm not afraid," he whispered to himself.

It was dark now, so Jesse was probably just trying to save his horse by moving slow.

"I'm goin' down thar." Nate didn't cotton to waiting. The sooner he found sign of Kristy, the better. Every minute she was stuck with those outlaws, her life was in danger. Nate was willing to risk himself getting caught. He almost didn't care if anything happened to him. After all, it seemed he was going to lose his family. What the marshal had said about Judge Prescott advising Pa didn't leave Nate with much hope of staying in Gray Rock.

He started to shift his weight to slide down off Buck, but Hattie wouldn't let go of him, holding him there.

"Let go of me."

"No. My sister's gone." Hattie turned her face into her shoulder and wiped tears off her cheek. "I don't want you to get taken too."

"I'll be so quiet that no one'll notice me." He unpinned the badge on his shirt and handed it to her. "This badge always gives me strength, makes me feel brave." He sweetly grinned.

She accepted it, squeezing it in her hand. Even so, it took a few more minutes of arguing, some convincing of his experience with such situations, and a solemn promise that he'd be right back before Hattie finally released her death grip on him so he could slip into that so-called town.

On his tiptoes, Nate peeked in one of the side windows, his nose barely above the sill. It was a saloon all right. Brown bottles of whiskey sat on a shelf behind a long bar at the far end of the room. A burly, gray-haired man with a Texas longhorn mustache that curled on the ends poured a drink from behind the counter. On the other side was Flynn, leaning on an elbow. There were a few round tables with chairs tucked in around them. The fat man wasn't there, but there were two other fellas with tied-down guns. Nate hadn't seen either of them back at the cabin where he'd seen Kristy, but that didn't mean they weren't part of that gang.

The piano and the man stroking the keys sat just inside the door to the left. Not far from the music was a set of stairs. Maybe the big guy was up there keeping an eye on Kristy.

Nate looked around for some way to scale the side of the building and have a look-see in the upstairs window. There wasn't even a tree close by that he could jump from onto the roof and get in from above. He cursed under his breath. A couple of crates were stacked near the back door, but they weren't big enough to put him in range of the second-floor window. What were the chances he'd get caught if he just slipped in the back door?

"Hey, kid! What are ya doin' back thar?" The voice had come out of nowhere behind Nate.

He whipped around, tripping himself, and stumbled back into the crates, rattling them. Shit! It had to be one of the men from inside. Who else was around? This was the only place that seemed to contain any life.

Nate's breathing was all off at being startled, and he couldn't seem to regain control of his wobbly legs and started to fall. The man was running toward him. Nate wanted to scream, but nothing came out, though his mouth was wide open. Suddenly, the back door flung wide, and light spilled out. A burly figure was silhouetted in the doorway, and an arm reached out and grabbed him by the scruff. Nate squealed and, as a result, got hastily shaken limp.

He was dragged inside kicking and squirming. All he could think about was Hattie. If she'd heard him scream—and she probably had—then she was sure to be panicking.

Lord, please don't let her come after me. If Nate had one wish left, it would be that Pa, Jesse, and the marshal would show up right then.

NATHANIAL

The bartender smacked Nate down into a chair at one of the tables just as the tall man from the alleyway shouldered through the swinging door while hiking up his zipper, then adjusted his gun belt. So Nate got caught because that guy had to take a piss. That was some poor luck.

Nate had been in plenty of tight fixes before this. That didn't mean his heart wasn't racing. At least he had control of his breathing so, on the outside, he maybe didn't appear as scared as he actually was, wishing he was almost anywhere but there. Being that there were only two weather-beaten buildings and a rickety old barn, it was doubtful that many kids were around. Since it was a house of sin, as Ma called the saloon back in Gray Rock, families certainly didn't frequent the grungy hole in the wall.

The tall man grabbed a handful of Nate's hair and yanked, pinching the skin on the top of his head, and a high-pitched yelp bounced off the ceiling. His hands instinctively flew up, smacking at the fella's arm.

"Where'd ya come from, kid? Who's with ya?"

Nate was shaken so hard his teeth rattled. He kicked out with both feet and thumped that mean fella's shin. He let out hollering and cursed at Nate while rubbing feverishly at his leg. The others chuckled. Nate wasn't amused. His head hurt where his hair had gotten yanked, and he was still half dizzy from being shaken. The man was scowling something fierce, and Nate expected a hard slap for riling him. These men were suspicious for damn good reason.

Nate recognized Flynn from the cabin, so Flynn hadn't seen him for sure. Otherwise, he'd be dead already. It appeared that the tall man was the leader. Flynn stood by his side, and the other fella was standing next to the barkeep, both within arm's reach of Nate, and all eyes were scrutinizing him, including the piano man who had stopped tinkering. The atmosphere in the room seemed strangely quiet without the music playing.

"Ain't no one with me! I came alone!" His voice packed a wallop to the ears. If he couldn't convince them, then Hattie might be found.

These were cautious, trail-wise men who had likely slipped away from more than one posse, and they would probably take at least a quick gander. Nate might get sliced to ribbons if they for any reason believed he lied. He tried to keep a poker face. Hopefully, Hattie was still well hidden in the woods just off the roadway, surrounded by a thick cluster of evergreens. If she got curious or too scared and started nosing around, it might mean the end for her and him.

It was dark, too black for this gang to take any chances. If they thought anyone was out there, they weren't going to politely ask a name. Any detection of movement could become a target. It wasn't unlikely that she could be mistaken for an enemy. Outlaws tended to shoot first and then have a closer look. Nate doubted they would care about killing an innocent bystander, except earlier, she had been in their possession and could have meant a profit for them.

The queer looks that passed between the roughnecks were ones of disbelief. Nate could rightly guess what each of them was questioning. He was too young to be way the hell out in the middle of nowhere by himself. Someone had to be with him. If Jesse wasn't hurt, then he couldn't be too far behind, closer than Pa and the marshal anyway. These outlaws wouldn't know that, though. Jesse might be outside watching for his chance from some vantage point. The thought of being rescued and seeing this gang arrested brought a smirk to Nate's face. Then he pictured Hattie, who had no experience with life-and-death situations. Nate crossed his fingers that Jesse had discovered her hiding place and she was now being guarded by him or he'd relocated her to a better spot. That was all based on the assumption that Jesse had won the gun battle. If he hadn't shown up yet, then Nate had an idea about how to baffle, perhaps profoundly confuse, this hard lot, and by doing that, he might keep them from going out hunting and possibly finding Hattie.

"I'm looking for Walt... I mean Walter." Nate guessed the name had been shortened, a nickname, such as Nate rather than Nathanial. It hinted that he knew what the hell he was talking about, or so he hoped. Although, it was the furthest thing from the truth. Walt was the name Nate had heard shouted before those men who lit out from the cabin with Kristy, and they'd seemed worried about quickly catching up. And if those hard cases were anxious to join Walt, it could be because he was the boss of this women-stealing outfit. These others must be waiting to hear what the next move would be. Even among the lawless, there were pecking orders. Strength and brutality usually decided the rank. Whoever came out on top typically was also smarter than the others, though sometimes not by much. Nate hoped this ruse would fool them.

Jesse, please get here.

"I'm Walt. Who the hell are you?" The tall man leaned down and stared straight into Nate's eyes. There was nothing friendly about his look.

Nate swallowed hard. *Think.*

"My name's Walt too... after my daddy," Nate shyly added. "I come to find him."

Laughter boomed inside the room. Only, that Walt fella wasn't laughing. He looked meaner than a bear in a trap, as if he might kill someone. Everyone else was clearly amused. Flynn hardily slapped Walt's shoulder in a mock congratulatory manner, a shitty smirk on his face.

"If my count's right, this little bastard makes six for ya." Flynn chuckled. "I'm sure that hotheaded woman of yours'll have lots to say about this."

Walt turned an evil eye on Flynn. "Shut the hell up. Ya really gonna believe that cockamamie story?"

Flynn grinned. "Well, like I already said, you got five. It ain't that hard to believe you fathered one more. Besides, you ain't exactly faithful to that little bitch you left back there in the mountains with all them heathens."

Walt's face screwed up, and he seemed to transform into some sort of maddened beast. Without warning, his right hand, all five knuckles, landed square on Flynn's chin, sending him spinning away. Flynn toppled over a chair and whacked the floor with a thud. Then Walt turned, shoulders back as if he was ready to strike again, but this time his glare was aimed at Nate.

Nate's heart skipped a beat or five. Then suddenly, an image of the thin, pissy-tempered woman popped into his head. "Your woman, she's the one who sent me here. How else would I find this place?"

Walt stopped midstep, an arm outstretched to grab hold of Nate. Flynn was off the floor and rubbing at his jaw. The barkeep and the other fella stood stock still. No one seemed to breathe. While Nate had them thinking, he'd best keep on spinning this windy, or Walt might just wring Nate's neck. He possibly would anyway.

"She's a skinny lady, not too tall, with dark hair. The oldest boy is probably my age, eight. They live in a shack near…" Nate snapped his fingers a few times as though he couldn't recall the name, then said, "Gray Rock." He was taking quite a gamble. If Flynn's earlier details about Walt's life hadn't been about the thin woman, then Nate was as good as dead.

Walt hoofed a chair so hard it flew across the room. "She knows better. Why the hell would she send ya to me?"

Nate kicked a chair. It didn't go sailing, but it toppled over. "Couldn't rightly tell ya. She just did." He didn't know what else to say. His mind was suddenly blank. He hadn't expected the man's temper to explode the way it did, and Nate was fighting to keep from shaking all over. So he modeled Walt's

NATHANIAL

behavior for whatever reason. It just felt like the right thing to save himself.

The barkeep grabbed a handful of Nate's white hair. "He don't look a stitch like ya, but he's got your temper." A soft, almost unnoticed snicker slipped out from between the barkeep's lips.

Walt glared at him. The barkeep let go of Nate all-fire quick, and his hands went up, signaling that he'd meant no harm.

The room was still. No one said a word. Their faces gave off an air of strained concentration as Nate's accurate description of the cantankerous, impish woman and her brood settled into their heads. Walt also might have been doing some quick math. Had the timing been right that a child Nate's age could have been produced? Had Walt been with anyone other than the thin lady in that time period?

The cuckoo clock opened, and the bird popped out and sounded. Everyone jerked around and looked at the sudden noise. At that moment, Walt also drew. His pistol had jumped into his hand smooth and quick, aiming at the chime. Nate slapped his hands over his ears and squeezed his eyes tight shut, waiting for the bang inside the room to deafen him.

"Don't shoot! That clock come from Germany," the music maker roared as he sprang off the piano seat as though he were about to throw himself between a bullet and that stupid clock. Nate had almost forgotten the man was there. He'd kept quiet so far.

Most importantly, everyone's focus wasn't on anything outside those four dingy gray walls. Nate silently sent up a quick prayer that Jesse, Pa, and the marshal were sneaking up on this rough outfit right this minute, that he would soon be safe with his family, and that Hattie was okay.

Walt shoved his gun in its holster and, in the same breath, snatched Nate off the chair by his shirt collar, giving him another hard shake. "Who's your mama?"

Nate's birth mother had been a whore and a friend of the thin woman who was the mother of Walt's brats. Chances were he knew Lucinda. Though, it wasn't the first name that had rushed to Nate's mind. Kate was his mother, but the name Kate Crosson, the wife of a famed lawman, would not fit in this lock. If Nate wanted to escape, he had to be smart. He held his tongue, knowing that if he said too much and clued these edgy fellas in to who he really was, it might cost him his life.

"This is Deputy Sheriff Jesse Adams. Send the boy and woman out."

CHAPTER 19

JESSE WAS ALIVE. Thank God. Nate now had a good chance of getting out of there with his hide intact. Although, Jesse sounded anything but pleased, and Nate reckoned once Jesse got his hands on him, he would get his behind tanned. Nate knew better than to go after bad guys by himself, but he hadn't wanted to risk losing Kristy's trail. He hadn't meant to get caught, but because he did, Jesse had then lost the element of surprising this gang at his timing, which was even worse since the odds weren't in his favor. Nate had certainly messed up. What if it cost Kristy getting rescued? Apparently, Jesse had found some sign of her being there somewhere because he'd ordered her to be released along with Nate.

Nate ran for the door. All he could think about was saying sorry to his best friend and partner.

"Oh, no ya don't." Walt's fingernails bit into Nate's shoulder, holding him there.

Nate jerked his arm, trying like hell to squirm away, but the tall man now had both his big, thick hands slapped on him like iron shackles.

"Let go of me!" he screamed.

Without warning, the door behind the bar at the back of

the room flew open. Pa stood there with his Colt aimed at Walt's forehead.

"Pa!" The cry had just slipped out of Nate.

Walt wickedly snickered, and his mean grip tightened on Nate's arm. After bursting in, Pa's eyes had narrowed to no more than two small slits, focusing on the man holding Nate. Nate swallowed hard. If Walt wanted to live, he'd best let go of him in the next few seconds.

The marshal, holding his pistol ready, ducked in behind Pa and quickly moved off to the far end of the bar, covering that side of the room. A squeak from the swinging door to the right of Nate turned everyone's attention but Walt's, whose gun had appeared in his hand within a mere blink. It was jammed into Nate's side, and he wanted to cry.

Jesse was a broad-shouldered figure of justice standing in the doorway, and with his finger on the trigger of the Winchester, it was clear he wasn't there to negotiate. None of the lawmen were.

Flynn, who had backed against the wall at the rush of the posse, held a six-shooter in one hand. The music man was now on his feet but cowering at the side of his piano nearest the corner while holding tight to a small pocket gun, which looked out of place. With arms stretched up into the air, the only thing the bartender had in his big mitts was a dirty rag. He didn't appear to have a weapon.

The piano player took a slow step toward the stairs.

"Don't make another move, mister. I ain't feelin' forgivin'," Jesse said through clenched teeth.

As though the music man hadn't heard the warning inside the ten-by-twelve room, he up and ran for the staircase. Jesse's Winchester exploded, rattling the windows. His bullet ripped into the man's back, splattering bloody guts through his bellybutton. He dropped in a heap at the bottom step.

NATHANIAL

His gun was sent spinning across the floor toward the bartender. The fool lunged for it. Marshal Huckabee's pistol stabbed flame. No one else moved. If everyone started shooting, this could become a deadly crossfire that no one survived. None of them wanted that. The bartender hit the floor on his knees, his apron staining with blood. He gripped his chest while cursing the marshal and watching his life drain all down his front and drip red on the floor. A few labored breaths later, he fell over on his face, dead.

"What's going on down there?" The boards of the balcony above them groaned loudly with each hurried step toward the stairs. At the top, the fat man appeared. His scatter-gun swung up as he pumped the lever.

Jesse dove behind a nearby table as the buckshot barely missed him and bit into the wall above the piano, which drew everyone's eyes in that direction. That's when Pa rushed forward toward Nate. In a flying leap, he tackled Walt and somehow managed to knock Nate spinning out of the way. He fell, bouncing across the floor, and Jesse grabbed him, throwing him under a table for cover.

"Stay there!" Jesse left him and ran for the stairs. He was probably thinking of Kristy. Why else would the big man be up there when his buddies were all downstairs?

Pa and Walt rolled across the floor, punching each other.

One and then a second pistol cracked. Nate whipped around. The marshal had hurdled the bar and was hunkered down. Then he popped up and fired again. Flynn, whose shoulder was bleeding, squeezed the trigger of his revolver just as the marshal's bullet drilled into Flynn's other shoulder. Flynn's bullet smacked into the bar, splintering the wood. His next shot shattered the bottles along the wall. The marshal's pistol jerked in his hand. This time, his bullet hit Flynn's chest, and he stumbled backward, crashing through a window. He was suddenly gone from sight.

The marshal hurried past Pa, slugging it out with Walt, to the broken window where he looked out. He turned and focused on the knuckle-crunching fight Pa was in. A boom rang out from upstairs. Then a retort of fire bellowed. Pa and Walt flipped over a table, and in a tangle, they hit the floor with a spine-jolting whack.

Marshal Huckabee glanced at Nate. "You okay?"

Nate stiffly nodded while wiping the tears off his face. In four or five long, hustling strides, the marshal reached the stairs and took them by twos toward the top, his pistol in hand. No more shots had been fired, but Jesse might need help up there, especially if Kristy was there as suspected. She might have gotten hurt or at least was probably near frightened to death. Nate was pretty scared himself and wanted those two upstairs to hurry down and help Pa.

Pa got kicked in the gut, doubling him over. Walt struck with a nasty blow up under Pa's chin that sent him flying backward on wobbly legs. He hit the floor sitting on his ass. Nate's breath cut off. Pa was down, and Walt drew his gun in no more time than it took to blink. Nate's eyes flicked to Pa's Colt aimed at Walt. Both guns blasted, then again. Pa hollered and grabbed his side. Walt timbered toward the floor with a hole in his forehead and another right between his eyes.

Nate scrambled out from under the table and scurried across the bloodstained floor toward Pa, clinging to his sleeve. He was only bleeding in one spot, so Walt's second shot must have missed. Pa grimaced, then regarded his hand covered in blood.

"Help me up." Pa gripped his side and didn't seem to be able to move. He wasn't breathing too well either.

Boot steps sounded on the stairs. Marshal Huckabee appeared, rushing across the room, and got both arms under Pa's shoulders, easing him to his feet. Nate sniffled, wiping his sleeve across his face.

"Let's have a look at that wound." The marshal wasn't asking.

Pa lifted his shirt.

All Nate could see was red. That was a lot of blood. His shirt was soaked through. Nate started to cry harder.

Sobs carried down from upstairs. Someone was crying harder than him. Was it Jesse? He hadn't come down yet. Had Kristy been killed?

Footsteps, plenty of them, clicked on the balcony above. That wasn't boots. The noise was too dainty. And there was more than one pair and more cries. Who else was up there?

Nate couldn't focus on Pa, who was moaning as the marshal fingered around his wound. All that red churned up a violent wooziness in Nate's gut. He cupped a hand over his mouth to keep his stomach down, and he turned away and watched the stairs.

Jesse came down, Kristy at his side. Her arms were around his middle, and his one arm was wrapped tight around her shoulders. That wasn't the surprise. Behind them trailed three more young women, all of them teary-eyed and dirty from their ordeal. Relief probably hadn't fully sunk in, and they were all still shaking.

One glance at Pa and Jesse let go of Kristy and crossed the room in an all-fire hurry to where Pa had slid into a chair. His face was white, and his head sagged forward, his chin nearly resting on his chest. Jesse put his face right in there with the marshal's, and they both gingerly eyed the bleeding hole in Pa's ribs.

Nate grabbed Jesse's hand and squeezed. He couldn't hold it in anymore and burst out wailing. "Pa'll be okay, won't he? Ma will patch him up."

No one said anything to comfort him. The ladies all stood in a huddle, wiping at their eyes and sniffling.

Jesse glanced over at the marshal, who returned the same worrisome grin.

"We're gonna have to dig that bullet out," Huckabee said.

With a groan, Pa pushed forward off the back of the chair. He wavered as he sat there catching his breath, then brought one hand to Nate's shoulder and weakly tugged him in close. Pa rested his forehead against Nate's. His eyes were closed, and his face wrinkled with the awful pain he must have been feeling.

Pa's eyes rolled up, and he straightened a mite and looked into Nate's teary baby blues. "I ain't plannin' on leavin' ya, boy. I'm just in a bad way right now. Jesse and the marshal will have to fix me up. I can't ride while leakin' this much blood." Pa fell a few inches against the chair back.

Jesse grabbed Pa's shoulder, keeping him from falling sideways out of his seat.

"Partner, you go on outside while the marshal and I patch up your Pa." Jesse gave Nate a slight shove toward the door.

Nate didn't want to leave Pa's side, but he wouldn't argue. That would just waste time. Time Pa didn't look like he had to spend.

Jesse slipped an arm under one of Pa's shoulders while the marshal did the same on the other side, and they lifted him out of the chair. Pa's head dangled, his hat fell off, and his feet dragged along the floorboards as they carried him to the bar where, together, they heaved and got him situated lying flat on top.

Nate couldn't stop staring. His feet had rooted to the floor where Pa's blood trail started. He now lay like a gray corpse on the bar top, and his arms hung limply over the sides. His feet rested in an outward floppy position, and the rise and fall of his chest could barely be seen. The sight of Pa looking so much like death petrified Nate.

"Jesse!" he wailed.

"Git him outta here!" Wetness glistened in Jesse's eyes as he snapped at Kristy.

She snatched Nate's hand, yanking him toward the door. He twisted around in her grip, looking back at Pa as she dragged him outside. She scooped Nate up into her arms and then plopped down on the end of a long bench. The other ladies filed out and sat down one at a time in a row along the same bench where he and Kristy sat.

A blood-curdling yell exploded through the door that Nate recognized as Pa. It jolted them all to their feet. No one took a breath.

"Kristy, git in here. We need help."

Nate choked, unable to draw air into his lungs.

Kristy threw him at a dark-haired young lady that he didn't know. "Don't let him come in." She ran inside. One of the other ladies followed on her heels.

"I want my pa!" Nate howled.

Pa's pain-filled holler mercilessly squeezed the air out of Nate once again. He jerked and twisted, but the dark-haired girl wasn't letting loose. He briefly thought about biting her hand or kicking her a good shot on the shin, but she wasn't the bad guy. She hadn't hurt Pa, nor was she really doing any harm to Nate. He just wanted to be held by his father, but that couldn't happen.

Nate crumpled into a ball and rocked himself.

CHAPTER 20

THE WOMAN WHO'D been holding to him was now standing at the swinging door, peering in over the top. Her face stiffened, and she lost all color. The other lady returned to the bench, and her face was buried in her hands as she cried. Nate felt all alone. The people he loved were inside, and he was stuck outside with strangers. It wasn't where he wished to be. Though, he was kind of afraid to see what was actually going on in there. Was Pa bleeding out? Did Jesse, Huckabee, or Kristy know enough about bullet wounds to save him?

"Nathanial." The soft, tender, quivery voice came out of the dark somewhere behind him, and Nate glanced over his shoulder. The pale moonlight cast a haze around Hattie. Her body was shaking, and her eyes were bloodshot.

Nate uncurled, slowing getting to his feet, and they hugged, holding one another tight for a long time. With all the killing and Pa getting shot, he had forgotten about her.

She gently pulled back from him. "What's going on? Jesse said he'd be back for me, but he never came. I got

NATHANIAL

scared during all that shooting. Then it stopped, but Jesse still didn't come."

Nate wiped at his eyes. "Pa got shot. Jesse's in there tryin' to save him. Kristy's inside too, lendin' a hand."

Hattie grinned at the news that her big sister was alive. Yet as she studied Nate's tear-streaked face, she sobered. "I hope your pa will be okay." She handed Nate's star back to him.

He pinned the badge on his shirt. Somehow it made him feel closer to his father. "They won't let me in to see, and no one's told me anything about what's goin' on in there." Nate shivered. He couldn't recall a time when Pa had ever been hurt so badly.

Hattie glanced between the two women. Nate's gaze followed. The one was still sobbing into her hands, completely oblivious to Hattie's appearance. The other one's back was facing them, as she was focused on the grim scene inside.

Pa wasn't screaming anymore. That could only mean one of two things. He'd passed out or... Nate hated to think that his father might have bled out. Strained voices floated out now and then, but no word came of Pa's condition. Nate only knew it wasn't good.

Hattie hastily took his hand, and before he realized what was happening, the two of them slipped into the dark around the side of the building and stood at the back door, which was wide open. From where he stood just outside, Pa's legs were visible. It didn't seem that he had moved since Nate had last seen him. Together, Hattie holding his hand, they stepped in but stayed out of the way. Nate didn't want to be noticed and once again be told to leave. Hattie's tight grip on his hand made him feel a little bit brave, though not brave enough to stop shaking all over.

There was a pile of blood-soaked rags at Kristy's feet, and she used long tweezers to fish around inside the hole in Pa. Blood squirted out onto the front of Kristy's dress, but she kept working and never batted an eye, hands covered in red. Pa must have passed out. He wasn't fighting the pain, and what Kristy was doing had to hurt.

Nate's side ached just watching, and he glanced away for a second or two, breathed deeply, then refocused. Even with Pa lying limp, Jesse had his weight over his shoulders, and Huckabee was over his legs. The dark-haired lady who was supposed to be watching him now held a basin of water and sponged the blood away while Kristy did her best to save Pa.

"Got it." Kristy tossed aside the lead ball.

It rolled over the floorboards and stopped at Nate's boot toe. He stared at the small, round, bloody hunk of lead. How could something so small and simple-looking be powerful enough to rob a man of his life? He picked up the bullet that had torn into his father and sullenly regarded it.

"Hurry up and get him stitched," Huckabee snapped.

Nate shoved the lead into his pocket.

Kristy worked feverishly, though her hands were good and steady. A few minutes later, Jesse held Pa under the arms and the marshal took him by the legs, and they carried his limp body slowly up the stairs. Pa never opened his eyes. With all that jostling, although they'd been gentle, he should have come awake.

Nate didn't care if he got yelled at. He followed.

Pa was eased onto a bed. Jesse stayed knelt beside him, maybe silently praying. It was certainly what Nate was doing. Kristy covered Pa with blankets. Marshal Huckabee flopped down hard into a chair that was stationed in a corner near a tall dresser that held a porcelain water bowl and pitcher. He ran his fingers through his hair, then shoved his hat back down on his head and let out a heavy sigh that they all understood. They had been through the wringer, and not one of them felt good about where this day had ended.

NATHANIAL

Jesse's head was bowed. He sniffled, and seeing tears on that tough guy's cheeks made Nate cry. Nate knelt next to Jesse at Pa's beside. Together they could fight through anything and would. Pa just had to live. It wasn't his time to go. Both Nate and Jesse needed him, loved him. They didn't want to let him go. Pa was a tough man, tough as they came. He'd beat this, and Nate and Jesse would be right there helping him.

A shadow fell over Nate. He looked up as the marshal placed a hand on Jesse's shoulder and gave a squeeze. Jesse looked up.

"Son, I know you're upset. I am too. But we still have a job to do." A slow grin spread across Huckabee's face. "I know Nolan. He'd want you to focus on keepin' these women safe and seein' to his boy."

To Nate, it sounded just like something Pa would say. Jesse must have recognized that too because he wiped a sleeve across his wet face. Nate had never seen Jesse cry that hard. It scared him, and he clung to Jesse's arm.

Marshal Huckabee fed shells into his revolver. "We don't know where or to whom these women were to be sold. When they don't show up, whoever's in cahoots with the dead fellas downstairs might come huntin' for trouble."

At that, Jesse pillared up like a brick wall, inadvertently carrying Nate with him. Jesse followed Huckabee's lead and reloaded his Winchester. Kristy gasped at the mention of there being more fighting.

Nate tugged on Jesse's sleeve. "Why can't we just take Pa home?" He had seen a wagon near the barn, and he wanted to be where Ma could take care of both him and Pa. He didn't want to run away anymore.

"If we try to move your pa, it'll kill him. It's too far to travel in the shape he's in. He'll need at least a few days to rest and heal some before we try," Jesse said grimly, then turned to follow Huckabee out the door.

Before he could go, Nate caught hold of his hand and held him there.

"I love you." Nate needed to say those words as much as he suspected Jesse needed to hear them.

Jesse grinned and winked. "Ditto." He squatted in front of Nate while gently peeling his hands away. "The marshal and I have plannin' to do, and we need to bury them fellas we killed. You stay here and keep an eye on your pa. I'll only be a holler away."

He must have sensed Nate's insecurity by how tight he'd been holding to him. He didn't want Jesse out of his sight.

"I won't let anything happen to ya, partner. You know as well as I do, though, that I got a job to do. Huckabee's right. Your pa wouldn't want me to forget my duties."

Nate nodded.

When Jesse had gone, Nate touched at his badge, thinking of the moment Pa had pinned it on him. He glanced at his father and felt lost without hearing the man's voice.

Kristy lifted Nate's chin. "I'll fetch some water. Let's see if we can get him to drink something."

At Kristy's persistent urging, Pa's eyes rolled up. Nate hovered, and Pa gave him a weary sort of grin. It was enough to give Nate some confidence that Pa was hanging in there. He drank each time Kristy lifted the cup to his lips. After a few minutes, he closed his eyes and slept.

"Why don't you try to get some sleep? Hattie's in the next room if you'd like to go over there," Kristy said in a motherly tone.

Nate shook his head. He didn't think he'd sleep at all, too worried about Pa, but he did nod off.

When he opened his eyes and sat up, the pink of morning lit the sky, and Kristy was sponging Pa's head. Nate was stiff from sleeping on the floor. Kristy or someone had covered him with a blanket, and he pushed it off as he sat up.

A few minutes later, Jesse showed up in the doorway. His gaze fell all over Pa, who was soundly sleeping. The rise and fall of his chest seemed stronger to Nate than it had hours ago before he had fallen asleep.

Jesse went to the window. The trail into town could be clearly seen from there. He and the marshal were cautious men. At the moment, they were responsible for many lives, and probably neither would let his guard down. Not until they had all returned safely to Gray Rock.

Kristy wrung a towel in her hands. "How many do you think will come?" Her voice shook.

None of them knew for sure that anyone would show up, but it made sense that someone would. After all, five men had been killed there. Plus, the man in the red shirt had been killed back at the cabin. Jesse had taken one down during the gun battle in the woods when Nate had rescued Hattie. That was seven dead. Someone would miss them. It was sensible to think it might be the person waiting to buy the girls. Why wouldn't he come hunting his goods? And who was to say he wouldn't bring some men willing to fight for a price?

Nate stared at Pa, who needed all his strength for healing. He wasn't in any shape to fight for anything but his life. Nate sniffled.

Jesse turned and looked at him. "I need your help. Come on." He headed out the door, and Nate obediently followed.

Pa was asleep, so Nate reckoned he was okay leaving his side. Besides, he needed to do something other than worry.

At the bottom of the stairs at the window stood Marshal Huckabee, eyes circled in darkness. The man obviously hadn't slept a wink.

"How's Nolan doin'?" The marshal glanced toward the room upstairs.

"He's still asleep." Jesse pushed through the door with Nate on his heels.

They headed into the barn. Chickens, six, seven of them, scratched and pecked around the dirt floor. Jesse grabbed one of the squawking things, pulled his knife, and off flew the bird's head.

"Get another one."

Nate did as he'd been told and tackled the bird closest to him. It flogged its wings and pecked the heck out of his hands. The stupid thing screeched, and soon, all the chickens were yelling. Nate fought down the bird's wings. Feathers flew into the air along with lots of dust off the dirt floor. It took a few minutes of rolling around with the dumb bird and he got a few more hard pecks, but finally, the clucking hen was tucked under one arm like a ball.

Jesse handed Nate his knife. Nate hesitated, though not because he was afraid of killing the chicken. At home, he used a stump, then chopped the head off with a hatchet. He'd just watched Jesse slice a throat with one swipe of his blade. Nate still wasn't so sure he could do it that way. He had a pocket flip blade that Pa had given him, but it wasn't as long or sharp as this pig sticker of Jesse's.

"Lay the chicken on the floor, but keep your knee pressed into him so he can't get away."

Nate intently listened and did precisely as instructed, though the chicken was not cooperating very well and Nate was getting scratched.

"Now, stretch his neck out and give it a hard whack with that knife." Jesse didn't move to help. He was teaching him how it was done. Nate was expected to try. If he failed, then Jesse would show him exactly how and finish the job.

Nate swung his arm and hacked down on the chicken's neck, cutting off its squawking.

Jesse picked up the dead bird, holding both headless hens by their skinny legs. Blood dripped out of their necks. "You look around for eggs. I'll gut these."

Nate rooted in the hay and looked everywhere inside the barn that he thought a chicken might lay. After ten minutes of hunting around, he ended up emptyhanded. He found Jesse outside, cleaning the birds.

"Here." Jesse handed him the raw meat still covered with feathers. "Take those inside to the ladies. I'll be in shortly."

"Where ya goin'?" Some sense was telling Nate that Jesse was leaving. He was going after the fight before it came to them. Pa had done that a few times, and Jesse was too much like him.

Jesse spun Nate around toward the building everyone else was holed up in and gave him a hard swat on the bottom to go on. "Don't you follow me. I'll whip the hide right off your behind."

Nate shot off running, his face burning red. Pa was near death, and now Jesse was going to go off hunting trouble. The kind of trouble that could get him killed. Nate burst through the swinging doors.

The marshal caught him by the arm. "What's wrong?"

"I think Jesse's gonna go searchin' for whoever's waitin' for these women to show up. You gotta stop him." It was bad enough that Nate might lose Pa. He couldn't lose Jesse too. What if there were a lot of bad guys?

The marshal straightened, then looked out the window at Jesse who was on his horse. Huckabee nodded. Jesse tipped his hat, spurred his horse, and left along the same path that Nate had come into town only last evening, which felt like a lifetime ago. So many things had changed since then, and not for the better. Nate didn't want anything else bad to happen, especially to Jesse.

"You shouldn't have let him go!" Nate was about to pitch a fit. He hoofed a chair, which rocked for a second or two.

Two of the ladies were standing at a potbelly stove in the corner opposite the bar. One was wiping out a frying pan. The other was stuffing the stove with kindling. Hattie and the third lady were playing a solemn game of cards, in which neither looked all that interested. Everyone stopped and stared all wide-eyed at him, so he kicked the chair again. This time, it fell over.

He didn't care what any of them thought. His father might not live another hour, and Jesse, who was the next best thing to that man lying in the bed upstairs, had left Nate. Not that the marshal couldn't take care of things there, but that wasn't who Nate wanted.

"You're the marshal, the boss. You could have ordered him to stay!" With one mighty swing, Nate chucked those chickens across the room.

Hattie and the lady with her ducked in their seats as the birds whipped by.

"Nathanial! What are you doing?" Kristy stood on the steps with her hands fisted on her hips, looking too much like Ma. "Go pick up those birds."

He stomped a foot and stood his ground.

The marshal cleared his throat. "Boy, do as the young lady says. I know your pa wouldn't put up with this kind of behavior, and I doubt he'd mind if I give ya a lickin'."

Nate marched over to where the headless chickens lay and begrudgingly snatched them off the floor. Huckabee raised his chin toward the ladies at the stove. Nate handed over the birds, then headed for the stairs to go check on Pa.

Huckabee stepped in front of him. Nate looked up. The marshal didn't look happy, and Nate had an awful feeling he was about to get that licking.

"We need to have a talk." The marshal jerked his head toward the door. Nate went with the marshal, mean tears in his eyes. "Have a seat," Huckabee barked.

Nate plopped onto the bench. His shoulders slumped, his gaze on his boot tips. If he wasn't getting spanked, then he was

NATHANIAL

in for a hell of an ear-chewing, which was better than having his ass smacked.

Huckabee sat next to him, letting out a deep breath of frustration. "I know you're scared and worried. I want your pa to pull through this too. So I will overlook your tantrum this time. If there's a next time, I'll take my belt to ya 'cause I do believe that's what your pa would do." The marshal lifted Nate's chin. "Do you understand me, boy?"

Nate nodded.

After taking a breath, the marshal went on. "Now, as far as Jesse's concerned, based on the things I've seen here and all the braggin' your pa's done on him, I don't doubt he can handle himself. Your pa has taught him all he knows about bein' a good lawman, and I think he is one. If I didn't trust that he could handle what he might run into, I would've gone myself and ordered him to stay here." The marshal patted Nate's knee.

Kristy flew through the doors. "The sheriff's sitting up and drinking broth." She beamed.

Nate jumped up off the bench, running for the stairs. Huckabee took the steps by twos right behind him. They both breathlessly hit the landing, and in a few running steps, they were at Pa's bedside.

Sure enough, he was sitting up. He was still pale and was somewhat slumped on the pillows, but his eyes were open and he was holding the bowl by himself.

"Pa." Nate smiled and carefully slid onto the bed next to his father.

Huckabee pulled up the chair. He, too, was smiling.

"Where's Jesse?" Pa's voice sounded pitifully weak.

As Huckabee explained, Nate curled up closer to Pa and thanked the good Lord that he wasn't going to die, or at least it didn't seem that way.

All that day, Pa slept off and on and drank more broth. Jesse hadn't returned by the time Kristy chased Nate upstairs to bed. She'd been teary since Jesse left, and her temper was short.

Huckabee was at the window with his rifle. One of the ladies kept coffee going for him while the others slept. Nate pulled his blanket around his shoulders, curling up on the bed near Pa's feet where he wouldn't bump his wound, and he fell asleep.

Three days later and with the number of chickens in the barn dwindling, Nate found himself next to Huckabee, sitting on the bench outside, picking at the eggs on his plate, and watching the trail for Jesse. Nate was worried. Pa was doing better, and that was a big relief. He wasn't out of bed yet, but he was steadily keeping more broth down.

A horse whinnied, and all the others in the corral lifted their heads. Their ears had perked straight up. Out of the trees along the trail rode Jesse. In tow, he had a man wrapped in a saddle blanket and tied facedown over the saddle and two others who were still alive and tied to their pommels.

Nate leaped to his feet.

The marshal stood, eying the rough-looking lot riding toward them.

Nate tore off. "Jesse!"

When he got close enough, Jesse grabbed his wrist and swung Nate up into the saddle behind him. He gave Jesse a big squeeze around the middle, relieved that he wasn't dead.

"How's your pa?" Jesse pulled up reins in front of Huckabee.

"Gettin' better every day." Nate couldn't have been happier. Pa was on the mend, and Jesse had returned safe and sound. His family was okay. Ma would surely be happy when they all got home.

The thought made him recall that real soon, his home might be with the Fletchers. He'd almost forgotten them.

NATHANIAL

The next day, Jesse hitched the wagon from the barn to the bay and mustang. Pa was helped into the bed, where Kristy and the ladies handmade him a soft pallet of blankets. Kristy took the reins, her little sister at her side. Nate rode in the bed with Pa, who slept most of the time. Jesse and Huckabee guarded the prisoners, and the other ladies all rode the horses of the bad men buried back yonder.

The closer they got to Gray Rock, the more Nate's thoughts drifted to what awaited him—the Fletchers.

Late the following day, past suppertime, the sun not yet down, they rode as a weary group onto the street of Gray Rock.

The first person Nate saw was Judge Prescott, who had just stepped out of the hotel with Mr. Graham, the town lawyer. They hustled toward the wagon. Kristy pulled up reins. It was suddenly as though the whole town had come alive like bees swarming around a hive. Kristy's ma and bothers were there out of nowhere, her Pa too. Lots of Nate's friends and their folks stood by gawking into the wagon bed at Pa, who was much paler than he had been yesterday. Someone called for somebody else to fetch Doc Martin.

Mr. Pike peeked over the back of the wagon and stared at Pa. Somehow he was sleeping through all the ruckus. The jarring wagon ride must have beat what strength he'd gained out of him.

Big John, the Hendersons, and other townsfolk rushed forward. The wagon was surrounded. Lots of jumbled voices asked too many questions, and in Nate's mind, it was one big ball of noise. He didn't like them staring at him or Pa. He didn't want to give them answers, not now. He was tired. He wanted Ma.

Jesse was reined in next to the judge, talking to him. Huckabee took the prisoners ahead to the jailhouse. Hattie was happily crying, as were others. It was all too much for Nate. He buried his face in the blanket covering Pa and sobbed.

A hand smoothed his hair, and he looked up, expecting to see Jesse. It was Deloris Fletcher. Nate screamed as if she'd lit him on fire.

Jesse hopped off his horse into the back of the wagon. In one jump, he was standing on the ground between Nate, Pa, and the Fletchers. "Keep your goldarn hands off him."

Judge Prescott hurried around to where Jesse stood, Mr. Graham with him. They placed themselves between the feuding parties. Nate didn't know what was going to happen. Jesse's fist was drawn back. Mr. Fletcher was yelling over the judge and into Jesse's face. Mrs. Fetcher paled as she looked around nervously at all the scowling faces.

Pa started to stir. A low moan seeped out of him, and everyone went quiet. No one moved.

Jesse turned to Kristy. "Take him to the house."

"No," Kristy's pa interjected. "My daughter's comin' home with me."

Nate could understand Shorty's concern. He'd just gotten his two missing daughters back. It was a moment he probably wouldn't forget, and he didn't want them out of his sight.

"I'll bring her home, then. She's safe with me," Jesse snapped.

Nate could also see Jesse's side. Jesse and Kristy were engaged. She wasn't officially his woman, not yet, but close enough. She wasn't a little girl. Soon, she'd have a home of her own and probably kids. She was a grown woman.

"Boy, you look like you haven't slept in days. She's coming home with her mother and me." Shorty wasn't backing down.

He and Jesse eyeballed one another, not in a friendly way. This was no way for a soon-to-be father and son-in-law to behave toward one another. Nate was only eight, and he knew that much. But everyone's emotions were riled up. When Nate was upset, he sometimes did dumb things, and he suspected grown-ups were no different.

"I'll take him." Doc Martin hastily pushed through the crowd. He helped Kristy down, then quickly climbed up onto the seat. Without warning, he slapped leather to the team, and the wagon lurched forward.

Nate didn't want to leave without Jesse, who thankfully swung into the saddle and fell into pace next to the wagon.

The Fletchers just stared after them.

CHAPTER 21

WHEN THE WAGON rattled into the yard, Ma must have heard them coming or been keeping watch since they had all gone missing. She was throwing open the door of the house before Doc Martin pulled up on the reins. Ma held her skirt up, rushing down the stairs, and burst through the white picket gate. Her eyes were teary, and Nate knew why. The bay Pa always rode was hitched on a wagon, no Pa in plain sight.

Ma ran to the back of the wagon, breathless when she stopped. Jesse opened the bed gate, slowly lowering it so Pa was not jarred. Ma gasped, cupping a hand over her mouth. Pa was deathly white, and dried blood covered his shirt and pants. He might have looked worse to her than to the rest of them who'd seen him right after getting shot.

"Mama." Nate's voice was soft only because he didn't feel strong. He was panicked by the grief and look of strained disbelief all over Ma's face. One glimpse at Pa, and the pink of her cheeks had drained right out. "You can fix him, right?"

Anytime one of them got hurt, Ma was the first to doctor them. Only in rare cases, such as a high fever or broken bones, did she seek Doc Martin's advice. Usually, she could patch any injury they brought to her. There was a shock in the rigid way she stood while taking in the god-awful sight of Pa, so still and unaware of his surroundings, that for a first, it dawned on Nate that his mother couldn't mend everything. The sad way she longingly stared at the man she had married, the father of her children, made Nate believe Pa might never recover, as though Ma had lost all hope in ever seeing him open his eyes again.

Would Pa die? The horrible, dreaded thought shriveled Nate's belief. His heart shattered, and tears burst out of him. If Ma, who was always the encourager, was unsure about Pa's condition, then how could Nate think otherwise?

Tears streamed down her cheeks as she crawled into the wagon bed alongside Pa, where Nate was knelt beside him. She laid a hand to Pa's chest and gently rubbed. "Nolan."

If misery ever had a sound, it was Ma's sobbing voice choking out Pa's name.

Nate let out a wail. Why was life so cruel sometimes? Until the wagon ride home, Pa had seemed as though he was getting better. What had changed?

Nate was glad Doc Martin was there. Ma definitely wasn't in the frame of mind to do much good. She was a sobbing mess, and Nate wasn't any better. Even Jesse had wetness on his face and was blinking back more.

"Let's git him inside." Doc Martin coaxed Ma to leave Pa's side. She was hunched over him, clinging to his shirt.

Jesse, who seemed anxious to do something other than cry, nodded while wiping at his eyes, then reached for Ma's hand to help her out of the wagon. Nate scooted out behind her, sticking close to her side.

Doc took a firm hold under Pa's shoulders while Jesse held his legs. Before they lifted him off the wagon, the sound of a group of horses trotting into the lane lifted their heads. Three men rode toward them. Marshal Huckabee was on the left, Judge Prescott led by half a horse length in the middle, and on the right was none other than Mr. Lem Fletcher. What in the hell? Surely, Nate's eyes were lying to him. His tears instantly dried up from the sheer shock of seeing that bug-eyed toad.

"Holy hell!" He stomped a foot.

This couldn't be happening now. Had they come to take Nate—lawman, a judge, and the jackass who wanted custody of him? No. Nate couldn't believe Pa's best friend would do that, especially now while Pa was on death's doorstep. And Huckabee had watched over him the entire ride home.

From all the times he'd worked alongside Pa, Nate did understand that even if a lawman didn't always agree with a particular ruling, he was bound by his oath to uphold justice as the law had been written. In some matters, a man wearing a badge might not like what he had to do, but he had to act accordingly anyway. It was his duty, and Nate knew Pa took that serious, as did Huckabee. As close and chummy as those two were, Nate figured Huckabee would unpin his badge before he would rip away the son of his best friend. But just in case Nate was wrong, he snatched up a rock and took aim.

"Hold your fire." Jesse had turned away from the wagon and Pa, who should have been inside in a bed, being tended to, and faced the official-looking trio.

Nate held ready to let loose with that stone.

"I see ya brought the fox to the henhouse." Jesse shook his head at Huckabee and Prescott, disgusted. He pulled Nate behind him and stood with shoulders wide and feet apart. It was a solid sign that no one was getting past him.

Nate kept his rock poised.

The marshal stepped down from the saddle, reins in hand. "Son, it ain't like that." He walked toward the wagon where Pa's body lay. "It took a bit to break up the crowd after the wagon left. Everyone wanted to know about their sheriff and,

NATHANIAL

of course, the details about rescuin' the women since we rode in with extra ladies and prisoners. People want to know if there's reason to be fearful." Huckabee looked over the side at Pa. "I put Big John to watchin' the prisoners."

Nate thought he could see the marshal's heart jump into his throat as his Adam's apple bobbed, trying to swallow the fact that his friend might not be around tomorrow. "Damn you, Nolan. Don't you die on me." Huckabee kicked at the dirt. He looked away then and studied Jesse. "The judge and I left town in such a hurry that it wasn't 'til we'd turned into the lane that I caught sight of Fletcher followin' us." Huckabee suddenly chuckled.

Nate didn't know what that laughter was about, but he didn't think it appropriate, not at a time like this. There stood Ma crying into her apron at the side of the wagon next to Pa. Doc Martin looked sorely irritated that if he didn't get help to carry Pa inside in the next few seconds, he would do it himself.

Nate was ready to bean Mr. Fletcher with a rock at the next twitch, and Jesse had the look of wanting to kill someone. There wasn't any guessing who that would be. At the moment, though, Jesse snarled at Huckabee.

"I don't find him bein' here one damn bit amusin'." Jesse was dead serious. His eyes narrowed, and he pointedly glared at Lem Fletcher.

"Oh, it ain't. I was mad when I first seen him and briefly thought about lettin' him ride in here on his own. Except I imagined myself havin' to arrest you…for murder." The marshal patted Jesse's shoulder. "Don't worry. I warned him that if he don't mind his manners as far as Nate's concerned, I'll stomp his face into the ground a few times, then throw his ass in jail."

Judge Prescott slid off his horse, minding what he was doing while probably choosing to ignore the conversation that had just taken place. Fletcher swallowed hard and stayed astride his horse. He seemed to be waiting for Jesse's invite. Nate would be disappointed if he didn't get to burst the dandy's lip with the rock.

"Kate." Pa's voice was a gargled simper.

In one swift move, Jesse grabbed Nate, lifting and carrying him while taking two stretching strides. In a breath, they were at the side of the wagon with Ma, looking inside. Pa's eyes were open, and he weakly raised a hand.

Ma intertwined her fingers with his. Nate could see her knuckles blanch as she gave Pa's hand a squeeze. "Nolan."

Pa's eyes rolled. Then after a few heavy blinks, he focused on their faces. "Boys." A hint of a grin turned up one corner of his mouth. It was the best thing Nate had seen all day. He couldn't help but smile through his tears.

"You hang in there, sir," Jesse said confidently.

A few seconds later, Pa's eyes fell shut.

"We've wasted enough time," Doc snapped. "We need to get him inside."

Jesse passed Nate to Ma, and he was glad to be held. He was scared. There had been too much commotion, and he could feel Fletcher watching him.

Jesse, Doc, the marshal, and Judge Prescott lifted Pa off the wagon and carried him toward the house. Ma hurried ahead of them, Nate wrapped in her arms. They were both sniffling and teary. She threw open the picket gate, then held the house door open as they shuffled around to get Pa inside without bumping him on the doorframe. A few minutes later, Pa was in his bed.

Ma put Nate down and went to work with Doc, stripping Pa to examine his wound.

"Nathanial." Ma called him out of his dismay. "Fetch hot water."

"Yes, ma'am." He ran toward the door between all the bodies in the room, not even realizing at first that he'd zipped past Fletcher. Nate didn't want that man in his house, but he

NATHANIAL

needed to hurry and do what he was able to in order to help Pa.

"Get towels," Ma hollered after him. Nate was just touching a foot on the steps to race down the stairs.

"I will," he yelled over his shoulder, not wanting Ma to think he hadn't heard. Even with Doc Martin there, Ma's brain was probably racing. Nate's was. If he could take one little thing away from her to ease her worries, he would.

Ten minutes later, after the water had come to near a boil, he carefully carried a big bowl into the room without sloshing any. Doc was poking around the seeping stitched hole in Pa's gut. Ma hurried over and took the hot water and clean rags from Nate, setting them on the night table.

The skin around the wound was awful red. It hadn't been like that before, and every time Doc pushed on it with his finger, Pa groaned and a fair amount of buttery-looking gunk oozed out. Was that what Nate smelled? Whatever the odor, it was foul like something rotting. Pa wore a shirt and was covered in blankets when he'd been carried home in the wagon. Could be that was why the god-awful rancid odor hadn't been noticed before.

"I need everyone out. Now!" Doc thundered.

Nate began to quake. Something was very wrong. Pa now had the glisten of sweat on his face and all over his bare torso. And Doc never got mean and yelled.

Nate didn't understand what was going on. He just knew it was bad. "Mama," he whimpered.

"Baby, you stay with Jesse." Ma turned Nate toward the door. She never called him baby. She was acting different. All this stress wasn't good for any of them. Everything seemed out of place.

Tears filled Nate's eyes. The marshal and the others all hustled, filing out the door in front of him. An odd thought popped into his head. Maybe it came to him because Ma had called him baby. Could all this constant worry that she had probably been doing since before Pa got shot hurt the baby in her belly? This wasn't the time to ask her, but he hoped not.

Nate wiped a sleeve across his eyes, then followed the trail of heavy footsteps into the hallway. Suddenly, he noticed Jesse was missing. He glanced over his shoulder in time to see Jesse talking quietly with Doc and Ma, but only for a few seconds. Then the door snapped shut, and Jesse stood in the hall with Nate. There was wetness in his eyes. He said nothing about what was going on behind that closed door. Though, hurried, rustling noises slid out through the crack below the door.

"Ma asked me to check on Elizabeth. She's napping." Jesse gave him a nudge.

Nate waited at the top of the stairs. Jesse was only in Elizabeth's room a minute or two, then appeared in the hall. She must have still been asleep. Nate followed on his heels down the stairs. Each footfall of Jesse's boot sounded like a weary sigh.

Nate couldn't take not knowing for one more second. "Is Pa gonna die? Is that why Doc kicked us all out and Ma ain't herself?" He wasn't sure he wanted to hear the answer.

At the bottom, Jesse turned and hunkered down, facing Nate eye to eye. "None of us knows the hour the good Lord will call us home. I won't guess if your pa's gonna live or die. I just can't say for sure. Wish I could promise ya everything will turn out the way we want, but..." Jesse's voice trailed off, and he studied Nate as though deciding whether he should say more or not.

Nate wasn't a baby, but he was a little kid. He didn't rightly understand lots of big people stuff. Though, he did want Jesse to try to explain this to him. That was Nate's father lying upstairs.

"Jesse, I'm scared." He threw his arms around Jesse's neck and buried his face in the collar of his shirt.

NATHANIAL

A big hand rubbed Nate's back. Then Jesse pulled him back and nodded. He'd made his decision to tell him something. Maybe not every detail, but he wasn't leaving him in the dark to wonder what was happening to Pa.

"I'm scared too." Jesse faintly grinned. "Doc has to operate on your pa. That bullet wound is infected. He's gonna try to drain the pus out."

"Then Pa will get better?" Nate innocently asked.

"Maybe." Very little confidence radiated out of those words. "Your pa is a strong man. I can't help but believe that he'll somehow beat this. Reckon that's just wishful thinkin'." Jesse straightened, and no more was said.

They found the others sitting on the porch. Huckabee and the judge were discussing Doc's quick course of action, and both seemed to predict a good outcome. Maybe they were saying that for Nate's sake since he was still wiping at his eyes or just to make themselves feel better.

Fletcher was quiet, keeping whatever he was thinking to himself, averting his eyes anytime Jesse looked in his direction. Nate wished that man would go away. Fletcher didn't belong there. He wasn't a friend or neighbor or even an acquaintance. He didn't care one iota about Pa. Nate wanted to be sad without some stranger sneaking glances at him, which just made him feel more ill at ease.

There was no escaping the crushing ache in Nate's chest. He couldn't stop fretting about Pa. He could, however, lose sight of Mr. Fletcher. He looked over at Jesse, who sat on the porch steps in gloomy silence, his head hanging between his hands, shoulders drooped, and every inch sapped of strength.

"I'll tend to the horses," Nate offered to get away. Buck and the bay were still hitched to the wagon, and Jesse's gelding stood with his reins dangling to the ground. Nate shuffled toward the animals, occasionally giving the dirt a hard kick when the urge to let out frustration hit him.

"I know just how ya feel, kid." Jesse had followed him.

It took only a few minutes for the horses to be unhitched and pastured. Nate then went into the barn, slowly working at his chores until he was finished. A couple times, he had mindlessly forgotten what he was doing as he was doing it. All he could think about was Pa.

Nate closed the barn door behind him. It wasn't yet dark, but the sun had sunk lower since he had gone into the barn. Long shadows reached out from the trees and made the yard appear as though it were wearing black prison stripes. The orange hue of the sky somehow felt cold to Nate. It wasn't giving off that warm, peaceful glow his family usually enjoyed after supper each evening while gathered on the porch, relaxing in one another's company. The men who'd been sitting there earlier were gone, but their horses stood tied to the rail outside the picket fence. Fletcher hadn't left the ranch.

Inside, the marshal was bouncing Elizabeth in an effort to soothe her cries. Jesse was scurrying about the kitchen, hastily trying to heat up stew. The judge and Fletcher were sitting peacefully on the settee. They weren't speaking, just sitting there burdened by their own thoughts, or so it seemed, considering the long faces. Judge Prescott was flipping through one of Pa's law books, and Mr. Dandified was staring at the framed photographs that lined the mantel. Nate ignored it, walking past into the dining room where the marshal had his hands full with the screaming Elizabeth. Nate scooped up his little sister's rag doll off the floor. It was her favorite toy. A godsend for the rest of the family when Ma wasn't nearby.

Nate danced the doll in his hand. "Ticklebug is comin' to git ya."

Elizabeth giggled. The crying instantly stopped, and she reached for the dolly.

Nate, being a big brother, had to do a little teasing. He had named the faceless cotton doll Ticklebug. It was a front for the merciless torment he so enjoyed overpowering his sister with. She loved it. He held Ticklebug in hand, hopping toward her. Elizabeth squealed, balling up in the marshal's arms, her fat rolls already shaking. She knew what was coming because Nate had played this game with her about a million times.

"Ticklebug," he sang a few times while quickly skipping the dolly all over Elizabeth's little belly. Using the rag doll, he poked in that sensitive spot right above the hip bone, the fatty gut part. Elizabeth's laugh was so deep it must have roared right up from her toes. In return, Nate laughed.

The marshal chuckled too. "Good job." He winked at Nate.

Jesse came in from the kitchen with a plate of stew in each hand. He plunked them on the table. "Here." He reached to take Elizabeth. She was hungrily chewing on Ticklebug. As soon as Jesse picked up the spoon, Elizabeth opened her mouth wide. "Partner, have a seat. That other plate is for you."

Nate wasn't hungry. His sister was too young to fully grasp all that was going on that evening. Their father might die, and the horrible man who had every intention of stealing Nate away from their family was in the next room. Fletcher was still stiffly sitting in the same spot, looking around as if inventorying the contents of their home. Nate really didn't care what the jackass thought about anything. He was honestly only concerned about one thing—their father.

"I ain't hungry," Nate said with some serious sass.

Jesse scowled. "I wasn't askin'. Now sit down and eat."

He was barely shoveling it in fast enough for Elizabeth. There was stew smeared on her face, and drips stained her dress where Ma always tucked a bib.

"I'm gonna get coffee." The marshal, looking about as beat as a man could get, went into the kitchen. "Jesse, you want some?"

"Make it strong," Jesse answered. He looked hard at Nate. "Git your ass in that chair and start eatin'."

Ma was usually the one who nagged him about his weak appetite, but since she was busy tending Pa, it appeared that not only had Jesse stepped into Pa's boots as head of the family, but also Ma's. Nate didn't always listen to his mother and father either, so that meant Jesse could kiss his big toe. If he wasn't hungry, which he wasn't, then he was not going to eat. And no way, no how was Jesse going to make him.

Nate could be bossy too. He smacked his hands to his hips and sternly stared at Jesse. "I don't see you fillin' your gut. Where's your plate? If I gotta eat, why don't you?"

His argument was sensible the way he figured it. Jesse had a big appetite like Pa. It wasn't unusual for him to have seconds, sometimes thirds. He was a pig there at home. His lack of appetite meant only one thing. Jesse was too worried about Pa to nibble a crumb. So why did he expect Nate to be hungry?

"Ma will ask if you kids got fed." Jesse pointed to the plate of food that sat waiting. "Git your behind in that chair."

It didn't seem like Nate had a choice.

Fletcher's voice carried in from the parlor. He twisted at the curled end of his mustache while talking to the judge, who was sitting erect and nodding his head slowly with each utterance flowing out of Fletcher's mouth. Judge Prescott appeared to be hanging on to each word as though it were life-sustaining.

"Why is he still here?" For a second, Nate forgot about food and arguing with Jesse. Not that he'd meant to change the subject, but he was at wit's end with this whole blasted day. He was mentally drained, which made him grumpy, and he realized he was fiercely irritable because he didn't usually get smart-mouthed with Jesse. At the moment, Nate felt like throwing both his plate of stew and Lem Fletcher right out the window. He wanted to hear Pa's deep voice, not the sissified tone of the enemy.

Jesse finished wiping Elizabeth's mouth, then turned and stared at Fletcher as if seeing him for the first time. Nate reckoned with all the worry, taking care of kids, having prisoners to deal with at some point, and stranded women, plus with Pa half dead, Jesse undoubtedly recognized those increased responsibilities at home and his duties at work had just grown a hundredfold. On top of all that, the trial for Nate's custody was looming over them like a dark thundercloud. Jesse most likely was feeling completely exhausted too, so much so that it had momentarily blinded him to Fletcher's presence.

"Here. Watch your sister." Jesse thrust Elizabeth at Nate.

She was a toddler and quite a squirming armful for him. Good Lord, she must have been twenty-five pounds, near half his weight. She wasn't built tiny like him. He juggled her in his arms the best he could without dropping her.

Jesse stood from the table. His manner was now stiff, and his face had contorted into something ugly. He took a step toward Fletcher in the next room.

Marshal Huckabee, who had been sipping at his coffee close by, caught Jesse's arm. "Hold up." The marshal glanced at Fletcher. Then his gaze came to rest on Jesse's hardened face. "Don't make him mad."

"Just why the hell should I be worried about that?" Jesse jerked his arm out of the marshal's grip, though he didn't move toward Fletcher.

Huckabee, like Pa, had lots of experience with dealing with people, good and bad. When Pa had taken Jesse under his wing as deputy, one of the things he had taught him was how to read people, to develop that sense of whether a person shaped up to be decent folk or a conniving slime ball full of lies and treachery. He was still learning.

"He ain't quiet 'cause he has nothing to say," Huckabee said under his breath. "He's been watching, taking mental notes. He hasn't been aggressive in any way, so I say we let him have a long look."

They knew what Fletcher wanted, the reason he was in Gray Rock, but they'd all been so preoccupied with Pa that no one had discovered exactly why Fletcher was there at the Crosson ranch at a time when things were at their worst. Why hadn't Fletcher just stayed behind in town? Was he just curious? Did he think the fight for Nate would be easier if Pa were to die? Could be he had a hankering to see how Nate had been living, his home life, who he really was. The marshal's reason for stopping Jesse from booting out that disliked man dawned on Nate. Seeing the strong bond in that home, how they worked together and fought, that made them family. If Fletcher recognized those ties, perhaps he'd be less likely to cut them. It was a long shot but the only one they had at the moment. Even if Fletcher didn't change his mind, Nate had no intention of going anywhere with him and that wife of his.

Jesse's face softened, and his shoulders relaxed. He must have come to the same conclusion.

"Boys." Ma was at the bottom step and coming toward them. There was bright-red blood on her apron. Her eyes were crimson from all the crying she'd done, but there were no tears on her cheeks at that moment.

Nate's heart raced. Was Pa going to be okay?

CHAPTER 22

NATE PRACTICALLY THREW his sister at Jesse, then ran headlong for Ma. Before she'd gotten halfway through the sitting room, Nate plowed into her, throwing his arms around her waist, hugging tight. "How's Pa?" His voice quivered.

Jesse and the marshal rushed in around Ma. Judge Prescott and Fletcher both had bolted to their feet. No one seemed to be breathing. Everyone waited to hear. Nate's shaky fingers were crossed.

Ma smoothed Nate's hair. "Your Pa isn't awake, but he has made it through the operation. Doc thinks he got all the infection." There was a hint of relief in her voice. Her face, though, was still showing strain.

With Elizabeth in one arm, Jesse threw his other around Nate and Ma, pulling them close. They stood huddled for a minute, taking in the comforting scent of one another, of family. A sense of togetherness came over Nate. It was a strong feeling that alone, not one of them had the stamina to overcome this dreaded obstacle, but as a unit, they could not be defeated. It planted in Nate a fertile seed of hope. Pa would live. He just had to.

"Kate, I need more bandages," Doc called downstairs.

Ma pulled away and hustled to work. She retrieved linen from the standing cupboard, along with her scissors, and on her way back upstairs, she gave Nate a pointed look. "Eat your stew."

Nate's jaw darn near hit the floor. How did she know? She had told him once a long time ago that she had eyes on the back of her head. He didn't doubt that. Somehow she just always knew what he'd been up to.

Jesse passed Elizabeth to Huckabee. She was just as unhappy about it as she had been the first time he'd been holding her. This time, instead of screaming, she was chewing madly on Ticklebug's head.

The marshal gave Nate a nudge toward the dining room where his supper was probably cold from sitting too long. Jesse followed Ma to the stairs. If he was going to see Pa, then Nate wanted to go too.

He turned to run after them, but the marshal snagged his hand. "Your ma will tell ya when you can see your pa."

The marshal, the father of Nate's best buddy, never put up with much sass from his son. Even if Nate were to have a fit, he doubted he'd win that argument. Defeated, he slunk into his chair. No steam rose off the stew on the plate in front of him. He miserably picked up his spoon and stirred his food.

"Excuse me, Marshal Huckabee."

Nate's head snapped to attention at the sound of the city dude's voice so close, practically breathing down the back of his neck. His hair there tingled. Mr. Fletcher stood not an arm's length away.

He didn't look at Nate. He spoke directly to the marshal. "Please offer my sincerest sympathies to Mrs. Crosson and do thank her for allowing me to be present today. I'm sure, given why my wife and I have traveled to Gray Rock, my presence was no comfort." Fletcher expressed a weary grin. "Let her know, too, that given the state of Mr. Crosson's health and her delicate condition…"

Nate's brow abruptly rose, as did the marshal's. How did Fletcher know about Ma's pregnancy?

As if he'd read their minds, he said, "Judge Prescott kindly explained some details that I would otherwise have been unaware of." Fletcher fiddled with the derby hat in his hands. "I have requested that Judge Prescott suspend the hearing for a week or two. Mrs. Crosson doesn't need the added stress of that so soon."

The words "so soon" rang in Nate's ears. He comprehended that the trial for his custody would come. It was just delayed for a short time to see if Pa lived or died.

Judge Prescott walked into the room. Perhaps he had overheard the conversation. He sadly looked at Nate and began to roll his lips. Nate suspected he had something to say, but either he wasn't sure how exactly to say it or he didn't want to. Either way, he remained quietly chewing on his thoughts. It was probably bad news, and Nate already had his fill of awful crap for one day.

Nate exploded, bolting upright out of his chair, knocking it over. His fists balled at his sides. His body shook. Everything that was going on inside that house, inside him, had boiled to the surface. He couldn't take all the possibilities, the not knowing. Pa's future, Nate's future, it was all up in the air. Who knew how any of it would turn out? Tomorrow, if Pa died, things could be vastly different for them. That didn't mean Nate would just give up and go away with the Fetchers. He still had a mother, and Jesse loved him. What wasn't the judge telling him? It had to be about the Fletchers.

Nate glared at Mr. Fletcher. "Don't bother waitin'. I don't care what the judge says. I won't ever go with you!" With both hands, he shoved Fletcher. The man fumbled back a step or two.

Elizabeth started bawling, probably at Nate's sudden screaming, and the marshal was jostling her around, trying to get her calm.

A no-good thief was what that fella Fletcher was. There was no way in hell he was getting Nate.

The judge stepped toward Nate. There was a sympathetic glassiness to his eyes as he stooped, arms outstretched toward him as if Nate would be comforted by him. Fletcher closed in too, dabbing at his glistening forehead with his silky handkerchief. It was obvious that he didn't know what to do. Had he ever been around kids?

"Don't touch me!" Nate screamed louder than before.

All of a sudden, Jesse was standing lock, stock, and barrel between Nate and those two. "What the hell's goin' on?"

Nate mirrored Jesse's defensive stance.

Huckabee stepped into the mix, still holding Elizabeth, who was reaching for Jesse and Nate. Tears streaked her face, and her cries rose. Marshal Huckabee stood between Jesse and Prescott and Fletcher. They were all arguing at the top of their lungs. All the noise mangled together. Nate was positive that someone was going to get punched.

"Git out! Every one of ya!" Ma wasn't a big woman, but that day, she stood taller than any man in the room—and both Jesse and the marshal were over six feet. She was head and shoulders over the whole mean, arguing lot of them. The harsh words, the arrogance of some, the hateful tones—it all had abruptly stopped. They stared uncertainly at Ma. Her cheeks were as red as her hair, and there was a gleam of fire in her pale eyes. Nate had never seen her so mad.

"Nathanial, sweetheart, come here."

Nate tore away from the crowd and threw himself into the folds of Ma's skirt. It was a soft, safe place, and his emotions were so mixed up he didn't know how to feel. The only spot he felt more secure was in Pa's lap or Jesse's. Ma held out her arms, and Huckabee immediately delivered Elizabeth. She kissed her face a few times, hushing her cries in less than a minute.

"Kate, I do apologize." It wasn't the marshal's fault that things had gotten out of hand, but he had been part of it. His soft face begged her forgiveness.

"Joseph, we're all feeling unsettled right now. I can excuse Jesse to a point. He's acting like an irrational son, losing his temper. But you—Nolan was the best man at your wedding. He wouldn't let your family fall apart like this if that was you lying up there in that bed. I expected better." Ma wiped at her eyes. "Nolan's awake. He would like to speak to you." Ma briefly paused, then through gritted teeth said, "I can't believe I have to say this." Before saying another word, she pointed a straight finger at Huckabee. "You don't say a word to that man up there about whatever started this brouhaha down here. I have my suspicions, and he don't need to worry about anything but getting well."

Marshal Huckabee humbly removed his hat. "Yes, ma'am. Not a word." He quietly headed up the stairs. His spurs didn't even clink.

"You." Ma's straight finger now pointed at Jesse, whose eyes widened like a kid about to get his ass whipped. She jerked her head toward Pa's office. "I'll talk to you in a minute." Then she eyed Prescott and Fletcher. "After I see these gentlemen out." Ma went to the door, toting Elizabeth on her hip and Nate hanging tight to her skirt. She opened it wide. "Gentlemen."

"I apologize, ma'am." Fletcher dipped his chin as he passed by Ma, and Nate retreated deeper into the warm folds of her skirt. Fletcher disappeared out the door. Nate wished the man would never come back.

Judge Prescott stopped in front of Ma. "Kate, I need to speak to you. It's vital."

"Not now. Please." Ma's demeanor had softened. She looked like she might drop in pure exhaustion.

"Kate, this can't wait," he begged.

Ma let out a troubled sigh. "Jesse," she called over her shoulder. He came hustling out of Pa's study. "Take the kids into the kitchen and get them milk." She gently passed Elizabeth off.

"Yes, ma'am." Jesse took Nate by the hand. With ease, he pulled him off Ma, and the three of them went toward the kitchen.

Nate twisted in Jesse's grasp and looked over his shoulder. Ma and the judge were engaged in deep conversation in a low tone so it wouldn't carry to the ears of anyone else. Ma looked over at Nate. Tears made her eyes bigger than they naturally were. She gave the judge a small nudge. He, too, was now looking worrisomely at Nate. Then together they stepped outside, out of earshot. The door clicked shut.

"Jesse, what are they discussin'?" Nate's gut tightened. He knew it had something to do with him. That look Ma had given him before she'd signaled for the judge to go outside where they would have more privacy, that look was one that made him believe that someday soon she might never see him again.

"Hard to tell." Jesse handed Nate a glass of milk.

He drank it while Jesse fed Elizabeth hers. When their glasses were empty, the three of them gloomily waited in the study for Ma to return. Nate sat in Pa's chair behind the desk. Jesse was in one of the cushioned chairs, using his hat to play peek-a-boo with Elizabeth. She was the only one to find something to genuinely smile about. It seemed like forever until the door finally opened.

Ma lumbered into the room as though she were in a trance. She plopped down hard into the only open chair and stared into the space between Jesse and Nate. It was as if she didn't even see them, as if they weren't there and she was a hundred miles away.

"Ma." Jesse sounded nervous.

Nate's grip on the desk chair tightened. His knuckles were white.

She snapped out of her deep thought, then looked from one to the other of them. "Sweetheart, come sit with me. There's something very important that I need to talk to you boys about."

Nate hesitantly pulled himself out of Pa's chair. This was odd. Ma had never called them tight together like this. She always just came out with whatever she had to say. The formality of this felt more like a proceeding like he imagined court would be. Ma's grimly lined face scared him too. He crawled up onto her lap. She bear-hugged him for a minute and sniffled.

She drew in a long breath, at which point she sobered. "Mr. and Mrs. Fletcher will be coming to visit tomorrow."

"What?" Nate gasped. Tears burst out of his eyes. He shook his head. In the same instant, Jesse leaped out of his chair. His lips thinned, and Nate could tell on the tip of Jesse's tongue was a big argument.

"Sit down, young man." Ma was using her stern motherly voice.

Jesse dropped back into the chair without a word said.

"I know right now you're the man of this house. But there are times when you need to listen to me. This being one of them." Ma rubbed a hand down the side of her face. Tears began to roll out of the corners of her eyes. "I don't know how to say it."

Nate quivered. Jesse was on the edge of his seat with Elizabeth, who was yanking at her dolly's yarn hair.

Ma cleared the choke in her voice. "The Fletchers will be visiting for a few hours every day until the trial."

"Why?" Jesse asked without hiding his agitation.

Nate didn't understand either and felt just as irritated. If the trial had been postponed, then what reason could the Fletchers have for being there? It wasn't concern about Pa; that was for sure.

"A Mrs. Walter Gill has come forward and is willing to testify on the Fletchers' behalf." Ma began to sob.

"Who the hell is Walter Gill? I never heard of him or his wife." Jesse was now scowling. Not at Ma, but it was evident that he was sorely disturbed by this entire situation.

"No!"

It had suddenly hit Nate. Walter Gill. Walt. The man Pa had killed. The man involved in stealing Kristy, Hattie, and those other ladies. The thin lady's husband. Mrs. Walter Gill was that skinny mountain woman who'd been friends with Lucinda. Now it seemed she was getting chummy with the Fletchers.

"No," he repeated several more times, the pitch rising until he didn't recognize his voice. Nate was feverishly shaking all over. Ma rocked him, trying to calm him. He couldn't catch his breath and choked on his cries.

"Will someone tell me who those people are?" Jesse snapped and smacked a fist down on the corner of Pa's desk.

Nate and Ma jumped, but Jesse's frustration was reasonable given the teary state produced by the mention of Mrs. Gill's name.

Nate wiped his eyes, staring at Jesse. "She's the thin woman we went to see. The one with all the kids. The man that shot it out with Pa, that's his widow."

The color drained out of Jesse's face. He had heard the thin woman that day at Blue Sky Lake. He knew the connection between the woman and Lucinda and how she knew the relationship between Deloris and Nate's birth mother. Her testimony would certainly hurt their defense in court, but would her word be good enough to guarantee Nate's removal from his home? The thin woman's actions reeked of revenge against Pa, but she had seemed to like Nate. So why would she purposely hurt him? Besides, her man hadn't been any good. He reckoned that didn't mean she was without feelings for the bastard.

Other than Elizabeth babbling to her dolly, the room was mournfully silent. Everyone, Nate suspected, was sadly reasoning through the same thoughts, except his little sister who was too young. Nate wiped at his eyes. Pa, upstairs fighting fever and infection, didn't know he might soon lose a son.

Ma smoothed Nate's hair while rocking him on her lap. He nestled his teary face into her bosom and didn't care if he looked like a baby. It wasn't something he normally would have done. He wished for a miracle. He prayed for Pa's health to return. Maybe Nate would feel braver if Pa was well and was there to lead them all through this.

Jesse was well capable, but simply put, he wasn't Nate's father. He was a close second in every way. However, it was Nolan Crosson who had found Nate almost two years ago. He had then given Nate the Crosson name, a home, provided for him in ways no one ever had. Nate trusted and believed in that man more than any other, and the idiot Fletchers were attempting to sever that tight bond. Nate wanted strength to come to his pa more than he wanted the Fletchers to hop a stage and head back east where they belonged.

"What about the trial?" Jesse asked grimly. "Even if that skinny bitch does rattle off what she knows, Nate's already been adopted so we gotta have a chance with that on our side."

"Jesse, watch your mouth," Ma scolded. She then kissed Nate's head. "The day Nathanial was adopted, Judge Prescott assured me that Jim Younger would sign away his rights to Nathanial." Ma blew out a deep sigh. "The judge checked the paperwork before coming to Gray Rock. He made a mistake. Jim Younger signed his rights over to the court, not to me. I was awarded the adoption."

"So Prescott wants us to go along with these visits 'cause he's convinced that the Fletchers are holdin' all the cards," Jesse said dryly, his tone completely flat. "Well, I won't allow it." There was a hard manner about Jesse that said he had readily stepped into Pa's boots and there would be no argument on the matter. He had made the decision, and that was final.

Numerous times, Nate had seen Ma and Pa talking things out. Both opinions were carefully weighed, but in the end, Pa was the head of the family so the choice and the responsibility fell to him.

Ma nodded, but not in an agreeable way, more that she understood Jesse's protectiveness. "I'm afraid if we do that, then the Fletchers will push for the trial date to be set sooner rather than later." Ma patted Jesse's hand as she gave Nate a squeeze with her other arm. "You boys and Elizabeth are the sun, moon, and stars to that man upstairs. If he starts to come out of this and then finds out that one of his sons has been taken away, it'll kill him."

What Ma had said made perfect sense to Nate, although he didn't want to have to spend a minute of time with the Fletchers. But for Pa, he could do just about anything. Pa needed more time for healing.

Jesse swallowed hard. That lump of pride that he'd forced down was surely turning his stomach. Nate felt a little sick himself. They had no other choice than to grant the judge's request and allow the Fletchers visitation.

"I hadn't looked at it that way," Jesse said sorrowfully. His shoulders drooped to a beaten measure. "Okay." He shook his head in disgust. "But I won't allow Nathanial to be alone with them. So if they want to get to know him, they'll do it with me right there, or they can shove off."

"Mama." Nate looked up into her tear-streaked face. "Do you think the Fletchers will win me?"

Ma slowly shook her head. "I have no idea. Unfortunately, Deloris Fletcher—" Ma choked up. "Shares the same blood as you. That might make a big difference in a court of law."

"So what?" Jesse stammered. Nate knew what he was thinking. None of the three of them carried the same blood, but that didn't mean they weren't family.

"In a court of law, that relationship, though unfamiliar to Nate, binds him and the Fletchers. The judge confided that he has contacted some lawyer friends to seek precedence in this matter, and there isn't any. Not one law or ruling on behalf of the adoptive parent nor the blood relation. But if I had to guess, I'd say any court would try to keep a child with kin when able." Ma cradled Nate tighter into her bosom and wept.

He bawled harder than he ever had.

CHAPTER 23

AT BREAKFAST, Jesse burned the eggs, stuck fast to the skillet. Ma whipped through the kitchen, fetching broth for Pa and coffee for Doc.

Nate had heard some strange mumblings coming from Ma and Pa's room last night when he was supposed to be sleeping. When Nate's cries had reached Jesse's room, he came and explained that Pa was delirious with fever. Nate knew enough to understand that wasn't good. He was happy this morning that Pa had made it through the night. But even so, he hadn't beaten this yet. Nate had no appetite for eggs or even his bacon, which he loved. He picked at the vittles on his plate.

"Why don't you go get some fresh air? Do your chores while you're out there." Jesse picked up Nate's untouched plate of food.

Nate shuffled toward the door.

A few minutes later, Jesse, with Elizabeth held in his arms, joined Nate on the porch. "Did you feed the horses?" he called.

"No, sir," Nate grumbled. He didn't feel like doing chores. He wanted to go back

NATHANIAL

to bed, get up on the other side, and this time, Pa would be up and around and just fine.

Jesse jerked a thumb toward the barn. "Go on."

Nate pushed up, thinking that Buck was probably anxious to see him. He took real good care of his horse. Maybe he would take Buck for a ride today.

He finished the barn work, gave Buck a pat on his soft nose, then returned to the yard with Jesse and Elizabeth, toddling through the grass. Jesse was a step off her pace, his arms outstretched in case he needed to save her from taking a tumble. Nate dropped onto all fours next to his sister. He barked and hopped along while gumming at her ankle, making her wobblier.

"Stop it. You'll make her fall." Jesse was a grump. He had been up all night the same as Nate, but Jesse wasn't getting any breaks and he wasn't used to taking care of Elizabeth, not this much anyway. That was typically Ma's work.

Nate kept up his torment, ignoring Jesse's scolding. Elizabeth plopped on her behind. Jesse was quiet. He hadn't even tried to catch her. Nate turned and looked in the direction that Jesse's eyes were narrowed on. A fancy black carriage creaked as it turned into the lane. There was no guesswork in figuring out who that was. Had Nate been smiling, it would have fallen right off his face. He got to his feet and stood tight next to Jesse as the solemn-looking carriage treaded closer. Nate suddenly felt cornered, as though he were under attack. His pulse quickened. He looked up at Jesse, who rested a hand on his shoulder.

"It'll be all right, partner." Jesse walked toward the gate. There was nothing casual or friendly in his mannerisms. His dislike of the Fletchers and this entire situation was plainly observable all over Jesse's scowling face.

Mr. Fletcher halted the carriage outside the picket gate. "Good day," he cheerily said and gave a wave as if they were all old friends.

Nate and Jesse looked at one another and likely were thinking the exact same thing. That Lem Fletcher was plumb out of his damn head.

Jesse didn't offer a welcome. Nate sat down next to Elizabeth. He wasn't willing to get anywhere near those two. Mr. Fletcher stepped down, then took his wife's delicately bent wrist and aided her out of the carriage. Her white polished shoes clicked on the step down, and to Nate, the noise was the same as nails on a chalkboard. He was annoyed, and they had only been there for about ten seconds. This was going to be a long couple hours. Hours delivered to him straight from hell.

Mrs. Fletcher held up the hem of her hooped yellow dress with all its puffy lace trim away from the dirt as she proceeded to the gate arm and arm with her immaculately polished husband, who wore a dark pinstriped suit and black tie. He was the picture of a sober man who lacked humor. Together, they gave off an air and appearance of having an agenda, as though they were going to some sort of fancy gathering, a party, or to meet the president. Pa and Jesse didn't even wear a tie to church half the time unless Ma made them.

Nate glanced at the upstairs window where Pa was fighting fever.

Ma stood in the window. Her lackluster gaze was on the Fletchers. She was a strong woman to deal with it all. Nate was a fighter too. He'd never been taught to give up. Besides, it just wasn't in his nature. Inwardly, he sneakily grinned. An idea was growing in his head. He wasn't defenseless against the Fletchers, and it was time he stopped acting like it. For his plan to work, though, he'd have to do something that he was a little bit scared to do. It required him to be alone with Mr. Fletcher.

NATHANIAL

Nate scooped up Elizabeth and bounced the two of them over next to Jesse. The Fletchers had stopped outside the gate where Jesse stood on this side of it. They appeared hesitant to pass through, and Jesse wasn't moving to open the entry for them. Hopefully, Nate's grand idea would work and he could rid his family of all this unpleasantness.

"Hi." His voice was too high. He was out of practice. Once upon a time, long ago, he was taught by his outlaw father to use his cute face and sweet little boy voice to swindle people. Nowadays, his ma and pa would blister his hide for even thinking about pulling those kinds of rotten stunts. On the other hand was Jesse, and as much as he would probably deny it, Nate was usually able to work him over until he caved in and gave Nate what he wanted. And honestly, it didn't ever take much convincing. So he might be able to get away with his plan and escape punishment. If he could chase off the Fletchers, then it was well worth the risk of Jesse tanning his hide.

This time it was the Fletchers who stared at one another as if Nate had gone crazy. And it was true he wasn't acting like himself. But he needed to convince them that he was perfectly content.

"I have a horse." He forced a big smile. He loved Buck. In no way did Nate have the least little desire to tell these two about Buck, but he was counting on his plan to work. So along with his toothy grin, he ever so sweetly batted his long lashes.

"Isn't that nice?" Mrs. Fletcher tilted her head, taking in the sight of Nate's fluttery baby blues.

Mr. Fletcher was not smiling like his stupid wife. His brow was set in a deep furrow. Nate needed to not lay it on so thick. He handed his sister to Jesse, who also stared at Nate as if in agreement with the Fletchers that he had lost his mind. Jesse, no doubt, was wondering what in the hell Nate was up to. But he stayed quiet and likely was waiting to see how this trickery played out.

"His name is Buck. He's the best horse ever." Nate went on in a singsong voice. "I was gonna take him for a ride today." Nate leaned against Jesse for the strength he needed to say what he had to next. "Why don't ya go with me? You could ride Pa's horse, Sugar."

"What?" Jesse coughed a few times to cover his snicker.

Pa had called his horse every name but Sugar. That big bay could be quite spirited when it took a notion to be. He had never sent Pa sailing off his back, but a man with fewer horse skills could easily be dropped on his head.

Jesse cleared his throat and regained control. He patted Nate's shoulder in mock sympathy. He likely had a good idea of what he was scheming. Not that Nate wanted Fletcher to get hurt, because he didn't. He just wanted the man to see that, like that horse, Nate required a certain someone who knew how to handle him.

"I told ya, kid. I will be supervising these visits, and I aim to do just that." The firmness in Jesse's voice was put on, but the Fletchers didn't hear it.

Mr. Fletcher's face smoothed as the realization of what Nate asked sank into his brain. They would be alone, just the two of them—well, three if his wife went riding with them. But Nate didn't believe for a minute that she would sit astride a horse, maybe not even sidesaddle. She was too used to having a fancy carriage under her seat.

"I have work around here to do. I can't be gallivantin' to wherever." It was Jesse's way of asking Nate where he planned on taking Fletcher. With that knowledge, he would piece together more of the plan.

"But Jumping Fish Canyon is so pretty this time of year. I could pick Ma some flowers." Nate thrust out a lip, faking a big pout.

Jesse nodded. He remained quiet, so it might have looked to the others that he was thinking it over.

NATHANIAL

Nate and Jesse both knew that Jumping Fish Canyon was one rough spot to take a horse. The rabbit path to get there formed a maze around tree clusters, boulders, and a scattering of fields and much smaller canyons. It would be easy for a man unfamiliar with the area to get lost. Then the trail through the mouth wasn't too bad, a little rocky, but once inside the boxy walls, that was another story. Three of the four sides were sheer cliffs that stood close to two hundred feet high. The remaining side was sloped at a rough, steep angle, and what made it worse was it was shale. The flimsy, unreliable mineral could give way under any amount of weight.

It wasn't hard to figure out what Jesse was pondering. On a dare a few months back, while Nate had been fishing in the canyon with his buddies, he had risked the fall while riding Buck and made it to the top. It was on the way down that Buck had faltered, rocks sliding out from under them, and Buck's hindquarters sank. Nate went tumbling, and when he finally stopped rolling and coughed all the dust out of his lungs, he painfully found out that he could hardly stand on his one leg. Worse than that, Buck had hurt his leg and was limping.

As soon as Nate got home and Pa took one hard look at them, somehow he knew. Nate got his ass wailed that day. Jesse had been mad too. But if Nate could slip out over the rim of that cliff, it would likely take Fletcher all day to find his way back to the ranch. A sneaky little giggle slipped out as he pictured Fletcher wandering around until dark.

"Not Jumping Fish Canyon. Maybe Bear Meadow," Jesse said in with an air of uncertainty, which wasn't fake. Bear Meadow was beyond Jumping Fish Canyon, so Nate could still lose Fletcher, but the risk of the fall wasn't there.

"We should stay close," Fletcher said, then added, "I have no ill intentions. I will agree to any terms you wish to set."

Nate was taken aback. There was a ring of oath-giving in the man's voice. It honestly made Nate believe him.

What was he thinking? He couldn't trust that man. Fletcher was the meanie who was trying to take him away.

Deloris Fletcher cackled. "Dearest, what are you doing?" She lightly touched her man's arm. "Since when do you ask permission or compromise? We both know Nathanial rightfully belongs to us. I find this entire visitation setup highly annoying. You shouldn't have had the judge suspend the trial. The sooner we return to New York, the better."

"You bitch!" Nate's mean temper exploded. Hell would freeze over before he went anywhere with them.

Jesse slapped a hand over Nate's mouth. Deloris Fletcher gasped. Her eyes were stretched unbelievingly wide. Jesse didn't offer an apology, nor did he make Nate give one. He did keep his hand covering Nate's feisty tongue.

"Darling, we spoke about this," Lem Fletcher calmly said as he fanned the air with his palm for a few seconds to help his wife breathe.

"Hello." Marshal Huckabee trotted his horse up to the hitch rail where he stepped down. He nodded at the Fletchers, then at Jesse. "How's Nolan?"

"Last I looked in on him, his fever was awful high. He didn't know who he was or where he was at." The words caught in Jesse's throat, choking him up.

Huckabee took a deep breath. He had obviously been hoping for some uplifting news. That Pa was getting better, not worse. "Judge Prescott took my testimony this morning. He needs to hear your side of what happened when you brought those prisoners in since it was just you. I'll watch things here if you wanna ride into town now and be done with it."

"Sounds good." Jesse handed Elizabeth to Huckabee, then headed for the corral to fetch his horse.

"Jesse," Nate called. "What about that ride?" He nodded toward Fletcher.

"No, not now, partner. I got something important that needs taken care of. Maybe another time." Jesse was no longer pretending to be serious. He meant what he said, and Nate knew the difference by the sharp tone. It seemed that Jesse could only focus on one big thing, and although he would have been keeping an eye on Nate at a fair distance, it appeared that space had grown too far when Jesse's duties as deputy took him off the ranch and into town. He hustled his horse into the barn where his saddle was stored.

The rest of them headed into the house. Nate watched at the window and waited until Jesse was gone. He turned to the marshal who was talking to Doc. Fletcher had his ear turned and appeared to be listening but kept quiet. Mrs. Fletcher was dreamily watching Elizabeth rolling around the floor, biting on Ticklebug.

"Marshal Huckabee." Nate interrupted, which probably wasn't the best way to get what he wanted, but he was growing impatient. Jesse should have just given Nate permission, and it sort of irked him that he hadn't.

Huckabee looked down at Nate. "What is it?"

Nate squirmed a little. He was taught not to tell lies. But if this worked to get rid of the Fletchers, everyone would be happier, including Pa's best friend.

"Right before you got here, Jesse said me and Mr. Fletcher could go for a ride." Nate uneasily shifted. Lawmen had an uncanny way of knowing when someone was lying, or at least Pa seemed to have that gift.

Nate couldn't keep his gaze on Huckabee. He looked over at the Fletchers. The man was eyeballing him suspiciously. He was aware of Nate's fib but said nothing to contradict it. Mrs. Fletcher was grinning proudly as if they had won Nate over and he was now theirs. Dumb broad.

"He did?" Huckabee scratched his chin. "I heard him tellin' ya no."

"He meant no, he couldn't go. I wanted Jesse to go with us."

Huckabee didn't seem to know what to think. Nate didn't like the Fletchers, Huckabee knew, and neither did Jesse. So he was probably asking himself why Nate would want to go alone for a ride with the man they all considered the enemy. "Where'd he say you could go?"

"Bear Meadow." Nate took Jesse's earlier suggestion.

He and the marshal didn't have the same internal dialog that Nate and Jesse had. He and Pa had taken Huckabee and his son fishing in the creek inside Jumping Fish Canyon, so he knew exactly what lay within those four stone walls. It wasn't flowers like Nate had hinted earlier when trying to convince Jesse to let him take Mr. Fletcher there. Plus, Nate doubted that the marshal would allow him to play such a trick. Pa wouldn't have liked it either, but none of that was going to stop Nate. He'd made up his mind. He would win this battle with the Fletchers, and to do that, he needed to play by his own rules.

"We should be back by lunch," Nate added with a touch of honey on his voice. He would worry about facing Jesse later.

Fletcher must not have thought of that since he hadn't spoken up to thwart Nate's plan. Fletcher slid to the edge of his chair, waiting to hear whatever Huckabee said. His eager posture sort of had Nate thinking that maybe he wasn't the only one pulling a shenanigan. Maybe that Fletcher fella was up to something. Nate suddenly wasn't so sure he wanted the marshal's permission. Maybe him going off alone with Mr. Fletcher wasn't so smart. Perhaps Jesse had been right, and Nate should just stay at home.

"All right. If you're sure you want to go." The marshal must have sensed Nate's uneasiness.

In his lifetime, Nate had dealt with much worse than Fletcher. That thought gave him the kick in the butt to get going. He was wasting time, time that could be used in driving the Fletchers away. Mr. Fletcher hadn't shown himself to be hateful like some of the men from Nate's past, so he wasn't worried about Fletcher hurting him. But Nate's gut was tight anyway.

When he pulled the bay out of the stall by his lead rope, the big horse snorted. Somehow Nate just knew Pa's horse was feeling contrary. "I ain't strong enough to lift the saddle on his back. You'll have to do that and my horse too."

"Oh." Fletcher looked baffled as if he'd never lifted a finger toward a menial chore in his life.

Nate pointed to where the saddles were kept. Fifteen minutes later, which felt like an hour, he had talked Fletcher step by step through saddling both animals. They were finally ready to go. Nate led Buck outside the barn. Fletcher followed with the bay.

"Why did you lie to the marshal?" Fletcher eyed him curiously.

"Because I wanted to ride my horse. I ain't allowed to go too far without havin' someone with me. You know, to protect me from all those dangers out there like grizzly bears, cougars, and Indians or maybe even bandits. You brought a gun, didn't ya?" Every word Nate had said was horseshit, but he'd put a good spin on the hum of it so it sounded quite believable to him.

Fletcher shrewdly eyeballed him. Likely, he was trying to figure out if Nate was telling the truth or not. Why not confuse the man a little more?

"A small white lie will never hurt anyone." Nate winked at Fletcher. "Don't tell Ma or Jesse, but I lie all the time. I think it's in my blood. You know I was born to an outlaw." That was information Fletcher already knew, but Nate was doing his best to make himself sound as bad as possible. Maybe if he seemed like a huge headache, then the Fletchers would back out of the trial.

"Is that so?" Fletcher said without humor. "I believe you know exactly what you're saying, right down to the very point of asking if I would like to take a ride with you. I own gaming horses and hunt for sport. I can ride." The pompous ass was too sure of himself as he stepped up and swung a leg over the bay.

And cantankerous that horse showed himself to be. He arched his back and bucked a few short hops. Fletcher flew up into the air, then hit the dirt on his back. Dust puffed up in his face.

Nate snickered. "I reckon Sugar"—Nate drew out the word—"ain't no gamin' horse."

"Isn't a gaming horse," Fletcher snapped.

Nate rolled his eyes, then climbed up Buck's tail as he did most times to mount his horse.

Fletcher got up, dusting off his slacks, then once again stepped up into the saddle.

They rode out of the ranch yard to the south. The fresh air brushing Nate's face as Buck trotted did feel good. The mustang's ears were up, and he flicked his tail. He seemed eager to go.

Nate patted Buck's neck. "You wanna fly, don't ya?" Nate wasn't really asking. He also had that urge to soar over the land, but they couldn't. Not with Fetcher this close to home. Nate didn't want to lose him so soon, or Fletcher would just turn around and find his way back to the ranch. So Buck would have to wait for his chance to run.

They'd gone three, four miles when Fletcher suddenly spoke. "I understand that you like to read."

Nate shrugged and kept his eyes on the trail ahead of them.

"Deloris and I have a library in our home. Over four hundred titles."

Nate turned and stared. There probably weren't that many books in all of Gray Rock. "Have you read them all?"

"No, not all of them. A good many, I have."

They rode a few minutes in silence.

"Do you like school?" Fletcher looked over at Nate.

NATHANIAL

"Sometimes. Mostly, I think it's boring." Nate didn't say it, but usually, the work was too easy. He liked a challenge.

"We spoke to your teacher, Mrs. McKay. She said you're a straight-A student. Gifted is what she called you."

"Huh?" Nate wrinkled up his nose. Was he in trouble for something he didn't know about? And why the hell had his teacher said a word to those people about him? She shouldn't have done that, not without Ma and Pa's permission, which they probably would not have given.

Fletcher chuckled. "Gifted just means that you're very smart. Did you ever think about someday attending a university?"

"No," Nate said.

Ma and Pa could never afford that. Plus, Nate wanted to be the next sheriff of Gray Rock, and he didn't have to go away to a big, fancy school to learn that. He was being taught by Pa and Jesse every day. Nate was planning on being an even better lawman than Pa.

"With the right resources—"

Nate jerked up on the reins, abruptly cutting off Fletcher's words as he then halted the bay. So that was it. Fletcher's hidden agenda. He aimed to buy Nate, win him over with the expensive things that Ma and Pa could only ever dream of giving their kids. Well, this ploy would not work on Nate.

"I ain't impressed by money." Nate knew what it was like to be dirt poor, and he was grateful for what he had now, which was a loving family. That was much better than anything money could buy him. He was happy until this trial business started. He didn't need anything more than was given to him under Ma and Pa's roof.

Fletcher stiffened. "I meant no insult to Mr. and Mrs. Crosson."

Nate hadn't mentioned his folks. This fella was good at reading him. Nate didn't like that.

"Don't you mean my father and mother?" he corrected, barely restraining his temper. What he wanted to say in the worst way was that Mr. Lem Fletcher could go bunk with the devil. Instead, Nate nudged Buck and chose to ignore the fact that Fletcher was riding next to him.

Nate turned onto the trail into Jumping Fish Canyon. From that point, they had to ride with Nate leading and Fletcher a horse length behind. The path had narrowed, and Nate was glad for the little solitude. In a half mile, they would be at the small mouth of Jumping Fish Canyon. The trail inside was three-quarters of a mile in length and dotted with sage. Here and there, rocks had crumbled down off the sides, narrowing the trail more. Buck had been on this deer path quite a few times, so his feet were sound. The bay too was familiar with his rough surroundings and didn't balk at the long cattle shoot-like line ahead of them. Had Fletcher been riding a timid horse, this trail wouldn't have been so easily navigated. Nate should have given him Ma's horse.

Inside the belly of the canyon, the creek trickled on their right along the western wall. A beaver slapped its tail, warning them not to come closer. Nate kept Buck walking straight ahead. It was three miles, if not more, to cross to the other side where the slope stood that Nate had ridden up only once.

"This trail doesn't seem to lead anywhere," Fletcher remarked as he twisted in the saddle, looking every which way. "Are you sure this is the canyon? I don't see any flowers. You said—"

Fletcher's head snapped around. His face hardened, and the veins on either side of his neck popped out. They were thirty feet from the cliff that Nate was about to chance. It must have dawned on Fletcher what Nate had been planning.

His eyes narrowed. "You wouldn't dare."

NATHANIAL

Whether the man was asking about Nate risking his neck to climb that cliff or wondering if Nate was about to leave him, the answer to both was yes.

"Enjoy the ride back if ya can find your way." Nate hammered his boot heels into Buck's sides.

His horse leaped forward and shot off at a run straight at that cliff. Buck didn't hesitate. His hooves clinked on the rocks, and a few times, his back end dipped when stones slid under his feet. His neck was stretching and he snorted to breathe as they climbed higher up the rocky wall. There were grooves and some sunken pockets where Buck could have broken a leg had he stepped there. Nate didn't remember it being so rough the last time. Buck hopped at the sound of crunching rocks, which sent them stumbling sideways. Nate's grip on the reins tightened, along with all his insides.

From below, a cry arose. "Hang on!"

As if Nate needed to be told. Buck had regained his footing and was steadily climbing toward the rim. Nate couldn't seem to take a breath. One of Buck's front hooves, then the other struck the crest. Buck's powerful shoulders pulled while his back end scrambled for a toehold. Nate was sure his heart was going to give out. Then Buck lurched forward, and they were safely standing on the rim.

Nate looked down. Buck had been lucky to make that steep climb. Nate rubbed his head. He could've killed his best friend. He should've listened to Jesse. What he'd done was stupid. He'd been so blinded by the satisfying thought of Fletcher having to find his way six miles back to the ranch that he hadn't thought too much about the consequences if his plan went wrong.

"Sorry, boy." Nate patted Buck's neck.

"Are you okay?" Fletcher had his hands cupped around his mouth, shouting. Why was he concerned? He hadn't turned his back and gone as Nate suspected he would. Nate had meant to be mean to him. He'd left him.

He put up a hand, signaling that he was fine.

"I'll see you at the ranch," Fletcher hollered up. He didn't even sound mad. Nate couldn't believe it.

Fletcher turned the bay, and Nate could tell by the way the horse was moving that Fletcher had given him his head. Nate had been outsmarted. Fletcher knew enough about horses that he was aware that the bay would lead him back to the barn.

Nate nudged Buck. He and Fletcher would probably get to the ranch about the same time. The trail Nate had to take was a mile or two longer, but Fletcher likely would be moving at a slower pace since he wasn't all that familiar with the area. Maybe then, if Jesse was home, he'd think they had just gone for a nice ride.

No way would Jesse believe that, and Nate wouldn't dare lie to him. He was in big trouble.

It was after lunch when Nate rode into the yard. He didn't see the bay. Was Fletcher there? The appaloosa was in the corral, along with the marshal's horse. Doc's buggy was still there and the Fletchers' carriage. Was Pa's horse in the barn? Had Fletcher told Jesse what Nate pulled? If so, he was done for.

"Nathanial!"

Nate jerked on the reins, spinning Buck.

Fletcher loped the bay out from among the trees toward him. Under his full black mustache, the man was actually grinning. "I'm glad to see you made it back in one piece."

Nate raised a brow. "Why aren't you mad? You know I tried to get you lost."

"Mrs. Fletcher and I had a son. He liked to play tricks. Harmless things like jumping out from behind a chair to scare you. Nothing as serious as what you did today. You could have been hurt. I can't condone that."

NATHANIAL

"Condone? Why don't you use words that I can understand?" Nate smarted off, but he was rolling around in his head what Fletcher had said—that they'd had a son.

"Let's just forget it," Fletcher said dryly.

"What happened to your son?" Nate might have been nosy, but Fletcher had brought it up.

Was he to be the replacement? He suddenly felt sick in his stomach. Was that the reason they'd come hunting him? It wasn't that they cared about him. They were thinking of themselves.

Fletcher was quiet for a long minute. "Ashton drowned. He fell into the Hudson River. I jumped in, but the current was swift and when I got to him, it was too late."

Nate understood loss and felt bad for the Fletchers. "I'm sorry," he said and meant it.

"It's okay. I've done my grieving. But Deloris has never been able to fully let go of her sadness, has had a broken heart ever since. And it's been nearly two years."

In silence, they rode into the yard side by side. Nate didn't see Jesse anywhere but expected to catch the devil once he did. Nate helped Fletcher store the tack. Then he rubbed down the horses before leading them to the corral. It wasn't until he turned toward the house that he caught sight of Jesse leaning against a porch post, watching him. Jesse's mouth was set in a thin line, and his arms were folded tightly across his chest. Nate gulped.

Mrs. Fletcher stood from the porch swing with a drink in her hand. "Did you have a nice ride?"

"It was eye-opening," Fletcher coolly remarked as he and Nate walked toward the house.

Jesse's face was growing redder. He was stewing and obviously had been for a while. If Fletcher was worried about anything Jesse might say, it wasn't showing. Nate was wishing for a hole to curl up in. His ears were about to get the worst tongue-lashing ever.

They had just reached the gate when Jesse stomped down the steps, pointing his finger at Nate. "Boy, I told ya to stay put, and you run off."

"He was with me," Fletcher interjected. "I am his uncle, whether you want to recognize that fact or not. The child is fine. I did him no harm, nor would I."

"Shut up!" Jesse snapped.

Fletcher took a step back. His missus froze midstep across the porch.

Nate cringed. Jesse was really pissed, madder than Nate had ever seen him.

"I'm guessin' by the lather on that horse when you rode in that you climbed the cliff at Jumping Fish Canyon." Jesse wasn't asking.

Nate stayed quiet. His gaze fell on his boot toes.

"Did you not hear me when I told ya no?"

Nate was sure everyone within the territory could, at the moment, hear Jesse.

He grabbed Nate by the arm. "Answer me, boy."

"Yes, sir." Nate sniffled.

Never would he have guessed Jesse would get so riled up about this. Yeah, Nate had taken a stupid risk. He had learned his lesson when he thought of Buck possibly getting hurt or worse. He wouldn't ever do that again. Everyone knew how much he loved Buck.

"You could have been killed." Jesse was seething.

"But he wasn't." Fletcher dared to timidly speak.

"Stay out of this." Jesse damn near snarled at him. Fletcher's face paled. Jesse's focus turned back to Nate. "I reckon you know what's coming to ya. Go on to the barn."

Nate burst out crying.

NATHANIAL

"What are you planning to do to him?" Fletcher stepped forward and pushed Nate behind him, placing himself smack dab in front of Jesse, which wasn't a good place to be because Jesse was boiling.

"I don't see that it's any of your business. But I'm gonna cut a switch off that bush and whip his bottom with it." Jesse shouldered past Fletcher as he pulled his knife and grabbed a long, wispy branch.

Fletcher turned on his heel. "I will not allow you to beat on him with a stick."

Jesse shoved his knife into its sheath on his belt. The branch was in his hand. Nate was rooted in place, not knowing what was going to happen between those two. Why would Fletcher stick up for him? On top of that, Jesse had only ever given Nate a hard, quick swat on the bottom now and then when he needed straightening out. He had never actually given him a real licking.

"Mister, I ain't gonna beat on him. But he will learn a lesson so the next time I tell him to stay on this ranch, he'll listen." Jesse took hold of Nate's arm, marching toward the barn.

Fletcher was on Jesse's heels, which was only severing to irritate Jesse more because the hand holding the switch balled into a fist, and his grip had tightened to the point that he was sort of pinching Nate's arm.

"Let go of him." Fletcher caught hold of Jesse's shoulder and spun him. "I won't let you hit him."

Jesse looked as if he was going to punch Fletcher. What stopped him, God only knew. "The way I see it, the boy is getting off easy. Had it been his pa who caught him, his ass would be feelin' the sting of a leather belt instead of a hickory switch."

"This is barbaric. I'm sure there is another way to punish the child. We never spanked our son, not once." Fletcher was now red-faced.

His wife hurried across the yard in a full-out twitter. Her arms were waving, and there were tears in her eyes. She was chirping funny, "Oh my," noises.

"Ain't no punishment better that I can think of. He'll think twice next time." Jesse shook the branch in his hand and seemed to overlook the fact that Fletcher had just admitted to once having a child. "Now I'm done talkin' about this. So one of two things needs to happen. You either get off my back so I can tend to this ugly business, or you step up here and try and stop me. Then I'm gonna flatten ya into the ground, and after that, Nate will get his ass whooped."

"I can't match your brute strength," Fletcher hissed. "But I can and will stop this from ever happening again." There was a confidence in his tone that spoke of always getting his way. It scared Nate.

"What do you mean by that?" Jesse's eyes narrowed.

"Judge Parker is due in on the stage tomorrow. I'm going to revoke my agreement to suspend the trial. The sooner we take Nathanial out of this setting, the better."

"Judge Parker?" Jesse said out loud to no one.

Nate was also stunned. Move up the trial? This day had gone all wrong. Nate had hoped to push the Fletchers away. Instead, it all worked out that he had indeed pulled them closer. This was awful. Damn bad luck.

"Did you really think I wouldn't protest if Prescott was the presiding judge?" Fletcher grinned.

Jesse boldly stepped up close, towering over Fletcher by a head and a half. His jaw was tight, and his nostrils flared. Jesse wasn't a man to take being pushed in any way.

"Git off this ranch and don't come back."

Both the Fletchers turned with their noses high and marched off toward their carriage. Lem Fletcher cracked leather to the buggy horse, and they were gone. Dust hung in the air where the wheels had spun through the dirt.

NATHANIAL

Nate threw himself around Jesse's waist. He didn't have to say it. Jesse knew Nate was afraid of being ripped away.

Jesse peeled him off. "I am upset with you."

Nate reckoned he wasn't getting out of trouble. Jesse led him into the barn where Nate was bent over Jesse's knee. After three, four smart licks, with Nate bawling his head off, Jesse stood him on his feet. Nate ran off and climbed the ladder into the loft. Jesse left the barn, slamming the door behind him.

CHAPTER 24

Jesse marched toward the corral where his horse was drinking from the water trough. He opened the gate, then lifted his bridle off a fence post where he'd hung it earlier.

He patted the appaloosa's nose. "It's about time I give ya a name." The gelding nudged his shoulder as though agreeing.

"How about Freckles?" He rubbed his hand along the horse's shoulder. It was a silly, fun name that made him smile, and he needed that.

Partner had gotten himself in trouble, and as much as Jesse had hated to do it, the boy needed to be taught a lesson, so he didn't feel bad about that. What had him sort of off balance was that Fletcher had mentioned a son. Nathanial had told Jesse every detail about his encounters with the couple while in Birch Creek. No kid was mentioned or sighted there in Gray Rock. It could be he was back east with a nanny. When the Fletchers had left New York, they wouldn't have had any idea how long it would take them to find the person they were searching for.

According to the information the sheriff had collected

from his different run-ins with the couple in Birch Creek, they had been slowly working their way west, following tidbits of information about Nate's past fed to them by a person in one town or another. That amount of time added up fast from weeks to months and months. Why not bring their child instead of leaving him behind for the better part of a year or more? He had an idea about that, and there were two people he needed to speak to.

He crossed the bridge into Gray Rock. The busyness of people walking along the boardwalk, in and out of shops, and wagons and horses being steered through the street normally brought about a sense of community and well-being. Today, it all seemed like a headache, one he didn't want to deal with on top of everything else. He would because it was his job, but he hoped there was no pressing trouble in town that would distract from the real reason he was there.

He pushed down his hat, and with any luck, no one would make eye contact. Every time he had come to town, it seemed like a thousand people would ask how Sheriff Crosson was doing. Jesse understood the concern, but after so many times, he was tired of repeating that the sheriff was no better off, barely hanging on.

Prescott and Mr. Graham, the Crossons' attorney, stepped out of Graham's office. As luck would have it, those were the two he'd wanted to talk with, and they were together. All the better. This might go faster. Jesse pulled up reins in front of them.

"I talked to Doc earlier, but how's Kate holding up?" Prescott reached across the rail and rubbed Freckles' jaw.

"She's tired, don't sleep hardly at all, and is snappish with everyone. I can't say that any of us are doing all that well." He was honest.

"If there is anything more I can do…" Prescott offered. He was working with Mr. Graham, preparing a defense, and he held the midnight post, relieving either Huckabee or Big John at the jailhouse, giving one or the other a breather from guarding the prisoners. Jesse couldn't ask any more of him.

"Do either of you know anything about the Fletchers having a son?"

Graham looked over at Prescott. Obviously, that was news to him.

Prescott touched at his mustache. "I was in the city when the accident happened. It hit the front pages of every paper. Later, I'd heard rumors that his wife had fallen into a deep depression. That she'd tried to take her own life."

"Then she comes huntin' for a long-lost nephew," Jesse said without humor.

"It appears that would be some of the reason. Don't forget she also lost a sister. Those are two big losses," Prescott said.

"Did any of those papers run a picture of the boy?" Graham faced the judge.

Prescott thought for a minute, then slowly began to nod until his head bobbed with vigor. "His hair was white, and he had big blue eyes. I'm sure of it."

"Partner," Jesse said aloud but was talking to himself. It was a dead-ringer description of Nathanial.

"Excuse me, gentlemen." The man dressed in the coat with tails was oddly short. His arms had the same stubby stature, but his hands were huge. He thrust one toward Prescott, who accepted and firmly shook.

"Might I have a word with you, Judge? And if this is Mr. Graham, counsel for the Crossons, he should be present too."

Jesse began to step down.

"Your services will not be required, Deputy." Whoever that was, he turned his back, heading for the door. Was that his way of telling Jesse he wasn't welcome to join the meeting?

He stepped onto the boardwalk. "Wait just a minute. Who the hell do you think you are?" No one would exclude him, and

NATHANIAL

why would they? The Crossons were Jesse's family. Everyone knew it. So if the conversation about to take place was about them, he had every right to be there.

"I'm Judge Parker," the man said with a smirk on his face. "I know exactly who you are, Deputy Adams, and as far as I'm concerned, you have no business in this meeting. Let's be honest. You may live with the Crossons, but you're not kin. Therefore, I have nothing to discuss with you, only those family members directly involved." He snapped around and disappeared inside with Graham following.

Jesse's fists balled at his sides. God, he wanted to punch that man's head off. Not family, not directly involved? The wee man was wrong. He didn't know much about Jesse, other than he wore a badge. He spit in the dirt.

Prescott put up a hand. "Wait here." The door clicked shut behind him.

Jesse paced the boardwalk, feeling like a caged animal. What was being said in there? It wasn't like Graham and Prescott wouldn't tell him. He was anxious to know, to have this trial business over. And what they'd found out about the Fletchers possibly looking at Nate as a replacement child certainly had to help their case.

Jesse had to do something other than rack his brain. He was starting to get a goldarn headache. Across the street, Orris was killing the tune he was attempting to play, as always. It was nice that some things never changed. Although, not so pleasant on the ears.

Jesse crossed the street. Inside were but a few cowboys playing cards and drinking beer. They gave him a friendly nod as he walked toward the bar.

"Pete, give me a beer."

He filled a mug, then placed it in front of Jesse, clearing his throat.

Jesse dug a coin out of his pocket and dropped it on the bar top.

Pete picked up the money. "Shorty was in here earlier. I'm sorry to hear the wedding's off."

Jesse choked on his swallow, slamming down his beer, sloshing liquid out of the top and all over his hand and the counter. "What did you say?"

Pete took a step back. He was a barrel-chested, surly man who wasn't prone to be afraid of anyone. "I'm just repeatin' what I was told. If you got a problem with that, go talk to Shorty."

Jesse would do just that. He swallowed what remained of his beer, then marched outside. He was swinging a leg over his saddle when the door to the law office whisked open. Parker came out first and passed by Jesse without a glance. The drawn faces of the other two men were glum. Whatever Parker said, it hadn't been good news

Prescott handed three or four folded pieces of paper to Jesse. Lem Fletcher had really done it. Not that Jesse had doubted him, but he'd almost forgotten the threat. Two days. It was all they had. The trial would start on Thursday. So soon. Jesse shoved the documents at Prescott.

"The only reason we're getting a couple days' notice is that Parker likes an audience. He's giving folks time to come into town. The bigger the crowd, the more of a show he'll put on." Prescott shook his head. "I've never liked him."

Jesse grinned.

"There's something else," Graham said. "I will talk to Mrs. Crosson directly, but I'll tell you now." He lingered a moment. "Parker said he will throw out any testimony about the length of time it took the Fletchers to find Nathanial. He doesn't believe that's relevant. He seemed more concerned about whether or not the Fletchers could prove kinship through blood ties. His belief is that eventually, the courts will and should consider that first and foremost in matters such as these."

"And I wouldn't put it past that pompous ass to set the precedence just to elevate himself." Prescott glared toward the hotel entrance where Parker had gone inside.

Jesse turned his horse. There was nothing he could say. Life seemed to be crashing down around his family. For them, he would never tire, never give up. Each day, as he had been doing, he would give his very best to support those he cared about by doing whatever he could and then some. There was something else he had to deal with too.

CHAPTER 25

JESSE TIED HIS HORSE AT THE HITCH RAIL, walked up the porch steps, then knocked. Mrs. Short opened the door. Of course, she didn't smile.

"I'd like to talk to Kristy. She home?"

Mrs. Short glanced over her shoulder as if contemplating whether her daughter should be summoned or not. This was lighting a fuse in Jesse.

"I'll get her." She shut the door.

He was never not welcomed inside, even by her. Something had definitely changed where he was concerned. Surely, Pete had been wrong.

For the second time, the door popped open.

Kristy's eyes instantly glistened. "Hello, Jesse." She didn't take a step toward him and had kept the screen door closed.

The greeting was too formal, completely unlike her. She usually gave him a big hug and kiss if her ma wasn't in sight.

He pointed to the porch swing. "Can we talk?"

She hesitated, then walked out and sat stiffly at one end of the swing. He wasn't typically nervous around her, but he was sweating and his heart was pounding.

NATHANIAL

"I'm sorry I haven't been around much. With the sheriff down and Nate's trial looming, I ain't had any time for me, for us. It won't always be that way." He wanted her to understand that he hadn't forgotten her. It wasn't as though he was ignoring her on purpose. She had been there when the sheriff was gunned down. She should have realized Jesse's responsibilities had grown a hundredfold.

As she sat there staring at the pocket on her apron and the more he thought about it, it sort of irked him. It wasn't like he was being selfish.

"I'm not mad," she finally said.

The house door opened. "Kristy, I could use your help in the kitchen." Mrs. Short didn't even glance at Jesse, but certainly, he was the reason she was out there making her presence known.

Kristy began to rise.

Jesse caught her by the wrist, noticing for the first time his ring wasn't on her finger. "Where's your ring? I expect you to wear it. We're engaged, and people should be aware."

"Take your hands off my daughter," Mrs. Short boomed.

"Stay out of this," he bit back.

She huffed inside, slamming the door.

"I took it off. I was washing dishes," Kristy said, unable to meet his gaze.

"Well, you ain't washin' dishes now. So it should be on your finger." He was fighting down his temper. "You got something you'd like to tell me? 'Cause I heard a rumor."

She raised her head. "Jesse, I can smell beer on you. Let's not discuss this now." She pulled out of his grip, heading for the door.

"Can't a man have a drink? Or has your ma brainwashed ya into believin' a man shouldn't be allowed to wet his dry throat now and then or that it's bad or will hurt you in some way?"

Jesse was now talking about their relationship. That he wasn't the one for Mrs. Short's daughter.

Shorty stormed out the door, his face red, the missus on his heels.

Jesse ignored them for the moment, facing Kristy. "I spilled beer on my sleeve. That's why you can smell it."

Shorty shoved himself between Jesse and his daughter. He pointed a finger in his face. "Git off my ranch."

The two women were huddled in the corner nearest the door.

Jesse could almost hear the words *I told you so* rolling in the mind of the cattleman's wife, and he was sure Kristy would hear just that once he left.

"What did I do? At least tell me that." He looked Shorty squarely in the face.

"I've changed my mind," Shorty said. "I'm inclined to agree with my wife. I don't want my daughter marryin' a lawman. No one can stop talkin' about Sheriff Crosson and poor Kate. I don't want to see my daughter in those shoes."

"Kristy." Jesse stared longingly at her. His heart was breaking. Him being a deputy and the risks that came with it weren't a surprise to them. This was nothing new. All but the missus, they had accepted it before.

"I could never dig a bullet out of you the same as I did Sheriff Crosson. I couldn't let on then, but that about killed me. I'm not strong enough to be your wife." She paused. "Only one other time have I been forced to treat a bullet wound, and that was when Tipsy, that outlaw, shot you and Ma and me patched you up." She shook her head. "That ain't the life I want."

He was stunned, struck utterly dumb. It was the opposite attitude shown by her just a week ago at the picnic. Her ma must have been working on her since returning, playing on those emotions Kristy was having after the whole ordeal of being kidnapped and seeing men shot and killed.

"Daughter, go get the ring." Mrs. Short gently nudged Kristy toward the door. She disappeared inside.

"Happy with yourself?" He stared at Mrs. Short, who said nothing.

He believed that some of what Kristy had said was her true feelings. As much as they loved one another, it might kill her to see him in the same shape the sheriff was in, but no one could see the future to know for sure that would ever happen to him. God willing, it wouldn't.

"Why don't you let Kristy make her own decisions? She's old enough. Instead, you baby her. She's stronger than she thinks, but you'll never let her believe that." Jesse could feel heat rising in his face.

Shorty shoved him toward the stairs. "I think it's time for you to leave."

Jesse towered over Shorty. He'd always been respectful to Kristy's folks, and he was trying his best to do that now and to understand their point of view, but he didn't. They had insulted him and his badge, and dammit, he'd been pushed too far. He had saved their daughters, brought them home safe. Where was the thank-you? That wasn't why he did it, but they should recognize what he and the sheriff and the marshal had done, the risk they had taken.

It hit Jesse then. That was exactly what they did recognize. That it could have been him, not the sheriff. Or both of them. He could be dead. Even so, Jesse wasn't about to let fear rule his life, and he was too riled not to put Shorty in his place.

"Shorty, don't ever make the mistake of thinkin' I'm afraid of you or any other man. 'Cause it just ain't true. And if the sheriff dies, I'll pin on that badge and keep things going just as he would have wanted, which includes protecting you and your family."

He turned and started down the steps toward his horse.

"Jesse." Kristy's soft voice called him back. She hustled down the stairs, her palm out flat, arm extended toward him. The sun glistened off the opal. Her dark hair lifted from her shoulders in the breeze. He couldn't help but think her beautiful, even if her eyes were red.

"Don't do this. Please." A man would only beg for something he truly wanted, and he wasn't above that.

Tears streaked down her face. "I love you." She took his hand, placing the ring gently in his fingers. Then she turned and raced into the house, her sobs echoing behind her.

He blinked back the wetness in his eyes. One glance at Shorty and his gaze darted another direction. Silently, both he and the missus filed inside. Jesse was left standing with a ring in his hand. Freckles blew, maybe telling him it was time to go home.

CHAPTER 26

TWO DAYS AFTER JESSE had told them that Kristy had broken the engagement, Nate crawled up onto the wagon seat and flopped down next to Ma. She clucked at the team and flicked the reins. It would soon be nine o'clock... more like the eleventh hour. Nate had wanted to stay home in the worst way for more than one reason. Pa's fever had broken overnight.

After breakfast, which Nate only picked at, he was allowed for the first time to see him. His time with Pa had been short, only a minute or two, but he surprised Nate with a weak grin and a few words of encouragement about today's proceedings.

The wagon bucked forward, then steadied into a roll. Jesse was riding the appaloosa next to the wagon. Overhead, the sky was a bright blue, the exact opposite of their moods. Nate  grumpily tugged at his tie. This morning, it seemed to be choking him. He was having difficulty taking a deep breath. Why Ma was forcing him to wear his white church shirt to a court hearing that he didn't want to go to anyway was beyond him. She was wearing her best skirt that allowed for her growing belly, and Jesse had polished his boots and donned a suit coat before leaving the house. It wasn't going to be a party. Seemed dumb to dress up.

The wagon turned onto the coach road. In a short two miles, they would have to walk up the steps of the schoolhouse, which was serving as a courtroom, and Nate would have to talk in front of what might be the whole town. His past wasn't something to brag about, and most folks didn't know all the details. That was the way he wanted it. He couldn't have been sweating more.

"Remember what your pa told ya this morning?" Jesse must have caught sight of Nate's nervous wiggles.

Nate grinned.

In a hoarse whisper, Pa had said, *"No matter the outcome, you are my son and always will be. Nothing can change that, so you hold your head up high."*

Pa was right, but Nate was still scared. He wished Pa was well enough to come with them, but his health wasn't anywhere close to even sitting up in bed. Doc had stayed behind with him.

Nate touched the deputy's star pinned on his shirt. It was like a piece of Pa was there with him.

The wagon rattled over the wooden bridge and into the street. There were a lot of people standing in small groups outside the so-called courthouse. Some of those folks Nate didn't recognize, hadn't ever seen before. An anxious hum of voices buzzed through the air. Other folks who were along the street, making their way toward the courthouse, stopped and stared as the wagon passed by. Nate shrank into the seat, wishing he could disappear. His insides felt like mush, except his heart. It was pounding.

Both Ma's and Jesse's spines straightened.

Jesse gave him a quick flick on the nose. "Don't fret, partner." There was a fierceness about Jesse that made him think

NATHANIAL

if anyone bothered him with even a simple matter, he might just tear that person apart limb by limb.

Ma's face was also stone sober. She didn't glance one way or the other. Although, they were getting plenty of looks. She just steered the wagon straight, then reined in next to at least a dozen or more other wagons parked in the schoolyard.

Nate took a deep breath and hopped down behind Ma where he wanted to stay hidden in the folds of her skirt, but he wasn't a baby and wouldn't act like one.

He wasn't sure his legs would hold up as the three of them, with him sandwiched in the middle, made the walk across that yard with more than a hundred eyes on them and then up the steps where other onlookers stood staring.

Jesse led the way inside. The crowd, jammed into the not-so-big room, turned as a collective group when the three of them entered. Everyone hushed. One look at Jesse, and as if that packed house were one person, the lot of them stepped back, producing a wide aisleway. The parting of the Red Sea came to Nate's mind. Maybe he, too, would escape, but he didn't want to wander in the wilderness for forty years.

Jesse pulled out a seat for Ma next to Mr. Graham and Judge Prescott who sat at a long table near the front of the room. Nate could be wrong, but Ma's round belly appeared more pronounced today.

Adjacent to them was a second long table. The Fletchers and their lawyer were huddled over papers and talking in hushed tones. The desk that Nate's teacher used sat where it always did, only there wasn't any documents or books sitting on it. There were a plaque and gavel.

"Sit down, partner." Jesse pulled out a seat for Nate, then sat himself.

People began to talk again, but it just seemed like a lot of noise to Nate. Why did they all have to be there? None of this was their concern. But as he glanced around, he took notice of

J.B. RICHARD

the people who did care about him. Shorty, the missus, Kristy, and the other kids were all there. Old man Pike stood in the back of the room at the door. Marshal Huckabee made his way in and sat directly behind them. He gave Nate's shoulder a little squeeze. The Filson and Henderson families took up an entire bench seat. Even crusty Pete, the saloon owner, had slicked down his hair, and his shirt wasn't wrinkled. Orris, Pete's piano man, was sitting behind the barkeep. It appeared the whole town and then some had turned out for the trial.

A man in a dark-gray suit and black tie walked in and straight down the row until he was behind the desk used by Nate's teacher.

"Order," he hollered, and immediately, everyone shut up. He took his seat, straightening his clothes for a few seconds, then looked out over the room full of folks of varying size and backgrounds. "We all know why we're here. Let's get started."

He looked over at the Fletchers' lawyer, a balding fella with big ears and nicks on his face where he'd cut himself shaving. The man wore a blue suit closely matching Mr. Fletcher's. He didn't look as scary as Nate had thought, but looks could be deceiving.

"Mr. Thatcher, call your first witness." Judge Parker relaxed back into his chair.

The Fletchers' lawyer turned stiffly toward the courtroom and announced, "Mrs. Walter Gill."

The thin woman stood from her seat. She wore new clothes, ones that fit, and her hair was combed and neatly pinned up. Not a speck of dirt smudged her cheeks like the other two times Nate had come face to face with her. Her pistol wasn't strapped on her either. She didn't look like her wild, rough-talking self at all.

Nate glared at Mrs. Fletcher. This had to have been her doing, making that mean bitch presentable. When she walked past, he wanted nothing more than to spit on her. She sat down like a lady in a chair next to the judge's desk. She must have really hated Pa to go to all that trouble.

Mr. Thatcher picked up a tintype off the table where the Fletchers sat, then handed it to the thin woman. "Do you recognize either woman?"

She nodded.

"Please speak to the courtroom," Thatcher said in a flat tone.

"Yeah, I know them." She kept her eyes on Thatcher, not once glancing at Nate. Perhaps she was feeling a pang of guilt, or it could have been Jesse's cold stare keeping her from looking in that direction.

Ma's eyes glistened with tears.

"What are their names?" Thatcher held up the photograph, showing it to everyone.

"That one"—she pointed to the younger image of Mrs. Fletcher—"is Deloris Fletcher. Seated right over there." The thin woman jerked her head toward the Fletchers. "The other one"—she pointed a second time at the photo—"is Lucinda Rineheart, Deloris's sister."

The entire courtroom gasped. Ever since the Fletchers had come to town, rumors had been flying. Nate had overhead Jesse and the marshal bitching about it. Everyone was aware that this trial was for Nate's custody. But until this moment, no one beyond those at the front tables knew the evidence stacked against him. And they had all just learned that he had a blood relation other than his outlaw father and his brothers who were all in prison. Lots of whispering ensued.

"Order!" Judge Parker smacked down his gavel. Everyone quieted.

"What is your relationship with the ladies in the photograph?" Thatcher theatrically straightened his tie and tugged on the cuff of each sleeve before he returned to his seat next to the Fletchers, whose faces glowed with satisfaction. This was their star witness. Their hopes of winning were wrapped up in her testimony.

"Lucinda and I worked in the same cathouse."

There was an uneasy shift in the courtroom. The sound of clothing chaffing the bench seats seemed louder than normal.

"We were the best of friends, more like sisters. We took care of one another. Even found ourselves pregnant at the same time." The thin woman chuckled crudely.

Ma's face held a flush. Nate glanced around, noticing most all the other ladies in the room either wore the same red staining her cheeks or were fanning themselves to breathe.

"Being as close as sisters, were you there the day Lucinda gave birth?" Thatcher asked as though it would be ridiculous to think otherwise.

"I delivered that boy." She spat out the words. "Lucinda didn't want him. Told me to go throw him in the river."

The courtroom erupted with loud murmurs.

Nate jumped to his feet. "That ain't true!" He wanted to scream that Lucinda had loved him.

The judge banged his gavel for quiet. But then what Nate had thought really sank in. Lucinda. Not Ma or Mama. What little he remembered of Lucinda, he did recall that she insisted on him calling her by name. Why hadn't the inclination been there in his mind to call her mother? That wasn't hard to figure out. She'd never been a mother to him. All the times she had pushed him away rushed to mind, things he must have blocked out until now.

Ma sprang out of her seat as if she'd sat on a tack and pulled Nate close. Tears streamed down his face.

The thin woman stared past ma, giving him a hard look. "You suckled from my tit the first few weeks of your life. I'd given birth a week earlier, so my milk was in. Lucinda was so upset that Jim wouldn't marry her. She prayed all those months to give him a son. What man don't want a boy to carry on his name? Jim Younger must have been the first. Lucinda hoped he'd change his mind. That didn't happen. That bastard actually got on his horse and left just after Lucinda's water broke, so she had no use for you."

"Stop it!" Ma screeched. Her fingernails clawed into the table as she leaned threateningly toward that thin she-devil. Ma's hateful glare bore into her. "What a vile thing to say to a child. You disgust me."

Cheers rose. Folks applauded. There was a bustling inside the small room. People were on their feet. That made it feel even tighter, and Nate gulped air between sobs. Jesse grunted loudly while eyeballing Thatcher, who wore a broad smirk. Jesse's face was pinched tight, and as he began to thunder up out of his chair, Huckabee's hand slapped down on his shoulder, throwing him back into his seat before all hell broke loose.

That bitch of a mountain woman was tougher than leather. Nate had known that the moment he'd met her. She didn't bat an eye at any of the ruckus. Being a saloon girl at one time, she was in her element with arguments and near fights breaking out around her.

"If it wasn't for me, Nathanial wouldn't be alive," she barked at Ma. Her face was beet red, as crimson as Ma's, and based on her steamy breath, she wasn't about to let it drop. "Who do you think changed his diapers or rocked him at night when he woke up cryin'? It sure as hell wasn't Lucinda, least not 'til she come outta her depression. All she did was drink. Some women was never meant to be mothers. You can hate the sight of me. I don't give a shit, but I wouldn't ever hurt no kid. Nathanial didn't ask to be born."

"Mrs. Crosson, take your seat. Everyone, settle down," the judge bellowed, shaking the windows. He hammered his gavel a few more times.

Mr. Graham and Prescott were speaking in a hushed tone at Ma's side, reminding her to retain civility. Ma did not like what Mrs. Gill had to say—none of them liked it—but she had a right to speak. Ma would soon get her say.

Ma slumped into her chair. The mass of folks who had pressed in to get their share of the entertainment plopped into their seats. No one made a noise. Nate alone could hear the rapid drumming of his heart. Ma and Jesse were sitting near that maybe they could hear it too, and that's why they'd inched closer to him.

"Proceed, Mr. Thatcher," Judge Parker said. His neck was still awful red.

Thatcher produced a letter from inside his vest pocket. Nate couldn't imagine what horrors it would tell of. It made him feel gooey inside. He wiped at his eyes. He was still stunned after just learning that the thin woman had been more of a mother to him than Lucinda.

"This is a letter received by Deloris Fletcher—" Thatcher started to say.

"I already know what that is," Mrs. Gill snapped, cutting Thatcher off.

Why was that skinny witch doing this to Nate? It was Pa she hated for killing her man. Nate hadn't done a damn thing to her. In fact, he'd been nothing but nice to her, and this was what he got for it. He'd gone against his old instincts about not trusting people he didn't know. Now look at him—sitting in a sweaty courtroom, waiting to hear if he would be shipped east with two strangers and never see his family again.

"I recognize that fancy stationery. Deloris sent a pack of it to her sister so she'd write." She smirked. "If I had to guess, I'd bet that's the letter I sent for Lucinda right before she died."

Everyone must have been holding their breath, waiting to hear what had been penned on the sheet, what awful event would be revealed from Nate's past. Not a peep or rustle of clothing was heard.

"That is correct," Thatcher said loud and clear.

NATHANIAL

The thin woman took the letter, tracing her fingers around the edge, but she didn't open the envelope. She could have been remembering the day Lucinda had handed it to her. It was strange to think that Nate could not recall this woman ever being involved in his life. He'd been very young, but she must have been the one who let him look at the picture book. In his memories, he couldn't even produce an image of Lucinda's face. There were so many awful things in his past that he wished to forget. Some he had blocked from his mind. Mrs. Gill, or whatever her name had been back then, she was one of those lost and better forgotten recollections. She stared nostalgically at the envelope with Deloris Fletcher's name penned on it.

"Why don't you read it for us?" Thatcher's request didn't strike Nate as odd, given that the Fletchers' attorney was trying to hammer in that this Gill woman knew Lucinda's last wishes for what would be done for her child. There was, however, something in his tone that hinted of devilry.

Mr. Graham, the attorney working for Ma and Pa, came to his feet to interject. "How do we know that letter wasn't just written? Perhaps Mrs. Gill wrote it herself. Who's to say the handwriting on that paper belongs to Lucinda Reinheart?"

Nate thought those were fine points. The Fletchers didn't look worried. Sweat glistened on Jesse's brow, and Ma closed her eyes tight for a few seconds. Perhaps she was praying.

"Judge," Thatcher said while walking to the table where the Fletchers appeared calm, at least on the outside.

Ma and Jesse, sitting on either side of Nate, looked flustered, so Nate reckoned their guts were as tight as his. It was hard to tell what crazy thing Lucinda might have put in her will. That was, after all, her last testament written days before she died. Who would go against that? Nate had to fight the urge to jump up, run out, and hop on Jesse's horse since he hadn't ridden

Buck to town. Then he would take flight and go someplace the Fletchers couldn't find him.

Thatcher picked up a stack of envelopes. All of them were the same size, shape, and cream color, not like any mail Nate had ever seen. He would bet those were the letters Mr. Fletcher had told Pa about that day in Birch Creek, and inside were other correspondences between Deloris and Lucinda. Thatcher opened several envelopes, presenting Judge Parker with the evidence. The judge adjusted the spectacles on the end of his nose while studying the handwriting. Both Mr. Graham and Prescott, as representatives of Nate's side of this battle, went forward and also examined the sheets.

Before any of them said a word, their noses stuck in the papers spread across the judge's desk, the thin woman broke the silence in the room. "I can't read or write. But I can tell ya what that letter says."

All eyes were now on her. Nate's stomach flipped. He was sure he was going to vomit. He took a deep breath and swallowed hard. Jesse put an arm around his shoulder, giving him a squeeze. Tears teetered on the rims of Ma's eyes.

"She wanted her boy sent back east to her sister. I don't know why. They didn't get along for shit," the thin woman stated matter-of-factly.

Mrs. Fletcher gasped. Nate reckoned she hadn't expected that to be revealed. All his dirty laundry was aired. Why not hers?

Judge Parker smacked his gavel down. "Mrs. Gill, I never thought I'd have to say this to a woman. Stop with the profanity. There are women and children present."

"I just meant that Lucinda and her sister, all they did was squabble in those letters. Lucinda would read them to me." The thin woman looked down at the gold band on her left hand. "Toward the end, she hated Jim. That hateful prick actually cursed her for gettin' sick. He bitched that thanks to

NATHANIAL

her, he'd have to start payin' to have a sweet time. Suppose she finally figured out what an asshole he was."

"Mrs. Gill!" Judge Parker shook his gavel at her. "No more cursing. One more...slip and I'll hold you in contempt."

Nate didn't care about the bad words. Wetness spilled down his cheeks. What a thing, an awful thing, for his friends, who were sitting in that courtroom with their folks, to hear. Every ugly part of his past was being exposed. Horrible circumstances that he hadn't even known were coming to light, and he hated it. He hated what he'd been born out of. It certainly wasn't love.

The thin woman glared at Judge Parker. "It's the truth! No matter how I say it," she barked right back at him. "Deloris Fletcher, accordin' to Lucinda, was the lesser of two evils."

There was sudden restless stirring among everyone. Nate didn't look around. Instead, he just stared at his boots, wishing he could disappear, and the whole time, he could feel all those eyes on him. Too many sad eyes that were filled with pity. He didn't want them feeling sorry for him, and he didn't want to hear any more. What he wanted, god-awful bad, was Pa. When no one cared a lick about Nate, Nolan Crosson had taken him in and given him the Crosson name. Where were the Fletchers then? They'd never been part of his life and never would be.

Mrs. Gill loudly cleared her voice. "Here's a little information that I'm sure that bitch"—she looked at Deloris—"didn't tell anyone."

Deloris Fletcher squirmed, taking hold of her husband's arm. Lem Fletcher stared at his wife, as he didn't have a clue. Even their lawyer's brows were raised, and he waited to hear.

"She wired Lucinda, saying she didn't want Nathanial. She had a child of her own to raise and feared that the offspring of an outlaw might be too wild. Guess she changed her mind."

"Wait just a minute." Thatcher pointed a finger in her face, and she smirked. She was on no one's side but her own.

Mrs. Fletcher was on her feet as if ready to argue otherwise. Her mouth opened, but nothing came out. Then she dropped back into her chair. The crowd was humming with whispered opinions.

Nate wiped his sleeve across his eyes as he looked up. Behind the judge, the rear door to the schoolhouse was open, allowing a breeze to flow through. It wasn't more than ten, eleven feet to freedom.

"That is enough from you, Mrs. Gill." Judge Parker hammered away on the desk. The banging was deafening, and everyone was focused there.

Although the unfettered muttering within those four walls rose above the hammering, it seemed that none of the preconceived ideas were taking shape. Those who knew Nate, and even those who didn't, what had they expected to hear? He wasn't born to sunshine and rainbows. His outlaw father had treated him no better than some no-name bastard child. And he now knew that the whore who'd given birth to him was no better a person. He wanted to forget all of it. He wished he had never heard a single word about his time spent with Lucinda. Why couldn't his past stay buried?

"Shut up! I don't wanna hear any more!" Something inside him snapped. Nate was on his feet. His body shook. Was it fear of what might happen to him or pure anger? Either way, he'd had enough.

Ma sprang up beside him. "Nathanial, sweetheart."

Nate jerked away from her and bumped into Jesse, who stood protectively on the other side of him. He just wanted to be alone. He needed air. He couldn't take a deep breath. So many faces looking at him, staring at him.

"Order!" the judge shouted over all the noise.

Thatcher glared at Nate. "You keep quiet."

That was all it took, and Jesse hurdled the table. Two long strides and Jesse was almost in Thatcher's face as he drew back to punch him in the mouth. Huckabee dove from where he'd been standing, knocking Mr. Graham and Prescott spinning in either direction, and somehow he managed to tackle Jesse before he walloped Thatcher.

Mr. and Mrs. Fletcher both popped out of their chairs, drawing in a deep, gasping breath. Thatcher was now wide-eyed and looking like he might piss himself. The thin bitch sat there snickering. The judge might as well have saved his voice. Screaming at everyone to settle down wasn't paying off. The crowd was riled up. It seemed everyone had picked a side. Opinions roared back and forth across the room. The judge should have just thrown his hammer right out the window for all the good it was doing him. No one was listening or cared to. Ma was crying into her hands as all the commotion whirled around them.

Jesse and the marshal tussled across the floor. Nate's partner was hungry for a piece of Thatcher in the worst way. Jesse lunged at the lawyer, the marshal grabbing with both hands to hold him back. They both hit into Thatcher, who fell backward into the table where the Fletchers stood. The two of them where knocked stumbling ass first into the crowd, who didn't hesitate to push in return. There was lots of grumbling. Too bad Nate couldn't stay and watch Thatcher get his. Ladies and kids where being quickly ushered toward the door. War was about to break out.

Nate looked over at his mother. He would never forget her. He was sorry he couldn't go home and say good-bye to Pa. "Ma," he said timidly while hoping the motherly sense that always told her when he was up to something didn't kick in. A lot was going on around them and none of it good.

She sadly stared down at him. Tears streamed down her face.

"I'm sorry." It was all he could say. All this trouble, he hadn't meant for any of this to happen. It was his past he felt the need to apologize for. Things that had happened years ago, things that should have been behind them and were now hurting the people he loved most. His leaving would hurt her too, and Pa and Jesse, but Nate saw no other way. More importantly, he wanted Ma to get the hell out of there before she got knocked into or accidentally hit.

"Go!" Nate said and dashed for the back door.

Behind him, Judge Parker was nearly bringing down the roof, yelling like an Indian on the warpath, threatening everyone with contempt of court.

"Nathanial!" Ma's shrill voice cut through all the other voices and noise and pierced Nate's heart. If he even dared to glance back at her, he'd stop running.

CHAPTER 27

JESSE HALTED in the doorway, catching his breath after his tussle with the marshal. Nate was running as fast as those little feet would carry him across the schoolyard toward the wagon. Jesse's horse was tied there, and he knew precisely what that boy was thinking.

"Partner! Stop! Come back!"

As he kept a fast pace, Nathanial threw a quick look over his shoulder but ignored Jesse's plea. That child was a damn good rider, and Freckles could run almost as fast as the buckskin. If he got on that horse, there would be no catching him. Nate was light and the appaloosa young and filled with stamina. A bad combination given the situation.

Jesse darted toward his little partner. Others were quickly filing out behind him and down the stairs. The noise and voices, including the Fletchers, Judge Parker, all the lawyers, and Prescott, briefly drew his eyes. Ma was standing at the top of schoolhouse steps, wiping at her eyes. Some of her lady friends were gathered around her.

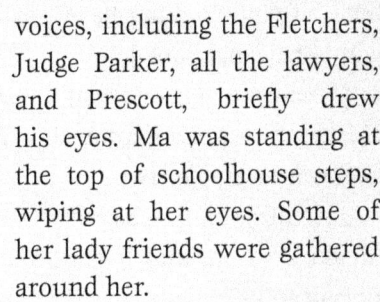

Jesse focused ahead. Nate was too little to step up into the

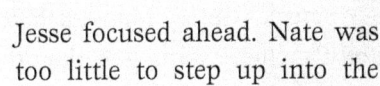

saddle without help of some kind, which would slow him down, perhaps giving Jesse time to catch hold of him. He quickly crawled into the wagon bed, then hopped over onto the saddle. He madly kicked the sides of the appaloosa, and away they flew as though that pony's tail were afire.

Jesse stopped at the side of the wagon, bent over and out of breath from the short spurt. What was that boy thinking, running away? What was that going to solve? Well…Jesse had almost punched a lawyer and a judge because he'd been upset. This was probably just the kid's knee-jerk reaction, or so he hoped. Once the kid calmed down, likely, he'd come home. Jesse stood there watching the boy go until he disappeared into the tree line.

Without warning, Jesse was shoved, struck in the middle of his back, and flung forward but didn't fall. He spun on his heel, not knowing exactly what to expect. But what he saw, or rather who he was looking at, definitely wasn't what he expected. Lem Fletcher stood before him. The man's face was flaming red.

"This is your fault!" Fletcher pointed an accusing finger at him. "If you wouldn't have started the fisticuffs, none of this would have happened."

"Horseshit!" Jesse wasn't about to let Fletcher crowd him. He gave Fletcher a hard push to back off, and the gent danced backward a step or two.

Fletcher's hands balled at his sides. Every man had his breaking point, and it appeared this dude had reached his. Lots of folks, mostly men, bunched in around them. Was this round two?

"Knock it off!" Marshal Huckabee barged between Jesse and Fletcher, eyeing one, then the other. It was a warning for the two of them to restrain themselves.

NATHANIAL

The brawl inside the courtroom had been enough. There was no reason to bring it out into the middle of town. Jesse was just too worked up to let it drop.

"It ain't no news flash that Nate wants nothin' to do with you. Why can't ya leave the kid alone? My God, you heard just a snippet of what that boy has lived through, and now that he's got good folks who love him, a family, something he ain't ever had, you wanna go and rip him away from it." Jesse cursed under his breath. "If you think that boy is just gonna roll over and let ya scratch his belly, you best think twice 'cause he don't warm up to people too easy."

"We are his family!" Mrs. Fletcher snapped, her nose in the air. "Eventually, he'll get accustomed to our ways. He'll come to see that this is for the best."

Had she not been a woman, Jesse would have smacked that highfaluting better-than-you smirk right off and enjoyed it. Instead, he grinned, but it wasn't friendly, not in the least. "If what you say is true—that you're his family—then why the hell is it that he jumped on my horse and ran off? Shouldn't he have run to you since you're what's best for him?"

Mrs. Fletcher swung a flat hand to slap Jesse's face. He caught her by the wrist.

"Don't forget the judge hasn't made his decision yet. I only wish I had that telegram to shove in your face. Didn't want him, huh?"

She yanked her hand away.

Mr. Fletcher barreled between them. "Go after him," Fletcher angrily demanded. Spittle flew every which way.

Jesse wiped his chin.

Fletcher's eyes narrowed. "It is your duty as deputy sheriff." The corners of his mouth triumphantly curled up.

Jesse was plumb out of patience with this asshole.

Ma had come to the wagon with a huddle of women all fussing over her. Her hands were supporting her lower back, which was arched in a way that pushed her belly out, showing her condition, and Ma looked downright beat. Her eyes were red, and her shoulders shook with each sob.

Jesse wouldn't hit Fletcher, not with Ma and the other ladies present. He unpinned his badge, regarding it a second or two. Taking it off wasn't an easy thing to do. He loved his job and loved the man he worked for. The man who somehow always kept Jesse thinking straight when otherwise he might have let himself get too riled up and done something stupid. Like now. But Jesse couldn't help himself.

He tossed the tin star in the dirt at the Fletchers' feet. "You want Nathanial, go git him yourself."

As Jesse turned toward the wagon where Ma waited to be helped up onto the seat, Huckabee caught him by the shoulder, spinning him. "Son, don't do this. Think of Nolan. He wouldn't want Nate left to run free on his own, nor would he be okay with you quittin'. I know for a fact that ain't who he taught you to be."

Jesse didn't want to hear it. Yeah, what Huckabee said made good sense and was true. But Jesse felt selfish. He couldn't pin that badge back on knowing he might be helping the snide city couple secure what they wanted. Although, that depended on the judge's ruling. If Judge Parker gave Nate to the Fletchers... There was simply no way in hell Jesse could hand over his little partner. He didn't possess the strength for it or the gumption. It'd be a fight. And it would take an army to pry that kid from Jesse's fingers. Just thinking about it took some wind out of him. Jesse suddenly felt as tired as Ma looked.

He met Huckabee's gaze and shook his head. "I can't." He wouldn't go after Nathanial unless Ma or Sheriff Crosson wanted him to. Jesse turned toward Ma. "Let's go." He took her hand.

NATHANIAL

A few minutes later, Ma had herself situated on the seat, and Jesse raised his arms about to slap leather to the team of horses and circle the wagon toward home.

Marshal Huckabee ran his horse past, on Nathanial's trail. Jesse shook his head. His partner was a miniature sheriff when it came to reading sign, and he was no dummy when it came to hiding hoofprints. He was better at it than most men. Pure dumb luck was what it would amount to if Huckabee found the boy. But Jesse suspected Nate would eventually come home. The kid never strayed too far without Buck. He would return for his horse.

"Wait a minute!" Judge Parker hustled up next to the wagon. Mr. Graham and Prescott were with him. The judge cleared his throat. "This trial has become a damn circus. Well, it ends today. I've already spoken to the Fletchers. Court will resume in two hours. The sooner a decision is made, the better for everyone involved. Dragging out this mess another day will just make the situation worse. I'm thankful no one pulled a gun in there."

Parker dabbed a handkerchief across his glistening brow. He looked solemnly at Ma. "I am sorry, ma'am. I sympathize, given your condition and what you had to endure hearing in that courtroom today. I am also aware of why your husband, Sheriff Crosson, was not present today. None of this can be easy on you and now, with the boy missing, I'm sure you're not in the best frame of mind to testify this afternoon, but I hope you can understand my position regarding having this trial over and done with. Tempers have gotten out of control." Parker pointedly looked at Jesse.

Ma nodded, wiping at her red eyes.

Jesse would be the first to admit that he wanted this trial over fast, but weren't they all forgetting something, something pretty important? "Doesn't Nathanial have to speak?"

The judge shook his head. "That little one is obviously upset. He's run off, and kids will oftentimes say things that will get them what they want, which isn't always what's best for them."

Jesse scowled, inwardly disagreeing. The boy's wishes should matter.

Judge Parker threw his hands up. "I'm not saying the Fletchers are what's best for the boy, nor am I calling Nathanial a liar. What I am trying to get across to you is that right now, in the state of certain shock, given what the child heard from Mr. Gill, and the grief that young one must be feeling because of it, his testimony wouldn't stand up."

Parker wiped his head a second time, then inhaled deeply. "Plus, anyone with eyes can see his attachment. I don't need to hear it. I know the boy wants to stay. The fact that he sat planted between the two of you during court like there was no safer place says a lot. Every time I caught sight of him glancing at the Fetchers, more tears glistened in his eyes. But I must warn you both. I am duty-bound to the law, and I will rule as the law governs me to. Mrs. Fletcher has proven that she is a blood relative, and that is substantial." Parker turned on his heel, marching toward the hotel.

The crowd had gone. Only Graham and Prescott stood there.

"Kate, you've seen how Thatcher operates. Don't let him trip you up. He's slick. The judge hasn't heard your side of it yet. Whatever you do, think before you speak. I don't believe Parker has his mind set one way or the other, but he is determined to end this trial," Mr. Graham said with little confidence.

"We can help prep you if you feel up to it." Prescott piped up.

Jesse needed a break to breathe some fresh air, to listen to the birds tweeting. Ma's eyes were half closed, and she was rubbing at her temple. She needed rest, some sound sleep.

NATHANIAL

"Excuse us, gentlemen." Jesse clucked at the team.

Not far outside of town, Ma reached over and squeezed his hand. "I'll bet Nathanial is in the hayloft right this minute."

Jesse grinned. "Could be." It was the boy's thinking spot, and after all the stuff he'd heard, there was a lot to think about. "If he ain't, I'm sure he'll be home before dark. He's probably just out running Freckles' legs so the next time we race, the appaloosa won't have a chance against Buck."

Ma hinted at a smile, leaned over, and kissed Jesse's face. By nature, Jesse was sometimes a little silly, a big kid, and in this case, it helped mask his nervousness. He wasn't so sure Judge Parker wasn't leaning toward the Fletchers. If that was the final ruling, then his little partner might really run away.

When Jesse steered the team into the yard, Doc Martin was standing on the porch, puffing a cigar. Small smoke rings floated up. "How'd it go?" he called to them.

"Hard to say." Jesse wasn't going to open up his can of fears in front of Ma. She likely had a stirring gut full of them herself. He halted the wagon, then jumped down.

"That's strange. When I asked Nathanial, he said everything was fine." Doc wore a puzzled expression, and his lips tightened around his cigar.

"Nathanial is here?" Ma opened the picket gate. Her steps quickened.

Jesse was right behind her, and for the first time today, he smiled.

"Well... no, he isn't." Doc spoke out the side of his mouth not pinching the stub of his cigar.

Ma stopped midstep, and Jesse nearly rammed into her. They looked questioningly at one another. Had Nathanial truly run away?

Jesse spun toward the corral. Buck wasn't there. He'd been rolling on his back in the dust when they'd left that morning. Freckles was there now, drinking from the water trough.

"Did he say where he was going?" Ma's voice quivered.

Doc removed the glowing stub from between his lips, holding it in the seam of his first two fingers. He flicked the ash off the end. "No. He asked to see his pa. I let him for a minute or two. Then he switched horses and rode out. I assumed he was heading back to town."

"He ran off," Jesse said to no one.

Doc jerked, dropping what was left of his cigar. "Dammit." He stomped the remnant with his heel. "If I'd have known, I would've nailed his boots to the floor."

Ma desperately threw open the door. "Perhaps he said something to his pa that will clue us in to where he might have gone." She had a foot on the stairs when Jesse caught up to her.

"Ma. Look!" What had made Jesse glance toward the dining room, God only knew. But a single sheet of paper centered on the table had caught his eye.

They rushed through the sitting room and into the dining room. Doc joined them. Ma snatched up the paper. First, she read it silently while Jesse looked over her shoulder, and Doc was trying to steal a peek too. Ma's eyes filled with tears. She turned and sadly stared at them. Then she crinkled the sides of the paper in her hands. As if it wasn't real, as if she didn't believe whatever was written on it.

> *Dear Ma and Jesse,*
>
> *I said my good-bye to Pa. He didn't wake up, so I'd be grateful if you would tell him for me that he is the best father ever. Ma, I think you're the best mama. Jesse, my horse will always be faster than yours.*

The boy had drawn a little smiley face.

> *Sorry, I don't have much time to write anything else. I hope when Elizabeth is chewing on Ticklebug, she thinks of me.*
>
> *Nathanial*

NATHANIAL

Ma's cheeks were tear-streaked. "Jesse, go fetch Nathanial."

"Yes, ma'am." Jesse turned and ran out the door. It would be easier for him to track the marshal, who had no reason to hide his horse's prints. But that would mean riding to town first. Maybe, by the grace of God, Huckabee had caught up to Nate. Jesse threw his saddle on Freckles.

With him on the trails, that meant Ma would have to return to the courthouse and face the Fletchers alone. Not only that, but if the judge ruled against the Crossons, that blow might feel ten times worse without kin there to lean on. Jesse was torn in two. But Ma had asked him to go. She was thinking of her little boy, so that's where Jesse would stay focused—on finding that kid.

He sank spurs.

CHAPTER 28

JESSE TOOK A QUICK LOOK around the yard, found the freshest hoofprints belonging to the mustang, and followed them out the lane. At the T where the coach road met with the wagon trail leading to or from the ranch, sign of the boy and his horse disappeared into the tree line ahead. If Jesse had the timing figured right, he should also come across Huckabee's prints in there. The marshal had left town long enough behind Nate, a solid fifteen or twenty minutes, that he would've had time to stop quickly at the ranch, do the things he did, then be at least ten minutes in front of his pursuer. And the kid certainly had the smarts to know that someone would come after him.

Jesse nudged his horse. Not far inside the trees, sure as shooting, he spotted a hoofprint. And Jesse was just as positive that it was the track of Huckabee's gelding.

Half an hour later, Jesse pulled up reins at the edge of Blue Sky Lake and let his horse drink. He took a swallow from his canteen. It would soon be time for Ma to head back into court. He couldn't fret about that now. First, find Nate. Then worry about the other crap. He capped his canteen.

NATHANIAL

About four miles later, Huckabee's trail turned sharply south. Why had the kid, who was leading them, suddenly changed direction? Jesse jerked up on the reins and took a good, hard look around. Buck's hoofprints were there on the ground, and not just a small hint of one. That was something new. So far, Nate had done a fair job of hiding any sign he'd left behind. So why stop covering his trail? The only reason Jesse could reasonably consider was that the boy had thrown an over-the-shoulder glance and spotted Huckabee somewhere along his backtrail, perhaps not too far off, and that was why the kid now seemed like he was in a hurry by not covering his tracks. And switching directions might slow the marshal down. Huckabee would have to watch the ground more carefully to make sure Nate didn't switch directions again and again.

Jesse spurred Freckles. If Huckabee was closing in on Nathanial, Jesse wanted to be there when he caught up. The boy obviously had his mind made up about running away. Jesse had talked Nate out of trouble a few times before. Maybe he could get him to be sensible this time. If not, it would be easier for two to bag that little rascal. Nate was a tough little bugger. It might take some real tussling to get him to return to Gray Rock—where the Fletchers might be waiting for him.

As Jesse followed the zigzag trail he suspected the kid to use to try and fool them, he looked into the sky several times. Hours had passed since he'd left the ranch. Ma was either celebrating or crying her eyes out right now. The custody trial surely had ended. His gut tightened, and he wished he knew the final verdict. But what he needed to do was focus before he missed a turn.

Jesse stepped his horse into a creek that was just deep enough to splash his boots with each stride of the gelding. There were no hoofprints on the opposite bank. Nate had stayed in the water to shake off the marshal. It appeared that the marshal had caught on to the trick and was also somewhere in the stream. There was no sign to clue Jesse which way to go. Should he follow the current or bet against it? So far, it had seemed that Nate was just leading them in an effort to escape.

Jesse rubbed thoughtfully at the stubble on his chin. He was starting to think the kid now had a plan and knew where he was going. Even though his partner had been leading them one way, then another, in general, they were still heading on a southerly route. Why south? Did he have some connection there? Jesse turned his horse.

By nightfall, his stomach was rumbling, and he was tired. His horse was holding up fairly well for as many rocky miles as they'd put behind them. Every now and then, the animal had halted of his own will, his nostrils flaring wide. Jesse had then gambled and given the horse his head. He couldn't track in the dark. The appaloosa followed whatever scent had caught his attention. Jesse was crossing his fingers that it was either the somewhat familiar smell of Huckabee's mount or Buck that put a mite of giddy-up in Freckles' stride.

The moon overhead gave light to his path, which helped keep Freckles from tripping. They had left the creek and rode over a tall butte dotted with the black forms of trees. Stars twinkled overhead. Nate's coat had been hanging on its peg when they'd left the house that morning, and it was unlikely that he'd thought to grab it. The air in the hills got cold after sunset, and that boy was in nothing more than a cotton shirt. If the shivers came upon him, the kid would probably hole up somewhere smart where a small flame couldn't be spotted so easily against the darkness.

Jesse wasn't overly familiar with the area. He could think of no good hiding place the boy might make camp. One thing he knew for sure: Nathanial loved his horse. It was unlikely that he would push Buck through the night. According to the shift of the stars, the hour was past midnight, way past the boy's usual bedtime. He should be getting awful tired if he wasn't already asleep. Jesse was counting on the kid to develop an awful case of lazy haze. The feeling when ya think you just can't hold your heavy lids open one more second, when you're not seeing straight anymore and your chin bobs on your chest every other minute. That's when the boy would stop running and find a place to rest. No way would the boy risk Buck getting hurt if he wasn't alert enough to lead him, especially at night. Jesse just hoped that would give him the right amount of time needed to catch the kid.

Off in the not-too-far distance, there was a speck of orange on the ground. As he rode closer, slowing his pace, Jesse caught a whiff of smoke. He didn't know whose fire that was, but it wasn't Nathanial. The kid would never have set up camp in such an open area. There were some trees and a scattering of brush, but otherwise, the spot wasn't all that concealed. A horse whinnied. Freckles' head lifted high, his ears standing at attention, and his nostrils flared. Jesse felt him bloat his belly. Then he whinnied.

"Hello," Jesse called out, not wanting the sudden sound of a strange horse coming out of the dark to jolt whoever had built that fire into popping off a shot at him.

"What changed your mind?" Marshal Huckabee stepped out from behind a tree, his rifle held down at his side. He, too, was a cautious man. It kept a fella living longer. Apparently, he'd been ready for any trouble that might have been coming had it not been Jesse.

"When I saw the boy had taken his horse, I knew then that he planned a one-way trip."

Jesse picketed Freckles next to the marshal's horse where there was grass for them to eat. He stripped off his saddle, then carried his gear over his shoulder and joined the marshal at the fire. The coffee smelled good, or at least it would be hot.

"Help yourself," Huckabee said as he tossed a few sticks into the flames.

Jesse did just that. Maybe now his stomach would stop its growling.

"That damn Nolan is too good a teacher." Huckabee grinned. "That boy of his threw every trick a man can use to hide his trail and then some at me. Shit. I never even caught a glimpse of Nathanial. I didn't think it'd be this hard to catch him."

Jesse chuckled. "Yeah. Out and out, the boy is his pa." Jesse sobered. "You got any ideas of where he might be headed?" After following him all day, he figured Huckabee might have some clue.

Marshal Huckabee nodded. "Sure do." He set down his cup. "You have probably heard the story of how Nathanial and my son, Deputy, ran off and ended up in Buttonwood."

"Sheriff Crosson told me that Nate had gotten jealous around the time Elizabeth was due to be born. But Buttonwood is where Nate had run into that killer, Tipsy."

"That's correct." Huckabee confirmed what Jesse had already known.

"Tipsy's dead, but don't you think the kid would shy away from a place where perhaps another no-account from his past might show up? Buttonwood's a rough town." Jesse wasn't convinced that Huckabee was right.

"What Nolan might not have shared with you was that Nathanial and Deputy received a fat reward for Tipsy's capture. Five hundred dollars apiece. Plus, since they returned the Wells Fargo money Tipsy had stolen, each of the boys got a thank-you in the amount of two hundred and fifty dollars. That's fifteen hundred between those two knuckleheads."

"So." Jesse shrugged. That was a lot of money, but he didn't see how any of that related to this.

"What do you think kids who are feeling rich and suddenly find themselves loaded down with lots of money are gonna do?"

"Spend it," Jesse said. If that'd been him, that's what he would have done.

NATHANIAL

"What do you think they'd spend it on?"

Jesse was annoyed and wished Huckabee would get to the damn point. But as Sheriff Crosson had always done, the marshal was making him think out the answer. People thought differently, and the more he knew about how to figure out a person's true motive, which couldn't always be seen by facts on the outside, the better lawman he would become. Tracking people was a big part of his job. Usually, it was criminals. In this case, it was a little boy that Jesse cared a lot about.

Jesse thought a minute. What would a kid buy with all that money?

Jesse smirked. "Candy."

Huckabee laughed. "They did buy sweets. But at that point, the boys had been gone for two months. Other than the train ride from Three Springs into Buttonwood, the boys had hoofed it nearly three hundred miles."

Jesse straightened. "They would have bought horses." He still wasn't seeing the connection between Nate and Buttonwood.

"Nathanial bought the mustang he's riding now. Purchased him from a man by the name of Graybill. That fella's wife's maiden name is Harper."

Jesse nearly sprang to his feet, sloshing his coffee onto his pants. "The same Harpers that Nathanial had been dumped with after Jim Younger was sent away to prison."

"The very one," Huckabee said dryly.

"Well, then Nate wouldn't head there. He hated those people. None of them ever treated him right but the girl, Jenny, who Nathanial watched get gunned down."

Huckabee dropped his hat on his bedroll, then ran his fingers through his sandy-colored hair. "Nate and Deputy had taken their horses and were gone by the time Nolan and I tracked them to Graybill's livery. Mrs. Graybill recognized Nolan, said she'd apologized to Nathanial for all the wrong she'd done him. He was welcome to come visit anytime."

What the marshal said did make sense to Jesse. The Graybills' home would be a good place to safely rest, get fed, and from there, if they didn't ask Nate to stay with them, the kid could probably use that cute face of his to swindle the price of a train ticket out of them. If that happened, then he and his horse could speed away on the steamer and end up just about anywhere. How would they track him then?

Jesse looked across the fire at Marshal Huckabee. "Are we gonna keep trackin' him, catch him before he gets too deep into Injun country? Or will we ride straight for Buttonwood and intercept him once he's there?"

The many miles between there and Buttonwood were dangerous. It was Cheyenne country, and those red bucks weren't known to be friendly with the whites.

"We need to catch him. I haven't had any word of recent attacks on settlers who were simply passing through the area. But Nolan made mention that there'd been a few sightings of a war party stirrin' about. The kid might slip past, but I'd hate to be wrong." Huckabee pushed his hat onto his head, stood, then rolled up his ground blanket. "The horses are probably rested. Let's go."

CHAPTER 29

THEY MOVED ALONG SLOWLY through the dark to the south with the hope of finding Nate sometime soon. Ma had to be worried out of her mind since neither Nate nor Jesse had come home. Jesse hadn't taken time to get an update on the sheriff before he'd left, so he was worried about that too. And he was about ready to eat one of his boots. The coffee he'd drunk hours ago wasn't holding him over.

As dawn began to streak the day with hues of pink, something else in the sky caught Jesse's eye. A thin line of smoke. They turned their horses into a shallow gully following the hillside down toward the smoke signal. Under Jesse's arms, the pits of his shirt were getting sweaty. *Please don't let it be a Cheyenne war party.* He just wanted to find the boy. Perchance Nathanial had gotten reckless and built too big of a fire, but Jesse didn't believe that was true. Maybe it was just some hunter.

Their horses scrambled over a rocky hump, out of the gully, and onto a flat patch of ground thickly lined with trees. Between the branches, Jesse spotted, one, two, three... six, nine... a dozen ponies grazing. His eyes were good, and there was no missing the paint markings on those horses. About ten yards from the animals, just as many Indians sat around the fire Jesse had spotted from the hill. He and the marshal both jerked up on the reins. Neither of them dared to breathe. This would be a fight to the death if they were seen.

Huckabee backed his horse up a step or two, then turned the gelding and disappeared into the gully they'd just come out of, behind the hillside.

Jesse started to turn his mount. Freckles' nostrils flared. Jesse's gut tightened. "No, boy." He chanced a whisper out of desperation. Freckles bloated his belly. In that split second, Jesse's entire body tightened into a knot. His horse whinnied. Those dozen ponies all lifted their heads, and they weren't the only ones.

"Ah shit!" Jesse hissed between gritted teeth. He jabbed his spurs into Freckles' underbelly, spun the animal, and shot off into the gully. Behind Jesse, screeching words that he didn't understand flew in what sounded like every direction.

Jesse crested the hilltop not far behind the marshal. They were running their horses as fast as they could. Two against twelve weren't good odds, especially when it came to fighting Indians. They had no rules of engagement, which made it harder to figure out what they might do next. Jesse threw a glance over his shoulder. The whole mad pack of them were thundering across the ground on their horses only fifty yards off his heels. Their war cries filled the air.

"Over here." Huckabee gave a sharp wave.

Jesse jerked on the reins. Up a steep hillside, their horses weaved between crags of brush and boulders, following what might have been a deer path. It certainly wasn't more than that. The horses were both breathing heavily. The climb had slowed their pace. Behind them, the Cheyenne had closed in by twenty yards at least.

Jesse followed Huckabee into the dark space between two tall boulders. It was a narrow alleyway just wide enough for a horse to fit, but Jesse had to lift his feet out of the stirrups the same as the marshal. Once inside the long crack, the Indians had been cut off from sight. They went about fifteen feet when, without warning, a small valley opened up before them. There was a camelback of steep tree-covered ridges on each side. Here and there along the skyline stood boulders as big as the ones that guarded the entrance to this hidden treasure. It was a natural fortress. Too steep and rocky in lots of places for a horse and rider to cross over the top to come at them. That meant there was only one way in and out.

"Git up there!" Huckabee pointed as he wheeled his horse toward the opposite ridge side. He didn't have to say more. Jesse figured out what Huckabee was thinking and knew the plan.

He'd just gotten to the spot and jumped off his horse with his Winchester in hand when the first of the Indians came charging through the gap into the valley. Jesse took aim and squeezed the trigger. His bullet drilled right into the chest of the red buck and sent him flipping backward off his horse. Those red boys had no time to react. The horses at the end of the line must have been pushing the ones in the front, making clear targets of their riders.

Jesse fired a second time. Another warrior was torn off his horse and ate dust when his face planted in the dirt. Huckabee's rifle boomed once, then twice. Jesse squeezed the trigger. A hail of gunfire was making that pack of scalp hunters spin every which way. Two more Cheyenne lay dead before they got their horses turned and tucked tail back into the gap between the boulders.

The dead Indians' horses quickly trotted away from the smell of death. Farther down the floor of the valley, there was tall grass, and the riderless mounts headed there. Jesse stayed hunkered amid rocks and shaded by the trees. His canteen was full and there was a cool breeze flowing through the hills, so he was in no hurry to move. It was hard to tell if what was left of those red bucks would try again or just wait until dark, slip in, and collect their dead. By then, Jesse hoped he and the marshal would be long gone. And going back through that gap wasn't an option unless they wanted to lose their hair. It seemed they were stuck trying to ride up and over. Yet Huckabee might know another way out. It didn't seem like chance, him finding the place.

After a few hours of holding himself ready to fire upon anyone that stuck so much as their nose out from between that gap, Jesse's legs were starting to cramp. He was tall, too long to be squatted in a tight spot for what felt like forever. He slowly stood, stretching his muscles. He raised a hand at Huckabee, who in return gave a nod.

The marshal's rifle was propped on a fallen log and aimed at the black space between the big rocks. While Huckabee was keeping watch, Jesse glanced at the horses feeding below. There was a pretty black in that bunch. His coat shimmered in the sunlight. Beyond the small herd of horses, the valley appeared to narrow again. There stood a single grazing horse. A buckskin. Jesse's heart leaped. From that distance, he couldn't tell if it was Buck. Jesse jerked in Huckabee's direction, then gave a sharp whistle. Huckabee got to his feet. Jesse pointed to the buckskin. When Huckabee looked back at Jesse, they were both grinning.

Glorious day if it was the boy. It didn't matter how he'd gotten in there without them seeing him. Perhaps he'd been there the whole time. Could have been he found his way in before they had. But that didn't seem likely. He would have heard the shots and known someone was close by, someone that might be hunting him. Buck was an easily recognizable horse. The kid wouldn't have left him grazing on open ground where he'd be seen if he thought anyone might be watching.

NATHANIAL

Nate was a savvy little cuss. He probably had come there to hole up for a few days, thinking if he made no tracks, no one would find him. Had those Cheyenne not chased them in there, Jesse and the Marshal would have ridden right past this place. Smart kid.

Jesse wasn't dumb. He motioned for Huckabee to ride along the hem of the ridge. The marshal knew to stay back among the trees, out of sight. If Nate saw them, he'd run for it. If it was even him. It might just be a wild mustang. The hills were full of unclaimed stock.

Jesse snaked along the foot of the other ridge. As he got closer, he grew more positive that was Buck. His heart pounded. Where was his partner? Had the boy gotten hurt? Maybe the Cheyenne had chased Nathanial in there, but then where were they? Jesse pulled up reins next to a small seep of water. In the mud around the hole were child-size boot tracks. The kid was somewhere around. Those prints were made in the past fifteen minutes.

On a jetting of rock about ten feet away sat the kid's small saddle. Jesse had to be close. His heart now raced. Twenty paces or so above that and off to the right a good ten yards was the rocky mouth of what looked like a cave or small dugout that had been naturally formed by the earth. The roof was a sheer rise of rocks. That was a good place to search first. If the kid had just gotten there not long ago, as Jesse figured he had because of the freshness of those tracks at the seep, the boy probably left his saddle sitting until he had a good look-see and decided where best to make his camp. Why drag heavy tack around?

Jesse dismounted, tied his reins to a limb, then quietly crept up the hillside toward the cave. There weren't any boot prints, but he found a wet spot and reckoned the boy had taken a piss. Jesse was careful not to scrape his heels on any rocks. Nor did he get close to any brush that might snag his clothing.

His partner had keen senses. He'd hear any noise that wasn't natural to his surroundings. Any sound possibly made by a man would put him on alert.

He was now within eight feet of the opening, but he was hidden in part by the aspens. His legs were still a little stiff, so he was not inclined to do any running if the boy were to see him first and take off. Jesse silently stepped inside. His eyes quickly adjusted to less light. No one was home. Jesse had expected to find Nathanial there. The cave body was deeper than he had first thought. It was more than just a dugout. An ominous-looking black hole the size of a horse stood in front of him. There was something mean-looking about it that made it appear hungry as if it would swallow man or beast. Had the kid seen him coming and decided to plunge deeper?

Jesse didn't have to think hard for an answer. A rock buzzed past his head. Instinct kicked in, and he ducked.

"Git out of here, Jesse! I ain't goin' back if I have to go with the Fletchers." The boy stepped into the light. His arm was poised, rock in hand. "That first one was a warnin'." He was waiting to hear otherwise, that the judge had ruled in his favor.

Jesse didn't know that answer, and the silence between them sat too long. That definitely wasn't the answer the kid wanted. The boy's eyes shimmered in what light filtered in.

"You find him?" Huckabee's voice carried up the hill.

The kid's eyes widened, panicked. He wildly searched for enough space to run past without Jesse catching hold of him. The space might have been six feet wide, not enough room for Jesse to miss.

"Yup!" Jesse called over his shoulder. "I'm sure the marshal has fetched Buck and hobbled him. There ain't no runnin' away." Inwardly, Jesse was happy. His muscles had relaxed a bit. The kid wasn't harmed, and they had him cornered.

NATHANIAL

"Damn you, Jesse. Why couldn't you just let me go?" Nate threw down his rock. In the faint light, the tears on the boy's cheeks glistened.

Jesse went to him. He did feel sorry for the kid. As of yet, they were unaware of the outcome of his custody trial. Nathanial threw his little arms around Jesse's waist, buried his face in his shirt, and cried. He patted the boy's back, but Jesse didn't know if things were really going to get better once they returned.

"When I left, the trial wasn't over yet." Jesse could only be honest.

A rustling noise behind them drew Jesse's attention. Marshal Huckabee stood just outside the entrance. "While we have a little light in the sky, I say we get movin'."

They turned and walked out of the cave. The kid's shoulders were slumped. Jesse kept a grip on Nathanial's arm just in case he got any funny ideas. He wouldn't put anything past that boy. He was a clever little devil. And he wanted to get him straight home to Ma, who had to be worried sick by now.

Jesse saddled the mustang, then lifted Nathanial onto his horse's back, keeping a tight grip on Buck's reins. He then stepped up and threw a leg over Freckles.

Two hours later, with the kid at Jesse's side pointing the way, the three of them exited the valley by another route, one much rougher than the path Jesse and the marshal had come in on. The trail had also led them farther south. Without a doubt, this was Cheyenne territory, a place they didn't want to get caught on tired horses, and their mounts were breathing awful heavy.

Since the path they'd followed had been so rocky, it also had slowed them down. The evening sky was now orange. They'd gone another mile when Jesse jerked on the reins, wheeling his horse away from the skyline above them some seventy-five, eighty yards.

"What's wrong?" Huckabee kept his voice low.

Jesse twisted around, pointing at the silhouettes of seven or eight warriors. He was afraid his horse might whinny again and give them away. At the moment, Freckles was nuzzling Buck's shoulder, who tolerantly swished his tail.

"Them ain't the same ones I seen earlier," the boy whispered. "I counted six, and one was injured. Seen the blood."

Jesse and the marshal both raised a brow, studying one another for the answer. And neither of them liked the fact that two war parties were stirring around the territory on the hunt.

Jesse looked over at Nathanial. "Where'd you see them other Cheyenne?"

"Cheyenne?" The boy wrinkled up his nose. "They were Sioux."

Jesse cursed under his breath. This was stacking up to be big trouble. The Sioux and Cheyenne tribes were not on friendly terms. Never had been. It seemed that they were riding through a clan war. The ranchers that Jesse was used to dealing with pushed at one another for water and land rights, and the Indian tribes did the same to claim better hunting grounds. And just because they were fighting each other didn't mean they wouldn't kill anyone who inadvertently got in the middle, as he and the marshal had found out earlier when those Cheyenne bucks had the mind to lift their hair.

"Why don't we find a good spot to hole up for the night? If those Indians are on the prowl at this hour instead of in their lodges eating supper, they might hunt well into the night. And it might not be just two war parties out there. I'd hate to run into one of them in the dark," Huckabee said.

Jesse nodded.

The sun was touching the top of the mountain when they finally found a suitable place to conceal them and hide the horses close by. They were all tired and likely testy, which came with being exhausted, though none of them had spoken.

NATHANIAL

Even the horses seemed grouchy, ears pinned, matched with an occasional tail flick. Jesse wore a frown that complemented Huckabee's deep, worrisome scowl, and Nate looked as if he was going to burst out crying any second.

"Get a fire going," Jesse snapped at the kid. "A small one," he said as if Nate needed telling.

Jesse was just concerned about the three of them getting out of there with their hides intact. He doubted he'd sleep tonight. How could he? Those raiding parties could be anywhere and sneak up at any time.

Huckabee picketed the horses on a find of grass. It took but a few minutes until flames danced and the coffeepot was on.

The kid spread out his saddle blanket and sat near the fire. "Suppose Ma's worried sick."

"Reckon so," Jesse said.

Huckabee handed Jesse a cup of steaming brew.

"How's Pa?" Nathanial's soft little voice was sad and quivery as he wiped at his eyes.

"Wish I knew." It was the only thing Jesse could say. He didn't like thinking about it.

With him gone, Ma was shouldering everything alone. The responsibilities of the ranch, tending to a sick husband—though Doc was probably still there helping—plus the outcome of the trial. It was too much for one person, especially when that person was with child.

Jesse took a swallow of coffee, then picked up the Winchester and headed out into the dark. "I'll take the first watch."

A few hours later when Huckabee came to take over, Jesse's eyes had to be red. He was god-awful tried. All he could think about was his family. Would Nate be taken away from them? They would soon find out. He should have been focused on listening for Indians, but he wasn't. It was a good thing Huckabee was there. Worrying would do nothing but rob Jesse of needed shuteye. He would try to sleep.

When Jesse's eyes fluttered open, the boy had, sometime during the night, curled up tight against him. He had done that many times at home when he'd heard a bump in the night and gotten scared. There was plenty there to be frightened of. The boy's future was unknown, uncertain in more ways than one. It could be that they'd all get scalped before making it back to town to find out.

Jesse rolled over. The fire was out. Not surprising. They'd kept it small in hopes of not attracting attention. The mountain air was chilly at this early morning hour. The sky barely held a hint of gray. At home, the rooster would be crowing.

Jesse sat up as Huckabee walked into camp with dark circles under his eyes.

"I spotted another war party, bigger than the other two. More Sioux." Huckabee pointed. "About a mile thataway down on the flat. We gotta move. Now."

Jesse shook Nate awake while the marshal quickly saddled the horses. There wasn't time for coffee. They needed to get the hell out of there. They lit out, not worrying about covering their trail. Their plan was simple: put as many miles behind them as fast as they could while running for home.

"Jesse, look." The boy pointed to a dark puff of smoke, then another, then two more spaced out by a few seconds.

Huckabee reined in next to them. All the horses were prancing nervously.

"There's another one." Huckabee jerked his head to the right where smoke spindled up off the ridge.

Jesse twisted around in the saddle, eyeing their backtrail. "We got company behind us."

More smoke signals took shape in the air. Whether those black rings came from the Sioux or the Cheyenne, the fact was they were surrounded on three sides.

"Holy shit!" Huckabee's jaw clenched.

NATHANIAL

The kid was shaking from head to toe, and his eyes were filled with water. Those two both stared at yet a fourth ball of smoke rising. It was on their left about a mile away from the first puff Nathanial had spotted. That made two war parties on that side. How many more were out there? And were they signaling each other, working together? Was this the same tribe, all Sioux or Cheyenne? Or were these warnings from one tribe to another?

Jesse could only come up with more questions, not answers. And he didn't like any of it. If they didn't soon get out of the middle, they'd be boxed in, and this was a fight none of them would survive. Sioux warriors liked white men less than the Cheyenne, and being a kid wouldn't save Nathanial. His hair, too, would fill a spot on a warrior's lance if they were caught. They weren't the target, but that wouldn't stop either side from killing them. Jesse believed this was just stupid bad timing, them running into a battle between nations.

"Come on." Huckabee spurred his horse.

Jesse's and Nate's animals fell into pace. It wasn't unreasonable to think they might be riding into a trap. Why were there no smoke rings floating up from ahead, the very way they needed to go to get home? It didn't make sense that no one would be positioned on that section of ground.

The highest peak loomed above them. Why not put a signal fire up there? The hillside below was thickly painted in different colors of green from the varying species of trees. All those leaves were some protection. The tree line was a barrier of sorts. A good defensive place. Jesse started to think about it more, but not as a battleground. That mountain was probably full of game. And they had stopped and watered their horses not far from there when they'd ridden in after the kid. So there was good water too.

Jesse yanked up on Freckles' reins. His horse halted. "Marshal, stop."

Huckabee did, as did Nate. They were both staring at him, probably waiting for more bad news.

Jesse swallowed the lump in his throat. "We can't go this way."

"There ain't no other way to go." Huckabee's tone was sharp.

"The first man to step foot on that land will start a war. I bet the Sioux and Cheyenne have come to claim that ground. Both sides are waitin' for the other to make the first move, and in the meantime, they're all callin' more tribes. Doubt they'll care that we're white and have nothin' to do with it. They're all itchin' for a fight."

"Jesse, I'm scared." Nathanial whimpered. He was shaking in his saddle.

"I am too, partner, but this ain't the time to panic. Right now, they're watchin' each other. I doubt they've spotted us, or some young bucks would've already had a try at us." Jesse didn't know how to console the kid other than to keep him from doing something dumb. He scooped Buck's reins out of Nathanial's hands. "I wanna keep ya close is all."

The boy didn't argue. He gripped the horn with both hands.

Huckabee's saddle creaked as he shifted uneasily, looking in every direction. "You're right," he said.

"What are we gonna do?" Partner barely choked out the words due to what Jesse suspected to be a bone-dry throat because he wasn't holding any spit either.

Huckabee studied the ridge side down toward the flat. "Gotta be a hundred of them between those two camps, if not more. We couldn't possibly slip past across that open ground without being seen."

"Might not be as many fighters up top. Only one fire up there." Jesse turned, glancing up the hillside to their right. Then he noticed something he hadn't before and pointed to a notch in the mountain where two hills came together, forming what appeared to be a ripple in the green that blanketed the hills. "Bet that's a wash. Depending on how rocky, maybe we could ride the horses up that. We might make it close to the top before they see us."

Huckabee nodded. "Could work. It's a chance anyway."

The kid didn't say a word, just chewed on his lip.

Jesse had been right, thank the Lord. That dip in the mountain where the treetops appeared to sit lower than the rest was indeed a wash. The ravine wasn't so deep that a horse couldn't get in or out of it. That long notch in the earth was, however, a good depth to keep them mostly hidden. The trees that hemmed the sides of the gully would help fort them. Their chance of escaping this trouble was slim, but if Jesse could somehow get Nathanial over the top to the other side, at least then the kid might be able to slip away. The Indians up there would be focused on this side where their enemies were stationed, so the other side of the mountain could be fairly clear as far as Nate running into any warriors. Jesse doubted he and the marshal would be so lucky. The area, at the moment, was too thickly populated with red bucks for them to go unnoticed. It was a matter of luck, and time was ticking until some warrior saw them. Then it would be a real fight.

Their horses were snorting, working hard to climb.

Out of nowhere, a god-awful cry cut through the air, stinging their ears. Jesse threw a look over his shoulder just as a Cheyenne appeared among the trees atop the edge of the ravine and took a running, flying dive with a hatchet gripped in his fist, no time for Jesse to throw his arms up. The warrior flatly tackled him, ripping him out of the saddle. That red bastard screeched bloody murder as they fell and whacked the rocky ground.

Shit, Jesse couldn't breathe.

Behind him, the kid screamed.

Jesse's fist jabbed up into that painted buck's throat, smashing his Adam's apple back into his spine. He choked, grabbing at his neck with one hand, which threw off the aim of the hatchet in the other. The glistening blade hacked into the dirt near Jesse's ear. Before Jesse sucked in a full breath, a bone-hard knee slammed his chest, dead center. Every bulky ounce of that red fella held Jesse down.

Out of the corner of his eye, he could see Buck rearing, kicking his front hooves out at a brave who was stabbing at Nate with a lance. Jesse arched with a jerk of his midsection to throw off his attacker, and as he did, he swung an arm, clubbing that devil upside the jaw. Jesse needed to get to the kid. The warrior's lower teeth shifted queerly to the side with a gut-sickening crack. With the blunt force of the blow, the Indian spun off him.

Where the hell was Huckabee? He wouldn't have left them.

As the buck rolled, he threw a wild chop with the hatchet, which nicked the brim of Jesse's hat, knocking it off his head.

Jesse sprang to his feet and turned, snatching his hat as he went. Huckabee was down. Blood gushed from his arm, and his horse lay dead. Over him stood a fierce-looking redskin with one long black braid down the back of his otherwise shaved head. Another redskin was charging, lance raised. That hard, leather-faced fighter who had Jesse winded was on his feet too and madly charged, wielding his ax like a crazy person. Jesse jumped back once, then twice, barely escaping getting butchered.

"Jesse!" Partner's panicked voice nearly made Jesse's ears bleed. The boy's pain was Jesse's pain, and he wasn't about to let anyone hurt him, not while Jesse had breath in his lungs.

He palmed his pistol. Flame blasted into the hostile's gut. He dropped to his knees, and the knife fell from his grasp. Jesse wheeled on his heel. He worked the hammer. Lead balls drilled the son of a bitch who jabbed at the boy. That bastard jerked one way, then the other as Jesse unloaded into him.

NATHANIAL

Huckabee's rifle boomed. Jesse twisted in that direction. Pools of blood surrounded the two Indian bodies. One had been killed with his own feathered lance sticking out of his chest, the other a shotgun blast to the face. Not a pretty way to go.

Three more warriors came running at them.

Jesse threw a glance at the kid. Nathanial's eyes were wide, and tears streamed down his face. Blood matted the fur on Buck's shoulder, and the kid's eyes were focused there. Dammit. If that horse went lame, Nathanial was as good as dead.

"Git out of here!" Jesse had just spit out the words when an arrow snagged his pant leg.

Nate smacked his heels madly into Buck's sides. The horse leaped forward, knocking one of the enemy rolling. While he was down, Jesse aimed and fired. That prick was going to kill a little boy. Something sharp struck Jesse's shoulder from behind, cutting into his flesh. An arrow stuck out from his skin. With one yank, he tore it out with a great agonizing yell.

Huckabee's rifle boomed for the second time, then a third.

Jesse twisted around. The one with the bow was dead, flat on his face in the dirt. Huckabee swung his rifle, batting one heathen alongside his ear. That son of a bitch got dropped like a hot potato. Around them, echoing through the trees, were a lot more shrill war cries, too many for two injured men to handle. Jesse grabbed up the reins of his horse and swung into the saddle. He grabbed Huckabee's outstretched arm and yanked him up to ride double.

Jesse spurred the appaloosa.

Huckabee fired upon two more who had pounced side by side out of the brush at them. Freckles was struggling to make the climb with full-grown men on his back. His neck stretched and he blew hard, but his feet were solid, digging in and propelling them onward. Amen. They were putting a little distance between themselves and the enemy. Ahead, Nathanial was out of sight. Jesse prayed the kid had made it through any trouble that might have been waiting.

Freckles stumbled, nearly pitching Jesse over his horse's ears. The gelding was tiring quickly. The climb was too steep, the footing rough and rocky, and the double weight would have been a lot for any horse.

A crunching noise rose out of the brush, and before their eyes, a painted pony and a buck wearing a soldier's hat slammed his horse into the side of Jesse's mount. Freckles' feet came off the ground as they flipped. Two horses and three men rolled back down the wash.

CHAPTER 30

NATE RAN BUCK. Blood spurted out with each torque of the mustang's shoulder as his gait stretched. Worse than Buck being hurt, Jesse and the marshal were still back there. Nate needed to get them help.

Gunfire repeated through the air. There'd been so many Indians. Nate couldn't calm his breathing or how badly he shook. It was too far to Gray Rock. He'd never get there and return in time to do Jesse and the marshal any good. They'd be dead before then.

Shots echoed. There had to be another way. What he needed was someone close. But this was lonely country, no homesteads. Maybe a hunter. But Nate had no idea where to begin looking, and that would take time. Too much time. Minutes counted. Seconds counted. The rifle booms were spaced out now by at least a hurried breath or two. Was that a sign of Jesse and Huckabee winning or losing?

Smoke—no longer formed in puffs, but a thick billowing line—mushroomed into the sky. That was it. Nate had found his help. It wasn't ideal and it might cost him his hair, but Jesse was worth the risk.

Nate spun Buck and charged the mustang straight down the mountainside.

Despite being injured, his horse covered ground with the speed of the wind. Buck was flying, and Nate was holding on tight. There was little cover in some spots, and that was exactly where Nate steered his horse. He wanted to be seen, recalling what Jesse had said earlier. That the first man to set foot on the ground that both the Sioux and Cheyenne wanted to claim would start a war. That was precisely what Nate was about to do.

He wasn't a man but he was white, and that might be enough to agitate the Sioux into coming after him. He would lead them straight up the hillside toward where Nate had last seen Jesse and the marshal. If he wasn't enough of a lure, Buck might be. Though he was hurt, the mustang was a fine, stout figure of an animal, pleasing to any eye. And Indians liked good horses.

Buck thundered out onto the flat not fifty yards from where those Sioux had the two signal fires burning. But now they were just brightly stoked bond fires.

"Hey!" he screamed a couple times and wildly waved his arms.

Dozens upon dozens of dark eyes drew upon him. Nate wasn't breathing, but his heart sure as hell pounded. He screeched his best imitation of the Cheyenne war cry. Every Sioux warrior seemed to stiffen. Nate let out hollering again. Then he jerked Buck by the reins, and they shot off up the mountainside. Nate hoped his effort wasn't too late. His eyes glassed over. Jesse had been hurt before he'd yelled at Nate to run. Marshal Huckabee had been bleeding too. Neither was in good shape, at least not for the fight they were in.

A rumble of thunder shook the ground. Nate dared to sneak a glance over his shoulder. Twenty-five or more Sioux were mounted and racing after him. Their horses were fresh, not

NATHANIAL

winded like Buck who was snorting with every breath. And the poor mustang was still trickling blood, but Buck was like Nate. He had no quit. Death would be the only thing that would stop them, and those braves were gaining ground too fast.

Nate made a beeline for the patch of level ground ahead. It was the spot where he, Jesse, and the marshal had entered the wash less than thirty minutes ago. That was a lot of time to be fighting for your life. Nate hoped with all his strength that Jesse and Huckabee, Nate's best friend's father, were still breathing.

Buck's hooves pounded onto the even spot. Jesse was there, Huckabee too. Nate's heart leaped with relief. Jesse was limping at a slow run toward his horse. Above his one knee, his pant leg had been filleted, along with the skin underneath. He was leaking red onto his boot. His Winchester lay on the ground, broken in two. Not far away, Huckabee was on all fours over a dead warrior, a bloody knife in his hand. His side had been sliced open, and he was bleeding from a cut under his left eye.

They both had lost the look of strength and must have been about done in. Nate's timing couldn't have been better. More Cheyenne, a damn passel of them, flooded in from above. Nate wheeled Buck to give another battle cry to hurry and lure the Sioux. Before he opened his mouth, the first ten braves of the bunch who were heeling him came flying on their mounts onto the flat spot of ground. In a brief pause, one side glared at the other. Then red bodies from both nations went at each other with arms raised and weapons bared.

Angry shouts carried everywhere. Screams of death followed. More Sioux came up the hillside, which would lead to but one thing—more Cheyenne racing down from the mountaintop. It was war.

As Nate spun his horse toward Jesse, who was now on the appaloosa and reaching to pull up the marshal, a shot rang out, then another. Nate was yanked off Buck and thumped on the ground. A lean-faced Sioux kicked him, rolling Nate out of the way. Then that devil started to throw a leg over Buck. Buck kicked and turned around, biting at the warrior.

A rifle boomed, and that rotten heathen jerked forward. His spine had blown out through his bellybutton, splattering Buck's side with blood. The shock of sudden death, so brutal, held Nate's stare, though he didn't want to see the mess. He wasn't on his feet, but just stupidly sitting there, not believing the slaughter all around him. The sound of battle was ferocious, the likes of which Nate had never heard. It was a terribly bitter song that would leave a scar on him perhaps forever.

"Nathanial!" Jesse screamed over the roar of fighting.

Panic streaked through Nate, and as he pushed up, he was scooped off the ground from behind. He kicked and hollered and punched. He didn't want to die, to get scalped or hacked apart like some of the grisly bodies around him. Nate tried not to look, but there were dead scattered all over the place. He expected to feel a hard blow from a hatchet any second. And too many more warriors rushed to replace the dead.

"Nathanial, stop it. I'm not going to hurt you."

Nate quit struggling and looked up. His eyes damn near bugged out of his cotton-picking head. Fletcher had him. They were on a sturdy brown horse, one from Mr. Pike's livery, and they were running from the battle. Nate then saw Pike, an old Indian fighter from way back. He was mounted and blasting away, keeping several braves off Jesse and Huckabee as Jesse madly kicked the appaloosa to run. Judge Prescott was there too. He had a rifle aimed at the savages and pulled the trigger

Fletcher ducked around a bend with Nate, and they flew through a patch of trees. He wasn't slowing the horse. Nate had to make sure the others got out of there. It seemed they were going to light out right behind Fletcher, but Nate needed to be sure. He hadn't risked that run-in with the Sioux and gotten between them and the Cheyenne to just turn and abandon Jesse and Huckabee back there, especially with both of them injured. Both were badly scraped up and bleeding.

"You gotta go back," Nate demanded.

Fletcher kept the horse running. Nate wasn't big enough to fight him for control of the reins, so he did the only thing he could. Something Fletcher, no doubt, would not expect. Nate shifted his weight off his ass and onto his heels and jumped before Fletcher could hold him back. Nate hit the ground rolling. It wasn't just the others he felt the need to go back for. He couldn't forget his horse.

Fletcher yanked up on the reins, swinging his mount and coming fast back toward Nate.

Nate stood his ground, not giving his hand to Fletcher to be pulled up into the saddle. "No. Go back. Help them. You got a gun."

There was a rifle on the side of Fletcher's horse, but Nate feared it was just for show.

"I won't leave without the others, without Jesse or Buck." Nate was serious. He stomped his foot, rooting into the ground. He'd be damned if he would go another step, not without those he cared about.

Fletcher glanced back the way they'd just come. Rifle fire boomed in the air. Then he glanced down at Nate. "All right. I won't shoot anyone, but I'll do what I can. You hide."

No shit, Nate thought while biting his tongue. This wasn't the opportune time to cock off. He had just talked Fletcher into returning for the others. The last thing he wanted was for Fletcher to change his mind.

"I know what to do. Just go!" Didn't that fool understand that success would take every man working together? That every gun would be needed to extract the others from the battle and hopefully all in one piece?

Fletcher spun his horse and disappeared back through the trees. What kind of help would he be? Not wanting to defend himself or anyone with a gun, the idiot would probably get himself killed.

Nate climbed the nearest tree as quickly as he could step off the swaying limbs bending under his weight. Evergreen branches, thick and full but a mite prickly, were a good hiding place, and he could see some of the fighting about a quarter-mile off. Gunfire echoed between the hills. Smoke whirled through the air when the wind kicked up, making details difficult to distinguish. He couldn't differentiate Cheyenne from Sioux, but white men wearing hats and holsters shouldn't be hard to pick out among the sea of redskins.

The booms seemed to be drawing closer. It was hard to tell from so far up at the tiptop. Then the sound of running horses caught his ears. Jesse and the others were coming. It had to be them.

Nate scrambled down the tree, slipping several times because he was hustling so fast. The Indians wouldn't be running away unless one side had decided to retreat, but most of them had been on foot, not mounted.

Out of the tree line charged a battered lot of riders. Prescott was leading the way by a horse length, an arrow sticking straight out of his left thigh, feathery shaft and all. Pain had hardened his face into an awful grimace. Right behind him was Jesse, who was sickeningly pale and slumped far over his horse's shoulder. Was he still bleeding? God, Nate hoped not. Tears stung his eyes.

On Jesse's tail and riding fast on Buck was Marshal Huckabee. His shirt on the entire one side was covered in bright-red blood, and he sat no taller in the saddle than Jesse. They were in piss-poor shape, but Nate couldn't help but smile as he dropped from the bottom limb onto the ground. Everyone was at least half alive, and Buck was there too. Fletcher and

NATHANIAL

old man Pike brought up the rear. Pike had his rifle in hand and kept twisting in the saddle, eyeing their backtrail.

Nate ran toward Jesse. Jesse pulled up on the reins, but he didn't put his hand out to pull Nate up, which he had expected. "Ride with Fletcher. His horse is in good shape, and he's the only one of us that ain't hurt."

Nate wasn't about to argue. Jesse's horse was scraped up, Buck was bleeding, and Prescott's mount had a cut above its hock. Pike's big roan wasn't injured that Nate could tell, but Pike's ear was bleeding and a fair chunk was missing from his hat. It appeared he'd come too damn close to losing his hair. Jesse wanted Nate to stay safe. The soundest horse and healthiest man would have the best chance of getting him out of there. Nate gave his hand to Fletcher and was pulled up behind him in the saddle.

"Let's git a move on, boys." Pike snorted.

They lit out as a bunch. Jesse led, spotting blood along the ground, showing their trail, and he wasn't the only one. If the Indians decided to come after them, they wouldn't be too hard to find. Pike hung a horse length back, watching over his shoulder while the rest of them were packed in the middle. Nate was scared. He didn't trust the city dude to keep him safe. But Jesse was close by, so Nate had to be satisfied with that for now.

They'd ridden a mile when Jesse yanked up on the reins, turned his horse, and guided the group of them into a hollow. There were a shallow creek and trees for shade and a rock cluster just big enough that if the Indians were to attack, they could defend themselves from behind a wall of stone.

"If I don't get stitched up soon, I'm gonna bleed to death," Jesse said. He looked over at Prescott. "We have to get that arrow outta your leg."

"I got a needle." Pike lifted his hat and pulled one from the lip inside. "Always carry one on me. Don't have thread, though. Used it." No one seemed to care. These were men accustomed to surviving on what was around them when need be. Nate had once been stitched up with a long hair from a horse's tail.

Ouches and groans circulated as each man slid off his horse. The animals were left saddled in case a quick need to escape arose, and though they had moved off from the direct fight, it wasn't unlikely they might encounter more warriors.

Nate helped Jesse lay out his ground blanket. "I'll get some firewood." He sprinted off. He knew to stay within sight so Jesse wouldn't worry.

Fletcher turned and watched Nate. The others were all settling down to rest a few minutes. Except Pike, who was propped behind those rocks with his rifle and keeping a lookout.

A few minutes later, Nate returned with an arm full of sticks weighing him down. He dropped the pile, fetched a pack of matches from Jesse's saddlebags, then blew until a small flame came to life. He put on coffee while Jesse and the marshal hunkered over Prescott, eyeing the arrow.

Pike joined them. "I think those Injuns have forgotten us. We'd have seen sign of them comin' by now." The old man looked over at Nate. "Fetch my whiskey." If anyone could guess what those savages might do, it was Pike. It'd been said that he had killed his first redskin at the age of nine. He'd been fighting them all his life.

Nate hopped to. Pike had barely knelt beside Prescott when Nate handed him the half-full bottle. Pike bit down on the cork and yanked it out. Without warning, he grabbed the feathered shaft, gave a jerk, and ripped it from Prescott's flesh. Prescott screamed. Jesse slapped a hand over his mouth while the marshal held the man back from punching Pike, who didn't seem a bit bothered. He then poured the whiskey all over the bleeding hole. Prescott cursed a streak through gnashed teeth and withered while being held down.

The old man sniffed the stone arrowhead. "Smells like cucumber. Copperhead poison."

"But we don't got copperheads 'round here," Nate said. Those were an eastern snake he'd read about in a book. It wasn't a deadly snake, but Prescott would probably get hellish sick.

"Every now and then, one will curl up in a Conestoga coming west. The varmint drops out on the ground somewhere along the trail, and the Indians take full advantage of it."

Pike pressed his lips tight around the bleeding flesh and sucked the poison out, then spit. He did that for better than a minute. Prescott's blood painted Pike's face more with each lip lock. Nate's stomach felt queasy. A couple times, Pike had to swat a fly away from getting between his lips and that bloody hole.

Pike looked around, searching for something. "Your shirt's clean. Cut it into bandages." He wasn't asking Fletcher. The ornery old badger pulled his blade from his belt and handed it to the wide-eyed city dude who was profoundly dumbstruck.

"What are ya waitin' for, Christmas? Git to it." Pike wasn't letting off just because Fletcher was out of his element and probably had never seen anything so gruesome before. Besides that, Pike was demanding the man disrobe his upper half. Good thing Fletcher was wearing a suit coat. It would be something to keep his lily-white skin from being sunburned.

Nate took the knife while Fletcher hastily unbuttoned his shirt. Everyone could see the blood spilling out of Prescott's leg. Jesse's leg was bleeding awful bad too. Nate took the shirt and sliced.

"Go yank some horse hairs." Nate lifted his chin toward the grazing animals while cutting the shirt.

Fletcher went.

Prescott was the first to be sewed up and bandaged. Nate couldn't help but notice the black grime under Pike's nails, at least the ones he hadn't bitten off, as he pulled the string taut through Jesse's skin. It made him think of Pa at home, fighting infection. Jesse had better not get sick too. Nate couldn't let himself think like that. Jesse would be fine. Pa too.

Then the marshal had his turn with Pike's so-called doctoring. None of the stitches lined up, and not all of them were tight together, allowing for a bloody discharge to seep out. Nate blotted at the ooze with a bandage.

"Git out of my way." Pike shoved at him.

"Then do it right, old man." There was a serious bite to Nate's tone. He wasn't pissing around.

These men needed taken care of correctly. They all had a long way to ride to get home. It would be tomorrow sometime before they got near Gray Rock, and bleeding over forty-some miles wouldn't get them to a real doctor any faster. Jesse, Prescott, the marshal, they needed their strength, so those leaks needed to stop.

Nate could feel Fletcher's eyes on him. That bothered him very little because he was so focused on helping tend to these injured men.

The blister of an old goat jabbed Nate with an elbow in the gut to git. "I'm doin' my best." He finished the last row, and to Nate's surprise, it was straighter.

The cut on the old man's arm wasn't bad, and Fletcher had been asked to do the sewing to give the other three wounded men time to handle their pain. They were all too shaky at the moment to do any stitching. Nate was glad when the doctoring work was done.

Everyone had coffee except him. Nate refreshed Jesse's canteen, drank from that, then filled everyone else's canteens as well. He brushed down the horses, and Pike stitched Buck.

Nate tried to shake off Fletcher's gaze, trailing Nate's every step. It was like having a nagging toothache. Fletcher didn't appear worried. In fact, he was expressionless. Instead, it felt like the man was studying Nate. Maybe he had something to say, something Nate didn't want to hear. There was only one reason for Lem Fletcher to be there, and that was to claim Nate. Otherwise, he'd be on a stage right now, headed away from Gray Rock. Judge Parker must have ruled in favor of the Fletchers. Nate tried not to think about it and ignored Fletcher the best he could. Old man Pike was leaned against a tree nearby, keeping watch while the others slept.

"Will we camp for the night?" Nate figured he'd unsaddle the horses if they were staying there. It would be dark in a few hours.

"No. We'll put a few more miles between us and that fight back yonder." Pike spit.

"Ya think they're still fighting?" Nate recalled that both sides had come at one another screaming like frantic lunatics and waving their weapons. He doubted either side would give up.

"By now, there's probably a winner. The loser will tuck tail and run. The winners will likely lick their wounds for a short time. Then they're gonna spread like locusts across this area, and if they find anyone who don't belong... well... Why don't you go wake those boys up? We should get movin'."

With a bum leg, it wasn't easy for Jesse, nor Prescott, to step into the saddle. Nate helped as much as he could. The marshal sat wearily on Buck, as did the old man on his horse. The day was catching up to him. Pike wasn't badly hurt, but he wasn't a young man either. Fletcher, with his suit coat buttoned to his neck to hide his bare skin, reached for Nate's hand. Nate didn't care if the locusts came. What time he had left would be spent with family, and that meant Jesse. Nate turned his back.

"Jesse." Nate pleaded with his baby-blue eyes. He didn't have to say more.

Jesse was smart. He knew why Fletcher had risked his life riding into Indian country. It wasn't to help Jesse or the marshal. Prescott had probably come to keep things civil between

Jesse and Fletcher, and Pike, Nate would bet, had been hired as a guide.

Jesse leaned down, took Nate by the wrist, and hauled him up into the saddle. Nate hugged Jesse's waist. Their time together was ticking away, and they both knew it. Surely, Nate would get to say good-bye to Ma and Pa before leaving Gray Rock.

He'd find a way to get away from the Fletchers. But with the threat of Indians, Pa barely hanging on to life, Jesse done in good, and Ma probably beside herself, it wasn't the time for Nate to pull any more stunts. Plus, he was just plumb exhausted.

CHAPTER 31

THE SUN WAS ALL BUT HIDDEN behind the mountain when they made camp for the night. No one said a word. The horses were picketed and chewing grass. Pike had built a fire. Everyone was spread around it on their blanket rolls. Jesse's head was pillowed by his saddle, and he was snoring. Prescott's eyes were closed. His face glistened in the orange firelight. Pike was sponging at Prescott's forehead. Marshal Huckabee stared off into the flames. He was probably thinking about his family. Pa had said lots of times that's what he thought about when stuck out on the trails, and Pa and Huckabee were cut from the same cloth.

Fletcher smartly stayed quiet and glanced around. It wasn't like he was a favorite among them. He had hardly been of any use, but he wasn't in anyone's way either. Except that he gave Nate a sad, lonely feeling for what he still had at the moment, a mother and father, but would lose real soon, maybe the very minute they rode into Gray Rock. Jesse, Huckabee, and Prescott all needed to be looked at by Doc, so that's where they would go. He curled up tight next to Jesse.

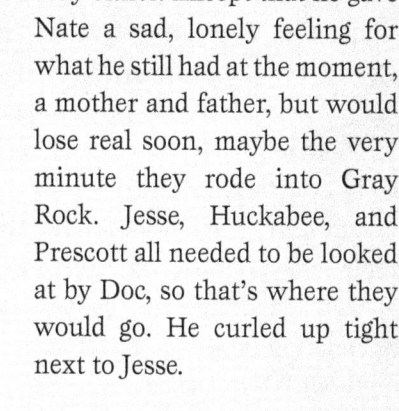

Nate's eyes fluttered open to Jesse shaking him awake. The hours passed too quickly as they made their way toward town. Nate's heart thumped harder with each mile put behind them. He blinked fast, fighting back the tears in his eyes. If anyone noticed, no one tried to console him. What would they have said anyway?

Everyone wore a grouchy look on their face, except Fletcher who rode staring straight ahead and seemed to be off in his own world, contemplating something that was going on miles from there.

Rooftops came into view. Gray Rock was still a few miles off, but not as far as Nate would have liked. He quivered. Jesse must have felt it and pulled Nate around to sit in the front of the saddle.

"Leave us," Jesse said in a stern voice.

Old man Pike and Prescott, who were riding side by side, passed them without hesitation. Pike turned and tipped his hat at Nate. That was about as much affection as the old man ever showed, though he had always been kind to him. Nate put up a hand.

Fletcher pulled up reins next to them. His lips pursed to argue otherwise. Jesse's face hardened. Before either could say a word, Huckabee shoved Buck between them.

"Move on, Fletcher," Huckabee barked.

"Like hell." Fletcher glared right back at Huckabee. "How do I know he won't let the kid escape again?"

"Ya don't," Huckabee said. "But we're gonna give them some time alone anyway. Might be the last they get."

Fletcher hesitantly turned his horse. Huckabee nudged Buck to fall in behind Fletcher.

"Wait," Nate called.

Huckabee pulled up reins, as did Fletcher, but that wasn't who Nate was thinking about.

NATHANIAL

He reached out and rubbed Buck's neck. "I wish you could go with me, boy." Nate sniffled. "Jesse will take good care of ya." Buck lifted his head and blew at Nate. He grinned through his tears. "Bye, boy." He patted Buck's soft nose.

Huckabee nudged Buck. A tear slid down Nate's face as the mustang walked away. Nate eased back, leaning against Jesse. This was the worst day ever.

Jesse steered his horse into the tree line. The path was one Nate was familiar with. He and Jesse had ridden this trail many times. It led to the overlook on the side of the ridge. All of Gray Rock could be seen from there.

When they got to the ledge, the spacious view seemed to take away all Nate's troubles. There was a whole big world out there, and he was but a speck of it. Jesse reined in. They sat quietly taking in the town a mile or so below them and all the green hills surrounding them. This was a spot Nate would never forget.

"Partner." Jesse broke the silence. Nate looked up at him. Jesse stared straight into his eyes. "I know you too well. I want you to promise me that you won't run away from the Fletchers."

What in the hell was wrong with Jesse? He had to be out of his mind if he thought for one damn minute that Nate would stay with those city folks. No way. Nate adamantly shook his head.

Jesse grabbed him by the shoulders. "I mean it, partner. I can't take the thought of you being out there on your own again, barely surviving. What if ya get hurt or get into some kind of trouble that ya can't get out of and get yourself killed?" Tears made Jesse's eyes shine. "Ma and the sheriff ain't in no shape to shoulder bad news like that. The Fletchers will at least take care of ya."

"Don't you want me to stay?" Nate's insecurities always surfaced when it felt he was being pushed away by someone he trusted, someone he loved.

"Hell yes, I want ya here. You know that. But... I need to know you're safe, and I ain't the only one. Your mother and father will both be a mess as it is."

Nate could imagine the worry on their faces. "Do you think the Fletchers will let me go home and say good-bye before leaving Gray Rock?" Nate really did want Jesse's opinion, but he had also cleverly changed the subject so he didn't have to lie. Nate couldn't promise that he wouldn't run away, not honestly anyway.

Jesse let go of him as he thought for a minute. "Don't see why they wouldn't. That'd just be ignorant if they didn't."

Nate supposed that was true, but the Fletchers had proved themselves capable of being heartless. After all, they were about to rip Nate from his family. Jesse turned his horse toward the trail to finish their ride into Gray Rock.

"I wanna hear ya swear it. No runnin' off." Jesse hadn't been fooled, nor had he forgotten.

Nate nodded. But he should have known Jesse wouldn't be satisfied with that. Jesse nudged him. He squirmed. Not because of the elbow jab. His gut had tightened. He didn't feel right lying to Jesse, but what choice did he have? Jesse would gripe the whole way there until he gave in, so he might as well just say it, though he wouldn't mean it.

"All right," Nate grumbled, hating himself for saying even that much. It wasn't a full-fledged promise, but Nate's word should be good. Pa and Jesse always did as they'd said when they'd given their word. So Nate had become an underhanded liar. His shoulders slumped for more than one reason. The lie, the Fletchers, it was starting to pile up on him.

"Hey, it's gonna be okay. We can write." Jesse encouraged him. "Maybe you can come visit."

That was a nice thought, but Nate doubted Mrs. Fletcher would ever come west again. And after all the violence Mr.

Fletcher had witnessed, Nate didn't believe the man would be in a hurry to return this way anytime soon.

Nate began to tremble as they neared the edge of town. "Jesse, I'm scared."

For the time he'd be alone with the Fletchers until he chose his time to bolt, he didn't know what to expect. What if they were mean to him? He had too much experience with that in his past. Mr. Harper had treated Nate worse than a dog, and his old pa, Jim Younger, had been cruel, as had most of the gang members. Who knew what that city couple was like when they weren't in public?

Jesse tucked an arm around him. "I would be too, kid." He was quiet for a minute. "Ya know... you might like the city."

Nate raised a brow. Hogwash. There'd be too many people for his liking. Wide-open space, that's what he'd rather have. Where would he ride a horse in the city? In the street didn't count because Nate liked to feel the wind whipping against his face. He wouldn't be skipping his horse merrily down the damn road—if the Fletchers allowed him to have one.

"There's production companies that put on plays. I seen a small version once at a theater in Kansas. It was like watchin' a book bein' read to ya." Jesse knew how much Nate liked to read. He was just trying to hornswoggle him into believing this move wouldn't be so bad.

"Suppose you're gonna tell me that in no time at all, I won't miss the mountains. That I'll be too distracted by all the new stuff, the different people and happenings, the styles, carriages, and tall buildings." Tears filled Nate's eyes, teetering on spilling over even though he had no intention of staying with the Fletchers for very long. He'd leave them before they left Wyoming. He couldn't come back here to Gray Rock where his life was. Fletcher had brains enough to assume Nate would run right home after escaping, so that was the last thing he could actually do.

They passed the church at the edge of town, then Netty's boarding house. It was of an hour that the main street was full of folks coming and going about their errands. As it was most days, horses spotted the hitch rail outside the different businesses. A wagon stood ready to be loaded with supplies in front of the general store. Several more buckboards had been parked close to the granary. People looked up and watched the two of them. Time seemed to stand still. Everyone had stopped what they were doing. All eyes were on Nate. He leaned back into Jesse.

"I'll come visit you." Jesse promised. "I'll take the train. The one near Fort Sherman connects and runs the whole way east."

Nate would never make it east, but hearing that Jesse was willing to go so far to see him did make him feel a little better until he noticed the stage outside the telegraph office. Mr. Fletcher was now dressed in a clean, unwrinkled suit. His hair once again was slicked and parted as straight as a ruler. He was handing luggage to Dutch, the stagecoach driver, who tossed it up top to Harvey to be strapped down. Mrs. Fletcher stood nearby, smiling and talking with none other than Kristy, whose eyes were red, and she didn't appear engaged in the conversation. Some people were so clueless, as Mrs. Fletcher appeared to be, that nitwit.

Kristy's ma and pa were there. Shorty was now helping Dutch lift a trunk to Harv. Kristy clutched a carpetbag and a handkerchief in her hands. Kristy's ma was also dabbing at the corners of her eyes. Hattie, Lenny, and Norman were there too. All of them looked sad. It made Mrs. Fletcher look stupidly happy.

"What in the hell?" Jesse muttered, more to himself. He stared at Kristy in utter disbelief. They weren't engaged anymore, but Jesse had said he'd hoped to work things out. It was pretty clear she was leaving.

NATHANIAL

Nate tugged on Jesse's sleeve. "Where's Ma? Don't I get to say good-bye?"

The stage door was held open, and Mrs. Fletcher was aided inside. If she was boarding, that meant Nate was leaving now, in minutes. Pa was ill. He couldn't come to town to see Nate off. Maybe no one had even told Ma what was happening. What if Nate didn't get to kiss his little sister one last time? No. He couldn't up and leave like this. It wasn't supposed to happen this way. None of this should have happened at all.

"I don't wanna go!" Nate wailed.

Huckabee was hustling toward them. "Your ma's on her way. As soon as I heard the Fletchers planned to leave on the next stage, I went to the house. She should be here any minute."

"What about Pa? I wanna see Pa." Nate sobbed. There was no holding back his misery. After all he'd been through in his short life, this is what God had in store for him? Couldn't one thing go right, work out the way he wanted?

Huckabee shook his head. "Your father's still too weak to git outta bed. He is a little better, but he ain't in the clear yet." The marshal patted Nate's leg as Jesse stepped down out of the saddle.

Jesse tossed the reins over the rail, and in two lengthy strides, he was standing next to Kristy and her family, who were dismally hugging all over one another.

Nate quivered as he bawled. This was a day from hell for everyone.

"Kristy, where ya goin'?" Jesse reached for her hand. She pulled away, then handed Jesse an envelope.

Nate kept his eyes on his big partner while waiting for Ma.

Shorty ushered the rest of his family off a few steps. The other passengers were boarding. Dutch and Harv were busy doing their jobs in the middle of all the commotion. No one but Nate noticed that Fletcher was walking toward him.

Kristy wiped at her eyes. "I'm going east to my mother's family. For a while anyway."

"Why?" Jesse's eyes were wide and glassy. He looked like a man who had just lost his whole world, and he choked while stammering out the one word.

Nate kicked at Fletcher. "Git away from me."

"It's time to go. I'm sorry it's sudden, but Deloris insisted on leaving as soon as you returned. I was hoping to give you some time with your mother and father before we had to leave." Fletcher sounded sincere, but Nate didn't trust him. They didn't care about him or they wouldn't be taking him away.

"I hate you!" Nate screamed. Everyone froze. Maybe no one breathed. Not even a horse flicked its tail.

"Let him alone!" Jesse stepped toward Fletcher, his fists balled.

Tensions were high, but Kristy caught Jesse by the arm as Marshal Huckabee stepped around Jesse's horse that Nate was sitting on and shoved himself between Fletcher and Nate.

"Jesse, ever since we got back, I can't sleep. My appetite is gone. I jump at every little noise." Kristy was crying as hard as Nate.

"You know damn well I'll protect ya," Jesse thundered.

Kristy's pa must not have cared for Jesse's tone. He charged in and pushed Jesse back.

A wagon rattled into the street. Nate turned. "Mama!" He jumped off Jesse's horse.

The marshal blocked any swipe Fletcher might make at him, but the man didn't move.

Ma halted the team. As she climbed down, Nate threw himself at her. They both nearly crumpled. Ma dropped to her knees, cradling him into her bosom, rocking both of them. Tears streamed down their faces. Curled together in a tight ball in the middle of the dusty street with dozens of eyes on them, they cried over one another.

NATHANIAL

Nate felt a firm hand on his shoulder. Both he and Ma looked up at Jesse. Wetness streaked his cheeks.

"Stand up," he said, though not unkindly.

Jesse plucked Nate out of Ma's arms, keeping him perched on his hip. Then he gave Ma a hand up. She brushed off her dress. Jesse held her hand, Nate in the other arm. Nate hugged Jesse's neck. As he walked them toward the stage, he must have known Ma wasn't strong enough to do it, to give her little boy over to another woman, to a different family. Jesse really had stepped into Pa's boots. It's what Pa would have done.

Dutch opened the door as they got closer to the stage. Kristy was inside. Fletcher waited near the step. Mrs. Fletcher poked her head out the window.

"We are going to be late to meet the train, young man." She huffed. "I'm sure no one else on this stage appreciates waiting either." She fanned herself exasperatedly, as though Nate's show of heartache was somehow embarrassing to her.

The whole town crowded around him. Trembling, he clung to Jesse. Ma was tight at Nate's side. One then another, friends and neighbors wished him the best. Some of his school friends were there waving good-bye, then wiping at their eyes. In a day or two, their lives would go back to the same. Nate's would never be the same again. He received a few pats on the shoulder from different people who knew him.

Mrs. Henderson, Phillip's ma who owned the store, handed Nate a small brown bag. "Gumdrops. Your favorite."

Nate grinned.

Dutch cleared what sounded like a frog in his throat. "I don't mean to cut ya short, but... the stage has to go."

"It's about time." Deloris Fletcher's haughty voice carried.

"Deloris, be quiet," Fletcher snapped, shocking everyone.

There was an uneasy shift within the crowd. They'd seen both the Fletchers as enemies until that moment.

Nate tucked his face into Jesse's collar. "I hate her. Don't make me go." He sobbed.

Sniffles rose from the crowd, and Ma was openly crying, clinging to him as tightly as he held to Jesse.

"If there was any other way..." Jesse shook his head.

There was no getting out of this that Nate could see. He knew better but couldn't act now. At the moment, he just wanted to stay there, at home. Jesse began to peel him off. Nate squeezed him tighter. Jesse tugged, but he wasn't about to let go.

"Partner, it's time." Jesse gave a yank, but Nate was hanging on for dear life.

"No. Please don't make me go." Snot was starting to mix with his tears and smear across his face as he bore into Jesse's shoulder.

Jesse pushed with force. A team of horses wouldn't have the strength to pull Nate off. He had a mean grip.

"Mama!" Nate howled. "Don't let them take me."

Jesse had yanked one of Nate's arms free from grasping his shirt. He latched onto another spot before Jesse could wrench Nate's other hand free.

"Stop it, partner. You're killin' me." Jesse had never sounded sadder. Ma was bawling worse than a grieving mother.

Suddenly, Nate was ripped from Jesse. Marshal Huckabee had him.

Nate swung his fists. "You bastard! I hate you!"

Ma was reaching for Nate, but Jesse held her back. "Nathanial." She sobbed.

The crowd was still huddled around, but Nate hardly noticed them, what their faces looked like, what they were muttering.

"Jesse." Nate stretched out his hands. "Mama," he called over and over.

NATHANIAL

Huckabee thrust him up to Dutch who was sitting at the reins. Dutch twisted Nate around until he was locked in one big grizzly arm, though he kicked and squirmed.

"Dutch, you get that boy to the train. Don't let him out of your sight between here and there. Hogtie him if ya have to." The marshal turned to Fletcher. "Get in." Huckabee slammed the coach door behind Fletcher, then pointedly stared in the window. "You'd be wise to let Dutch handle Nathanial until ya reach Fort Sherman. Then you're on your own. For Nate's sake, I hope you're up to the job 'cause it ain't gonna be easy."

With one hand, Dutch slapped leather to the team. The stage lurched forward and began to roll. Only, Nate's heart had been left behind.

Dutch flopped Nate ass first onto the seat between him and Harvey, the shotgun rider. "You even think about jumping off, and I will tie you with the luggage."

"Kiss my ass." Nate didn't care about anything anymore. His life had been ripped to pieces.

He could feel Dutch's scowl. Nate ignored it and stood on his knees on the seat. All the luggage was stacked up too high. He couldn't see over it. He took a step to climb on top. Harv grabbed the belt of Nate's pants.

"I ain't goin' anywhere."

"Let him go," Dutch said

Nate hustled onto the highest part of the luggage where he could see the road behind him. Ma and Jesse stood in the middle of the street, watching after him. Jesse was practically holding her up. Ma was waving one arm and wiping a handkerchief across her face with the other.

Nate waved. "I love you!" he yelled from his mountaintop.

Jesse waved then too. Ma suddenly collapsed. Jesse's quick hands caught her before she hit the dirt, and he scooped her up, hustling toward the wagon. Jesse glanced over his shoulder one last time at Nate. Their eyes held. The stage rounded a bend, and Ma and Jesse were gone.

Nate shrank into a ball, holding himself and crying. Was Ma okay? What about the baby? Nate didn't even know if Pa would live. Would he ever see his family again? Elizabeth might forget him. She was so young. There was no fear of Jesse forgetting him, but he was, no doubt, just as broken as Nate felt. Kristy wasn't even there to lean on. Ma and Pa always relied on each other to pull through tough times. They couldn't do that this time. Nate wasn't sure that Pa even knew he had been taken on the stage. Last he'd heard, Pa was still in and out of consciousness. Nate's hate for the Fletchers grew, festering quickly.

By stage, it'd take ten, eleven days before they arrived at Fort Sherman. In that time, Nate would take it upon himself to learn some things that would help him slip away. Dutch had promised to get Nate to the train. He was a man of his word and he was well enough acquainted with Nate's history with the Younger gang to know his trickery, so Dutch would be watching closely. There was no use trying to escape before that. However, he would know the stage schedules, which probably closely correlated with train times. Nate was counting on that.

He had been taught at a very young age how to get a man talking, then to turn the conversation to what he wanted to know. If he out and out asked about the train schedules, Dutch would likely grow suspicious. But what man didn't like to brag on his profession? And Dutch, Nate knew, took pride in having one of the only coaches that had never been robbed. Attempts had been made, but never had the bad guys gotten away.

If the schedule worked against him and he couldn't hop on a different train than the one the Fletchers would get on, he'd have to steal a horse and run for it.

CHAPTER 32

THAT EVENING just before dark, Dutch steered the team into the yard of what Nate guessed had been a stage stop at one time. Now, though, the windows and doors were boarded up, and the roof had caved in. Weeds grew out of every plank seam. Some of the fence rails had fallen away from the corral and lay on the ground. There was a rusted pump for water—if it worked.

Dutch pulled up on the reins. The team halted. He jumped down. "We'll rest here for the night." He opened the coach door.

In single file, the passengers stepped out.

Mrs. Fletcher looked aghast. "Where are the accommodations?" She huffed.

Dutch stomped a foot in the dirt. "Right thar. Make yourself comfortable."

Mr. Fletcher took his wife by the arm and led her off a short distance.

Dutch looked up at Nate. "Help Harv with the team. And don't get any ideas about stealin' a horse."

"He is not an employee of this stage line or your slave. He's a child. So I doubt he'd steal a horse," Mrs. Fletcher snapped at Dutch before Nate had even crawled off the seat.

Dutch ignored her. He jerked a thumb for Nate to get going.

"Darling," Fletcher said. Nate was still within earshot. "Let the..." Fletcher eyeballed Dutch from head to toe, then hesitantly said, "Gentleman handle the boy. He is far more capable than we are."

"That is ridiculous." Mrs. Fletcher turned toward Nate. "Nathanial, come here. Let the paid men do the work."

Nate arched his neck back and spit at her. A big glob splattered the ground near her foot.

She gasped and jumped back. "Lem, do something." She was red in the face.

"What would you suggest, darling? Spank him? As I recall, you don't believe in that, or so we have agreed."

Nate chuckled.

"We made a mistake, Deloris. He belongs here. I tried to tell you after we escaped the Indians, but you wouldn't listen." Was Fletcher pleading Nate's case now that it didn't matter? Nate had been signed over to them. It was too late.

The other passengers politely made themselves scarce, working to build a fire.

"He is our nephew, Lem. He belongs to us."

"He is not a horse. He is a child. A very unhappy little boy. I saw him ride into the eye of battle without fear. Do you really think he will ever fit into our world?" Before she snapped a retort, Fletcher went on. "Well, I don't. He will be miserable. I'm already miserable. Nothing good can come from us taking him away from his mother and father. He didn't even get a chance to properly say good-bye. Do I really have to remind you of that awful scene?"

"They are not his mother and father. My sister was his mother."

NATHANIAL

"Oh yes, your dear, sweet, foul-mouthed harlot of a sister who fell in love with a wanted man, a killer. I'm sure Mrs. Crosson doesn't compare."

The slap across Fletcher's cheek cracked like lightning. Deloris was snorting and rubbed at her hand.

Nate found himself holding his breath. No one moved or said a word.

Fletcher drew air deep into his lungs, then exhaled just as long. "I watched them, Deloris. I sat in the Crossons' home, and I knew right then that Nathanial was where he should be. We are not what's best for him. But as always, I gave in to you, giving you what you wanted. I wish I hadn't this time. Had we not lost Ashton, I'm positive we wouldn't be here." Fletcher spun on his heel. He stared at Nate. "Do not spit at Mrs. Fletcher again, or..."

Nate grinned. "Or what?" He cleared his nose and was about to spit again when a big hand slapped down on his shoulder.

"Or I'll tan your hide." Dutch scowled at Nate. "The man asked ya not to spit at his wife, so don't. Your ma and pa would be embarrassed by such behavior. They didn't teach ya to act like that."

"Thank you," Fletcher said.

Dutch nodded.

"According to her,"—Nate pointed at the city bitch—"Nolan and Kate aren't my parents, so I reckon what I do doesn't matter."

Before Nate even finished the last syllable, Dutch spun him around and smacked his ass once, and Nate was already facing the big man again. Tears stung his eyes, but he wasn't going to let himself cry in front of the Fletchers.

"Don't let me hear you talk like that again."

"Yes, sir." Nate sniffled.

"There's a bucket tied under the coach. Get it, then pump some water so if the ladies want to freshen up, they can. After that, see if Harv needs your help with anything." Dutch nodded for Nate to go on.

At the pump with the bucket sitting underneath the nozzle, Nate let his tears fall. The handle creaked with each priming, sort of reminding him of old man Pike's knees when he stood up. He missed all his friends.

"Nathanial." He turned to see Fletcher standing behind him.

"Let me alone." Nate didn't want to talk about anything. He turned his back. Water gushed into the bucket.

Fletcher gently touched Nate's shoulder. "Please hear me out... I am sorry."

Nate looked up. "She won't ever give me up, will she?"

Fletcher shook his head. The water stopped.

Nate picked up the filled bucket, which was heavy. "You're her husband. Can't you make her return me? Why don't you sign me back over to Ma and Pa?"

Fletcher grinned. "Here, let me take that." He took the bucket from Nate. "It might be hard for you to understand, but believe me. Deloris, she means well. She loved her sister very much, and our son, and I have no intention of creating an unhappy marriage. So no, I can't make her. As far as signing our rights away, I wouldn't do that."

Nate abruptly stopped. "What? Why? But you just said I don't belong in the city."

Fletcher squatted in front of Nate so they were eye to eye. "Deloris isn't able to carry another child. She had trouble throughout the first pregnancy, and the labor almost killed her. You are our only heir."

Nate wrinkled his nose. "What does that mean?"

Fletcher chuckled. Nate wasn't sure if he was being laughed at or not. "You are a very wealthy little boy is what that means. Money will never be an obstacle that stands in your way."

NATHANIAL

Nate shrugged. "What do I need money for? I had me a good horse. That's all I ever needed to buy, except candy sometimes."

Laughter boomed from Fletcher.

Those sitting around the fire all turned and stared. When nothing appeared to be wrong, they all turned back to the flames.

"I can tell you with certainty that I've never heard anyone say that."

"Lem, could you bring the water please?" Deloris Fetcher beckoned.

Fletcher straightened with bucket in hand.

Nate followed slowly, a step or two behind. He was curious and a little confused. This man had him thinking. Fletcher didn't want to give up his rights to Nate, but he didn't want to take Nate to New York either. Was there a possibility hiding in all that? If so, Nate wanted it spelled out for him. And the only one who could do that was Fletcher.

"Nathanial, why don't you join us?" Deloris's prissy voice rubbed him the wrong way.

He rolled his eyes as she gently patted the blanket for him to sit. Hell would freeze over before he tucked in snug next to that woman. He would wait until Lem was alone, then talk to him if the chance arose. Nate didn't want within ten feet of Deloris or her money. She was only thinking of herself, her losses. Owning him wasn't the same as getting her sister back, or their son. Lucinda was dead, as was Ashton. How could Deloris not recognize what had been taken from Nate? Fletcher's eyes had been opened to it, but he was reluctant to stand up against his wife.

"I want to go home," Nate said as a matter of fact.

Everyone hushed. The only thing heard was the crackling fire.

"Oh dear God, don't start that again. Your home is in New York." She waved a hand as if brushing off what he'd said as pure lunacy.

"The hell it is!" he fired back at her.

"How dare you speak to me like that?" Deloris hissed.

Kristy jumped up, grabbing Nate's arm and dragging him off around to the other side of the stage where they were alone. She opened the stage door, nodding for him to climb in. She stepped inside, took a seat near the window, then pulled him onto her lap. Her arms wrapped around him. She was soft like Ma, and although it wasn't Ma, that tender touch made him feel better. They stared through the window at the others all sitting quietly around the fire. Stars twinkled overhead.

Nate's thoughts focused on Lem Fletcher. What did he mean when he'd said Nate was better off there, at home in Gray Rock with his family, but he would not relinquish his rights to Nate? How was that possible? Maybe it was just wishful thinking on Nate's part, shared custody. Such a thing probably didn't exist. Why couldn't he be the first? He knew the answer. It wasn't a matter of a judge hearing them out. Judge Prescott was a reasonable man. However, Deloris Fletcher was too much of a bitch to settle for any way but her own.

Nate turned his face into Kristy's shoulder and sobbed. She gently smoothed his hair and kissed his head. All of it made his heart ache more for his ma and pa. Being away from his family, missing them so much, was nearly killing him from the inside out, eating at him like a disease.

Would there come a day when the sun would rise and he would see his loved ones again?

EPILOGUE

AS SOON AS NATE was dragged inside by his arm, he was met with lace runners on every table, centered with large vases of long-stemmed red flowers. Sparkling chandeliers hung from the ceiling, and being that the passenger train soon to be headed east—the very steam engine that would carry him and the ever-annoying Fletchers to New York—wasn't scheduled to depart for twenty-five minutes, lots of people had crowded into the restaurant for a quick bite of lunch.

Great! He had an audience, a full room, standing space only at the moment and only five minutes to make himself magically disappear. At the top of the hour, the orphan train parked on the rails would leave Fort Sherman. He'd been ripped away from his mother and father and, as badly as he wanted to, couldn't go back to Gray Rock. The ache in his chest made it hard to breathe. This wasn't the time for him to lose his nerve. He needed to push away that bawl-baby feeling that took hold of him too often and turned him into a ball of mush, but he missed his family. The Fletchers certainly weren't his family and never

would be. Maybe they'd think twice about keeping him after this stunt.

The setup couldn't have been any more perfect. Nate's lips curled into a shit-eating grin, and a sneaky little giggle slipped out. Lem Fletcher's eyes narrowed. Dammit. That man could read him too well. Why couldn't he be as clueless as his dippy wife who was lost in a conversation about a mink stole? There was no hesitating. Nate had to move quick to make this work before Fletcher somehow fouled up his plan.

"Pa took Jesse and me to a magic show once," Nate said as he hustled toward the table smack dab in the middle of the place. He was just the right size to slip by.

Mr. Fletcher couldn't squeeze through the narrow aisle zigzagging between all the people seated at the dozen or more tables. His eyes were wide and all on Nate. He'd bet he was sweating too. The missus was too busy chatting with another waiting couple, her hands doing most of the talking, completely unaware of where or what Nate was about to do. What a dummy. She didn't know when to take good advice. Marshal Huckabee had warned them to keep a close eye.

At the center table, the family of six—a mother, father, two boys older than Nate by some years, a girl maybe Hattie's age, and a younger boy maybe a year or two older than him—cocked their heads, staring at him as if asking what he was doing standing next to their table. He'd show them and the Fletchers all right.

Nate looked over his shoulder at Fletcher as he latched onto two fistfuls of tablecloth. "Daddy, dear." His voice drooled with sickening sweetness. "Watch this!" His mouth curled into an ornery grin, and with an almighty yank, the lace runner holding plates of steaming food, filled glasses, a pot of coffee forgotten by the waitress, and, of course, the beastly pot of thorny flowers ripped off the table, flying into the air.

NATHANIAL

During the magic show he'd seen some months back, the magician had been able to slip the tablecloth out from under all the china without disturbing one utensil. That was not the case here, and that was exactly what Nate wanted.

All of it, every silver fork, spoon, knife, and morsel of food went flying above the customers' heads. Something brown, could be gravy, splattered the ceiling. Mrs. Fletcher, Kristy, and most all the other women gasped in unison in one high tone. After that, no one breathed for a few seconds until... *Crash!*

Dishes hit the tables, cups on the floor. A fork and spoon landed on an adjacent table, sending spits of their grub in every direction. A sandwich belonging to someone landed in a lady's lap, and she screamed as if it were a rat. Coffee sprayed the room. People popped out of their chairs, and all the glaring eyes were on the Fletchers for not controlling their child. Nate snickered as their roars began to fill the room. No one was happy, and Mr. and Mrs. Fletcher caught an earful.

"I'll pay for the meals and any damages." Lem Fletcher pled to the mob of hungry travelers surrounding him.

One man plucked a slice of tomato off his hat, flicking it at Fletcher. Mrs. Fletcher was hysterically crying into her hands. What Nate could see of her face was beet red. He reckoned she'd never been so embarrassed. Hopefully, she regretted taking him away from his family. Kristy was at her side, rubbing across her back sympathetically. If she wanted to work for them, she'd have to do it without Nate.

The clock dinged one.

Nate ducked through the crowd and ran out the door, hoofing it toward the orphan car. His past was a bad one. He never seemed to be able to escape it, and he'd tried hard. Why not just embrace it? No longer was he the son of a lawman, and there was but one other way of living that he was familiar with. Besides, his ma and pa would soon have a new baby and probably forget all about him.

Nate would search near Lee's Summit, Missouri. Jim Younger had never married that he knew of, but chances were there'd be some kin in that area since his father had been born there. How he'd come to know that and why it stuck in his brain was beyond him. He must have heard it years back when he'd ridden with the gang. Nate hadn't forgotten how to pull his weight as a Younger, though he might be a tad rusty at robbing stagecoaches and banks.

Unseen, Nate slipped onto the train, ready to start a whole new life... again.

ABOUT THE AUTHOR

J.B. Richard, author of the Western Promises series, resides in the Seven Mountain region of Central Pennsylvania, where her grandparents' farm is nestled, cultivating inspiration through her wild days-gone-by adventures with her many cousins. She is an avid outdoorsman who enjoys hiking and exploring Civil War battlefields. A highlight of her life was riding horseback on the same road that General Robert E. Lee had ridden into Gettysburg.

Visit J.B. Richard at www.jbrichard.com or on Facebook at J.B. Richard.